North To Disaster

An Alaskan Novel

Jim Craig

Bushak Press
Seward, Alaska

Published by Bushak Press
P.O. Box 46, Seward, AK 99664
www.bushakpress.com

Copyright © 2008 by Jim Craig

This is a work of fiction. Names, characters, places and incidents either are the product of the author's imagination or are used fictitiously, and any resemblance to actual persons, living or dead or events is entirely coincidental.

Cover design by Dennis Lee Treadwell, Starbird Studio, Seward, Alaska

All rights reserved.

No part of this book may be reproduced, scanned or distributed in any printed or electronic form without permission. Please do not participate in or encourage piracy of copyrighted material in violation of the author's rights. Purchase only authorized editions.

ISBN13: 978-0-9617112-1-4
ISBN: 0-9617112-1-3
Library of Congress Control Number: 2007901727

This work is dedicated to adventurous spirits everywhere. May your dreams be your guide.

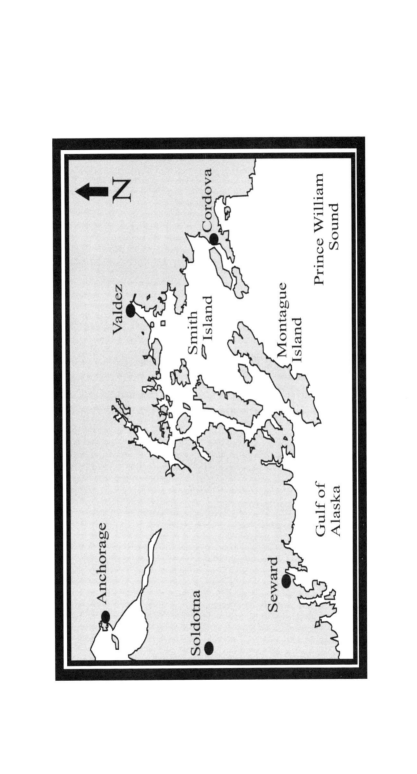

PROLOGUE

I've never really liked the taste of a Smith & Wesson. Especially when it was a forty-five caliber handgun jammed between my tongue and the roof of my mouth. It had a gritty metallic flavor with a touch of sea salt and sweat.

It didn't matter much that I was located in one of the most beautiful places in the world. In that moment I couldn't see any of the scenery. I was face down on the concrete floor and under a table in a corner of a dark hangar in Seward, Alaska. Within a couple miles of the blood stain spreading under my face stood majestic mountains, blue white glaciers, and brilliant white icefields. Wilderness spread in all directions where eagles soared, sea otters chortled, and humpback whales breached in the nearby Gulf of Alaska.

But like I said—none of that mattered at the moment. I couldn't see a lick of it. And none of it could see me. That was the whole point. Why else would I be huddled in the dark next to a pile of smelly airplane tires?

This wasn't a very heavily populated area. In fact there were only three people within shouting distance at the moment. They weren't interested in the scenery either. They were looking for me. They were trying to kill me. One of them was stretched out on the pavement just a few feet away. He was trussed up like a turkey dinner, and he wasn't saying much. Just a groan once in a while. Especially when I kicked him. The sonofabitch.

It hadn't been my idea to taste a high-powered handgun. It was his. Although it's true that it rains a lot in this part of Alaska, I wasn't suicidal just yet. Not on that night anyhow. No, suicide wasn't on my mind; homicide was.

The other two people were outside somewhere. And they were headed my way. One had a hunting rifle suitable for killing grizzly bears, moose, or an unlucky bush pilot. The other carried a twelve-gauge shotgun. Like the local scenery, she too was beautiful. And deadly. My ears were still ringing from the shot she'd taken at me. She'd missed but the blast tore a huge hole in the side of the metal building where I was hiding. I was starting to regret sleeping with her.

I hunched deeper into the corner when I heard footsteps outside and pulled a rusted-out muffler over me to cover my feet. The hangar was a mess. Boxes of greasy airplane parts and paper cups were strewn everywhere. The cups that weren't half full of old coffee were filled with nuts and bolts and sheet metal screws.

But for once I wasn't cursing the mess in the maintenance shop. Old Hubert McCormick was the mechanic that ran this disaster. All of us pilots on the field spent hours helping Hubert search for parts and tools to fix our planes. It's a good thing we all liked the guy. Otherwise, he'd have been found floating face down in the bay a long time ago. That night I fell in love with the old bastard. I was counting on his mess to save my life.

The huge body lying next to my hiding place groaned again. I thought about shooting him. After all, I was holding his forty-five caliber cannon now, quietly spitting out the tiny chips of teeth and dental work he had recently rearranged. I knew it was only luck that I'd been able to turn the tables on him. If I hadn't, I wouldn't be telling this story. I'd be pushing up blue lupines and Alaskan forget-me-nots in the Seward cemetery.

The cold concrete felt good against my cheek. It cooled the bleeding divot he'd left there with the gun barrel, trying to force me to give up the prize. My face would have felt much better if it hadn't been for the sand and the gas and the oil and the sheet metal screws I was lying on. Damn that Hubert.

The rest of me felt terrible. My hands were cramped and sore. More blood seeped from matching wounds on the front of both shins, and my feet cried out from multiple open blisters. My neck muscles protested the effort it took just to hold my head off the floor. I think I was in a bad mood too.

But I'm getting way ahead of myself. I wasn't lying there by accident. As much as I hate to admit this, it was my own damn fault. And I need to tell this story from the beginning.

CHAPTER 1

"Hey, Willie; you ever wreck an airplane?"

"Shit. You kidding?" He looked up at Mount Alice and her snow-covered slopes and shrugged his jacket up closer around his neck as if fending off the early morning chill. Or maybe the chill of a bad memory or two. He tugged on the bill of a bright red baseball cap and pulled it down tighter over the round globe of his skull. Tufts of bushy gray hair stuck out over his ears in a vain effort to escape the confines of the cap. A bristly white mustache set off his round ruddy face, which hadn't seen a razor in a couple of days.

I always watched Willie's eyes to monitor his mood. When they were dancing in all directions like hip hop dancers on the Red Bull express, I knew to shut up and wait. There was no point in talking when those blue orbs were doing their tormented tango. But on that day Willie's eyes were relatively calm. He stared at the ground and said nothing.

Moments went by. I waited. I was used to this with Willie. His mind was a mysterious wonderland of sidetracks and diversions. A tangled web of neurons and synapses, firing in random order in a twisted mockery of intelligent design.

We were standing on the airport tarmac in the morning mid-May sun, soaking up the rays and shaking off the lingering chill of another damp night in Seward, Alaska. The airport spread out in front of us. Mountains surrounded us just a mile away on all sides except to the south where the bay's cold waters filled its bowl like formation on the south edge of the Kenai Mountain range. The canyon to our west was filled with low-hanging fog. Resurrection River ran there, cold and loaded with grayish brown silt from the glacier upstream. Misty silver vapors swirled off its surface into the frosted morning air.

Willie was usually prompt about driving us into town for coffee this time of day. It was our routine. But something was different today.

My camper sat nearby on the pavement behind my SuperCub. She was tied down beside the office, a twenty-five-by fifteen-foot wooden A-frame set on cement footers in the black alluvial gravel. *Seward Air Services* read the big sign on top of the building. The front window detailed the rest: *Scenic flights of the Kenai Fjords, air taxi, and wildlife viewing. Johnny Wainwright, pilot and flight instructor.*

The morning had started normally. I'd crawled out of the bunk above the cab on my 1985 Toyota motor home, shivering in the narrow dark living space. My propane water heater was on the blink, and it was way too brisk for a cold shower. I pulled on jeans, sneakers, and a hooded sweatshirt, followed by a fleece jacket. Thank God for fleece—the perfect material for chilly, damp Alaska mornings. Zipping that turtleneck collar all the way up and feeling the soft texture against my skin can give a guy hope. I peeked out the window to see if Willie had pulled up yet.

When I saw he wasn't there, I went outside to check on the airplane parked beside my camper. My 1953 SuperCub sat right where I'd left her. Walking around helped warm up my cramped muscles. A Toyota motor home is not exactly the lap of luxury. Usually by the time Willie got here, I'd be halfway warmed up and jonesing for my first cup of coffee. I'd climb in his car and we'd ride two miles down the highway dodging the perpetual potholes to the Texaco station by the small boat harbor. Like I said, it was our routine.

Today something was different. When Willie pulled up, he got out of the car, walked to the front, and sat against the hood to stare up at the sky. Then he looked down at the ground. Instead of his usual jumpy self, Willie was quiet. He usually grunted "Morning" at me, but today he seemed more disconnected than normal. He said nothing.

I suppose I was different as well. There was something on my mind too. The phone call from the night before was still bothering me, and I needed to talk to him about it. But I knew better than to waste my breath when Willie was distracted.

Most of the time, if I waited a while Willie would eventually come back from his mental meandering and answer my question. Other times, he followed a side journey in his head, bringing up another subject altogether. This time was one of those times.

"My sister called yesterday," he finally said. "Said Mom wasn't doing so good."

"Yeah?" I replied hopefully. Willie and I were about the same age. Fifty-something. So his mom having aches and pains wasn't really breaking news, but I knew I had to play along. Had to wait for his neurons to get in the mood to align. To synchronize somewhat and arrange themselves in some kind of half-assed sense of order so he could address the issue at hand.

"Yeah, she said our mom's got the rutabaga real bad."

"Don't you mean lumbago?"

"What?"

"I mean, I'm sorry about your mom and all that, but I think a rutabaga's some kind of vegetable."

"What?"

"Lumbago?"

"Who's that?"

"Lumbago, Willie. It's some kind of ailment, like back pain, or some shit. I think you told me before your mom's got it."

"I did? I don't remember telling you about my mom. You sure?"

"Willie, for chrissake. Can we talk about airplanes for a minute?"

"Airplanes? Sure. Whatcha wanna know?" Willie's mind had just returned to the scene with apparently no recollection of the initial question.

"I asked you if you ever—"

"Yeah, I've wrecked one or two in my time. What about it?" His eyes glinted at me for a moment.

So he was just messing with me, the sonofabitch. And then that direct eyeball-to-eyeball contact. That didn't happen very often with Willie. Maybe it was just one of those tough guy things. You know, that whole thing about tough guys not looking each other in the eye. Not for more than a brief moment. Not unless there's a damn good reason. Some reason with heavy meaning, like, "I'm serious and you better damn hear me." Those looks carried heat.

Willie's look had heat. It did happen once in a while. I must have touched a nerve or some damn thing. I didn't know, and I really didn't care. I needed information, and I was getting anxious. Edgy. Not pissed off yet, but on the way.

I don't get irritated very easily. People usually think of me as a pretty easygoing guy. But I have my times. Like when I'm on a mission. Like when I need to keep moving toward a target with a hunger that won't be satisfied until it gets fed. Like right about now.

"Look, Willie. I don't mean nothing by this. This ain't about you. I'm just trying to find out what happens to wrecked airplanes."

"Oh yeah?"

"Yeah. I heard something yesterday, and it kept me awake most of the night."

"You heard something about what?" Now he was interested. He seemed to have moved past whatever triggered the sidetrack. Maybe I could get some answers now.

"I heard about a bunch of airplane guys getting ripped off. Somebody's stealing parts for some kind of black market or something."

"Well, hell. That shit happens all the time. What's the big deal?"

"I know it happens all the time, but they made it sound like this time it's different."

"Different how?"

"Different because eight airports right close to each other got hit over a three-week period and forty-nine airplanes were stripped."

"Holy crap. Forty-nine airplanes?"

"Yeah, forty-nine. Now what I'm thinking is—"

"I never heard about this. Where did this happen?"

"Down in the Lower Forty-Eight—Arizona, New Mexico, around there somewhere. But look, I was wondering—"

"What kind of airplanes got hit?"

"I don't know, Willie. Look, will ya wait a minute?"

"Okay. Go ahead."

"I got a second call last night, too. I might be able to make some money, and Lord knows, I need the dough."

"Yeah, no shit. You ain't paid me back for those beers from the other night. You need to drink cheaper beer anyhow."

"Yeah, right. MGD, the rich man's beer."

"Drink what I drink."

"I ain't drinking that moose piss. Will you just wait a minute? I'm in a hurry here." I glared at him. Hard. Tried to put some heat in my expression. I was getting pissed. Like I said it doesn't happen very often, but I was starting a slow burn.

Willie let a little grin slip, and his eyes, surrounded by laugh lines, twinkled. "Okay, okay, I'm just messing with ya." He grinned wider and glanced over at me like he was taking my temperature, checking my mood.

He was enjoying this, I realized. The sonofabitch was getting off on working me over. How did I give him that edge? I wondered. Okay, note to self: Do *not* let Willie know I'm in a hurry. The silly sonofabitch will use it for his own entertainment. And he has no sense of timing. I was not in the mood. I was not sharing his sense of fun. And I was not going to laugh along and make his game okay. My look must have worked. He dropped the grin.

"Okay, sorry, man. What's going on?" He sounded halfway sincere, so I decided not to kill him just then.

"I got a phone call from Steve Harkin, up in Anchorage. You know, the parts guy at Ballards? He told me about this airplane ripoff deal, and he's been called by some security people. They think the same group might be starting to operate up here."

"Up here? Really? That's weird. Why up here? That doesn't make any sense."

"He said there's a big black market for used parts overseas, especially for backcountry planes in places like China and Siberia. So these bad guys have figured out a way to grab all the parts they can and make big bucks."

"It's still weird. Why'd he call you?"

"He heard about what I did for those equipment guys by Merrill Field. Remember that? Anyhow, he says I'm the only person with an airplane who's in the recovery business, and he wants me to keep my ears and eyes open in case something comes up."

"Yeah, you're the only dumb bastard stupid enough to get involved in that crap. What are you trying to do? Be a bush pilot repo man or something?" The sarcasm rolled off his lips like day-old syrup dripping from a greasy counter at the diner.

I just shrugged and stared back at him with what I hoped were stone-cold eyes.

He returned my hard look. "How many times have I told you not to keep taking chances with that bullshit? You're gonna get yourself killed."

"Thanks, Mom. I love you too," I grunted at him. "Anyhow, I wanted you to know in case you heard something. Okay, Willie?"

"What kinda job you got?"

"Just a chainsaw recovery. It's supposed to be out at a cabin on Johnstone Bay."

"You goin' alone?" He scowled at me. More disapproval.

"You know I always work alone. And by the way, I'm flying out there in a little while. If I ain't back by three or four, come looking for me, will ya?"

"Yeah, whatever."

He walked around to the driver's side of his car, and I could tell he was trying not to shake his head, but I saw it anyhow. My imagination maybe. Or maybe not. I watched him long enough to see him check his watch. Then I knew my flight plan was good.

I could always count on Willie. We might bitch at each other, but this man was my friend. At least until five o'clock. Five o'clock pulled at Willie like the Kenai River dragging at a sockeye fisherman's knees. This particular undertow was named the Yukon Bar. To tell the truth, the place pulled us all in sometime during the evenings, but Willie's undertow had a deadline. If he wasn't seated on his favorite bar stool by five, the man might explode. Or turn into a pumpkin.

Riding down the road beside him, I wondered what was going on. Willie wasn't usually cranky in the mornings. He didn't normally criticize me about anything—even when I deserved it. I didn't blame Willie for getting frustrated with me sometimes. He always tried to look out for me. Got me settled in this north country when I first got up here. And he was always telling me all kinds of scary stories to try to keep me from killing myself with an airplane or getting eaten by a bear or something. I actually appreciated that about him, even though he made me crazy sometimes with all the mothering BS.

Reaching the Texaco, we made our way inside to get some morning go-juice, weak overpriced coffee for me and a plastic mug full of unleaded cappuccino for Willie. His stomach no longer tolerated caffeine. When he did drink it, he had to throw in a handful of antacid tablets too.

Back in the car, he told me about an airplane junkyard up in Anchorage where some wrecks end up. But he also said that most crashed airplanes in Alaska that he'd ever seen disappear little by little. Like a dead carcass picked apart by buzzards, or up here more like eagles.

That always surprises outsiders—to hear that the magnificent bald eagle, proud symbol of the United States of America, is a rampant scavenger, eater of road kill.

Anyhow, Willie didn't seem to want to talk about his own experience with wrecks. That was unusual too. Willie had a million stories about his bush flying days all over Alaska, and he frequently entertained all of us at the Yukon with one tale after another.

I wanted more information from him, but I was in a hurry to get going, and besides, he was preoccupied with something he wasn't ready to discuss. I figured I could get to the bottom of that later.

I changed the subject. Thought that might help get his mind back on something happier. "How was your trip out to Bristol Bay?"

He didn't answer. I waited and then glanced over at him while he drove. He was rocking his head slightly from side to side, and his lips were moving. But he wasn't making any sound. Then he threw one hand out in a gesture like he was having a silent conversation with somebody I couldn't see. He didn't seem to remember that I was even sitting there watching either.

I'd seen that before too. It was like he was deep in consultation with some inner advisor or demon of some kind. He never seemed to realize he was doing it, and the conversations could go on for several minutes. I didn't think they were visiting about the weather. I thought his invisible pals were prodding him about problems he should have been taking care of or things he needed to worry about.

"Say, Willie, I don't mean to interrupt, but this is our turn."

He looked up in surprise, then braked hard, so we could make the turn off the highway onto the airport road. I juggled my coffee cup to keep it from slopping all over his dash. There was a clunk behind us, and I looked back to see a heavy old duffel bag on the backseat pitch forward and fall to the floor.

I reached back to pick it up and when he saw what I was doing, he snapped, "Leave it!" I straightened up again and looked at him.

"Okay, man. Take it easy."

"That's another thing that pisses me off," he grumbled. "These goddamn work crews leaving their shit all over the place." He waved one hand at a pile of battered red cones laying on the side of the road. He reached over to grab his plastic mug out of the cup holder, took a loud slurp, set the mug back down, and wiped his moustache with the back of his hand.

We pulled up in front of my office, and I climbed out. Glad to be alone again, I shrugged off his cranky mood and gave him a wave. "Thanks, Willie. I'll see you later, and I'm sorry your mom isn't feeling well."

"Yeah, I hope it ain't some genetic shit. I don't want to get that crap."

"No kidding, me either. Gotta watch out for those damn rutabaggers."

"Screw you, Johnny." He pulled away, spinning his tires on the gravel. I looked after him wondering if he was okay. His extended middle finger waved at me through his back window. I grinned and turned to my Cub.

CHAPTER 2

I drained the rest of the Styrofoam cup. The coffee, weak as it was, got me going finally. But the best way to warm up in the mornings was to get busy with something.

The SuperCub sat in its tie-down spot looking like a caged beast waiting for a chance to leap into the sky. The white paint and red stripes gleamed at me in the morning light. My fingers were stiff, but it felt good to get them working to undo the ropes holding the little airplane. I left the other end of the ropes lying on the ground attached to the metal rings that were sunk into the pavement and walked around the plane. I always liked to make sure all her parts were still there before I went flying.

I peeked in the side window to make sure my survival bag was behind the backseat where it belonged. A glance at the fat tundra tires reassured me that they were sufficiently pillow like and plump enough to handle the landing I might be making on the beach at my destination. Quick looks at the fuel tanks and dip stick, and I was almost ready to leave.

Into the office and back with my twelve-gauge pump shotgun, I secured it in the black scabbard strapped under the right wing. I always liked the way the scabbard looked hanging there, like I was loaded for action with a rocket launcher or something equally lethal and macho. While I was attaching the bungee cords that held in the shotgun, I looked up to see myself reflected in the side window of the Cub. A guy in a sweat-stained dark blue baseball cap, dark beard, and prescription sunglasses stared back at me. No line trifocals, actually. Okay, so I'm vain. Sue me. If I flipped up the hood on my jacket, I could be the Unabomber, you never know. If that guy wasn't locked up in the SuperMax in Colorado, I might have to call the authorities. A faded black-and-white plaid jacket completed the bush pilot uniform. More like bush pilot wannabe, Willie was fond of reminding me. A guy had to spend a lot more years flying the backcountry to earn that exalted title in his mind.

Willie was a proud man and proud of who he was. He was a natural, an Alaska born and raised flyer since he was a teenager. He'd spent years flying SuperCubs and other small planes fish spotting and hauling cargo and people to all corners of the final frontier. A guy like that doesn't expect to have things handed to him. He made his own way. Solved his own problems with his own resources. Played by his own rules.

I stretched my right foot up to the step and reached inside to grab the reinforcing bar above the windshield. Then I swung up and inserted myself inside the cockpit. Settling into the front seat, I was reminded again that it was good to be a little guy when you're strapping on a SuperCub. I might not be six feet tall, in fact, I might not be over five and a half feet, but it didn't keep me from flying. It was actually an advantage. There was more room for me in the cockpit, and at a hundred and fifty pounds I could carry more weight in an airplane than my heftier colleagues.

The SuperCub's fuselage was an intricate network of lightweight steel tubing. It looked simple but the crossbars and braces connected in a carefully engineered masterpiece of design. I always loved that first sensation of sitting in the cockpit before a flight. I wriggled to get comfortable. My elbows touched the walls of the cabin on either side.

The instrument panel filled the space in front of me; the gauges and dials stared up at me like eyeballs set in the rough black metal face of the panel. One instrument had been removed some time ago—probably an engine temperature gauge. The empty hole revealed green and black wires and tubes behind the panel.

I took hold of the control stick between my knees by the round ball on its top end and gave it a shake. Moving it in all directions I twisted my neck around and watched the ailerons and elevator responding just like they should. The stick in the backseat moved in unison, too, in case I had a copilot back there. But I rarely did.

I looked down and made sure my feet were clear of obstacles where they fit against the rudder pedals. The brake pedals by my heels stuck up through the floor. Mud was caked against them from the last flight, and I kicked at them to break it loose.

Hooking up the seatbelts and running through the handy plastic checklist, I was ready to go: three pushes on the primer knob, master switch on, and a firm press of the starter button. The hundred and fifty Lycoming horses under the cowling seemed to wake up one cylinder at a time as they shook off the morning chill and began to shudder in harmony. In a few moments, the whole plane was rumbling around me. Making sure the oil pressure came up in the green, I took a minute to let her warm up while I gazed outside.

With clear blue skies out the windshield and the windsock indicating about five knots of wind from the north, my weather briefing was complete. There's not a lot of information available in the small communities of Alaska. Normally, the only way to find out the conditions on the other side of a mountain around here is to fly over there and stick your nose in it.

Pushing the throttle forward with my left hand, I could feel the lumpy doughnut tires reluctantly begin to move, and we began our taxi to the south end of the field. After a runup and another check of all systems and flight controls, we were ready to go.

It always surprised me how quickly she jumped into the air. With full throttle and a decent headwind, in less than a hundred feet, we were airborne. Snow-covered mountains lay dead ahead and on all sides, but a turn to the left pointed us toward open sky over the bay.

As the SuperCub pulled us into the morning sky, I could feel power pumping through my veins. Just like the fuel flowing through the gas lines from the wing tanks above me, the hungry engine sucked its life force into the carburetor and with many controlled explosions hurtled us up the west side of Resurrection Peninsula. Well, perhaps I should rephrase that: SuperCubs don't exactly hurtle, but we were making good progress.

The sleepy little town of Seward slipped by on our right, her three thousand residents moving through their midmorning routines. I looked over and wondered how many of them never had the opportunity to do what I was doing on a daily basis. It made me feel like one of the privileged people on the planet.

How lucky was I to be up here guiding my own machine through some of the world's most spectacular scenery? The only tradeoff was money. There wasn't much up here in the air. But on mornings like this, squinting into the sun with the engine roaring and my spirit soaring, I felt almost overwhelmed with riches.

Looking to my left, I saw the prison on the east side of the bay passing underneath. I wondered if the residents of Spring Creek Correctional Facility could hear me flying by high above them. I wondered if the sound of my freedom echoed in their sadness, but I didn't let my thoughts linger on that for long. I preferred not to think about how close I had come on more than one occasion to joining them. I supposed there were residents on both sides of the bay who felt trapped.

I pulled my thoughts back to the task at hand. Getting carried away was a distraction I didn't need. The plane felt alive around me, tingling with a sense of purpose. We had a mission today, SuperCub and me. Our goal was a small forested bay less than thirty minutes ahead. The airframe vibrated with a soothing rumble through the seat of my pants,

Flying through the wilderness gives a guy time to think. Sometimes that's a good thing. Sometimes not. As we gained altitude, the forested mountainsides gave way to rock faces and cliffs, then just big rocks and shadows. When I realized we were going to make it up and over the ridgeline, I banked left and turned toward the notch. This small opening in the skyline was only a couple of hundred feet wide. It saved climbing another thousand feet, so local pilots used it to save time. Besides, it was fun as hell. And reasonably safe—as long as some other crazy sonofabitch wasn't using the same notch at the same time coming the opposite way.

The blue expanse of Day Harbor came into view as we sailed through the rocks and over the ridge. I've seen whales in these waters before, but on that day I was thinking about the beach a few miles ahead. Ellsworth Glacier hunkered in the landscape off to the left.

At my altitude I was good to go to cross the wide and deep stretch of water below. If my engine quit I would still be able to glide to one shore or the other. It was habit to check for some kind of beach or clear spot like a meadow among the trees where I could make a forced landing, but in terrain like this I'd have to set her down in the water. Preferably close to shore. And hopefully close enough to shore that I could get out of the frigid water before my arms and legs quit moving.

I kept my altitude when I reached the far side of the bay and proceeded east over more forested mountain sides with rocky ridgelines around Whidbey Bay. The snow line was moving higher and higher up the mountains as summer approached, and bright sunlight reflected an almost painful brilliance into the cockpit. Then Mount Fairfield slid underneath us, and Johnstone Bay came into view. The land in this part of the Chugach National Forest was a series of troughs and ridges running north to south and jutting into the sea like bony fingers. High country to the left and north of us, and the wide expanse of the Gulf of Alaska to the right. Excelsior Glacier slid down from the Sergeant Icefield into an iceberg-filled lake. Between the lake and the long curved beach of

Johnstone Bay lay several acres of flat land forest at the base of the valley. A small river connected the lake to the bay gently curving its way through the forest. In the middle of these woods lay my target.

I thought back over last night's phone conversation. Stan Morgan with Alaska Rentals in Anchorage called me while I was at the Yukon Bar. I hadn't turned off my phone yet, which I usually do once I start drinking. Not only can I not fly anymore once I start with the booze, but I'm just not that interested in being called then anyhow.

Somebody asked me about that once when I was turning off my phone.

"Doesn't that make you hard to reach?" he asked.

I gave him my best Steve McQueen answer. "Yup."

But last night, Stan called before I shut her down. "Hey, Johnny; I need your help with something. You still doing repo?"

"Sure, Stan. What's up?"

"I got a guy who rented a chainsaw from us over two months ago. Said he was clearing trees from a place he bought on Johnstone Bay. His ID checked out, but he paid cash for a five-day rental, and I haven't heard from him since."

"Just a little overdue, eh? You want me to go get it?"

"Yeah, if you could. You're the only one I know with a bush plane that'll do remote repo."

"Yeah, that's my niche. Can do, Stan. And you're okay with my standard deal?"

"I pay you half of what it would cost me to replace the unit, right? It would cost me about seven hundred bucks, so we have a deal for three hundred fifty?"

"Yeah, that'll work. And don't forget, that's the fee whether it takes me five minutes or five months to get it back. You still okay with that?"

"I understand. You got to protect yourself if it gets messy. I don't blame you, and it's still a good deal for me. I could always write it off and buy a new one, but this model's discontinued and I want it back. Besides if you don't find it, I pay nothing. That still the deal, Johnny?"

"Yep, that's it. So give me the details. I need the guy's name and location, and the equipment make, model, and serial number."

He filled me in on all the info, and I wrote it all down in a little notebook I carried in the breast pocket of my jacket. I was hoping this job would be routine. I really needed the money. The nice thing about living in a camper was that there was no rent—if you kept moving, that is. But that propane repair might be expensive. And the bar wouldn't carry any credit. How unfair is that for struggling bush pilots? Ah hell, I shouldn't complain. No one wanted to listen to some loser in a plaid shirt bitch and moan. No one but Willie. He'd listen all night. As long as I was buying the beer. Damn guy.

I reached up to check my pocket again. Just to be sure I hadn't dropped the notebook while I was climbing into the plane. It was still there. I noticed the pocket of my jacket was dirt stained and greasy.

That reminded me that tourist season would be rolling around pretty soon, and I'd have to upgrade my clothes a bit. I liked the repo jobs since I could dress grubby. But when I did scenic flights, I tried to be a little more presentable. Not all the tourists appreciated the basic nature of the Alaskan bush pilot and our reputation for less formal attire, which actually meant grubby, hairy, and coarse.

I'd done several of these repossession jobs in the last few years. Some were routine, and others were a real pain in the ass. My success rate was good. Only failed once. Never could find that sonofabitch—or the generator he made off with. Some were out-and-out ripoffs, but others were just folks who forgot. Sometimes things came up. I understood that. But the equipment rental people needed the stuff on their shelves if they were going to make any money. That was the need I tried to fill.

I surveyed the location below me from two thousand feet so my subject wouldn't realize anyone was looking for him. That was my usual method. To arrive unannounced before they had a chance to take off or hide the equipment from me. I learned the hard way that if you approach these things straight up, you wind up chasing all over the place. Then you end up with nothing but a lot of wasted time and fuel. Damned expensive fuel. Over five bucks a gallon these days. With the deals I made there wasn't much payoff anyhow, so I had to be efficient to come out ahead.

My favorite recovery was when no one was home. Especially when the equipment was sitting in a backyard. All it took was a quick lean over the fence. Pick up and go with no hassle, minimum time, and just one plane ride to get it and one more plane ride to deliver it and get paid.

Stan was my favorite customer. He always paid right away, and he was a nice guy about it. Some of my other customers gave me attitude if they thought I'd made the money too easily. They didn't understand that some jobs were money losers for me, so I had to get a break once in a while with a profitable situation. It was the only way I could keep doing this. So far it was working out okay. It was a good deal for the rental guys. They got their stuff back cheaper than replacing it. They couldn't get it themselves most times. Or they didn't want to. So they called me.

Everybody was happy. I got to fly around remote Alaska and I got paid for it, and they saved time and money. Well, not everybody was happy. The crooks didn't like it much. That's why I had to be careful how I handled things. But screw the crooks. If they were trying to steal from hardworking folks like Stan and his wife, they deserved to lose the stuff they'd taken.

I could see the cabin down below where Stan said it would be. A blue tarp, remote Alaska's favorite roofing material, was clearly visible next to the building. I had already verified the name against property records before I left so I didn't waste a trip. A local Realtor buddy did that for me.

I couldn't see any activity or signs of people around. No boats tied up at the nearby lake shore, and no planes or vehicles around the beach area where I was going to land. The property actually had a short landing strip cut out of the woods right next to the little cabin. I could see evidence of recent tree cutting where the owner was probably using the chainsaw to improve the airstrip.

I thought about landing on his strip but quickly decided against it. Too many negatives. That would definitely alert any occupants of my arrival, and on private property I might run right into a hostile reception. All these guys out here had weapons and knew how to use them. Not to mention remote landowners in Alaska took a dim view of trespassers.

With no one in sight, I pushed the stick forward, pulled back on the throttle, and banked left to check out a spot to land. The glassy water on the lake and calm seas offshore told me I had no wind to worry about. The beach was deserted and the tide was fairly low, so I had plenty of real estate. A SuperCub doesn't need much. I concentrated on the far end, a good distance from where I saw a path leading toward the cabin.

I made my first pass at about twenty feet off the surface looking down the left side of the plane to find the best spot to set her down. I used as little power as possible to keep the noise level down in case someone was home. The cabin was about a mile away from the beach so if I was careful I could still preserve the surprise.

Everything looked good. The surface was fairly smooth with typical gravel and small rocks. Nothing to damage the prop or puncture the tires. And no big chuckholes or bad surprises either. A couple of driftwood logs were scattered here and there but I saw plenty of room to avoid them.

The next pass I slowed way down and let the tires roll onto the surface for a couple of seconds. It felt normal, but I lifted off again, banked left, and looked down one more time. The shallow tracks I'd left behind told me the surface was plenty firm to land on without bogging down in deep sand.

From just fifty feet up this time, I cut the engine to idle, turned to final, pulled the Johnson bar all the way up and the flaps helped slow us down to about forty-seven knots. Holding the nose steady, I craned my neck left to concentrate on the landing spot and let her slide. Just before touchdown, a slight nudge on the throttle gave me exactly the attitude I wanted. I waited for the tires to rumble on the bumpy surface of the beach. As soon as she touched down, I pulled the throttle all the way off again, and held firm pressure back on the stick.

My feet on the brake and rudder pedals started an automatic dance so I could keep the nose pointed straight ahead. Beaches always wanted to suck a plane into the water. Without any crosswind it was no big deal. I brought us to a stop.

 I couldn't help but smile. With a half-mile of beach left in front of me, I figured I'd stopped in less than four hundred feet. Plus, I had plenty of room in front of me to take off straight ahead, so I could leave the plane right where she was. That way if I needed to make a hasty departure with an angry mob on my ass, I wouldn't waste any time taxiing or turning around.

 I shut her down and climbed out to take a look. The first thing I noticed was the quiet. Only a gentle sound of small waves slipping up the beach to my left. Out on the ocean I could just make out the outline of one small fishing boat slowly working its way toward Prince William Sound. Otherwise, I was completely alone. An eagle screeched high overhead, letting me know my arrival had been noticed after all.

 I reached into the backseat and swung a small daypack over my shoulder. I looked at the shotgun under the wing but decided to leave it. I hadn't seen any bears on my approach into the area, and if I ran into someone, I preferred to appear defenseless to keep suspicions to a minimum. I hoped my decision about leaving the shotgun wasn't going to bite me in the butt. Besides, I had a can of pepper spray in the pack just in case.

 I started back down the beach to find the path I'd seen from the air. I went over the cover story I was going to use. I was planning to tell any unexpected people I ran into that I had heard this property was for sale, and I was just out to take a look-see. That way my snooping around and looking into things would sound halfway plausible.

 If bad guys don't think you're a cop, they tend to just growl at you and run you off with threats rather than doing anything drastic. That was my theory anyhow. It had worked for me so far, and I was sticking with it. Besides, the information Stan had given me had all checked out, so there weren't any obvious signs that I was dealing with a thief or any other kind of bad guy. This person probably just spaced out the chainsaw and forgot about it. He'd probably even be happy that I'd come to pick it up and save him the trouble. Well, he'd be happy until Stan came after him for the extra rental and recovery charges. But that part wasn't my problem. I found the path and started into the woods.

Then I spotted bear scat. A couple of brown lumps lay on the trail unmistakable in their shape. I wasn't going to stick a finger in to check their freshness, but I did take a closer look. They weren't recent, I could tell that much. At least several days old, I figured, from their appearance and lack of odor. But it still made me nervous. The trees were close together now, crowding the little trail and almost blocking out the sunshine. I started feeling a little vulnerable out there without a weapon. In the Alaska wilderness. Alone. In a dark forest.

Sometimes I sang out loud in places like this to make sure I didn't surprise the carnivores. Willie taught me that years ago. "Take Me Out to the Ballgame" was his favorite. But that would tip off my target too, so I picked up a stick and thumped it on some tree trunks as I moved forward more slowly.

"Knock it off," I grumbled at myself. "Stop being a wuss. Get a grip." I thought about the twelve-gauge again, but clouds were starting to appear over the mountains and the wind was picking up. I didn't want to waste the time to backtrack in case bad weather came in and trapped me here. So I moved on.

CHAPTER 3

The woods opened up ahead, and with relief I stepped out onto the small airstrip I had seen from the air. It was a nice setup. Someone had put in a lot of work making a nice landing field. Freshly cut tree trunks and piles of chopped firewood were stacked here and there—probably thanks to Stan's stolen chainsaw.

Turning to my left I spotted a cabin in the trees at the far end of the strip. I reached it after a few minutes' walk. There was no one around. The A-frame cabin had a nice deck in front; around back I spotted an outhouse, a work shed, and an elevated food cache built from logs that sat on stilts about twenty feet up a log ladder. There was no chainsaw in sight.

I made my way back around to the front door and looked it over. A cheap padlock secured the place from the outside, so unless the owner was running a prison, there was nobody home. That made me feel better. With nobody home I could relax and do what I needed to do. Even if an airplane came to land at the strip, I would be able to hear it well in advance and get the hell out of there. I could disappear into the woods, and they'd never see me.

With a deep breath, I slid the pack off my back and removed a small black leather case that held my lock picks. I liked this part of the job—when I got to play James Bond. I took off my sunglasses and pulled on a pair of tight-fitting gloves. Selecting two tools, I took hold of the padlock and inserted the wrench into the keyhole. With one hand I applied just enough pressure on the wrench to pinch the tiny pins in their respective cylinders. With my other hand I inserted my favorite pick and began to manipulate the pins.

When I watched TV shows about this stuff, I always chuckled when the hero sticks one pick in a lock and pops it open. Maybe the producers are trying to disguise the real process, but anyone with a clue knows that lock picking is an art. It takes tons of practice and a careful, painstaking touch to open even some of the simplest locks. And it takes two tools, for chrissake. How dumb do they think we are?

Sure, I could have just pried off the lock hardware on the door with a simple crowbar in five seconds, but I had my standards. I took pride in leaving a job with no clues left behind. No damage, no fingerprints, no mess. Nothing but the absence of the stuff they weren't supposed to have in the first place. What were they going to do? Complain to the police that their stolen goods were stolen? Sorry, dipstick, you're left with a big bag of nothing.

If you're a thief, I want you to be confused. I don't want to give you any direct evidence of my having been there. It's just a quirk, I guess. Call it method, maybe, or professionalism. Even a lowly repo man can have style.

So that's my trademark. You'll never know I was there. You stole some shit, but then all of a sudden it's gone. And you're right back where you started, dumbass. Without any clue about what happened. Crime doesn't pay, does it, moron?

But in this case, I was still giving the guy the benefit of the doubt. I was assuming it was just an oversight. So I come and get the stuff. No harm, no foul, everybody's happy. Johnny Wainwright scores again, flying the friendly skies of wilderness Alaska in his SuperCub, making money and having fun. I'm no cop. Don't want no part of all that BS, but I can deliver a little justice my way, and even make a living at it. Sort of a living.

There was another reason for my modus operandi, of course. Some people had the nerve to call my work habits breaking and entering. Or burglary. Those people had no sense of humor. They also tended to wear uniforms and carry badges and guns. Another good reason to avoid leaving signs of my visits. That way, I could always maintain that I just repo'd stuff. *Honest, officer, that chainsaw was just laying there in a public area. I heard it had been "misplaced," so I just picked it up and took it back to its rightful owner.*

Besides, a lot of laws are just protection for thieves and bad guys. If I had to cut a few corners to deliver real justice, where's the harm? Someone has to help out the victims of crime. Yes, sir, I had my rationalizations down pat. I took great pains to not have them tested.

It took a few minutes but soon the lock yielded to my touch, and I was in. I took a quick look around but didn't see a chainsaw. Since the coast was clear I spent more time checking every nook and cranny. Still nothing.

The place was clean and well kept. There were family photos on the walls. It seemed like a normal summer getaway cabin. The whole look and feel of the place made me even more certain that the chainsaw renter was just a space cadet, not a bad guy.

After making sure that everything was in its original place, I moved outside and locked the padlock behind me. I even made sure I hadn't tracked mud onto the deck. Then it was time to check the shed in the back yard. That's when the trouble started.

There was a small clearing behind the main house. The shed was on the left, its backside in the trees. In the middle stood a simple outhouse. On the right side of the open space, a big pile of something was covered with a blue tarp. Nothing moved. The surrounding woods loomed darkly like an old musty theater curtain hiding a thousand secrets. The stillness was deadly. Silence hung in the air like a heavy blanket. All of a sudden I was nervous as hell, and I had no idea why.

I tried to shake off the creepy feeling and walked over to the shed. To my surprise there was no lock, just a bar across the door to keep animals out. I looked around the clearing before moving inside the shed, but there was nothing to see. I sensed that something was watching me, but I didn't know what. I felt like I had walked onto an empty stage in front of an invisible, hostile audience.

The shed was small, only about six feet square. Without a window, it was dark as a tomb inside. I took a flashlight out of my pack, but it only flickered for about five seconds, then went out. Banging it on my knee did no good either. Damn it. So much for all that professional-style bullshit.

Just before the light went out, I spotted a battery-powered lantern hanging from the ceiling. Reaching up, I was surprised that it came on when I pushed the switch. I closed the door of the shed behind me. I liked to do my snooping undisturbed, and closing doors helped. It probably didn't matter much here in the wilderness, but it was habit.

The small room was full of tools either hanging from nails or leaning against the walls. There were axes, shovels, rakes, and a huge two-man saw. There was also an ancient scythe with a wooden handle and a long rusted blade hanging from a hook. Reminded me of the Grim Reaper. A shudder crawled up my spine.

Get over yourself, Johnny. You're just creeping yourself out.

I heard a noise outside, and I froze. Straining my ears, I listened trying to identify the source. I thought about the woods outside. If I had to, I could jump out the door and dash into the trees with a pretty good chance of getting away. Unless whoever had just arrived came into the shed. Then I'd be trapped. I moved quickly to the door and tried to peek through spaces between the boards. I couldn't see a thing. Then I heard another noise.

The blue tarp on the other side of the clearing was moving around with a jerky motion. A bear cub's head poked up behind the tarp. I watched as the little animal climbed up on top of the pile. Sitting on top it grappled with the material, clawing and ripping at its surface with its little teeth and claws. The stiff blue plastic crackled and crunched under the abuse. Then another cub climbed up and tackled its sibling, both of them growling and rolling across the shredded cloth.

Shit. Two cubs just twenty yards away. They couldn't have been more than a couple months old. This was bad news. Cubs meant momma had to be nearby. Sure enough, an enormous grizzly sow came into view standing over the blue pile watching her cubs. She stood on her hind legs and peered across the clearing, her eyes squinted and her nose twitched as she surveyed the area for threats. With her poor eyesight, I didn't think she could see me through the cracks in the door. But I forgot about trying to dash out the door into the woods.

There was nothing more dangerous in Alaska than a grizzly sow with cubs. And running was the worst thing you could do. It made you look like prey and triggered their "Let's grab some lunch" response.

The best advice: Don't act like food.

At least I was okay in the shed for a while. The walls wouldn't keep a bear out, but I didn't see any food in there that would attract them. There had to be a lot of human scent in the area, so I hoped she hadn't detected me yet. If I just kept my cool and waited a few minutes, they might lose interest in the blue tarp and move on.

Or so I hoped. Then one of the cubs started batting around a jar of something and licking its top. Momma noticed and took it away, but the way she continued to lick and bite at it, it must have been food of some kind. The smell on the outside of the jar had their interest. When it broke open all three of them started slurping eagerly at the contents.

The big grizzly tore back the rest of the tarp, and I spotted good news and bad news. Good news first. Stan's chainsaw was laying there in plain view. I could even see his business name, Alaska Rentals, on the blade. The bad news was there were at least thirty more jars, probably the same stuff, stacked beside the chainsaw.

Shit and double shit. A glance at the sky didn't help my mood any. Clouds were starting to block out the blue sky and the treetops were swaying in a heavy breeze. I thought about the SuperCub out there on the beach, not tied down. I thought about the shotgun under its wing instead of here where I needed it. I wondered how long I was going to be stuck there waiting for the bears to finish eating all the jam or whatever the hell it was.

I turned to have a look around inside the shed again and banged my head into the lantern. It swung violently from side to side, casting weird shadows on the walls. I grabbed frantically with both hands to stop the lamp from swinging and fought the urge to swear out loud. Since I wasn't holding the door closed anymore, the wind pushed it open behind me. I snapped the light switch off and moved back to the side of the door trying desperately not to be seen by the bears. In the dark I bumped against an old shovel and it clattered to the ground. I froze. All the noise outside stopped. All I could hear was the wind rattling branches and whistling through the treetops.

With my back against the wall of the shed, I didn't dare look outside and expose myself to the grizzly. I didn't move a muscle, but I could feel the bears staring in my direction. I was a dead duck trapped in the tiny room with no way out and five hundred pounds of angry grizzly in my way.

After a long wait the cubs must have gotten restless. They started to move again, and I could hear their growling sounds and the crunch of heavy glass jars.

Turning carefully in their direction I found a crack in the wall, and sure enough, momma bear was standing closer now, between me and the cubs. She was glaring hard in my direction. She must have been six feet tall, her ears were back, her head was swinging from side to side and she was clacking her jaws. All the classic signs of a nervous bear.

Slowly sliding the pack off my shoulders I reached inside for the pepper spray. It was a small can, just four ounces. Great, just enough for seasoning. I remembered that anything larger was prohibited from airplanes. Hazardous material rules, or some shit like that.

I looked closer at the can. I groaned silently when I saw the cap. That was going to make a noise coming off. No way to avoid that. I raised it up to my face to examine the trigger mechanism and saw the instructions on the side.

In case of a bear encounter, remain calm.

Yeah, right. Screw you. It was all I could do to not wet my pants.

I looked back through the crack. She was still standing and twitching her nose in my direction. I remembered for some damn reason that I hadn't showered that morning and kicked myself for it. But she must not have picked up my lousy hygiene, because she dropped down to all fours.

More seconds ticked by, and with one more look in my direction, she slowly turned and went back to the pile of food jars. I realized then that the wind was coming from behind them, so she couldn't get my scent. I thought about bolting from the shed into the woods. But that wouldn't get me the chainsaw.

The stack of jars was going to keep them busy for hours, and I was running out of time. When I saw momma turn her back to me, I reached over and pulled the door closed. Bears have great ears, and I hoped as hard as a guy can hope that the door didn't squeak. She would probably hear my heart pounding first anyhow.

As quiet as I could I pulled the shovel against the bottom edge of the door to keep it from blowing open again. I spotted another blue tarp folded up behind some boxes, and an idea came to me. I took a minute to think things over while I looked through the wall boards again. Then moving carefully around the room, I collected a long axe and a rake that I found leaning against the wall. I kneeled down and unfolded the tarp taking my time to keep it quiet. A drop of sweat dripped from under my cap and dribbled down the side of my nose. I wiped it with the back of one hand as I took out my Leatherman and silently opened a knife blade.

It took me a while moving that slowly, but when I was ready I carefully moved to the door and slid it open. Without revealing myself just yet and watching through the crack, I pressed my lips against the gap in the rough boards and started to call in a slow sing-song voice.

"Hello, Missus Bear. Hello. How are you?"

Three fuzzy heads jerked in my direction. Momma Griz stood up and started clacking her jaw and swinging her head again. She shuffled her huge feet back and forth positioning herself for a charge.

"Yeah, Missus Bear. I'm over h-here, and believe me, I don't want no tr-trouble with you." My jaw was trembling so much I had trouble keeping my voice low and calm.

Her massive head stopped moving when she spotted me, and her beady eyes stared daggers. The cubs reacted too. They watched their mom nervously and stopped slurping at the spilled jam. My mouth felt like it was full of dry sand.

She watched me intently, but so far she wasn't charging. I guess she was still trying to figure out what I was. Then I held up the shovel draped with the blue tarp and hung it out the door. I stayed inside so all she could see was the blue fabric sticking out the door. I waved it gently while I kept talking slow and easy.

"Hello, Missus Bear. Yeah, it's me over here, but it's okay. Don't want no trouble with you. You don't have to worry about me. I don't want your food."

Little by little I exposed more of my shape out the door. I had made a poncho out of the blue tarp with a hole cut for my head. The shovel and the pepper spray were in my left hand under the tarp, and the axe was in my right hand. I kept talking and slowly moved out of the shed until I was in full view, a huge crackling blue shape crinkling and scuffling slowly into the clearing like a big blue blob.

Thanks to the tools in my hands and the tarp, I must have been about ten feet wide—not to mention strange looking. Especially to a bear. My bulk made me over twice her size.

The grizzly stared at me in disbelief. She was either thinking, "Good grief, look at this silly chunk of lunch meat." Or "What the hell is this? Let's get outta here." I hoped it was the latter.

The cubs took one look at me, then turned and ran bawling into the woods. It was now up to momma and me to work out our differences.

I kept up the soft and slow patter and avoided looking her straight in the eye. Prisoners and grizzlies have that in common. No direct eye contact unless you're looking for trouble.

"It's okay, Missus Griz. If you'll just give me a minute, I'll be on my way. I promise. Then you can finish your snack there."

I stayed close to the shed in case I needed to jump back inside. She could have charged me at any second. I had the pepper spray ready even though I figured that would only piss her off. I had the axe ready too in case I needed to fight for my life.

She didn't seem to like the crackly fabric of the blue tarp around me. Every time I made some noise with it, she acted more agitated and looked around for her cubs. They were nowhere in sight. She made a sound as if calling them, and I heard the cubs squeaking an answer from the woods. Slowly, she dropped to all fours and starting backing away from me. She looked back and forth between the pile of jars and me but kept moving into the forest. Finally she turned and disappeared.

I started breathing again and moved quickly to pick up the chainsaw. The data tag was right where Stan said it would be, but it was covered with sawdust and grease. I had to swipe it with my thumb to see the serial number. It was the right one.

I didn't want to take any chances with the bears so I struggled out of the tarp fast. I folded it as best I could and put it back in the shed with the tools. I kept glancing into the woods for signs of bears but saw nothing. I put the crossbar back in place on the door and hoisted the chainsaw onto my shoulder. With a last look around, I headed for the airstrip again to get back to the plane.

As I moved through the grass, the reality of the bear encounter started to sink in, and my knees were shaking so bad I could hardly walk. I kept the pepper spray in my free hand the whole way.

It took a while but the walking helped me calm down. The chainsaw bouncing on my shoulder was just starting to feel heavy by the time I reentered the woods. But I didn't care about the weight. I was tweaking with the thrill of victory.

Score one for Johnny Wainwright, bush pilot repo man. I started dreaming about how good three hundred fifty dollars was going to feel in my hands. What a chucklehead.

When I reached the beach I was tired. I realized I'd practically run the whole way back. It was getting close to four o'clock. I had to get back to Seward before Willie started to worry about me. Happily, the weather was okay even though it was getting cloudy. Only one concern remained: Would the engine start? That last fear evaporated when the engine sparked on the first try.

The wind had shifted to the south, and the steady breeze off the ocean helped me lift the SuperCub into the air in about a hundred feet. The muffled roar of all one hundred and fifty horses reverberated through the fabric covered wings and fuselage like drumbeats urging us onward. Setting a course along the rocky shoreline, I was finally able to relax and enjoy the view for the thirty-minute trip home.

The airport was empty when I landed and taxied up to my tie-down spot. Except for Willie. He was waiting for me there in his car. I pulled the chainsaw out of the back of the plane and gave him a big grin and a thumbs up. I stashed the saw in the office and climbed in beside him.

"What the hell was that all about?" he asked.

I told him about the repo job and the bears as we drove downtown. He just shook his head. "I hope it was worth it, Johnny. You're gonna run out of luck one of these days, you know."

"Three hundred and fifty bucks, man. How much did you make today?"

I could tell from his expression that he hadn't worked at all. His on-call job with the Department of Transportation was part-time and very hit and miss. Mostly miss lately, so he didn't have much to say. But he did raise his eyebrows for a moment. "Three hundred and fifty bucks for a ride out to Johnstone Bay and back? Pretty easy money, I guess."

"Yeah, right," I grunted, remembering the grizzly's clacking jaws. "A piece of cake. So shut the hell up, man. Mister Moneybags'll buy you a beer."

CHAPTER 4

I don't know how Alaska became the world's drop-off collection point for eccentric people. But it had. And when eccentric people in this part of Alaska get thirsty, they go to the Yukon Bar. You have to suspend judgment to be a regular in the Yukon Bar. If you can't, you'll always be on the outside looking in.

Willie and I parked in his customary spot and walked around the corner. On the corner of Fourth and Washington, the Yukon Bar was a simple single-story structure with a rustic faux log cabin façade. All the standard neon beer signs graced the outside windows. A pool table and a fifty-foot bar waited inside for patrons. Crumpled dollar bills covered the ceiling of the joint, placed there by visitors who wanted to commemorate their visits, and the walls were filled with memorabilia. When more than ten customers were present, a pallid smokescreen hung in the air.

North To Disaster

Over the bar a prominent bear head leered at the customers, a ragged tennis shoe jutting from its toothy grin. Someone had added the caption, "Send More Tourists."

And tourists did frequent the bar, but May was a little early for most travelers to the north. Before the summer season started to hit its full stride, local fishermen, cannery workers, and working folk of all kinds spread out along the bar and filled the tables. When you spent your day ripping the guts out of fish, you needed a drink. Maybe several.

The Yukon Bar was unpretentious. Not much underground there. It was all on the surface. New faces appeared at times, but the usual suspects were implanted like fixtures in their regular spots. Especially before tourist season began in earnest.

"Hey, Willie. Hey, Johnny. You gentlemen having the usual?"

"Jeez, you'd think we were regular bar flies around here or something, Goldie."

"Aw, shut up and sit your asses down like you do everyday. Give me a freakin' break."

Goldie was your basic brassy piece-of-work Alaskan bartender. Short and stout, she flipped her long black hair behind her as she carried buckets of ice through the bar, trailing cigarette smoke and broken hearts behind her. Her bulging biceps and square jaw commanded respect. Quick with a joke or to light up your smoke, as the old Billy Joel song goes. When she smiled, it was usually a sarcastic smirk and her golden tooth sparkled like a construction zone warning light.

Goldie was also an expert in keeping a guy humble. She was unimpressed with the usual bullshit men brought to her plate, and she could single handedly serve an evening crowd with a live band and hundreds of customers overflowing into the street. She was also known for disarming monster lumberjacks on their way to the alley for a friendly knife fight.

She had us pegged, of course, and our beers were open and ready before we even sat down. Willie and I were regulars at the Yukon. Most any evening of the week, we could be found at the first corner of the bar as soon as you came in the front door. Willie called it the Revenue Corner. It's his theory that the majority of the bar's nightly money can be made right at that location. Willie considers himself quite the expert on such matters. In fact, he considers himself quite the expert on a number of topics, but the rest of us know he's mostly full of crap.

But his revenue corner theory makes some sense, so we all listened more respectfully than usual when he started expounding that point of view.

"You gotta see the logic here," he said, his first can of beer already half empty from the first powerful swig. "This spot right here is what everybody sees first when they come in the door. This here is what's called your first impression. This is where the truly thirsty motherfucker makes his first stop. If the bartender's fast, the money's gonna roll."

The rest of us suspected that Willie's frequent lectures were some kind of ruse to vent secret frustrations. Probably after he'd had to wait through an inexcusable delay—meaning more than a minute or two. But Willie couldn't help it. When he was thirsty, he was not a patient man.

I thought Willie liked the corner spot for a couple of reasons. First, the Yukon's owner usually sat there where she can keep her eye on things and greet customers on the way in. Sitting next to her let Willie provide his expertise on bar management whenever necessary. Plus, sitting in the Revenue Corner gave Willie early access to new information. Knowing things first was an important game in Seward, and Willie was one of the best at it. He knew more crap about more stuff than anyone in town. His cell phone was frequently busy as one friend or another notified him of the latest development in some local situation, business development, scandal, tragedy, or plain old gossip. He prided himself in this knowledge, and his station at the Revenue Corner was a key component.

Bugeyed Larry was leaning against the wall by the phone smoking a handrolled cigarette. It smelled reasonably legal for the moment, though later, the men's room would probably reek of dope. Larry looked like a halibut. There was just no nice way to put it. One of his eyes stared straight at you, but the other one had morphed closer to one side of his head and was focused on a point somewhere over your left shoulder and a hundred yards away. Not a problem unless you were trying to talk to him and couldn't decide which eye to look at. Both orbs bulged from his skull like he'd been hanging by the gills from a fish scale for the last week. Bugeyed Larry worked at the cannery, filleting the daily catch for hours at a time. Larry was okay; I just tried not to stand too close to him.

Bars in Seward, like bars all over the world where locals drink, are centers of social discourse and interaction. Like the sign at the end of the bar explained: "Beer—helping ugly people get laid for centuries."

I remembered Willie telling me one time: "Every bar has a personality. The Yukon is no exception. Sure, the building, the décor, all the trappings are important. But the people make the bar. When you walk in the door of a place like this, it's like meeting a stranger. Its personality starts to unfold. Sometimes it feels welcoming, sometimes hostile, sometimes indifferent. The bar has an immediate impact on each visitor whether they realize it or not. And just like any encounter between two personalities, what you bring is what you get."

"So if that's true, Willie, what's the most important thing about a bar?"

"The bartender."

Willie liked Goldie but would never admit it. He said in private, however, that she was a fast bartender. He respected that. He especially respected speed in a bartender when he was thirsty.

I was just starting on beer number two when Scooter, one of the only aircraft mechanics in town, came busting through the door. His bright red hair was long and kinky and pulled back in a tortured ponytail. Today he had it bunched up with a rubber band in a strange knot at the back of his head. He also sported a bright red beard that covered most of his face. The intense expression in his bright blue eyes and fixed stare intimidated most people, but we all knew Scooter as a gentle fellow who was kind of shy. Like a shy Eric the Red with chipped front teeth and high on crack cocaine. But Scooter didn't use drugs—or not very often anyhow.

He looked like he'd run all the way to the bar. Pulling up a stool beside us, he could barely contain his excitement. Scooter was a blinker. Like an uncontrollable tic, he would rapidly and repeatedly scrunch both eyes closed hard like his foot had just been stomped. It was worse when he was excited.

"Have you guys heard about the missing Cub?" Blink, blink.

"The one in Homer?" asked Willie. "Yeah, I heard about it."

"How'd you know about it?" I asked Willie in surprise.

"Homer called me earlier," he said.

"Homer?"

"Yeah, did I stutter? Homer."

"Homer called you, or somebody named Homer?"

"Yeah, Homer called me. You got a problem with that?"

"No, no problem. It just wasn't making sense to me. I mean, Homer's a place, right? And a place can't make phone calls. But if it's a guy named Homer, well, that's different. I was confused before, but now that clears it up."

"Well, I'm glad you're clear now."

"So which was it?"

"Which was what?"

"Guys, guys. I'm trying to tell you something," Scooter interrupted, blinking wildly. "I'll bet you didn't hear the best part. The FBI's involved and they think it's a ring of ripoff artists that's been operating in the Lower Forty-Eight. Now they're up here."

"I already knew all that," Willie smirked. "Even Johnny heard about that already."

"Well, I bet you didn't know this. They're targeting SuperCubs." Blink, blink, blink.

"Whoa, no shit? Why SuperCubs?" Scooter had Willie's attention now. He had mine too. There were only two SuperCubs at Seward's airport. Willie owned one and I owned the other.

"Think about it. If you wanted to steal SuperCubs, where would you go? There's more SuperCubs in Alaska than anywhere else." Scooter took a pull on his beer and wiped his mouth with his shirt sleeve. Alcohol helped slow down the tic, but the less he blinked, the more he talked.

"Okay, but why SuperCubs?"

"For the parts and for rebuilds or something. Hell, I don't know. The wings come off quick, you know. They're only held on by two bolts on each side."

Willie chimed in. "Yeah, that's right. There was this one time when I had one of my wings off for a repair, but then I needed to take it over to Soldotna to a mechanic there, and I couldn't find one of the goddamned bolts. So I shoved a big screwdriver in the hole and duct taped all around it to keep it from falling out. Then I flew it over to the repair shop. When the mechanic saw what I'd done, he started yelling and screaming. Called me a crazy motherfucker. I thought it was pretty funny. The screwdriver held it together just fine."

We all laughed. Willie was always telling some story like that about his flying career. It was a wonder he was still alive. We all agreed he was either the luckiest bastard we'd ever known or the best bush pilot in the world.

Willie raised his bottle and said, "Here's to Johnny. He rescued a chainsaw today. Snatched it from the teeth of organized crime and a pack of hungry carnivores. Alaskan bush pilot wannabe repo man."

"Gee, thanks, asshole." I gave him a look.

Scooter was interested. "So you're an airplane repo man, eh? Like taking cars back from the poor slobs who can't make the payments? But you do it with airplanes?"

"Nah, I don't do that shit. I take stuff back from people who are trying to rip off the rental people."

I told Scooter the story about the chainsaw, but he was stuck on the airplane angle. "Wasn't that guy that crashed in Ketchikan a repo man?"

"The one that crashed the Czech fighter jet? Yeah, I did hear he was repossessing it from that company in Anchorage."

"Well, very cool, Johnny."

"Yeah, but that's not what I do. Nobody's asked me to repo an airplane."

He looked disappointed, but then he brightened and grinned at me. "Not yet, man. Not yet. But, hey, who knows?

You could be flying all over the world, doing the repo thing, flying jets and shit."

"Whatever." I drank more beer and pretended to get interested in an old newspaper laying nearby.

Scooter wanted to know more about Homer. "So who got ripped off?" he asked Willie.

Willie looked glum. "A guy named Wally Simmons. He had a sweet Cub that was for sale over there, a fifty-six model, I think. Rebuilt it himself and had it for sale for eighty-five big ones. Homer Fogarty called me about it."

"Homer from Homer," I muttered. "What about Wally? Anything happen to him?"

"No, he just found his parking spot empty one day when he went out to go flying. He hadn't been there for a few days, so he's not even sure when they took it."

The news was unsettling. So much for our quiet little village in the north country. We'd always felt safe here, free from big city problems that plagued so many places down south. Little country airports are typically remote and peaceful havens out in the boondocks. Especially in Alaska. But not anymore.

Our corner of the bar grew quiet. We drank our beers and ordered more. A hockey game was on TV on the wall behind us, and I turned to check it out.

Scooter noticed and turned to watch with me for a minute. "I never could understand what the big deal was with hockey. Christ, the last time I was in Canada this time of year, it was on every TV set in every bar or restaurant I went into. People couldn't talk about anything else. Even the chicks."

"It's Stanley Cup season," I informed him. "The Canadian pastime. It's their obsession. Everybody's into it, and the girls know that if they want any time with a guy they better know a lot about hockey."

"I grew up in Arizona," he said. "I never saw the game until I hit Canada. So what's the big deal?"

"It's big sweaty guys on ice skates knocking each other down over a little piece of rubber. But much more than that. Look at the way these guys move. It's fast. It takes a lot of skill. They've got razor sharp steel on their skates and they're

carrying sticks to smash each other around with. Lots of blood in this game. What could be better than that?"
"And they let 'em fight, too. What's the deal there?"
"Oh, yeah, the fighting's the best part. When one guy fights, he fights for the whole team. He's protecting the stars or retaliating for a dirty hit. It's like he's defending their honor. Like the freakin' knights of the round table or something."
"You used to play?"
"Ah, not much. I played some a while ago just for the hell of it. I was never any good."
On the screen a group of players slammed into the end boards, everybody grabbing somebody, elbows and gloves flying every which way.
"See that? That's what I'm talking about. It's like warfare out there. Your teammates are with you in combat. You're trying to pound the puck past the other team, and they're doing their best to pound it past you. If the enemy bashes one of your mates with a cheap shot, it's your job. No, it's your duty to fight him. The sonofabitch needs to pay."
The play on the screen stopped for a minute. A camera panned across the faces of one team sitting on their bench. Every face was marked with a black eye or stitches in an eyebrow or some other kind of cut or abrasion. Every man was breathing hard, sweating profusely, and staring intently at the other team.
"Look at those guys, Scooter. They're warriors, dancing on the edge of disaster. It's the greatest game on earth."
I noticed that Willie hadn't said a word in a long time. His beers were disappearing about as quick as usual. But he was just leaning against the bar, staring at nothing.
"What's up, man? Why so quiet?" I asked.
"Aw, it's nothing. I just got a lot on my mind. I found a bunch of old bills today that I haven't taken care of, and the goddamn city sent me a tax bill that just about made me blow my stack."
"Bummer."

"I might have to get a real job or something. Bloodsuckers over there are bleeding me dry. And I got nothing in the bank, you know?"

"Maybe you worry too much."

"Shit. I ain't getting any younger. Where's the money gonna come from when I'm an old fart?"

"Dude, you can't let that bullshit get to ya so much. Here, I'll buy you another beer," I said, waving at Goldie for a refill. She noticed me after a minute and nodded. I watched her pouring drinks and making change, and I let my thoughts wander back through some old places where we'd been together.

Goldie and I had a history. Damn it all. I hate when I do that. But the memories were mostly good ones. Sometimes holidays or songs on the radio would bring them back resurfacing like old photos that you find in a dusty box in the basement.

She brought over some fresh beers and I asked, "So how've you been, Goldie?" The beers were making me bold. I was usually pretty quiet in public.

"I'm okay, Johnny; how about you?" She was more relaxed now that the early rush was under control. Her voice was soft and warm. She lingered for a moment, wiping down the beer tap, listening to me.

"I'm the same. Remember when I used to sit here and write you drunken love poems?"

She smiled and looked at me while she wrung out the cloth in the sink. "Yeah, I remember. It's been a long time." She turned away to tend to a customer on the other end of the bar.

I watched her for a minute and let those warm memories wash over me. I thought I saw her smile. The kind of special smile I remembered when she came home late at night. That smile reminded me of good times. Very good times.

Willie interrupted my prurient thought train. "Careful, hound dog. You're getting that look."

"Hey, a guy can dream, can't he?"

"You know better. It's like eating chocolate cake. You have one slice, then another. A little voice says, 'Slow down, dumbass,' but you ignore it and have one more. Maybe even number four. Then all of a sudden you're fat and ugly, wondering what happened."

"Yeah, maybe, but at least I have the satisfaction of eating the whole damn cake. No man is an island, Willie."

"Okay, I'll remember that the next time I hear you puking your guts out and bitching at me for not stopping you."

"Am I puking? Am I bitching? Gimme a break."

"Well, you ain't now, but you sure were back when Goldie dumped your ass."

I turned away from him and drank my beer, staring at the bottle between sips. I looked over at Bugeyed Larry to see if he was eavesdropping, but he was leaning against the wall like usual, his head back, eyes half-staff and unfocused, puffing on a lumpy roll-your-own cigarette, surrounded by smoke.

At first I was irritated. I'd been enjoying my little mind game, watching Goldie work and remembering. And Willie was supposed to mind his own business, drink his fourteen beers, and leave me alone. But he was right, he was always right. Goddamn Willie. Goldie's smile was probably just my ego giving me a stroke. Pure imagination, hallucination, self-gratification. I quit watching Goldie and took a look at Willie.

He didn't look any better, and then he stood up and said, "I'm gonna take off. You wanna ride?"

"Nah, thanks, I'm going to hang out a while longer. Why you leaving so early?"

"Ah, the beer ain't doing me any good tonight. I got a lot on my mind, and now we got thieves to worry about. I'm gonna go check on the airplane. Oh, and my daughter's coming in sometime tomorrow."

"Okay, man. See you in the morning."

Willie left. Wait a minute. A daughter? I didn't even know he had a daughter. Is that what was bothering him? What the hell? Since when did Willie not talk about the shit bothering him? Man, just when you thought you knew a guy.

My head was full of fuzzy cobwebs. I took a look at the cold bottle in my hand, moisture running down the dark glass neck. What the hell was I doing drinking so many beers? I should have taken Willie's offer of a ride, but something made me want to spend some time alone.

I didn't usually drink more than two most evenings, but I had just ordered number four. Way past my limit. My judgment must have been screwed up.

Willie was upset, and I was too drunk to see it. I'm a stupid jerk, I guess. Besides, watching Goldie was distracting me. Sure, she was a cutie pie, but my three-beer buzz had her on a pedestal I couldn't climb with three ladders.

Scooter elbowed me and motioned to the TV with his chin. I turned around to see a Victoria's Secret commercial on the screen replacing the sweaty hockey guys. The almost naked young women bent and moved their bodies to the music surrounded by velvet and feathers and fuzzy see through thingies. Scooter and I looked at each other and clanged our beer bottles together.

"Skol, brother," he said to me in a half-loopy, slurred voice.

"Yes, sir," I slurred back. "Life be good here in the big city."

Scooter swung around abruptly and scowled. "I can't watch that shit no more. It just makes me horny."

"I thought you had a woman, Scoot." I was kidding. Scooter had the social skills of a cross-eyed moose in a staredown contest.

"Who, me? Hell, no. I ain't had…." He looked away and muttered, "It's been a long time."

"Tell me about it, cousin." Okay, so I was pretty drunk. I can always tell I'm loaded when I start hearing myself say "dude" and "cousin" and talking like I was some kind of hip guy from the streets—or at least trying to sound like one.

Scooter drank and stared around the bar. "Look around here, Johnny. There's what, three women in this bar? And maybe twenty-five guys?"

"Yeah, so? You're just now noticing there's a shortage of females up here?"

"No, I've been thinking about doing something about it." He leaned over toward me and dropped his voice, like he was letting me in on a major secret.

"What, Scoot? You gonna order up a wife from one of them catalogs?"

"No, hell no. Have you seen the Bulgarian babes that are working over at the cannery? Foxes, man, unbelievable. But they're gold-diggers, looking for American husbands, to get the citizenship, you know. They don't want nothing to do with lowlife scum-sucking poor bastards like us."

I laughed. "Hey, man. I'm no low bastard scum life, blah, blah, blah. Shit, I can't talk right anymore."

He laughed at me and went on. "No, I got a better idea. There's not enough women up here, so I'm gonna build an artificial one."

I stared at him and stared at my beer. Goldie came over and pointed at it with raised eyebrows. Bartender code for did I want another.

I shook my head and reached in my pocket to find some bills for a tip. Then I remembered what Scooter had been saying, and I shook my head to try and clear out the cobwebs. Did I really hear what he just said?

"What are you talking about, Scooter?"

"I'm gonna make me an artificial woman."

"Well, hell, you can do that this summer. There'll be plenty of those right here in the bar when the tourists start coming."

"No, man, I mean like a doll. It's gonna be made out of a new material I discovered. I'm gonna make a woman's body out of it."

"You mean like an inflatable doll? You can buy those on the Internet."

"No, no, no," he protested.

I ignored him and continued. "I thought you already did that once. Got too rough with it one time, and it exploded. Almost blew your dick off as I recall."

"Very funny, jerkoff. No, I'm serious, this is a hot idea. There's nothing better than snuggling up to a fine behind, spooning with your woman between the sheets. It's the feeling that's important. Does the reality matter if the feeling is good?"

That made me think. My mind drifted back to the feel of fleece on a cold morning. I thought fleece was made out of something real, you know, cotton or some shit, one of the basic materials of the natural world. But imagine my surprise when I learned that most fleece is made of polyester. So maybe Scooter had a point here. Something artificial can give comfort after all. But, come on, it was still strange. This was private stuff, not something I wanted to talk about with a guy like Scooter. I was pretty open-minded, but this was too eccentric.

"Okay, I know you think I'm nuts here, but hear me out for a minute. You're going home to a cold empty bed tonight, right?"

I glanced down the bar for Goldie but she had stepped into the back office—probably to fix the CD player that was stuck. Either that or Eric Clapton had developed a nasty stutter.

"None of your business. I might get lucky."

"Yeah, right. But anyhow, for those lonely nights when it's been too long, think about coming home to a warm hunk of woman in your bed. It can be there for you any time, and feels just like the real thing. The best part is you don't have to talk to her, or pay any attention to her at all unless you feel like it. How cool would that be?"

"Just the torso, huh? What's that mean?"

"The basics. Butt, snatch, thighs."

"What about boobs?"

"Nah, who needs 'em. I just want to spoon and get off, not fall in love."

"You're a sick and twisted man, Scooter."

"You know how some broads can get so annoying, nagging and going on about some stupid bullshit. What's the definition of a blow job?"

I looked at him wondering how I could gracefully escape. "What's that?" I played along.

"Ten minutes of silence."

"Or ten seconds in your case." I laughed.

Scooter turned beet red. "Hey, don't get personal. No, man, I've put a lot of thought into this. I got this friend who deals with plastic skeletons, you know, the kind they use for med schools. There's not enough real cadavers to go around and the plastic ones are cheaper. Anyhow, the key is the pelvis, man. The way it moves. You gotta have part of the backbone attached and part of each leg bone, the femur, you know. So he gave me the parts, and I found this liquid foam rubber stuff that feels like real flesh, and I took the wiring out of an electric blanket to imbed in the rubber so the warmth feels real.

"Oh great," I interrupted. "'How did Scooter die? Oh, he was humping an electrical outlet and hit the main line.'"

"C'mon, Johnny. This is a good idea, especially up here in Alaska. All these horny single guys? Way outnumbering the females? Then think of the secondary market with the military. All those horny young guys overseas? What do you think their number one pastime is? Whacking off, that's what. And they don't even hide it anymore. Every platoon would get issued at least one of my girls. They could pass it around."

"Yeah, I knew a girl like that once."

He laughed. "Now I need some investors, to help me finance all the development costs."

"You might want to keep this idea to yourself, Scooter. Women might get offended hearing about it."

"No way. They'll like it. Think about it; it'll spare them the phony attention of all the jerks with loaded hard-ons that are only being nice to them on hopes of getting laid. Besides, they've had artificial men forever. You know, cucumbers and dildos and all. You want another beer? I'm buying."

"No thanks. You know, man, I think I know why you're single." I stood up and looked for Goldie, but she was busy. I turned to leave and tripped over a scurrying shape on the floor behind my stool. A big dog was lurking there in the shadows just below the bucket of free peanuts, probably looking for a handout.

"Sorry, Goober. Didn't see you there. It must be tough being a black dog in a dark bar." I stooped over to scratch behind her ears. Goober was a Yukon Bar regular too, a black lab owned by a guy playing pool.

She licked my hand in forgiveness. I slipped her a peanut and stepped outside.

I filled my lungs with the moist night air in a deep breath. I was hoping a long walk in the cool breeze might sober me up. I wasn't looking forward to waking up with a hangover. I didn't know that would be the least of my problems.

CHAPTER 5

Before starting my trek, I looked out over the bay. Seward is built on a flat plain of alluvial deposits nestled against the west side of the natural bowl around the bay.

The town sits at the end of the highway from Anchorage, which is about two hours north. It was also the end of the route for most of the cruise ships that came up from Seattle or Vancouver before they turned around and returned south. And it was the end of the railroad line, too. Maybe the end of the line for a lot of us.

The rest of the bowl was filled with chilly water. The flat land to the north held the airport runways. That was my destination. About three miles away. The airport was my home. At least, that's where my home was parked for now.

Fourth Avenue in downtown was the main drag, and I set off to make my way north. A few doors down I passed DJ's Wheelhouse, another of Seward's fine drinking establishments. The crack of pool balls floated out through the door as

I walked by. Two guys were arguing over something, and the lights of the game machines flickered in the background.

A group of Coast Guard sailors filled the sidewalk ahead on their way toward liquid refreshment. They'd already had plenty and were stumbling arm in arm singing the old Johnny Horton song "North to Alaska," but with different words.

"North…to disaster, we're going north, the rush is on." They shouted in drunken mirth and laughed loudly into the night. My head was still spinning and the hint of an omen flashed past before I could notice.

I crossed the empty street and continued up the block, passing Starbird Studio and a couple shops along the way. Up ahead, the First National Bank stood on a well-lit corner across from a travel agency and an office building. Before I got that far, I turned into a gap between two buildings and found the alley. Gravel beneath my feet made the walking a little more uncertain, but the air and the exercise were already starting to clear my head.

I liked alleys. Dumpsters, back doors, few lights, the underside of any town. In Seward, they were mostly unpaved and rutted. When it rained, the puddles were substantial. I didn't care. I felt more at home in the shadows that night.

Seward has its mix of haves and have-nots. The big shots owned a couple of the fancier hotels in town, and the larger businesses—charter boat operations, gas stations, hardware stores, the dry dock, et cetera. I walked along watching the ground in front of me. Haves and have-nots. I knew which group I was in. I wondered if the haves ever walked through these alleys.

Passing by City Hall and the police station, I thought about the struggles that go on in little towns like this. Depending on the tourist trade for big dollars, Seward was split into two factions: One group wanted more tourists and business, and the other group didn't. Almost every new idea meant a fight. Prosperity versus preservation. This part of downtown was the center of the old school folks.

I could understand both sides. Growth would be good for me, since I got some business from eager tourists every summer who wanted to see the sights from a small plane. But

I liked the traditional small town stuff, too. Hell, Seward didn't even have a traffic light, and I liked that.

I stayed out of politics. Let the big shots fight that out. I'd make my way the best I could in the meantime with whatever might float my way. Besides, I thought the struggle was boring as hell. Especially since I couldn't make any difference. Who was going to listen to a guy living in a Toyota camper?

At the top of a small rise north of downtown, I made my way past some of the largest buildings in town, AVTEC, the vocational school, and its dormitories. The term was almost out for the summer. The mostly Native young people would go back to their villages in the bush. Lots of Natives lived in Seward, but they generally kept to themselves. I only knew a couple. The overall population was somewhere between two and three thousand people, and most of it was lily white.

Small homes lined the streets in this part of town. Most had pickups parked nearby or small boats of one kind or another. At its basic foundation, Seward was a fishing town, and fishing was the number one reason people came to visit. From the small houses in this area, residents could look out their windows and check conditions on the bay under the backdrop of towering mountains.

Churches were scattered here and there throughout Seward. Willie liked to joke with the tourists that there were fifteen churches in town and fifteen bars. One winter a church burned down and the locals damn near panicked wondering which bar would have to be sacrificed to maintain the match.

I kept plodding north. My feet slapped lightly on the side of the road, kicking up dust whenever cars came up behind me. Otherwise, I stayed on the street. There weren't a lot of sidewalks in this part of town. I remembered how Stephen King got flattened by a drunk driver while walking along a highway in Maine. I crossed to the other side of the street.

By now I was passing a motel and descending into the other group's part of town. I sensed travelers sleeping nearby, dreaming of high mountains with snow-capped peaks. Wild animals, rushing rivers and blue skies. And big fish bending a pole.

The small boat harbor held the marina, the major tour boat companies, and fishing boat charter operators. The harbormaster has an office there, and there were a couple of hotels and dozens of shops and restaurants spread through the area.

I thought about dropping by the Breeze Inn. Willie often stopped there on his way home for one more. Or two. But I didn't see his car. He liked to park in the yellow zone right in front daring the local authorities to give him a ticket. Willie Maxwell, beloved local outlaw. The man was basically harmless, but no one wanted to stir up one of the last great rabble-rousers of the frozen north.

The main reason to drop in at the Breeze Inn was to ogle the bartender. But I knew Rainey was already gone for the night. I'd have to exchange snippy barbs with her some other time.

In fact, I didn't want to be noticed through the big picture window, so I turned into the alley behind the Breeze and made my way by in solitude, kicking a stray can out of my way. Having second thoughts, I bent over and tossed the empty beer can into the dumpster beside me. The least I could do for the town.

Why did I live here? A good question to ponder on a long walk. I guess some people felt trapped by their circumstances, but others stayed for the rewards. Whether through work, business, or pleasure.

But why did I stay? I could ply my trade in plenty of other locations around Alaska if I wanted. Why Seward?

I walked on and turned into the road past the petroleum supply company down to the railroad tracks. A dirt road from there would get me to the airport without worrying about traffic. The back road was deserted and dark, a perfect match for my frame of mind.

The beer was wearing off, and so was the euphoria from earlier in the day. What would tomorrow hold? It started to rain, just lightly, but I cursed the distance I still had to go. I was going to get thoroughly soaked. The long walk was about to become a long ordeal. I tugged my cap lower over my ears, pulled my collar closer and picked up the pace.

Life around here could be exhausting. A continual struggle to make ends meet. The beauty of the place was its main appeal. Oh yeah, and the people. Well, some of the people. I could get through many a lonely night as long as a friendly voice said hello once in a while the next day. Or the day after.

The rain picked up. The rain. The goddamn rain. It just took you over. If you couldn't get out of it, all you could do was give into it.

The coastline of the Gulf of Alaska is a wet place. Warm low pressure systems churned their way across the northern Pacific and met cold air descending from the Arctic. The result was a condensation collision centered on Seward. The mountain ranges that ringed the gulf trapped those rain swollen clouds and held them in place for days at a time.

The bowl that holds Seward and the bay is a catcher's mitt for clouds. Layers of the thick wet stuff regularly covered every feature in sight that was more than a hundred feet high. Then there was no scenery, no mountains, and no sky. Sometimes the clouds were so thick they seemed to seal off the town's access to the heavens. No wonder there were fifteen churches full of worshippers straining to reach through to the Promised Land.

On days like that life in Seward was like living in a Tupperware bowl. With the lid firmly attached. All sound was muffled and absorbed by the cotton fluff of fog and impenetrable cloud. And the rain. All day and all night, the goddamn rain.

I walked on. Water was filling the ruts in front of me now, and my path weaved left and right. Not from intoxication. I was almost sober by then. I was zigzagging to avoid the puddles and racing a date with pneumonia. I had on my flying shoes—a pair of old scuffed up walkers that I thought looked cool when I bought them. But they weren't waterproof, not even water-resistant. The cold water laughed at me as it crept through the seams and crevices of the ancient footgear.

Every now and then I stumbled. It was dark on the back road. My toes banged into stones hidden in the shadows. I was getting closer to the airport. A tall line of trees lurked in the darkness ahead.

I became aware of a pair of headlights behind me crawling slow along the same dirt road. Then I heard the sirens and looked over to the highway. Two police cars and an ambulance were moving fast past the Safeway. With no traffic in their way, they moved quickly out of sight heading north.

I figured it was a car accident. The Seward Highway to Anchorage was notoriously dangerous. Not because it was a bad road. Mostly because people drove it stupid. Too much speed, passing on curves, passing on solid lines, not slowing down for rain or snow. What was the big hurry? Drive like hell, you'll get there.

Distracted by their passage I stumbled and stepped right in the middle of an ankle deep puddle. The lights behind me were closer, but whoever was back there wasn't driving much faster than I was walking. Looking back I stumbled into another puddle.

Shit. I was cold and I was wet. The wind was biting the back of my neck. I was probably gonna get sick.

It would be several more minutes before I could round the corner and get back into dry clothes in the camper. I pushed my way forward with my head down, shoes squishing and shoulders hunched almost to my ears. I tried to keep the rain from sliding down my back but only succeeded in cramping my neck and shoulder muscles.

Then the car pulled up beside me and stopped. It was Willie. He rolled down the window and grinned at me. His face was bright red. As red as the baseball cap he wore twisted forty-five degrees to one side. His eyes were twinkling like a Christmas elf overdosing on eggnog.

"Hey, man. What the hell you doing out here in the rain? Ain't you got no sense?"

I opened the door and climbed in. "You see those flashers?" I asked.

"Yeah. Shit. I thought they were coming after me. I'm drunk as a motherfucker."

"Is that why you're driving five miles an hour and taking the back road? You scared the crap out of me."

He threw his head back with a big, silent, open-mouthed laugh. Instead of saying something, he let his foot off the brake, and we rolled toward the airport bouncing through one puddle after another.

"I stopped at the Breeze for a couple," he said. "Harv and Tom were there, and they started buying me beers. Damn guys got me loaded."

"Want me to drive? I'm half-sober again."

"Nah, I got it. Hell, we're almost there. I'm glad I found you. You can help me check on the airplane."

"You worried about that stuff Scooter was saying?"

"About what? Oh. Nah. I always check on my airplane on the way home. Let's go do it."

"Sure, whatever. Just let me get a raincoat out of the camper."

When he got there I jumped out and fumbled my way into the dark interior of my home on wheels. It was cold and damp inside, and I cringed at the thought of crawling into the cold bed. Then I heard Willie put his car in gear, and by the time I got back outside he was driving slowly toward his airplane on the other side of the hangar.

Damn guy. Must have forgotten me. I wrapped the raincoat around me and zipped it up over my wet clothes. I pulled the hood over my baseball cap and started trudging toward Willie's receding taillights. At least the walking was easier on the asphalt surface of the tarmac.

Before I could even reach the hangar, I heard Willie's horn blare and a shout. I picked up my pace wondering if he was just letting off steam or if there was something wrong.

Around the corner of the hangar I saw Willie's car stopped beside a black SuperCub I'd never seen before. Willie's headlights were still on and the engine was running, but I couldn't see him anywhere. Ignoring the chafing from my cold wet clothes, I started to jog toward his car.

When I got closer I spotted Willie under the wing of his airplane. Some big guy had him by the front of his coat and was shaking the hell out of him and yelling in his face.

"Where is it? Where is it? Who do you think you are? Stupid loser. You leave my shit alone. You got it?"

"Fuck you, asshole. I don't even know who the hell you are!" Willie shouted back and tried to swing at the guy. His hat fell off and his white hair tossed left and right as the stranger easily manhandled him. The guy was tall and the way he had Willie in his grip there was no way to fight back.

"Oh, you must think you know me. I saw you today out there with this red and white SuperCub. What makes you think you can screw with my stuff?" The guy was screaming in Willie's face from two inches away like he was going to leave powder burns.

Before Willie could answer, the big stranger punched him in the jaw and Willie dropped.

"Hey!" I shouted and ran toward them. But before I could get within ten feet, another huge shape came out of the dark beside me. I caught a glimpse of a fist coming at me. It disappeared in my gut, and I went down hard. Black gravel smashed into my face and open mouth. I had no breath. I couldn't even groan.

Huddled on the wet gravel, I could only twist in pain and watch as the two men worked Willie over and kicked at his face and head. Before I blacked out I heard the guy yelling in between kicks. "Don't mess with me, repo man. You couldn't leave it alone, could ya? I'm just trying to get by, do a little business, keep to myself, but you had to come along and fuck it up."

He landed another vicious kick. I saw Willie's body lurch across the ground and lay still. Before my lights went out, I could still hear their voices.

"You really think we should take his plane?" asked a new voice.

"Yeah, the bastard's gotta pay. We can use it to run supplies or part it out."

The last thing I saw was Willie's still form lying beside one of his big tundra tires. I thought he was dead. I thought I was next.

* * * * *

I don't know how long we lay out there in the rain, but when I came to, I was sucking in huge breaths of air and rubbing the pain below my ribcage. Police lights were flashing red and blue all around me. The black SuperCub was gone. So was Willie's. And Willie was nowhere in sight either.

There were cops walking around the area with flashlights searching the ground. I struggled to a sitting position and grimaced at the pain. Another officer was talking to somebody in the front seat of his cruiser. One of the cops walking around with a flashlight noticed me.

"Are you all right, sir?"

I held up my hand to block the flashlight beam he was shining in my eyes. "Yeah, I think so."

He helped me to my feet and opened the door to his cruiser. I sat inside and shook my head trying to clear the cobwebs. "What the hell happened? Where's Willie?"

"Hang on, sir. I'll get the sergeant for you."

In a few minutes a police woman came over and pointed the flashlight in my face.

"Whoa, Johnny," she said in recognition. "You okay?" It was Betty, one of Seward's finest and a friend who owned a Cessna 180. She was a regular at the airport when she was off duty.

"What the hell's going on, Betty? Where's Willie?" I gestured toward the empty space where his plane should have been.

"You had me worried there for a minute," she said. "You need an ambulance? We already sent Willie to the hospital, but you didn't look as bad."

I felt like I'd been run over but nothing was broken. "I'm okay."

"I'm afraid I've got some bad news for you." She got in behind the wheel and closed her door. The holster and heavy leather belt around her waist creaked as she sat. She put the vehicle in gear and started driving back down the tarmac toward my office. I started to panic, thinking they'd done something to my plane too. But when we got closer I could see nothing wrong with it. The white paint gleamed in Betty's headlights. Even the red stripes and numbers looked clean, freshly washed by the rain.

"Willie's been hurt, Johnny. I hope we got to him in time. It's been about twenty minutes since we got a call about a fight out here."

"Did you see the guys?" I asked.

"No, the gentleman back there talking to the other officer was out walking his dog. He says he saw a plane land and taxi over like the pilot was going to get fuel. When he got closer to the hangar, the guy says his dog got all excited, running back and forth along the fence line there. He heard some yelling and saw three guys fighting where Willie's plane was tied down. By the time he could grab his dog and put him in the car, the planes had started up and left. He found you and Willie all beat up and called nine-one-one."

"Did he get a look at the guys?"

"No, too dark I guess. I'll take you to the hospital if you want. We can see how Willie's doing."

"Yeah, yeah, sure. Jesus, I can't believe it. Why Willie?"

"Good question. You know everything we know so far."

We rode in silence down the highway, listening to the windshield wipers slapping back and forth in a vain effort to beat back the rain. Only the police radio's garbled words broke the quiet.

I stared straight ahead trying to make sense of it. Betty drove the speed limit, turning occasionally slightly left and right to dodge potholes. I spotted my reflection riding beside me in the side window glass. The face looking back was frowning. Eyebrows knitted together in a puzzled knot. The eyes were dark and haunted.

The mystery was starting to come together. The guy had been yelling about Willie's red and white SuperCub, but he'd gotten it wrong. He was talking about me. He'd gotten the wrong guy and the wrong plane.

The silence grew uncomfortable after a while, and Betty interrupted my thoughts. "See that guy coming our way weaving all over the place?"

"Yeah, I see him. Drunk driver?"

"No, we never stop the weavers along here this time of night. The ones we stop are the ones that hit every pothole. Driving straight as an arrow, trying too hard not to weave."

Betty chuckled for a moment. So did I, but then we lapsed into silence again remembering where we were headed.

"How do you think he is? Is it bad?" I had to ask as we made our way down Third Avenue approaching the turn uphill to the hospital.

"I don't know. He was out cold and...." She didn't finish.

"And what? Come on, he's my best friend, for chrissake."

"I'm sorry, I'm no doctor. I don't want to say anything else. I just don't know. We need to see what the doctors say."

Willie was somewhere in the emergency room complex. A nurse directed me to a waiting room while they worked on him. She took Betty in back, but she was back out in a few minutes with nothing new to say.

"I still don't know much, Johnny. I'm sorry. They're working on him. He's got a couple of broken bones, but the worst part is his head. He took a pounding and may have a fractured skull. He's hooked up to a bunch of equipment. You want to wait here?"

"Yeah," I muttered.

"Okay, I've got to get back out there, but I'll check back by here when I can. You hang in there, okay? He'll pull through. Willie's a tough old bird."

It was almost midnight and being a Wednesday night, the emergency room was quiet. I was alone in the waiting room. Alone with my thoughts and my soggy clothes. I found the heat register and pulled off my raincoat and soaked jacket and arranged it on a chair to dry. Then I took off my shoes and wrung out my socks over a trash can. The rain water made a puddle on the floor where I'd missed the can.

I thought about stripping off my wet jeans too but decided that would be pushing it. I slumped into a chair, one of those hard plastic things they put in waiting rooms so you don't get too comfortable and overstay your welcome. My feet looked horrible. My toes were like tortured albino prunes, and as I tried to rub some life back into them, they ached like hell.

Sitting there I thought about what had happened. Tried to make sense of it. Poor Willie. What had he ever done to anybody but try to help them out? Who the hell were these guys? Was this connected to that theft ring that Scooter was telling us about?

I felt weak. Almost too tired to keep my head up. I wanted to hide. Somehow the thrill of the afternoon's escapade had lost its glow. Everything yesterday had been simple. But now I couldn't escape the thought that somehow I had opened a door to an unwelcome stranger, and the simple life was gone.

We had a peaceful life here in Seward, Willie and me and our friends. We didn't bother anybody. Well, not much anyhow. Maybe some folks thought we made too much noise with our airplanes, but we honestly tried to make sure we stayed a respectful distance from houses and businesses. The airport was like a little island in the countryside, isolated from town. We were only trying to make a living out of the flying game, and if we could help some folks get from place to place or to see the sights, well, that was what we loved to do.

And now, here was Willie, fighting for his life because some assholes decided to invade our territory and help themselves to what we had. Hell, it could have just as easily been my airplane they grabbed. In a strange way I wished they had. Then I'd only have myself to blame. Instead I had to carry Willie's pain too.

We never did much to protect ourselves against theft out at the airport. None of us had ever seriously worried about it. These guys took Willie's Cub thinking it was mine. The injustice of it all. Did they have any idea what they had done? Did they care?

Time went by, and my thoughts were wearing me down, not to mention the physical aftermath of the long, wet walk. The shock was losing its grip on me, and a bitter rage was starting to boil. I wanted to hit something. I wanted to break something. I wanted to hurt somebody.

But this was more than just some body. That screaming guy was a psycho. I mean, I can understand being pissed off, but Jesus. Talk about an overreaction. He was the one in the wrong. What had I done? Shoved a stick in a goddamn bee's hive. That's what.

Now Willie's plane—Willie's life—was being dismantled, taken apart, torn from limb to limb while I sat there rubbing my pruney feet and wondering what to do.

Where'd they go? Alaska's a big place with lots of places to hide. It was too much to think about. Screw it. I leaned against the wall and went to sleep.

I don't know how long I was out, huddled next to the warm heat register leaning against the blue cinderblock wall. My head must have fallen forward, because I awoke with a start. My eyes bugged wide open for a moment while I tried to figure out where I was. My neck was killing me, cramping up like crazy. I stood up and took a look at my watch. It was just before four in the morning.

I couldn't just sit around there anymore. I had to know something. Pulling the door open to the inner sanctum of the emergency treatment area, I saw a nurse at a counter and she told me they had moved Willie down the hall into another room. She didn't seem to mind when I padded down the hallway barefoot, looking like I just crawled out from under the dumpster out back. They must have been used to seeing folks in rough shape in the middle of the night.

It didn't take long to find Willie, but I wished I hadn't. I couldn't recognize anything about him. He was surrounded by machines, and tubes were coming out of him from every direction. One of his legs was hanging from a pulley from the ceiling, a large cast encased him from knee to toe. And his head was wrapped too, completely obscured by the bandages. In fact, his whole head was framed by a massive neck brace made out of plastic and foam.

I stood there and stared feeling more helpless than I ever have in my life. I hate hospitals. I hate the pathetic look of patients in beds, totally vulnerable and unable to take care of themselves. Too many bad memories came flooding back. Of too many hospital rooms and too many lost souls in beds just like this one. Lost souls that never found their way out again and left this world strapped down and staring mindlessly at a TV set blinking through reruns of *I Love Humping Lucy* or *As the Stomach Turns*.

The nurse stopped in to check on him. "You want to stay? You can sit in here as long as you want. He's in a coma, so I don't think he's going to say much."

I couldn't take my eyes off Willie. "Is he going to make it?" I finally managed to ask. But she was gone.

I couldn't leave my friend lying there alone. The pasty white flesh of his thigh above the cast reminded of the jeans he sometimes wore—the pair with the big tear behind the knee. That same pasty flesh was staring back at me now, and it wasn't funny the way it was when I teased him about it back at the airport. Nothing was funny now. This guy who lived to make other people laugh and have a good time looked like he was checking out.

I couldn't leave him there and I couldn't stay. When I got back to the waiting room and started pulling on my damp socks, Betty came in, the rain dripping off her rain slicker. I filled her in on Willie's condition.

She drove me out to the airport through the rain and stopped beside my camper. I tried to rub and stretch the cramp out of my neck, twisting and turning it in all directions.

"What happens now?" I asked her.

"I turned in a report and notified Anchorage. Since the airport is state property, we'll have to see who takes over the case. Probably the troopers, but maybe the FBI. I don't know yet. Probably won't hear anything until later today."

"Well, they need to move on this. That airplane could be history within a few hours, you know?"

"Yeah, I know. We'll just have to see what happens. I'll see you later."

The night air was cold compared to the suffocating warmth in Betty's cruiser. I took some deep painful breaths and climbed into the motor home. I flipped on a small electric space heater, but the chill still gripped me as I changed into dry long johns and wool socks and crawled into a sleeping bag. I shivered in a fetal position, waiting for my body heat to spread through the goose down enough to calm me. The bag was zipped all the way up, with just my nose and mouth sticking out, trying to keep as much heat inside the bag as possible.

But my eyes were wide open, staring into the darkness. I listened to the drone of the heater and the rain beating a steady pattern on the aluminum roof six inches above my face. I thought about two guys flying two airplanes through the Alaska night headed who knows where.

CHAPTER 6

A locomotive whistle woke me. My neck was still cramped, and I grimaced when I rolled over to look out the camper window. I halfway expected Willie to drive up for our coffee run at any minute. Then I remembered and closed my eyes. Damn it. The vision of Willie in that bed flashed past, and I felt sick.

I thought about getting up, but instead I just laid there for a while listening to the rain. There was too much junk piled in the chairs to sit anywhere anyhow. Sometimes, I thought about cleaning it up, but maybe another day.

I found it both comforting and unsettling to listen to the rain. The sound of it was soothing, and occasionally the wind rocked the camper gently, lulling me into a semi-napping lazy frame of mind, daydreaming about stuff. Like old memories, old girlfriends, past victories, conquests, adventures, the highlights of a pretty interesting life.

But then listening to the rain could be unsettling, because those other memories rose to the surface too. Like ugly greasy bubbles of bad mojo. Stuff I didn't want to remember, things I wish I didn't have to think about. Old defeats, times I wasn't proud of, things I regretted, things that still pissed me off when I thought about them. Times when I was betrayed. The stuff that alcohol helps people forget. Or drugs. Whatever. The escape medicine that distracts us from the shit. The life that could have been. The opportunities lost. Dreams unfulfilled. Lusts squandered. That sweet smile across the crowded room that could have been mine if only I had done something about it. Taken the time to pursue. Had the balls to say hello even. The guy that invented Chinese water torture probably grew up in Seward, Alaska. The sonofabitch.

When I can keep the bad stuff away from the door, I enjoyed daydreaming. One of my favorites was when I thought about how I could have been a movie star. That one came to me once in a while when I was sitting alone or walking somewhere. I knew it was dumb. I'd waited too long. Should have started when I was a young guy. When I was full of myself, when I knew I could walk on the moon if I had set my mind to it. When I could stroll onto a movie set, lean against a brick wall, wait for the lighting guys to get ready and the director to say, "Action!" and then conjure up that cockeyed smirk, stare into the camera, and say, "You talking to me? You talking to me?" my head shaking just slightly with a dangerous bravado barely under control and simmering just beneath the surface, my muscles bunched and ready to explode. The guy I was talking to wouldn't stand a chance. Remember what Robert DeNiro said when he was Travis Bickle in *Taxi Driver*? "I want to do something...something big."

Yeah, I coulda been great. Coulda been so real, so alive, so amazing. People would have paid a lot of dough to watch me. They would marvel at my talent and bathe me in gratitude for entertaining them. For distracting them from their own disappointments. That's what happened for me anyhow. When I see something good, hear something good, feel something good, or drink something good, the emptiness fades at least for a little while.

Yeah, I had those thoughts sometimes. Stupid. I know, but my thoughts were my only company when I was alone. And eccentric company is better than none at all. Especially on mornings like that one, when the rain drops were splashing on the camper roof just inches from my face. They lulled me into remembering. The last thing I ever wanted was to do was lie in my final bed remembering bad shit, wishing I'd done things I never had the guts to try. I don't want to lie there trying to forget, trying to dream up a nice fantasy instead. Don't get me wrong; I liked fantasies, but too often they left me disappointed with myself and depressed.

I rolled out of the bunk and stretched my neck out some more. Enough of this feeling sorry for myself, I decided. I had to go see Willie. Maybe he'd be awake by now. I had a lot of nerve moaning and groaning about stupid stuff when Willie was all busted up. Maybe dying. The thought made me shudder.

I drove the camper into town and stopped for coffee at the Texaco on the way. The place felt empty. Either the coffee was weaker than usual, or I was. I picked up a package of Twinkies for breakfast. By the time I pulled into the hospital parking lot, the sugar was kicking in. I glanced down at the bay. A small patch of blue sky out over the gulf looked promising.

When I reached Willie's room, Scooter was there with a long face looking like he'd lost his pet dog. Mitch Woofley was with him. Mitch ran a charter boat outfit and had a place out at Lowell Point for the past several years. He and Scooter were sitting against the wall staring at Willie's still form. They looked up when I walked in, their worried eyes searching mine for answers.

"Any news?" I asked, afraid to hear the response.

"Not really," said Mitch. "A doctor stopped in, but all she said was that he had a serious concussion and was in a coma. And his right leg is busted."

"Yeah, no shit. That's pretty obvious," I muttered, gesturing impatiently at the sling hanging from the ceiling.

"What are we going to do, Johnny?" Scooter leaned forward, his elbows on his knees, staring up at me and blinking rapidly.

"What do you mean, 'what are we going to do?' What can we do? I told the cops about the chop shop and how they gotta hurry. It's up to them now."

Mitch frowned and grunted. "Fat chance that'll do any good."

The room smelled of medicine and disinfectant. That creepy hospital smell. I sank down in a chair beside Scooter and rested my chin on my hands.

A few minutes went by. We listened to the hum of the equipment plugged into Willie.

Finally, Scooter spoke up. "Johnny, you got that repo thing going. Can't you do something?"

"Like what? What the hell can I do?"

Blink, blink. "I don't know. Aren't you like a private investigator or something? We could fly out and look for those guys, I guess." Blink, blink.

"Yeah, right. You gonna buy the gas? And where we gonna look? That plane could be anywhere. Jesus, use your head."

"I'd pay for the gas," Mitch said quietly, not looking at either one of us.

"Ah, great. Now I gotta feel like a cheap, selfish bastard that won't even help an injured friend? Gimme a break, you guys. You know I'd do anything for Willie, but I ain't got a goddamn clue what to do."

"Well, somebody needs to do something." Blink, blink, blink. "This sucks. Aren't you gonna fight back, Johnny?" He was staring at me. And blinking.

I didn't say anything, but I could imagine Willie saying something like, "Well, you gonna do something or just stand around with your thumb up your butt?" Silver-tongued devil that he was.

"Who are these guys that Scooter's been telling me about?" Mitch asked.

"I don't know. I first heard about it from a guy in Anchorage."

"Well, maybe we could learn more about what's going on with that stuff. It might give us some ideas."

Mitch was the wise man of our group. Barrel-chested and bearded, it was easy to picture him at the helm of his boat explaining the sights to tourists and telling stories of the sea. Well educated and calm by nature, he was a thinking man. His wire-rimmed glasses made him look like a schoolteacher, and his vocabulary was better than you expected to find around the Yukon Bar. Certainly better than the rest of us jerkoffs.

Mitch was a hell of a nice guy too, and we all enjoyed his stories. He was a regular fixture in the Revenue Corner, hanging out at the bar after work and drinking imported beer. His cell phone rang regularly as he handled one situation after another, taking customer calls, making reservations, or arranging schedules for his crew. I figured him for a good guy to work for. Unflappable and thoughtful.

His calm voice started to register with me, and I took a deep breath shaking off the sleep-deprived sugar high that had been rattling my nerves. "Yeah, that makes sense. Sorry, Scooter, I've had a rough night."

"I'm serious about paying for gas. It's the least I could do, all the times Willie's helped me out," said Mitch, as he and Scooter stood up to leave.

Scooter stopped beside the bed. "Hey, Willie, maybe you can hear this, maybe you can't, but you gotta get better, man. The Yukon's boring as hell without your stupid stories."

"And the owner's going to experience a serious hit in her receivables if you're gone for long," added Mitch.

I watched them as they took a last look at Willie's bandaged head and left the room. I lingered for a moment, fighting off the dread. Was he ever coming back?

"See ya, man," was all I could think to say, pausing again before I left the room.

I caught up to Mitch and Scooter in the hall. "Okay, you guys, I'm going to check in with the cops. See what I can learn. Scooter, could you give whatshisname at Ballards another call and see if he knows anything else? And make sure he knows what happened down here so he can spread the word."

"Sure, Johnny, I'm on it," he grinned and blinked a few times before climbing in his car with Mitch.

Back in the camper, I drove to the police station and talked to the sergeant at the front desk. "Can you tell me the status of the incident at the airport last night?"

The stocky officer with a Marine haircut wore a crisp, tight-fitting uniform shirt with starched seams. He was built like a fire hydrant. He looked me up and down. "And who are you?"

"My name's Wainwright. I'm a friend of the victim. We're both pilots out at the airport."

"Wainwright, huh? Yes, we have the report." he said, biting each word off like chunks of caribou jerky.

"Can you tell what's being done about it?" I asked, meeting his gaze evenly.

He looked at me for a moment, sizing me up. "Wait a minute," he said and disappeared down a short hallway.

After a few minutes he came back followed by another officer with lieutenant's bars on his collar. His name tag read "Hansen." He could have been the other cop's twin, only taller.

The lieutenant took over. "You're a friend of William Maxwell's?"

"That's right."

"Johnny Wainwright?"

"Yeah, that's right. What about it?"

His eyes narrowed. He stood as straight as he could, looking down at me. "I can't tell you much."

"You're not telling me anything. What's going on?"

"Look, Wainwright," he sneered. "It's under investigation. The troopers down the hall took the case, but the FBI might get into it as well."

"Well, is anybody going to do anything? Time is critical here. These guys cut up airplanes and disappear."

"So you know who they are? You didn't tell the officers that last night."

"No, I don't know who they are. I just heard about guys like this in Arizona."

He looked at the other officer standing beside him. Then he smirked at me. "So you don't know anything, do you, sir?"

This was going nowhere, and I was getting pissed. "You may already be too late. Do we have to do something ourselves to save the poor guy's plane?"

"Look, sir." He puffed himself up as large as he possibly could until I thought the buttons on his shirt might pop. His sidekick puffed up too, and the two of them glared at me from behind the counter like angry Michelin men twins.

"The proper authorities will be conducting an investigation, and if you do anything stupid or try to take things into your own hands, you're going to bring a world of hurt on yourself. Are we clear?"

"Oh, yeah, we're clear. It's clear Willie's never going to see his plane again. Not in one piece anyhow."

"Well, I'm very sorry, sir," he snarled sarcastically. "We're just not in the business of chasing around the Alaska countryside trying to find airplanes that the owners couldn't bother to lock up in the first place. Are we done here?"

I stared at him in disbelief. I wanted to say a hundred other things but thought better of it.

"Yeah, I'm done here all right," I said, turning on my heel. I could feel their hot glares on the back of my neck as I left the office.

Walking down the stairs, I felt stupid. I might need the cops at some point, and I had just blown any chance at their cooperation. I chalked it off to lack of sleep and worrying about Willie. I cringed at the thought of him waking up to learn his plane was gone.

I pictured those bastards from last night. Who the hell were those guys? It was a real violation.

Airplane people didn't screw each other. Up here especially, they helped each other. You could fly into a strange airport that you'd never been to, and if you had a flat tire or another kind of problem, somebody on the field would help you out. Pilots would pull out tools and nuts and bolts, whatever it took, to get you going again. Usually at no charge. Hell, I've done it myself for other pilots plenty of times. Even the dumbasses that fly up here from the Lower Forty-Eight on a lark. We all share our local knowledge of the terrain and the weather, or we help them with something on their planes when we can. We don't worry about shop charges or lawsuits. None of that crap. And Willie was always giving visiting pilots and their passengers rides into town from the airport.

Alaskans in general help each other out. That's why it was such a shock to discover other pilots stealing from us, attacking us and taking advantage of our relaxed way of life. I thought about the lieutenant and shook my head as I pushed the city hall's door open and walked down the stairs to the sidewalk. I made a mental note to try and find out who was actually going to handle Willie's case. But in the meantime if something was going to happen, we were going to have to do it ourselves.

It was a good thing we had Betty on our side. But then, she was a pilot so she cared about what went on out at the airport. But the bureaucracy couldn't care less.

And now, we had some group of idiots ripping us off. Okay, it was official. I was pissed. I knew they were pilots, but how could they be so different from the rest of us? They didn't seem to care about their brothers in the sky. They were just greedy cocksuckers who didn't give a damn about anyone but themselves and their crooked little racket. To hell with them. I was going to do something about it. Screw Lieutenant Hanson and his do-nothing bullshit. If I could locate the stolen airplane, it would force the authorities to do something about it or explain why they wouldn't.

I drove back to the airport, and as I turned off the highway and crossed the railroad tracks the blue spot south of the bay had opened up. Only a few wispy clouds clung to the mountaintops and ridges. The windsock indicated a southerly breeze off the ocean at about eight knots. Perfect conditions for a flight.

I decided I had to do something. The cops wouldn't do anything, and Willie's plane could be sitting just thirty minutes away from here, being cannibalized. Gimme a break. I couldn't just sit around and let it happen.

CHAPTER 7

I made a quick sandwich and washed it down with a soft drink while I got the Cub ready to fly. I wracked my brain trying to remember what I'd seen out at Johnstone Bay.

What had I missed? Obviously, I'd missed a lot. I didn't think that airstrip had been used for a while, and the cabin hadn't looked occupied either.

A simple plan came to mind. If I could spot these guys and Willie's plane, I could make an anonymous phone call to the cops. Or get someone else to do it. For some reason the Seward police didn't like me. What had I ever done to them? I went through a list of possible things that might have irritated them. There was that file folder I lifted from their office last year during a case. Hell, I'd needed that information to track a guy in Kenai. They wouldn't share. Didn't I return the folder later? Oops, maybe not.

Then there was the time they found my surveillance camera set up in the restroom in city hall. It wasn't anything weird like they were trying to say. I was just trying to record voices, nothing else. Geez, what did they think I was, some kind of pervert? And hey, it had worked. A couple of cops taking a leak were talking about the case while they thought they were alone. Gave me just the lead I needed to find the deadbeat I'd been looking for.

Maybe I could do something to get back in their good graces. At least Betty still talked to me. Airplane people, you know. We stuck together out here in the wild.

That reminded me of the guys who beat us up. Shit, they were pilots. Had to be to fly both SuperCubs out of there. What the hell?

Since I was going to spend a lot of time over the water, I tossed in a life vest just in case I had to set down in the drink. I also got a handheld radio from the office and put it in my survival pack. Marine band. That way I could talk to boats below and ask if they had seen a black SuperCub as well.

I stood on a ladder feeding hundred octane low lead fuel into the wing tanks. I also wiped off the windshield before I left. The rain had cleaned most of the bugs off the glass, which made my job easier. The sun on my neck felt like a million bucks. Sunshine sparkled off the small puddles along the taxiway, and I watched a Harrier hawk hovering low before pouncing on a fat lemming deep in the grass next to the runway. Loud screeches high in the air above made me look up to see at least a dozen bald eagles soaring in circles on the air currents over Salmon Creek and Resurrection River.

It wasn't long before the SuperCub's engine was rumbling smoothly and pulling us into the air again to join the eagles. With sun glare in my eyes, I squinted into the distance and climbed past the face of Mount Alice. Before I turned to the east to cross the ridgeline, I glanced toward Seward and spotted the hospital nestled against the far hillside next to Mount Marathon. I thought about Willie lying there missing this glorious day and set my jaw, jerking my thoughts back to the task at hand.

With two tanks full, I had plenty of fuel. If I needed to, I was going to use them both flying low along the beaches out to Chenega Bay and back. If I couldn't see any airplanes, maybe

I could spot tire tracks or something. What would I do if I located Willie's plane? Good question. But first things first. For now I just had to look. I'd worry about answering that question later.

I felt as excited as usual when I cut through the notch and pulled back on the throttle to descend into Day Harbor. The notch. What a great spot. Cut into the ridge between Resurrection Bay and Day Harbor, it was the perfect little passageway in the rocks to squeak a small plane through. The top of the ridgeline reminded me of a kid's set of wooden blocks. Huge boulders and chunks of rock shaped a massive ridge that ran for miles and formed the eastern skyline that we looked at every day from Seward. The pile of rocks was a solid wall as high as four thousand feet above the ocean. Except for the notch, which was a doorway through the wall hundreds of feet deep.

Once I popped through the gap, it wasn't long before I was over the water again. There were a couple of long sandy beaches on the north end of Day Harbor where I had seen hunters land airplanes. I dropped down to fifty feet above the water and cruised along the beaches staring down for any sign of airplanes or tire tracks.

Nothing. I realized that I was looking for a needle in a stack of needles. This was black bear season, and there was going to be spike camps all over the place. But at least I could make a note of them and check with the hunting guides I knew who used the area. The more I looked around the flat area between Day Harbor and Ellsworth Glacier where it swept uphill into Nellie Juan valley, the more I could see several clear spots where SuperCubs could land. It felt hopeless, but I pressed on anyway.

I pulled into a climb and gained some altitude to get a wider view. White airplane wings would be hard to hide. Especially if they were still attached to the fuselage. A SuperCub's wings are almost forty feet across and over four feet wide. Still nothing.

Along the east side of Day Harbor, there was no place to land. I headed toward the Gulf, turned around the rocky point at the south end and curved my way into the next inlet. Out the left window, looking past the fat tundra tire under my wing, wave after blue wave crashed against the rocks, white foam scattering in all directions.

It was moments like this that connected me to this land, this water, and this sky. I couldn't imagine living anywhere else. I belonged next door to this beauty, breathing in the salty tang of the ocean breeze. This was my life. I loved this place. Yes, the weather sucked sometimes, and the rain dragged me down. But what the hell. Sometimes it got to me, and other times it didn't. Bad moods were going to come and go. Kind of like the weather. So be it.

I spotted another small beach ahead that separated the ocean from a small lagoon surrounded by cliffs. A SuperCub could land down there, but it didn't seem like a logical place to hide. Too close to Seward and too much boat traffic nearby.

The next rocky point was called Cape Mansfield next to Whidbey Bay. This one had a long black beach but no lagoon. It did have some flat areas in the valley but very marshy and soft. No good spots to land a plane. There was a big house built on the west corner of the beach. Three stories high. A guy and his wife bought this place a while back for a possible lodge. He wanted me to bring him supplies, landing on the beach. But I never heard back from him. And I hadn't seen anyone at the property since that time either. That happened a lot up here. Dreams were easy. The realities were tough and the conditions were hard. Only the truly persistent and the lucky made it work.

I didn't usually let my mind wander like this when I was flying. At least not when I was low and slow, right beside the trees and cliffs. I usually left the daydreams for those long cruising high altitude flights when I could let my mind meander and slide. Below five hundred feet, it was better to stay focused and pay attention to every detail of the airplane. How it felt in my hands, how the engine sounded, how the wind was pushing me around as I worked my way through the terrain. Lack of concentration could get me too close to a rock. If I clipped a wingtip on a hillside or snagged a tire in the treetops, it would be all over.

I shrugged off the lapse and refocused on the sights in front of me. Seeing nothing in Whidbey Bay, I continued to the east. I passed over a tiny cove with a small beach and a parking area for one airplane and a cabin. I had always admired this neatly laid out piece of land and the pilot who used it every summer. It didn't look like he'd arrived yet. There were no tracks and no signs of an airplane anywhere.

Rounding the next point took me by rocky Cape Fairfield. A ship had crashed there a long time ago in a storm. She was a steamship named *The Yukon* with almost five hundred souls on board. Eleven people died down there in a bitterly cold scene of chaos and confusion in February 1946. I'd read that the wreckage was still there, just below the surface.

I looked down at the rocks again. Every time I flew out there I looked for signs of the disaster. But all I ever saw was beautiful blue waves and white foam spray at the base of magnificent cliffs. Harbor seals and stellar sea lions lounged in the sunshine just above water line. There was no sign of shattered lives or tragedy.

Then I was in Johnstone Bay again with its long beach and woods. I flew several circuits looking everywhere a small plane could possibly land. The little airstrip at the cabin was still deserted. I could see the remains of the blue tarp and the busted up pile of food jars but no sign of the bears. No one had been in there to clean up either.

I even searched the north end of the lake where Excelsior Glacier flowed down from the Sargent Icefield. There were a few landable gravel bars up there but no airplanes. My favorite waterfall was pumping thousands of gallons of frigid liquid down a thousand-foot cliff, its stream dazzling in the midday sun. As these spring days began to warm the terrain, snowmelt was accelerating. Small waterfalls sprung up everywhere returning melted snow to the sea.

I banked my wings forty-five degrees to the right, added power, and flew toward the glacier again. I watched the enormous chunks of blue ice floating below me on milky blue lake water.

A bad memory came to me. The year before last on a beautiful day just like this one, a careless pilot overloaded his

Maule on floats with five occupants and made a bad landing in this lake. The plane sank, and they had to swim. A seventeen-year-old boy drowned when his lungs and legs cramped up in the bitterly cold water. The others had to sit on an iceberg and wait for hours to be rescued. The airplane and the youngster sank hundreds of feet to the bottom of the murky lake and have never been recovered.

I shuddered at the thought of it. I was always struck by the cruel contrast of beauty and tragedy that exists up here side by side. In spite of the amazing scenery, death's specter is never far away.

Leaving the cabin with its airstrip behind, I flew low and slow into a small bowl in the mountains called Little Johnstone. It, too, has a landable beach and a small lake with a couple of cabins on the hillsides. The south wind pushed me gently into the pigeonhole opening, then the breeze was blocked by the steep side of the mountain. I had to adjust the controls to make sure I didn't fly into the side of the steep snow covered mountain that loomed over a thousand feet above me.

It's easy to lose perspective around these parts. The Empire State building is twelve hundred and fifty feet high. Mountaintops nearby ranged from sixteen hundred to over five thousand feet, in some places straight up. You could easily hide hundreds of Empire State buildings around here, and I was trying to find an airplane less than forty feet long.

Feeling discouraged, I flew around the small lake anyhow and looked down at the tiny flat meadow between the lake and the treeline. The water in the lake was high because of all the snow melt. There was another airstrip down there, but it was under water. No way to get a plane in there safely.

Coming out of Little Johnstone, I spotted tire tracks along the small river that connected Excelsior's glacier lake with the ocean. There was a wide spot down there that could hold a SuperCub. Or two. I kept my distance but flew in close enough to get a good look. When I was sure it was deserted, I slowed down and dropped to fifty feet. There was some trash and a fire ring. The way papers were blowing around I guessed they hadn't been there that long. They weren't waterlogged and matted down under leaves or other stuff.

Then I saw a trail that connected the campsite with the cabin where I'd found the chainsaw.

I landed on the beach and took the shotgun with me this time. As I hiked along the beach and headed into the woods my nerves were jangling. My eyeballs flicked right and left taking in every detail. Bears or bad guys, it didn't matter which. If anybody messed with me today, I was going to blast 'em. Shoot first, questions later.

It didn't take me long to find the camp after kicking through some brush. The turnoff in the trail was to my right where the forest opened up. Yesterday I must have been so focused on finding the cabin that I missed the turn.

Anyhow, there it was. A recent campsite with tundra tire tracks all over the place. It looked like the occupants had left in a hurry. Beer cans and plastic bags full of trash and coffee grounds were strewn everywhere. I took a bag and filled it with whatever printed materials I found. There were a couple of credit card receipts, a letter, and some other envelopes that looked like bills. I took it all with me to look at later. Whoever this was, they'd bugged out recently. The mess disgusted me, but the profile fit. In my experience, criminals were never good housekeepers.

On the way back to the beach I thought about my next steps. Where'd they go?

I put myself in their place and tried to imagine what I would do. They'd just stolen an airplane, beat a guy almost to death, and assaulted another. They had to think the cops would respond right away. That meant they had to get out fast. Plus, the screamer guy had said he'd seen me. That meant he must have been nearby. He was probably cussing himself for that. They could have roughed up Willie and swiped his plane without saying a word. The guy with the big mouth was probably the type who couldn't keep it shut. Had to yell and scream, broadcasting his power like some kind of a howler monkey in the jungle. But in the meantime they had to relocate.

I wondered about the cabin. What was the connection? They weren't staying there, but they were using stuff from there? There had to be some link.

I looked at the sky. I didn't want the good weather to go to waste. I decided to keep searching. It was time to head east.

I didn't fly over Prince William Sound that often. Not that many tourists wanted to pay what it took to get out that far and back. They preferred the close-in glaciers and the Harding Icefield, which was right next door to Seward in the Kenai Fjords National Park. Plus, I could almost always find bears for them to look at within fifteen minutes of the airport. The Sound is largely uninhabited, although the towns of Whittier, Valdez, and Cordova have sprung up on its fringes. There were also a couple of Native villages: Chenega Bay and Tatitlek. They both had excellent airports. At least I could fly out there and check them out.

I fired up the Cub and headed east. The next opening in the mountainous coastline was called Puget Bay, and it contained more than four cubbyholes with small beaches, maybe landable, maybe not. I searched them all but saw nothing. When I turned and flew back out of the bay, all of Prince William Sound lay before me. Low green islands were scattered across the brilliant blue expanse. I climbed to two thousand feet to make my way across Port Bainbridge and a stretch of three miles of open water. A mantra replayed itself in my head from years of repetition by the owner of the flight service in Moose Pass: Always stay within gliding distance of land.

Good advice over the Sound. Altitude is your friend if the engine quits. I reminded myself of the safety vest I had in the pack behind me and wondered if I should have put it on. I didn't want to think about trying to find it underwater, upside down in the dark, tangled in a seatbelt.

I pressed on. A cruise ship, probably out of Vancouver, was visible ahead making its way across the azure water. It was probably headed for Whittier on the northwest corner of the Sound. The massive ship looked like a bathtub toy from my altitude, but the wake it left behind was easy to see on a perfect day like this one.

I flew over Bainbridge Island and its thick spruce forests. Although some of these islands had been heavily harvested, those close to me were thick with mature trees and no flat areas or beaches came into view. Rocky shore lines, low hilly islands, and trees stretched in front of me as far as I could see.

My destination was the airport on Evans Island, just a few miles ahead. The native village of Chenega Bay was hidden from view behind low peaks, rocks and trees. All of these islands lay below the snow line, and I flew into a world of blue and green, leaving the land of ice and snow behind me.

As I approached Port Ashton and Sawmill Bay on the east side of Evans Island, I spotted the old San Juan cannery below. Red buoys in the water marked nets and oyster farms. I chopped power to begin a descent and watched the small houses of Chenega Bay come into view. Then I could see the end of the runway just above the waterline straight ahead. I made announcements over the radio just in case there was any traffic around, but no one answered. The village and its airspace looked as quiet and deserted as usual. I figured the wind was still out of the south, but to be sure I took a careful look at the orange windsock halfway down the runway. There were a couple airplanes with white wings parked below, and I felt my heart start to beat faster. I set up a downwind leg and then turned to line up into the wind on the long wide runway. Throttle all the way off, I pulled on full flaps and listened for the rumble and crunch of my tundra tires settling onto the surface.

The transition from flying to taxiing in a taildragger always gets my attention. All the visibility I had at two thousand feet looking out at miles of ocean, mountains and islands was now reduced to the confines of the instrument panel in front of me and a little bit of ground on either side. Gentle bumps in the runway bounced me gently in the seat. I grabbed the braces above the windshield and pulled myself up as best as I could to see further ahead, but zigzagging the plane as I taxied was really the only way to see straight in front.

I turned into the parking area and stopped beside the two airplanes. Only one of them was a SuperCub, but it wasn't Willie's. The other was an old Stinson, its fabric wings tattered and torn by years of exposure and lack of use. I scribbled down their registration numbers anyhow and climbed out of the plane. An old beat up backhoe was moving at the far end of the parking area, along the dirt road that led into town.

I walked in that direction, stopping behind the only building, which appeared to be some kind of maintenance shop, to take a leak in the weeds. Ten feet in front of me lay a fresh pile of bear scat. I zipped up and looked it over out of habit.

When I walked back around to the parking lot, the backhoe driver was standing beside his rig looking in my direction. I gave him a wave and he waved back, so I headed over to say hello. The native villages can be touchy about visitors—make that white man visitors—so I always tried to be careful about how I approached their turf. I've landed in several places where no one would make eye contact with me, a clear sign that visitors were not welcome.

"How you doing?" I offered as I reached him. He was a Native guy, or at least part Native, thin with long black hair tied in a ponytail that hung halfway down his back. He wore a red flannel shirt and a sleeveless blue down vest over blue jeans. He had a round friendly face and when he smiled back at me, I saw he had a single snaggle tooth and crinkled skin around his mouth and eyes.

"I'm okay," he said.

I made sure not to stare at him, looking around at the sky and trees instead. "Nice day."

"Yup," he spat into the grass. "It finally stopped raining."

"Yeah, no kidding. I'm from Seward. We've been getting lots of it lately."

"Well," he spat again, a brown string of tobacco juice arched into the grass. "It's that time of year."

"Not too busy around here, eh?" I ventured.

He shrugged and poked at the gravel with the toe of a battered work boot.

"You get many planes round here? It's such a nice runway."

"Nah, you the first one in over a week."

"Really, well, I guess the weather's been bad."

"Yup, and there's nothing here anyhow."

"Couple of nice ones you got parked here. Alaskan working planes, looks like. They belong to local guys?"

"Yup," he spat another brown stream, and wiped a brown drip from his chin with a sleeve. "The SuperCub's mine, but the Stinson there belongs to Andy. He's been in jail for a while, so it don't get flown much."

I waited a few moments, then decided I might as well get to the point. "A friend of mine's SuperCub got stolen last night from Seward, and I was wondering if maybe anyone around here might have seen it?"

His eyebrows rose in surprise, and he shrugged again. "Hmm," was all he said.

After waiting a few more minutes, I thought I'd heard about all I was going to get. "Well, okay, I was just out flying around and thought I'd stop in to see if anybody saw anything. Thanks anyhow."

I turned to walk back to my plane, but before I'd gone very far, he spoke up again like I hadn't left.

"Say, you know, the other night a couple planes flew over town really low."

I stopped in my tracks and turned back to him. "Oh yeah?"

"Yeah, that was different. It was foggy and raining real hard and they was real low." He pointed one hand toward the Sound. "Went that way."

"Could you see them?"

"Nah, just heard 'em. I was in the yard and they buzzed by overhead. I thought they was landing here, but they dint."

"Did they sound like SuperCubs?"

Another shrug. "Probably."

"Well, thanks. That might help. Here, if I give you one of my cards, would you call me if you see anything else like that?"

He ignored the card I offered. "We ain't got a phone on the island."

"Oh, uh, okay. Well, thanks anyhow."

He watched me walk back to my plane. When I taxied onto the gravel strip and lifted off, he was still standing in the same spot watching me fly by.

I banked to the east and felt my nerves starting to jangle again as I watched mile after mile of thick green forest and rocky shorelines pass below. "Patience, son, patience." I tried to calm myself. And I tried to ignore the little voice that kept telling me I was just wasting time and gas.

I thought over what I'd learned at Chenega. It could have been Willie's SuperCub going by, but it could have been anybody. Then again, two planes flying together during bad weather was unusual.

I looked out the side window to the east. Cordova and Valdez were in that direction. So was a lot of water and islands and the Copper River delta. Tons of places to land and hide. Shit.

I turned north and switched fuel tanks since the left one was getting low. The area I was crossing was mostly unpopulated and rough. Remote cabins sat here and there, mostly fishing camps. I hadn't flown over most of this. The best routes across the Sound were either north along the coastline near the Collegiate glaciers or from Chenega Bay across Green Island and the northern tip of Montague Island to Hinchinbrook Island and then into Cordova. That way you could stay over land as much as possible, connecting the dots from one island to another, avoiding wide open stretches of water.

This would be a good area to hide airplanes in, since most planes flying over would be too high to see much on the ground. Plus, it was less traveled and a long way from a real airport.

I banked left and pointed the Cub toward Port Nellie Juan and Kings Bay. The way back to Seward would take me across the north side of the Sargent Icefield and then down the south fork of the Snow River. I didn't expect to see anything along that route since it was fairly heavily traveled by airplanes flying from Seward to Valdez. It's also easily reachable by the floatplanes that operated out of Bear Lake and Moose Pass. I made a note to myself to call all those guys when I got back.

They might have seen a black SuperCub or any plane parked in an odd location.

When I lined up for a landing back in Seward the bay filled my windshield. Mount Alice was alive with color. Her bright green hillsides and snowcapped peak took on a pink alpenglow while three sailboats cut across the bay in a moderate breeze, their bright white sails flashing in the sun.

I parked the plane, checked for any messages in the office, and drove into town. I couldn't get used to the idea of the Yukon Bar without Willie, but I went anyway. What the hell else was there to do with a lonely evening?

Plus, there was always a chance that someone interesting might wander in some night.

CHAPTER
8

"I just want a girl who'll drop to her knees any time I need it, know what I mean?" Scooter was leaned over talking to Mitch when I walked in.

Mitch took a slug of his beer and nodded with understanding. He winked at me when Scooter wasn't looking. "Hey, Johnny. Big Red here was just expounding on the characteristics of an ideal relationship."

Scooter glanced at me and shuffled his bar stool to the left making room. He wouldn't make eye contact with me. He hesitated a minute as if deciding whether to continue with me listening. I noticed an empty shot glass next to his beer. He sniffed, blinked, and cocked his head toward me thinking about it. Then he continued.

"Yeah, man. I mean, a guy's thing is just so easy to get to. He can whip it out anywhere, in the car, in an airplane, at the breakfast table. I had a girlfriend once. I'd be getting out of the shower, and she'd be sitting there and just reach for me.

Right there, man, she'd work me over while I was toweling off my hair. She loved it, you know. Couldn't get enough of the old love muscle. God, I miss that. I need another girl like that."

"So what happened to her?" Mitch asked while Goldie brought me a beer, smiling and looking cockeyed at Scooter, letting me know she had heard enough of his bullshit.

"Oh, you know, 'irreconcilable differences,' as they say." He blinked hard a couple times, his whole face contorting with the effort.

"She didn't get bored with 'the old love muscle,' did she, Scooter?" I asked. "Maybe you weren't waiting outside of her shower often enough?"

He snorted. "It's different with women: Theirs isn't as easy to just whip out like that. It takes more effort."

"Well, we do have the more convenient plumbing. That's well established," said Mitch.

Bugeyed Larry was standing next to the wall phone, as usual. He must have been listening. He leaned across me and tapped beer bottles with Mitch. When he grinned, a line of rotten brown teeth appeared.

"Right on, dude," he said, a little too loud. His breath reeked of many beers and free peanuts. "Women like it too, you can bet your ass they do. I knew a guy once, went to a party. Didn't know no one there. So he's getting some chips and dip, and there's these four young hotties standing around. All of a sudden he up and says to himself, 'God, I love to eat pussy.' The women all giggled. He looks up like he's all embarrassed and says, 'Oh God, did I say that out loud?' The dude was surrounded by chicks all night. I've never seen him without a babe ever since."

We all laughed and clicked our beer bottles together and signaled Goldie for another round.

"Maybe you ought to try that approach, Scooter," I said. "Seems to be on your mind a lot lately."

"Yeah, no shit," he muttered, staring at his beer bottle and tearing at the label with a dirty fingernail.

"What's new with Willie, Mitch? You been over there since this morning?"

"Yeah, I checked a couple hours ago, but he's still out of it."

"He better not die on us."

"Yeah, no shit," Scooter chimed in. "'Cause if he dies, we'll have to have some kind of service and stand around talking about what a wonderful person he was."

Mitch gave him a quizzical look.

"You know what I mean. A guy dies and no matter what kind of half-assed life he's had and who he's screwed over, at his funeral, he's always a hero. You'd think he was a goddamned saint or something."

"Scooter, me thinks perhaps you're a bit too cynical tonight. Willie's a helluva good guy. Everybody thinks that."

"I'm not saying he isn't; I just hate funerals."

"Scooter's right about one thing," I mumbled. "Willie better not die."

Scooter and I nodded at each other and tilted back our bottles. I needed a change of subject.

"So, Scootie. How's the artificial woman coming along?"

He brightened at the question and launched into the details of his latest research. I was sorry I'd asked and went to the john. But Scooter didn't seem to mind. He just turned to Mitch and continued his rambling account.

When I came back a woman was sitting on my bar stool drinking a glass of red wine. I'd never seen her before, and the guys grinned at me watching to see how I reacted to my seat being taken by a pretty woman.

Mitch introduced us. "Hey, Johnny. This is Brandy. She's from Cleveland. We didn't think you'd mind if she sat here while she waited to use the phone."

"Of course not," I said. "Hello, Brandy."

She smiled shyly, nodding and sipping her wine.

I reached for my beer bottle awkwardly stretching between her and Scooter. I didn't mean to get that close to her, but I caught a whiff of something sweet. Her hair smelled like strawberries. I moved to give Goldie some space to get out from behind the bar to the main room. The place was filling up. Every seat was full by now and the tables were getting busy too.

I sipped my beer and looked over the new arrival out of the corner of my eye. She was a brunette with short-cropped wavy hair she tucked behind her ears. Thirty-something, I guessed, and very attractive. She was perched on the barstool wearing black jeans and running shoes and a lightweight suede jacket. Nice figure. She kept to herself and drank from the wine glass occasionally, running her fingertip around the rim between sips.

Scooter had turned his back to her, and he was still explaining his project to Mitch until I couldn't stand it anymore. I also realized that I had never seen Scooter with a girlfriend or any female for that matter.

"Scooter, have you ever been with a woman before, a real woman?" I thought I saw Brandy's eyes flicker just slightly.

"Oh, yeah," he answered nervously. "I've had lots of girlfriends."

"Hookers don't count, Scooter," said Mitch and we all laughed. Brandy didn't look over, but I saw her smile.

Scooter looked confused. He just stared at his beer bottle, blinking like crazy.

"That's it, isn't it?" I said with a big smile. "You've only been with hookers. Well, that explains a lot."

"Hey, don't knock hookers," Mitch said. "They provide a valuable community service."

"Well, if that's so, professor, why is it illegal?"

"In more advanced civilizations, it's not," he answered. "Like Amsterdam, Denmark, Australia, Canada, Nevada."

"So is that where you go every winter, Scooter?" I asked laughing. "Down to Vegas to the Chicken Ranch? To give 'the old love muscle' its annual tune-up?"

Mitch and I laughed, but Scooter's face was bright red. He pushed back from the bar knocking his stool to the floor with a clatter. He turned and disappeared out the door.

"Oops," I said, looking at Mitch with a sheepish grin.

Mitch returned the look. "Maybe we were a little too hard on the Scooter."

"Please don't say Scooter and 'hard-on' in the same sentence."

"Good point," Mitch chuckled. "I think our friend needs to get himself in a relationship."

"I don't know, man. Relationships take commitment. Like you and your wife, right?" I picked up Scooter's barstool and sat down in the space he'd left behind. "Scootie may not be ready for that. He may need to stick with the artificial variety for now."

"He might actually have a good idea there, you know?"

"Yeah, right, freakin' pervert," I swore and took a long pull on the beer. I filled Mitch in on my flight, and when he heard I hadn't seen anything, he grunted in resignation.

"Any chance Willie had insurance on the airplane?"

"No way. Willie didn't believe in insurance even if he could afford it."

We drank in silence for a few minutes. Heavy guitar riffs reverberated an old blues tune through the sound system. I thought about how Willie always sat here and bitched about the music being too loud.

"I really miss that sonofabitch," I finally said. My third beer was making me melancholy. "Remember that story he told about wrecking a SuperCub on a ridge one summer? He and a buddy were out in the boonies and he hit some rocks with the prop? Twisted the ends over like a pretzel. So he had the guy stand behind the prop holding a big rock, and Willie got another big rock and ran into him over and over until they finally beat the blades halfway straight. Then they flew it back home. Remember that one?"

Mitch laughed. "Yup, crazy bastard. The guy's a hell of a pilot."

I caught another whiff of strawberry shampoo and straightened up on the stool, glancing to my right. She was still sitting there, another glass of wine in front of her.

"Well, enough about all that," I said. Thinking about Willie was bringing me down.

"So Brandy, what do you think about relationships and commitment and all that stuff?" I was hoping a little trivial bar bullshit with a total stranger might lighten the mood.

She turned slightly toward us and smiled. "Oh, I'm not too good at the commitment thing either. I just stay for the fun parts."

"Oh? And what are the fun parts?"

"The sex, of course" she said with a grin.

I was mid-sip when she said that so matter-of-factly, and I almost sprayed beer across the bar. Mitch and I looked at each other wide-eyed and tried to keep our faces straight.

I turned to face her more directly. "Well, hello. I'm Johnny Wainwright. Welcome to Seward, Alaska."

She smiled. She had a very pleasant face; she wore no makeup or jewelry. She looked me straight in the eye for a moment like she was reading me, looking for a sign of something.

"What do you do, Johnny?"

"I'm a pilot—air taxi and scenic flights around the glaciers. Maybe you'd like to go up sometime? Do you like to fly?"

It was a good line. I'd used it on several occasions with good results. And the beer was working its magic on me. My usual shyness had disappeared completely, and I was warming up to this pretty woman in a hurry. Most people are impressed by pilots, and women seem to like adventurous types who flirt with the dangerous side of life. Thanks to the alcohol, I was very impressed with myself at the moment.

"Are you one of those bush pilots I've heard so much about?" she asked playfully, her eyes twinkling.

"Yes, m'am, I sure am. If you want, I'll fly into the bush anytime." I grinned at her, trying as hard as I could not to slur my words.

Mitch leaned in front of me to mock whisper at her behind his hand. "Better watch out for these local pilots, Brandy. Some have questionable reputations."

"Thank you, sir, but you don't have to worry about me. I fly Learjets out of Cleveland on medical charters. I know how pilots are."

Suddenly I felt about as small as the peanut shells laying on the floor beside us. If only I had been sober I might have come up with a witty response. Instead, I just stared at my beer bottle in numb silence.

Mitch laughed and elbowed me in the side. "Well, how about that, Johnny. Brandy's a pilot too. Isn't that nice? Now you have something in common to talk about. Don't forget to tell her about your budding private investigator career."

I wasn't amused, but I tried to hide it behind a grin. "Say, Brandy, didn't you say you were waiting to use the phone? It's free now."

She giggled and looked into my eyes again to see how I was doing. "Actually, I was waiting for a call. I'm supposed to meet my dad here, but he hasn't returned my calls."

Mitch and I looked at each other. "Who's your dad?" he asked.

"Bill Maxwell. He told me to come down here. He said the Yukon Bar's his hangout. Do you guys know him?"

"Know him?" I blurted. "You mean Willie? We've been talking about him for the past hour. Why didn't you say something?"

She looked at me puzzled. "Willie? I've never known him as Willie. We, I mean my family, we call him Bill. Where is he?"

CHAPTER 9

"How long has he been like this?" Brandy's lower lip was quivering. She held one hand over her mouth trying to hide it. Her other arm hung helplessly by her side. She looked at her father and then looked away, standing sideways at the end of his bed.

Willie was lying in the same bed in the same position. The only difference was a couple vases of flowers people from the Yukon had sent over. Brandy had driven us up the hill in her rental car to get here. My head was still fuzzy, and the friendly buzz I had at the bar was becoming a dark burden.

She walked to the head of the bed and looked down at her father. His head was still bandaged although the dressings had been changed and his eyes were visible now. At least he was recognizable. A nurse stopped in to tell us we couldn't stay. It was after visiting hours.

"What's being done for him?" Brandy demanded.

"We're doing what we can," the nurse explained. "But he may need to be transferred up to Anchorage. If you want to come back in the morning, the doctor will be in and you can ask her."

As we walked back to her car, Brandy started to cry. She seemed so small and vulnerable walking beside me with her head down. I put my arm around her shoulders.

"Oh, forget that," she snapped, shrugging away from me.

I raised my hands and backed away. "Sorry, sorry. I feel bad about it too."

"You don't understand the first thing about it," she grumbled and climbed in her car.

I thought she was going to drive away and leave me weaving in the parking lot, but after a moment she unlocked the passenger door, and I got in beside her. I pointed the way to my camper, and she drove in silence.

After the short drive back down the hill, she parked beside the Yukon, shut off the engine, and turned to look at me. "What now? You going back in for more beer?"

"Uh, no. I think I've had enough. I'm headed home. Anything I can do for you?"

"No, I really don't think so." She was looking me over and shaking her head.

"Look, Brandy, I'm really sorry your dad got hurt."

"Well, shit. What the hell happened here?"

I told her what I knew. I guessed I was making more sense now that the night air was clearing my head a bit. She listened quietly.

"So these guys were really after you and your plane? Lucky for you." She spat the words at me. And they hurt.

"I know, I know. It wasn't my idea for him to get hurt. Believe me. Everybody here likes Willie. There's no way he deserved this."

She wrapped her arms around her waist and glared out the window. "You didn't bother to clear it up with them, now did you?"

"Wait a minute." I threw my hands in the air. "Gimme a goddamn break. I got knocked silly before I could say a thing. To hell with this." I got out and walked to my camper. I sat there stewing. I felt bad enough about Willie already without this noise. But I couldn't back out. She was parked too close to me. So I was stuck, trapped between her car and the one parked in front of me. All I wanted to do was get away.

She wasn't going anywhere. I looked in the rearview mirror several times and could see her parked back there. I thought about honking my horn, but then I calmed down a little and thought better of it.

At first I thought she was blocking me on purpose. Out of pure meanness or some shit. Then it began to dawn on me that my mobility was the last thing on her mind. I took a deep breath and got out of the Toyota. When I walked back toward her, I found her leaning against the back of her rental car. Her arms were still wrapped tight around her chest.

I approached slowly and didn't say a word. I leaned against the car beside her and waited. I was in no hurry. And besides, damn it all, she was Willie's daughter.

Several minutes went by. I tried to read what must be going through her mind. Up here in Alaska, not knowing anyone except the father she came to visit, and he's seriously hurt. Might even die.

"Brandy," I said softly. "Willie's my best friend. I'm really sorry all this shit happened. Is there anything I can do?"

She let out a big sigh. "I don't know. This is a big shock."

"Yeah, no kidding. It's funny though. None of us even knew you existed until he mentioned the other day you were coming for a visit."

She dropped her arms to her sides and let out another sigh. She wiped at her face with her palms and fingers.

"We weren't close. He left us, mom and me, when I was five. He came for Christmas visits and brought presents and stuff, but that stopped when I was in high school. I haven't seen him for several years."

"This your first time up here?"

"Yeah, he sent me a letter a while back, and he seemed really impressed about my flying career. He invited me to come up and see Alaska sometime." She paused. "Anyhow, what about the police? You got any law enforcement up here. What are they doing?"

"That's a good question. I'm not sure what they're doing. I didn't get much of an answer when I asked the same question."

"What are you doing about it?"

"Me? What do you mean, *me?* What the hell can I do about it?"

"You're some kind of investigator? Isn't that what Mitch said?"

"Oh, he's just giving me a hard time. I do some repo jobs once in a while."

"Repo? You mean repossessing cars?"

"Nah, I stay away from that stuff. It's nothing, really. Sometimes I help rental stores get stuff back that their customers don't return. It ain't much to get excited about, really."

She turned her head and stared at the deserted street. We could just barely hear the music and the crack of pool balls drifting out of the bar. She rubbed her face with both hands and tucked her hair behind her ears.

She let out a big sigh. "Something's got to be done. That airplane was his life."

"You're right about that. I just don't know what to do."

She looked me up and down again. I knew I wasn't helping her feel hopeful. "Do you ever get sober, or is this your normal state?"

That pissed me off. "Hey, take it easy. I almost never get loaded. I was just drowning my sorrows, I guess."

She sniffed in disbelief. I started to leave again. I needed to get away from that shit.

She looked at me. "I'm going to get to the bottom of this. You can be all helpless if you want, but if you're really his friend, I'd think you'd want to help."

And with that she got in the car and drove off. I stared after her. Jesus Christ, what a bitch. I looked at the Yukon and thought about heading back in, but it was midnight, and I felt like French fried dog crap. I drove to the airport and collapsed into bed fully clothed.

Sleep was difficult. I kept waking up thinking I heard Willie's car pulling up beside me. Then the memory of him lying in that bed would come back, and I saw the frustrated look on Brandy's face again. I kept having one of those repeating dreams that never resolve. The one where I was in a fight with some enemy, and I was hitting him in the face as hard as I could. But he just smiled at me, mocking me, obviously unfazed by my best shots.

* * * * *

It was after ten in the morning before I finally got moving. I showered and put on some cleaner clothes than I had been wearing for the last couple of days. I looked in the mirror and hoped my face didn't look as fuzzy as I felt. The hangover was fading, but I sure wasn't firing on all cylinders by a long shot.

Coffee from the Texaco helped a little. When I pulled into the hospital parking lot, Brandy was just coming out the front door. She spotted me but there was no smile. Just a brusque hello on the way to her car. Then, in what seemed like an afterthought, she stopped. "There's no change," she said to me. "The doctor says if they don't see any improvement today, they'll ship him up to Providence Hospital."

I stopped in my tracks and looked down at my feet. "Damn it. This just sucks so bad."

"I checked with the police too. The case was transferred to the Alaska State Patrol, but when I went to that office I got some runaround about the chief being out on another investigation, and they're waiting for the FBI to contact them. I tell you, I've had about enough of Mayberry and Barney Fife around here." Her jaw was set and she was staring holes in me.

"Take it easy, will ya? You don't know anything about this town. I've been thinking about what you said, and maybe we can do some things." I kept my tone civil, but it wasn't easy.

"Who's going to do something? You?" She gave me that up and down look again.

I glared at her. "Okay, forget it," I snapped and turned on my heel.

I had the engine started and in gear when she waved me down. Reluctantly I stopped and rolled the window down.

"Look, I'm sorry," she said in a calmer tone. "I'm just upset, you know? Can we go somewhere and talk it over. I promise to lighten up."

I could hear the strain in her voice. I knew the type. Self-sufficient, strong woman. *I can do it myself. Don't need help from anybody, especially a man.* There were plenty of tough women like that in the aviation world. They could fly as well as any guy in most situations, but you better not get in their way. Not if you wanted to avoid footprints on your back. Footprints in golf cleats.

I supposed it wasn't their fault. Like a lot of professions, aviation has always been a male-dominated world. Any woman good enough to make it as a pilot has to be one tough cookie. Self-reliant, decisive, determined. Like any good pilot. It was no wonder many of them developed a hard edge.

I wasn't much of a hardass, so I gave in. I'm always giving in, it seems. Especially to a good-looking woman. And I usually regretted it.

We went to the Breeze and sat at a table in the back part of the big room. We were barely seated when she started in on me again. "You've got to know how important that damned SuperCub is to my dad. It's his life. You know that, don't you?"

I nodded. "You don't have to explain that to me."

She ignored me and went on. "I think his airplane was always more important to him than I was. He'd deny that, of course. But I always felt that way. Anyhow, if he loses that airplane, we might lose him altogether. He won't be able to overcome it. We've got to get it back."

I must have rolled my eyes or something. I was trying not to show a negative reaction to this speech, but it was getting a little too Oprah for me.

"If you let this slide away and these guys are never caught, Willie will never forgive you. You say you're his friend. What the hell kind of friend are you anyway? You're going to turn your back on him when he needs you the most?"

I blinked and looked at her hard. She wasn't kidding. What did I care? I didn't even know her. And who did she think she was? Somebody important to me? To hell with her.

Trying to lay a guilt trip on me like that. It wasn't my problem. *Leave me alone. Willie got himself in a mess. Too bad.*

I wanted to say all that to her, but she looked like she expected me to have some lame-ass thing to say. So I looked away, took a swig of my coffee, and kept quiet.

I looked at her again. She was still staring at me. Hard. Then she looked away just before I did. Damn it. I tried to ignore it, but I could see it. I could see her father's eyes in her when she looked at me like that. Willie's eyes. The disappointment in her face, the way her eyes dropped, like her faith in all mankind had just left the depot, hunkered down in the backseat of a dirty dog Greyhound disgusting busload of pain leaving for the coast.

Yeah, I tried to pretend I didn't care, but bullshit on that. Her words had sliced through me like a knife, its serrated edge jagging through my heart, shredding a path through my soul. And I was defenseless. I couldn't stop it. Couldn't stop the horror. Jesus. Why did I care so damn much what this little broad thought about me?

But it wasn't her. I knew that. To hell with her. I'd turned my back on pretty women before. It was Willie. I couldn't let the sonofabitch down. She was right about that. Goddamn it. This is why a guy shouldn't get involved with people. It makes you care, makes you vulnerable, makes you feel things you don't want to feel.

What did she expect me to do? I wasn't a cop. Didn't wanna be either. And for chrissake, who knew what these assholes were capable of?

I needed her to understand. I needed to explain myself. I was just a simple guy, there was nothing really complicated about me. I just liked flying my plane and helping people when I could. And hopefully I made a buck along the way. I loved Alaska, the outdoors, the wildlife, this beautiful part of Alaska around us down here in Seward, not the Seattle wannabe mess called Anchorage whose only redeeming value is its location, conveniently only thirty minutes from the "real" Alaska.

And I wasn't the richest guy in town. So what? I lived in a motor home at the airport and my best friend, Willie, lived in a leaky mobile home down by the river. I wore the same jeans for about two weeks at a time. My work got me dirty sometimes, so I usually had grimy fingernails and grubby hands. I ended every day at the Yukon Bar. I didn't drink a lot. Couple of beers, maybe three. Four on a night of wild abandon, but I was always sorry for it in the morning. And sometimes beer started to taste like crap after a couple, so I would switch to something tasty, like a White Russian or straight Baileys. When I was sipping on one of those, Willie would give me a funny look, then he tried to look away like he didn't notice. But I caught him exchanging glances with Mitch, who's usually sitting next to him. Sometimes I straightened my pinky for them, you know, just for effect, as I took another sip. And sometimes it was my middle finger. That always got their attention. Made them laugh.

They liked me, cuz I made 'em laugh. That was a good thing, I guessed. If people liked you and laughed at your jokes, they usually liked having you around. And sometimes they bought you drinks. Another good thing. Came in handy sometimes. Unless they started treating you like their personal clown. *Hey, Johnny, tell us about the time you thought you saw penguins.* How was I supposed to know there weren't any goddamned penguins in the Northern Hemisphere? *Hey, Johnny, make that funny noise you do.* What the hell was I? Their trained monkey? Gimme a break. I'd be funny when I felt like it. They couldn't just order that shit up when they needed a laugh. The audience didn't direct the show. The audience had to wait. When the talent felt like showing up, then they got a performance. If they were lucky. I got sick of people trying to push me around.

And sometimes I got scared. I had to fight through the fear—fear of heights, fear of turbulence, fear of bad visibility, fear of dying, fear of conflict. I wasn't a big guy, so I had to be careful about getting in fights, for fear of getting my ass kicked. I wasn't a hero. I would do a lot of things to avoid getting caught up in the stuff I was afraid of.

I wasn't particularly strong either. Wiry maybe, but I avoided fights and violence of the physical kind. I never saw much of a future in getting pounded by some drunken gorilla who took offense at a smart-assed comment I might make when I'm not in control of my tongue. Or even an innocent remark misinterpreted. Anyhow, in my line of work I used other skills to get the job done. You don't need to be strong to fly a plane. Or big. In fact, smaller people actually made better pilots. For a lot of reasons.

Like tiny cockpits. Did you know that some of the best fighter pilots of all time were little guys? Maybe because a little guy could strap on an airplane and merge it with his body and his soul. Not to mention that being able to see the enemy and watch his every move is the key to winning a dogfight. You had to be quick and agile to watch the enemy turn, dive, and roll through one gyration after another in a chase.

I looked up with a start. Rainey had stopped by to refill our coffee cups, and she was staring at me with a worried look. "You okay, Johnny?"

"Huh? Oh, yeah. I'm fine. I was just thinking about stuff. This is Willie's daughter by the way. Meet Brandy."

While they exchanged greetings, I realized that I'd been off in the ozone. Thinking about all the things I wanted to explain. Rainey left us, and Brandy was looking at me again, waiting.

After a moment, I met her gaze. "So that's how you lighten things up, eh?"

She sank back in her chair and laughed. "Aw, crap. I can't help it. I'm sorry, Johnny, I'm not usually such a total bitch."

"Shit, why me, Brandy? What do you expect me to do?"

"Who else, Johnny? The cops aren't going to help. Not anytime soon anyhow. You've got an airplane, and it seems like you have the time. And you know how to investigate and find people. And I'll help. We'll work on it together. I know your friends will want to help too."

I rolled my eyes. "Oh, brother. What are we gonna be, the gang that couldn't think straight? Gimme a break."

Her eyes were relentless. They wouldn't let me go. They were softer now and green, but I could see the hard edges too. Lurking behind the side curtains like a loaded trap, ready to strike. I tried to avoid her gaze. There was no way.

She was pretty, damn it all. I liked looking at her. But there was no way I wanted her to know that. And I was catching the glances of others across the room, wondering what old Johnny was doing with this young stuff. I liked the way that felt too. Shit.

"And," she went on, "you haven't run away yet, so there must be some reason you're still listening."

I didn't answer. What could I say anyhow? I knew I was hooked. I looked out the window past the bar. Rainey was moving along, serving coffee, and putting fresh napkins in front of new customers, handing out her daily ration of sass in equal portions. I just wanted to walk over there and flirt with her for a while.

I knew Rainey was safe. Didn't have to worry about losing my heart there. Rainey was a good friend. Rainey was taken. Her husband was a friend of mine. Flirting with Rainey was like reading the funny papers at the public library. Good for a giggle, but you didn't get to take her home. Forget Brandy, forget Willie.

Right. Like that was an option.

The spoon clinked in her coffee cup as she stirred in cream. "So maybe you are a friend of my dad's after all."

I took a deep breath. Glanced at the smooth skin of her face and the way her little ear lobes tucked in beside the soft hair above her collar. Damn it all, I was going to get involved here and probably wouldn't even get lucky either. I was an idiot.

"I gotta make some calls. You want to order breakfast?"

She made a slight smile and reached over to squeeze my hand. Then she got up to get some menus.

Her hand was warm. Damn it, don't touch me. Don't make it worse. But she was halfway across the room already. A couple of ruddy-faced fishermen looked up with self-conscious smiles and made room for her to reach over the bar for menus. I stepped into the lobby where I could hear better.

I called Moose Pass. Luckily Phil was home. Phil Bartlett was the owner of the company I flew for. He had six other planes that flew regularly in the area. I told him about Willie and asked him to be on the lookout for anything strange, especially out in the Sound. *No, not floatplanes, wheel planes. Yeah, I know that doesn't make a lot of sense in floatplane country, but that's what I think is going on here. Something strange. And spread the word, would ya? No, I'm not going to do anything stupid. Just looking around, that's all.*

Phil told me that a group of tourists was coming in that next week and wanted some scenic flights. For now, though, things were still quiet. No flights scheduled until then. And the air taxi job set for tomorrow cancelled.

Then I called Steve Harkin in Anchorage. I wanted him to know that I thought we got hit by the ripoff team he had warned me about. Steve was good at keeping people informed. He was like Willie that way—a networking guy with all the latest information.

"Yeah, Scooter called me about that too. Hang on a sec, will ya, Johnny? I just got something new on that around here somewhere." He put me on hold.

Rainey walked by with a tray full of dirty dishes. She stopped in front of me.

"So uh, you and little Miss Muffet?" She poked me in the chest and studied my eyes with a suspicious grin.

"No, no way. Are you kidding? She's Willie's daughter. Besides, she's not my type at all."

She put her hand on her hip. "Who you trying to convince. Me or you?"

I swallowed and glanced at her, then looked away quickly.

"That's what I thought. I got one word for you, Mister Hotshot Pilot. Keep it zipped."

"That's more than one word," I protested.

"Don't forget. I know you, Johnny." She pointed two fingers at her own eyes and then pointed one at me as she walked away.

Steve came back on the line. "Johnny, I got a name. I don't know if it means anything, but the people in Arizona say one of the suspects was named Anthony Baxter. I know it ain't much, but that's it, okay?"

I hung up and went back to the table. Brandy was returning from the bar. I watched her walk across the room with the morning sunlight backlighting her from the big picture windows behind the bar. Liquor bottles on the shelf along the window were illuminated by the sunshine, glowing gold and yellow, green and red. TV screens on both ends of the bar flickered silently and low country music filled the room accompanied by the sounds of breakfast dishes, utensils, and coffee cups like a million diners in a million towns from here to Dawson City. Well, maybe not a million, but several dozen anyway.

We ordered food. Brandy ordered pancakes. I got eggs over hard and hash browns. Energy food. Protein. I had a feeling I was going to need it. Washed it down with coffee. The mixture warmed me and filled me up. It was more than I needed, but I ate it all anyhow. Wiped the plate with the toast. Brandy ate slowly, pacing herself. We didn't talk for several minutes.

"When you're done, I need to get on the Internet," I told her. She looked up, intrigued.

"Oh, yeah? What are you thinking?"

CHAPTER
10

At the office, I logged on and connected to the FAA's website. There were two Anthony Baxters in the database. One Anthony A. and one Anthony L. Two different N-numbers, the registration numbers that all U.S. airplanes wear. One for a Beech Bonanza, the other a SuperCub.

I went further, looking up the information on the SuperCub. It was registered to Anthony L. Baxter with an address in Chula Vista, California. A quick check on MapQuest showed me that Chula Vista was a suburb of San Diego, not that far from Arizona and just north of Baja, Mexico, where a SuperCub was an ideal plane for its beaches and deserts.

The information was promising. At least, it made sense so far. But how did it connect to Alaska? I thought about calling airports in Chula Vista to see if I could locate the airplane parked somewhere. If it was down there, this lead was probably just a dead-end. Leading us nowhere. But I had another thought too.

I Googled "A Baxter Alaska" and got four hits, but no Anthony. Then I Googled "B Baxter Alaska" and got three more. Cutting and pasting as I went through the entire alphabet, in twenty minutes I had a list of fifty-four Baxter phone numbers in various places in Alaska, some nearby and the others all over the place from Juneau to Barrow and Bethel.

"What are you doing?" Brandy stopped inspecting the photos and brochures around the office and came over to see the printout.

I showed her the list. "We can start tracking these down. Might be relatives of Mister Anthony here. You never know."

She looked puzzled. "What do we do with this?"

"I'll show you," I said, picking up the office phone and dialing a number in Seward. "We've got two Baxters right here in town."

A man's voice answered on the third ring. "Hello?"

"Hi, is this Anthony?"

"No, you got the wrong number."

"Oh, I'm sorry. This number was left on a bulletin board with an airplane for sale by somebody named Anthony. That's not you, eh?"

"No, no Anthony here. You got a bad number."

"Sorry, then." I hung up and dialed the next Seward number. No answer.

I showed her the list. I'd scratched off the first Seward name and made a note about the no answer on the next one.

"Sheesh, what a pain." She plopped down and started flipping through an old copy of *TradeAPlane*.

"Welcome to the world of skip tracing and chasing deadbeats."

She tossed the magazine aside. "Well, I'm glad you know what you're doing. I'm going for a walk."

I pointed down the tarmac showing her where Willie's plane used to be. She left, and I went back to the phone.

Using the same routine I worked the list focusing on the nearest locations first. An hour went by with zero results. Brandy came back in while I was on the line to a number in Soldotna.

"Any luck?"

"Not so far. Wait...." I held up my hand as an older woman's voice answered. I went into my pitch asking for Anthony Baxter.

"Uh, no? Who is this?" Something about her tone alerted me.

"My name's Eddie Dergen. I met Anthony out at the airport a while ago. He was showing me his SuperCub and thought he might want to sell it. He gave me this number to contact him."

"Oh, well, uh, I don't know why he gave you this number. He doesn't live here."

"Oh, I'm sorry, m'am. Didn't mean to bother you. Do you know how I can reach him?" I must have passed the polite and respectful test. She seemed to relax.

"Well, Anthony's my grandson, and he came up for a visit, but I haven't seen him for over two weeks." She sounded confused. "I didn't know he wanted to sell his plane. That's odd." She seemed a little shaky but was probably a nice little old lady. I was guessing in her seventies or eighties.

"It is? Why's that?" I asked in my most wide-eyed innocent voice.

"Well, because he flew it all the way up here from California. Said he was going to use it to go fishing and hunting."

"All the way from California, eh?"

"Yes, he had some kind of trouble…. I-I shouldn't say. I just don't know about young people today."

"So he doesn't live up here?"

"Oh, no. They were just here for a couple of days. Didn't say when they were coming back."

"Okay. Well, thank you, Missus Baxter. Sorry to trouble you."

Brandy had leaned in close to listen to the conversation. The smell of strawberry shampoo filled my nostrils.

I hung up the phone and reached for the Soldotna phone book. It didn't take long to find the address next to the phone number. I didn't know my way around Soldotna that well, but I thought this place was an apartment complex close to the main drag. It was about a two-hour drive away. I could have flown over there in thirty minutes, but I was going to need a way to get around once I got there.

"Okay if I borrow your rental? The camper doesn't do long drives very well, and a couple of the tires may not make the trip."

"Why? You think you got something?"

"You never know. Might be nothing, but it might be something." I held my hand out for the car keys.

"Get in," she said, heading for the car. "What am I supposed to do, sit around and diddle myself?"

I didn't move. "Wait, that ain't gonna work. I do this kind of stuff alone."

"Then drive your camper, butthead. Or forget the Lone Ranger crap."

I didn't like it. I didn't like any part of it, but hell, what was I going to do? I climbed in beside her. "You always this disagreeable?"

She grinned and backed out of the parking space. "You're stuck with me, Johnny. Get used to it."

I glared out the window as she pulled onto the highway and crossed the bridge over Resurrection River.

"Shit, I am getting used to it. That's the problem."

She glanced sideways at me.

"You're just like your damn father. 'Cept he calls me motherfucker instead of butthead."

"He calls everybody motherfucker."

"That's true, isn't it? A sad lack of social graces if you ask me."

We drove on in silence. She handled the car competently, maintaining a steady speed even on hill climbs and descents. Passing RVs or slow trucks as needed and not scaring me. It made me think about her in the pilot's seat of a Learjet. I could picture her doing that, wearing a neat uniform or flight suit, going through the preflight, flipping switches and calling out checklist items. Then using light control pressures and the various instruments needed to manage the sophisticated turbine powered beast.

I would never tell her this, but I was impressed and more than a little intimidated by her Lear experience. Jet jockeys were the upper crust. Up there almost as high as fighter pilots or airline pilots in the status game of the aviation world. Learjets fly over four hundred miles per hour and they carry seven passengers. Both a pilot and copilot are required to fly the thing. My SuperCub is lucky to make a hundred knots with a stiff tail wind. The Lear has two turbo fan jet engines producing thousands of horsepower cruising along at forty thousand feet. The Cub pumps out just one hundred and fifty horses and usually at treetop level.

Not that I'm embarrassed by the SuperCub. No way. It was the perfect plane for what I did and for thousands of backcountry pilots like me carrying hunters and fishermen or cargo to remote bush areas. But when a Lear or a Cessna Citation comes into the Seward airport and my Cub is parked nearby, the contrast is like a beat-up dingy floating next to a huge yacht, a Chihuahua next to a sleek greyhound, a mosquito next to an eagle.

And this little woman sitting next to me, with her petite frame and a hundred and five pounds of well-packaged self-confidence was piloting that multimillion dollar jet and pulling down at least eighty grand. And me, in my tattered plaid shirt and scuffed shoes—I was lucky to keep gas in the Cub some months.

I stared out the window and tried to think about something else. No point in bemoaning the choices I'd made over the years. *I am what I am.* Geez, listen to me, Popeye the fucking Sailor Man.

It was another nice day. The miles passed easily as we made our way over Twelve Mile Pass. Kenai Lake was painted a brilliant blue and finally free of winter ice. Turning west at the Y, we headed downhill along the Kenai River to the flats west of the Kenai Mountains. High snow-covered peaks on the west side of Cook Inlet stood miles away in the distance.

We didn't talk much on the trip over, but I explained what I thought might be going on with the Baxters. Without anything else to go on, it seemed worth a try.

"What are you hoping to find over here?"

"I'm not sure, but something in the old lady's voice made me think she's worried about something. Like maybe young Anthony's been in trouble before or has had bill collectors trying to track him down or something. Or maybe his dad did—her son, you know. I'm not sure; it's just a hunch kind of thing. She seemed cautious, like someone told her not to answer questions."

"You got all of that out of that phone call?"

I shrugged. Some things couldn't be explained. "She's not used to whatever's going on. We're just going to drop in and say hello. See what's what. One time I did that. I was shooting the breeze with this guy, and his cousin, the guy I was looking for, walked right in the door."

I'd have rather been alone. I didn't work with a partner. Never had. Especially not a woman. For lots of reasons.

Think about it. There were plenty of times when I had to sit in a vehicle on stakeout for hours and sometimes all night watching somebody. A partner might complain or get grumpy. Who needs that? Or other times I had to do stuff I didn't want witnessed. A partner would know too much about what I was doing and if questioned by cops couldn't be trusted to keep quiet. Not only that, but the bad guys might get a hold of a partner too. Not good for either one of us. No thanks, no partners for me.

Brandy and I drove along without talking, passing the turnoff for Sterling. She broke the silence finally, reading my thoughts. "Is this bothering you?"

"What?"

"Me tagging along, doing the driving. Bugging you?"

"Nah, it's fine. I'm cool," I lied.

"I'm good with old ladies," she said. "Maybe I can get something out of her."

"What? I'm not good with old ladies?"

"Relax, Johnny. You don't need to be so uptight."

"I'm not uptight! What the hell kind of statement is that? Don't tell me to relax."

She started to giggle, looking over at me. Damn it. I tried as hard as I could to keep a straight face. How was I going to keep my distance if she kept being so playful?

"I'm good with old ladies because I've had lots of experience."

"Oh, really?" I grumped at her, suppressing a grin.

"Yes, my mom's not really that old yet, but she's got early Alzheimer's. I spend most of my free time taking care of her back in Cleveland."

"That's too bad. Your mom and Willie…?" I left the question hanging.

"Yeah, she started going downhill a few years ago. Some days she doesn't even know who I am. I'll come home from an all night flight, and she'll look at me and say, 'Can I help you?' like I'm a total stranger. I think Willie picked up on it before anybody else. That's when he quit coming around as often."

"Why'd they break up in the first place?"

"Well, he would never marry her. That was an issue. And she wouldn't move to Alaska. So they drifted apart, I guess. I remember how much he would talk about flying in Alaska. He couldn't stay away. That's probably what got me interested in flying in the first place. Now that I'm up here, driving around, I can see the appeal."

"Yeah, it does that to ya." I watched a caravan of pickups carrying bright orange rafts passing us in the other direction. Had to be headed for the world famous salmon fishing waters behind us on the Kenai River.

"You live with your mom?"

"Yeah, didn't want to put her in a home. She can still take care of herself pretty much. And after my divorce I had more house than I needed for myself. So it made sense to move her in with me. I'm gone a lot anyhow, so it's no problem."

I thought about that and quietly shuddered to myself. No way I could handle that kind of situation. I couldn't see Willie doing it either. But I didn't say anything. More power to her if she could deal with it.

"It doesn't get in the way of your flying?"

"Most of the time it doesn't. We have a nursing service that comes in and checks on her when I'm gone. So it's okay."

She was quiet for a minute. Then she said, "I miss my mom. The way she used to be. We used to be really close. Now we don't talk much, you know? She doesn't remember things

I've said ten minutes ago. So I just keep it to 'How you doing? Want anything? Want something to eat? Need a sweater?' Stuff like that. And she gets pissy a lot. If not outright angry."

"Sounds rough. I know I couldn't do it."

She drove in silence for a few more miles. The drone of the highway was making me sleepy. But she had more to say. "The hardest part is when she's mad at me. For nothing. Sometimes I just hate her for that. That's the hardest. Then I just want to run."

"Wow." Hearing her words shocked me. She was telling me stuff I hadn't expected to hear. "Why do you do it then? Isn't there another way to have her taken care of?"

"I don't know. I guess that's what you do when you love someone. That's what I've never understood about my dad. I mean, how could he leave us if he loved us?"

I squirmed in my seat. Wished I was driving. To give myself something to do instead of listening to the pain. Wished I was somewhere else. I was a wuss about stuff like that. I thought about changing the subject.

"I think I decided he didn't love us," she said. "Maybe that's why I finally came up here. To confront him, you know?"

I thought about that for a minute. Tried to picture Willie listening to this kind of stuff. I couldn't see it. My scalp started to itch thinking about that conversation.

"I don't know, Brandy. You're gonna have to work that out with him. Willie keeps a lot of stuff to himself. He's my friend, but I don't think even I know him that well. Some things a man keeps inside. Maybe cuz it hurts too much to let out."

"Yeah, maybe," she said. "Men are so screwed up." She let out kind of a giggle. Her way of shaking off heavy thoughts, I thought.

I thought about secrets. I'd always figured everybody had some. Most people kept some stuff private, didn't they? No one was an open book, were they? If they were, they were a pain in the ass. The kind of people you'd want to tell, "Shut up, dude. You're boring the hell out of me."

I thought about a young woman in a professional flying career. Family obligations could really bog down an ambitious pilot. I'd seen it mess up a lot of marriages. Flying jobs were easier when you were footloose and fancy free. But the life could be pretty lonesome. I wondered if her ex couldn't handle her success.

    I glanced over at Brandy driving. Her face was calm as she concentrated on the road ahead. I couldn't read her. Something told me a guy better have his shit together to partner with her. I was glad I didn't have to worry about passing that kind of test.

    "Well, maybe you can help with the old lady. We'll see how it goes."

    She giggled again, looking over at me.

    "What?" I couldn't figure her out.

    "Oh, nothing," she pretended to focus on her driving.

    I thought about asking her more about Willie's past. I was curious. He had hidden this part of his history from all of us as far as I knew. I wondered why.

    Before I could think of any good questions, we entered the outskirts of Soldotna, and I had to start looking for street signs.

CHAPTER
11

It wasn't long before we pulled into the parking lot of a large complex not far from the main highway. We walked between three different buildings until I found a Baxter on a row of mailboxes.

Before I rang the bell I briefed Brandy. "Okay, let's play it by ear and see what happens. Just follow my lead."

She nodded and I pushed the button. To my surprise the entrance door buzzed, and I pushed our way inside without having to say a word. I looked at Brandy and shrugged. Up one flight of stairs we found an apartment door open halfway down the hall. A little blue-haired lady was leaning out the door watching us walk toward her.

"Missus Baxter?" I asked smiling my friendliest but not too pushy smile.

She looked confused. "I thought it was my friend Betsy. Who are you?"

I chuckled pleasantly. "Oh, I'm sorry. I'm Eddie Dergen. I talked to you this morning. Remember? And this is my friend,

Brenda. After we talked on the phone, I realized that I had something of Anthony's, and I thought since we were in the neighborhood, I'd just stop by and drop it off."

I handed her an old sectional chart I'd brought with me from the office. She looked at it with a frown, then looked up at us. Brandy and I were smiling our friendliest "shucks, how ya doin'" grins. We must have looked irresistible.

"Well, okay, thank you," she said sweetly, pulling up the granny glasses that hung around her neck on a chain. She looked at the chart without a clue what it was.

"But like I told you, Anthony's not here and I don't know where he is. You didn't have to go to any trouble."

"Oh, no trouble at all. I didn't want him to be mad at me for not returning it. He seems like a really nice guy." Fishing, fishing.

"Yes, well, thank you." She started to pull inside the door, looking at the map again, turning it over and peering down at the small print.

I thought we were about to get closed out when Brandy piped up. "Gosh, Missus Baxter, are those forget-me-nots?" She pointed into the apartment at some overflowing flower boxes on a balcony.

"Yes, they are, dear," she smiled with pride. "They're the Alaska state flower, you know."

"Are they really? I didn't know that. Yours are lovely. How do you get them to bloom so well?"

"Oh, come in, come in. I'll show you." She led us inside and took Brandy by the hand leading her out onto the balcony for a closer look. "You're a sweetheart to ask about them. I just love my little flowers. They're such a delightful splash of color after the long winters are finally over, you know."

While they went out on the balcony I lingered behind and had a look around the little apartment. Family pictures were everywhere. But I stayed right by the balcony door so the old lady wouldn't get nervous.

I needn't have worried. She and Brandy were deep in a discussion about the plants, the fertilizer, the clipping. All that shit. I joined them after a quick inspection of the lounge chair and pile of papers and letters in front of the TV by the phone.

After listening to them for a few minutes, I interrupted. "Missus Baxter, I don't mean to interrupt, but do you have a bathroom I could use?"

"Oh, certainly, sonny. Right down the hall behind you." She turned back to Brandy to continue their talk, obviously cherishing the attention and the company.

I checked each of two bedrooms carefully for evidence of another person living there. I also checked out the pictures on the wall. In the bathroom, I used the john and ran the water in the sink while carefully opening the medicine cabinet for pill bottles with other names besides hers. Checked the trash can too but found nothing.

But on the way back through the living room I spotted a small daypack sitting behind a couch. The pack looked out of place in the tidy apartment. Checking to be sure Missus Baxter was still occupied with Brandy, I stooped to open it and found the kinds of things a guy carried around on fishing trips. Small tackle boxes, a roll of line, a pair of gloves, and a couple envelopes and pieces of paper. I stuffed the papers in my coat, replaced the pack where I found it, and rejoined the ladies on the balcony.

Brandy looked in my eyes, and I gave a quick jerk of my head toward the door.

"Well, thank you so much, Missus Baxter. You've done a wonderful job decorating your place. The flowers are such a delight. But I guess we should be moving along."

"Oh, you're so welcome, sweetie. And call me Sallie. All the grandkids do. You're about their same age. And thank you, Eddie, for stopping by with Anthony's map."

We all shuffled off the balcony into the small living room. On the way to the door, I pointed at one of the pictures on the wall. "Say, isn't that Anthony when he was much younger?"

"Oh, no, no. That's Michael, my grandson in Los Angeles. This is Anthony over here." She retrieved a desk frame with a family of four, pointing at one of the figures standing beside what looked like a sister and two parents.

I looked at the picture closely and handed it to Brandy. "Oh, sure. That's him all right. Pretty recent picture."

"Yes, he's my daughter's boy, and she always sends lots of pictures. Even now when they're all grown up. I guess it's just a family thing she likes to do. As you can see, we're a big family. And this little place just won't hold all the pictures of everybody anymore. But since my husband died, this is all I can afford."

She smiled at us again as she led us to the door. "Well, this was very pleasant. You all feel free to stop in and visit me any time. An old lady needs company, you know. Won't you stay for some tea, or maybe a little snack?"

We begged off and said goodbye. Making our way back to the car, I thought about the visit.

"That went pretty well, I think. You did a nice job with her. You get a good look at that picture?"

"Thanks, Johnny. Yeah, I guess so, but this Anthony guy didn't look unusual or anything."

"Yeah, I know, but I'm not that great at remembering faces. You think you'd recognize him if you saw him for real?"

"Maybe. What else did you learn? That was a pretty long bathroom break." She drove us back to the highway and we headed for Seward.

"You mean, besides the life history of the forget-me-not? I'm not sure, but knowing what he looks like is huge. That could really help us."

"You ever feel bad about lying to people like that? She was so nice."

"Lying? Hell, that ain't lying."

"I mean, the 'Eddie Dergen met Anthony at the airport' bullshit."

"Oh, that. That's just part of doing this kind of business. Whatever it takes to get the bad guy is my motto."

I thought about her question and wondered if she was getting the guilts. "Hey, sometimes you have to get creative. That's all. Besides, you were so friendly with her, you probably made her day. Where's the harm?"

"Yeah, I know." She drove and watched for traffic on our way out of town. "I don't think I could do what you do."

"I did manage to pick up a couple of other things that might help. Let's see what we got here."

I pulled the papers out of my coat. "I found a guy's pack behind the sofa. These were in it."

I had a crumpled brochure, a small piece of notebook paper with what looked like a phone number written on it and a package of photos. Like twenty or so snapshots.

Then I remembered the papers I'd picked up the abandoned campsite. There were in my other pocket. The name Lance Holcomb appeared on a credit card slip, but nothing else made any sense. A few forms and pieces of notepaper with numbers written on them.

Brandy was watching me examine the papers while she drove. When I finished looking them over, she reached for the two pieces of notepaper. One was from the campsite and the other I'd picked up in Sallie's apartment.

"Does the handwriting on these look the same to you?"

I looked closer. "Yeah, could be. And the paper looks like it could have come from the same notebook. These could connect this guy with the campsite."

I pulled out my cell phone and dialed the number. No answer.

"I'll check later to find out who this phone number's for. Or at least to see if I can get a location. I don't recognize the prefix, but I know it's not Seward, Soldotna, or Moose Pass."

"What's the brochure from?"

"Just some lodge on the Kenai. Don't know if that'll lead anywhere or not. But these pictures might be interesting."

I looked through them and found standard tourist fishing trip pictures. Guys and girls on a boat mugging for the camera and holding up fish they'd caught. There was a shot of Sallie Baxter and a guy who looked like her grandson in a baseball cap next to her. But nothing that showed airplanes in the bush country.

"Let me see those." Brandy held out her hand, and I handed her half the stack, glancing at the highway.

She caught my look. "Oh, relax. You think I could fly a Learjet without being able to multitask?"

"Okay, you're right. But then again, do you have to dodge many moose at thirty thousand feet? They'll jump out of the woods around here most any time."

"Okay, okay, I'm being careful."

And she was too. I grudgingly had to give her credit. She'd handled Grandma Baxter smoothly, and I knew she had to be good to do the kind of flying she did. She was very competent. Maybe she was more competent than I was comfortable with. *Note to self: Think about that some other time. You might learn something.*

"So how do you like flying a Lear?" I kept my voice neutral but interested. I didn't want her thinking I was jealous. Didn't want her to know the truth.

"You know, it's an excellent job. Sure took me a long time to get there though. I spend a lot of years beating around the patch in a one-seventy-two to get enough hours."

"Instructing?"

"Yep. Paying my dues. I tell you, when I was in school, all I could dream about was flying the big iron, you know? Had stars in my eyes. Brandy Fontaine, seven-seventy-seven captain. Then I met reality and spent years just getting to where I could fly right seat in a commuter. A couple years of that and finally the left seat, but that was still boring. And the money was terrible. But that's not the worst part."

"What do you mean?"

"Okay, so I'm finally a captain, thinking I'm hot stuff, but the airline gets in financial trouble and they lay me off."

"Wow. After all that."

"Yeah, I was lucky to have met a lot of people. So I was only out of work for a couple weeks, and a friend of mine called me about the job flying medical charters."

"Nice. That does sound like a lucky break."

She looked over at me. "I know what you're thinking, and you can forget it. I didn't sleep my way into the job."

I raised my hands in self-defense. "Hey, easy, easy. I wasn't thinking that at all."

She looked pissed. She looked over at me again, and I met her eyes directly, raising my hands palm up with a blank look.

"Okay," she said, softening her look and her tone. "Sorry. I've been accused of that too many times. It's so stupid. My friend is female. She and her husband own the company."

"Understandable, I guess. With a great job like that and so many guys out of work, I can see where people would get jealous and say stupid stuff."

We rode in silence for a few minutes.

"I'll tell you a secret, Johnny."

"Uh, okay."

"Flying a Lear isn't that big a deal. Everything is so regulated. The FAA is watching every move we make every second of the day. Every flight is an instrument flight and completely regulated and controlled by the air traffic guys. I envy people like you who fly up here with a lot more freedom."

That was a new idea. She was jealous of me?

"You're kidding. Broke all the time, flying beat-up planes we can't afford to fix?"

"No, I'm serious. The career pilots I know are mostly bored to death and in debt up to their ears. Flying careers are just not the field of dreams we all thought they would be."

"That reminds me of something your dad used to say. 'We always want what we ain't got.' His way of saying 'The grass is always greener….'"

"Yep, sounds like him. But please don't talk about him like he's dead."

"Sorry, I didn't mean to do that."

"It's okay. Keeping busy like this keeps me from worrying about him. I hope he's better when we get back to Seward."

A few miles went by, and we started the uphill trek into the mountains along the river curving and bending its way east to Cooper Landing. Afternoon sunlit snow covered the mountaintops ahead. Vast stretches of forest spread all around, spring leaves fluttering in the wind.

"Wow," she said as we came around a curve to find a long valley with color glistening from both sides. She seemed overwhelmed. I knew the feeling. "Dad always told me how beautiful it was up here, but I never really knew what he meant. I was always too poor to come up for a visit. And it was worse when I was married."

"What happened there, if you don't mind me asking?"

"No, I don't mind. He's a pilot too with the same struggles. When I got my big break, I don't think he could handle it."

"What, you doing good and him not doing as good?"

"Yep, that about sums it up I think. At least we were never the same after I got the Lear job."

She stared out the side window for a minute. "Then other stuff happened—and kaflooey. It was over."

"Bummer." It was the only sympathetic thing I could think of to say. I felt bad that I'd brought up bad memories. I could sense the pain. I'd been there.

"Yeah, bummer is right. Why are men like that?"

"Like what?"

"So filled with stupid pride and male ego bullshit, they screw everything up?" The hard tone was back. I could feel the edge of tears in her voice.

"Whoa, geez. I ain't no Doctor Phil here."

She wiped her nose and sniffed, raising her chin with a deep sigh. "Damn it. I thought this stuff was done with. I'm sorry."

"Ah, it's okay. And don't worry about me. I lost all my 'stupid pride' years ago." I gestured down at my raggedy shoes and worn plaid jacket.

We both laughed. "Yeah, but what about male ego bullshit?"

"Who, me? Male ego bullshit? Well, geez, you gotta leave me something."

We laughed again.

"This place okay for gas?" she asked, pointing at the restaurant and fuel stop ahead.

"Oh yeah. This is right next door to Quartz Creek. There's a big gravel airstrip right through those trees. Sits on the bank of Kenai Lake. You hungry? Why don't we get some lunch. Maybe Arnold's here. He's an old friend of mine I think you'd like to meet."

Seated inside in the cozy log building, we sat at a table looking out into the trees and ordered hamburgers. It wasn't busy. We were alone in the dining room. After our food came, an old Native man came walking toward us, wearing a sauce-smeared apron and a wife beater undershirt. He wore clear plastic gloves, which didn't hide the dirty hands and greasy fingernails underneath. His footsteps echoed on the old bare unfinished wooden floor.

"Hey, Johnny. You fly in for a burger?"

"Hey, Arnold. No, we're driving back to Seward from 'Slow Dotna.' Meet my friend Brandy. She's from Cleveland."

Arnold slowly took her hand and said hello, looking her over quickly, then glancing away in the customary Native manner. His gentle eyes smiled quietly at her again. "Welcome to Alaska."

"Thank you. I'm having a hard time getting used to how amazing the scenery is around here. On the way up just now I think I fell in love with it."

Arnold looked at her briefly, then gazed out the window. "You know, Brandy, my wife and I have owned this place for thirty years," he said. "I thought it was funny when outsiders would say stuff like that. I didn't understand."

"Understand what?"

"I guess when you're born here, it doesn't seem so special. But after watching so many folks over the years, I get it now. This country moves people. The way it changes with the seasons. But, you know, Alaska's not about the scenery."

"It's not?" Brandy seemed transfixed by Arnold's slow mumbling speech. She watched his mouth, trying to capture everything he said.

"No, it ain't the scenery. It's about the person moving through it."

That seemed to catch her off guard. Her head jerked slightly, and she frowned and looked up at him, captivated, yet puzzled at the same time.

He went on, saying more words than I had heard Arnold speak at one time ever. "I mean, some people come up here and look at it all, and think 'that's nice, very pretty' and they go home and never come back. But other people come up here, and the place grabs them by the throat. And it won't let go. And no matter what they do from then on, they either find a way to come back, or they live the rest of their lives wishing they had."

His eyes twinkled at her for a moment. "If you don't believe me, just look at this guy." He jerked a dirty thumb in my direction and smiled.

Brandy turned toward me with a curious look and then laughed as I started to choke on the huge bite of burger I had just stuffed in my face. By the time I got it swallowed and wiped the debris off my beard and mustache, Arnold was gone, the floor boards creaking as he crossed the room and disappeared into the kitchen.

CHAPTER
12

Willie was somewhat better. Some of the tubes and equipment were disconnected, and more of his face was visible. Dark purple bruising covered half his face, and both his eyes were swollen shut. A large bandage was still wrapped around most of his head.

A nurse stopped in just after we arrived and told us that Willie was still in a coma, but the doctor thought there was some improvement. I couldn't see it. The Willie I knew was nowhere around. And she told us that his leg wasn't broken after all. It was his ankle that was busted. It was still elevated and surrounded by a big cast that extended from mid-calf.

Brandy looked shaken, seeing her father's face for the first time in a long time. "God, he looks old."

"Those bruises aren't very attractive. But he's a tough old bird. Maybe he's gonna make it." I tried to sound hopeful.

"You staying?" She looked at me. "I need to go to my room for a while."

"Yeah, you go on. I'll stay for a bit, then probably head down to the Yukon."

She turned with a sad smile. "Figures. Okay, see ya."

"See ya." I watched her leave and turned back and sat down beside Willie's bed.

"Hey, man. You in there?"

I gave it a minute but didn't get an answer. I didn't expect one, but I talked anyhow. What the hell, you know. I'd heard people in a coma might still be able to hear stuff.

"C'mon, Willie. Dude, you gotta snap out of this crap. It's after five o'clock, you know. The guys at the Yukon don't know what to talk about without you around."

I pulled my chair right up beside the head of the bed, but I kept my voice low. No one needed to hear this but Willie and me. "Why didn't you tell me about your daughter, Willie? She's pretty cool. Smart, too. I would have thought you were proud of her, flying jets and all that. We're working together, she and I are, to find your plane. I know, I know. You don't want us doing that. Tough shit, bucko. We're not going to sit around on our butts while somebody takes your Cub apart piece by piece like vultures picking on a corpse. Maybe it's a good thing you can't talk right now. Now I don't have to listen to you being my big brother, trying to boss me around. I can just hear you ragging on and on about us taking chances and doing stupid stuff.

"Well, we ain't. But we gotta get your Cub back. And the cops ain't doing shit. You know how pissed off you get about stuff like that, I can just see you ranting and raving and waving your arms around bitching about it.

"Another thing, Willie. We finally got some halfway decent weather out there, and you're missing it.

"Well, I appreciate you listening to me talk about these things. Not like you have much choice about it. It looks like they're taking care of you pretty good here. You're not missing much down at the Yukon. Except for Scooter. I'm afraid that young man may be losing his mind, but whatever. He might be better off without it. I mean, look at you. Just kidding, pal. Don't get pissed at me."

I leaned in closer and started to whisper. "Seriously, Willie. Get better, man. We miss you. We care about you, too. Not me so much, you know. But the guys do, for some strange reason. And Brandy, damn, she really seems to care about you. She came all the way up here to see you finally, and you're laying here all wrapped up and not saying nothing. C'mon, man, you know that ain't right."

I got up and started for the door. Something stopped me, and I returned to the chair and stared at him for a couple minutes. Willie didn't make a sound. A heart monitor hummed in the corner, the only noise in the quiet room. Willie's chest moved with his breathing, but otherwise he was motionless. I put my hand on his arm, staring at the bed sheets, collecting my thoughts. Then I took a deep breath, let it out, leaned in and started to whisper again.

"One more thing, Willie. I promise you. I goddamn promise you, man. I will get your plane back. And if I can't, I'll get the people that did this to you. They're going to pay. You can take that to the bank."

I stood up and cleared my throat. In my normal voice, I said, "Now knock off the bullshit, you slacker. Quit goofing off and come back to the world, all right?"

I walked down to the bar watching the evening sun still illuminating the ridgelines on either side of Mount Alice across the bay. The dry dock lights twinkled on the water, and a dog barked somewhere nearby. A car or two went by but no one I recognized. A few gift shops were still open on Fourth Avenue when I turned the corner, and some tourists were doing their slow tourist meandering along the sidewalks on both sides of the street. Older guys sat on the benches while their wives cruised the shops looking at cards and t-shirts and souvenirs. Music from the juke box in DJ's wafted out the door as I walked past. "No Dogs Allowed" said the hand-lettered sign on the front door. I tried not to think about Willie, but I thought I saw him everywhere I looked.

I had a cold beer on my mind and not much else when I pushed open the door of the Yukon Bar. The place was almost deserted. Even Bugeyed Larry was gone. The Revenue Corner was surprisingly vacant too. *Damn it, Willie.*

Mitch walked back from the restroom just after I sat down. Goldie came over, quietly laid out a napkin, and set down a bottle for me. I made my best attempt at a smile thanking her. We made eye contact for a brief moment, then she turned and left us alone.

"You seen Willie?" I asked Mitch.

He nodded but wouldn't look at me. His eyes were cast down, his face slack. "Yeah, I was up there this afternoon. He just looks so…broken."

I didn't know what to say. I drank my beer. All I could think was Mitch better not cry. If he started crying, I was gonna lose it. How pathetic was that? A couple of old farts crying in their beer at the Yukon Bar.

While I was doing my best to maintain that rugged bush pilot stiff upper lip, Goldie came up behind Mitch and set down the dirty glasses and rag she was carrying. She didn't say a word, just stepped up onto the rungs of his barstool and put her arms around him. Looking down into his forlorn face, she leaned in and pressed her lips against the side of his head. Mitch said nothing, but I noticed he leaned toward her and took a deep breath with his eyes closed. She stayed there for a moment, the two of them ignoring everything else in the bar and beyond. Then she whispered something, brushing her lips gently against his hair.

When Goldie pulled away and moved down the bar, Mitch stood up, flipped a couple of bills next to his half empty glass and without looking at me turned and left. I swallowed more beer and watched Goldie wipe tables and collect glasses.

The door behind me swung open and banged against its stop by the cigarette machine. A friend of ours we called Hondo strolled in and took Mitch's seat.

"Hey, Johnny. What the hell's going on?" Hondo was a loud guy who owned a yard full of construction equipment and drove a dump truck around town. He was a massively built man of more than three hundred pounds though he stood only five foot eight or so. He looked like the bulldog emblem on his Mack truck. I don't know who first started calling him Hondo but the nickname stuck. The word was he had been a special ops guy, dropping inside North Vietnam by parachute, sneaking around and blowing shit up. Those guys had balls of steel. I couldn't even remember what his real name was at this point. Henry or some shit. Maybe he got it from his army days.

"Hey, Hondo. What are you drinking?" I was glad to see him and waved at Goldie to get him whatever he wanted. I was glad for any distraction.

"Yeah, tough shit about Willie, ya know? But that old fucker's gonna make it. You watch. The sonofabitch'll probably outlive us all." He wrapped a huge meaty fist around the beer bottle that Goldie brought over and drained half of it with two swallows.

"What you been up to, man?" I asked him, wanting to change the subject.

"Ah, it was such a nice damn day out there today. Shit. I couldn't work. Hell with that. I went flying, ya know? But the weirdest thing happened. I was cruising along, everything good, going through Resurrection Canyon, ya know, out by Exit Glacier? And all of a sudden the goddamn airplane flips upside down. I don't know how the hell it happened. I didn't do nothing out of the ordinary. It was weird, man. So I slammed the throttle all the way in, and shoved the nose forward and jammed the wheel all the way to the left. Somehow it turned over again but headed straight up. Then it stalled and the nose dropped until I was staring at the river coming up at me straight in the fucking face. It was wild, man." He waved his arms around imitating the gyrations of the airplane. Sweat beaded up on his broad bald head gleaming in the barroom's lights.

"Jesus, Hondo. You could have bought the farm."

"Yeah, fuckin' A, bubba." He took another huge gulp of beer and wiped his mouth with his sleeve. "You're an instructor aincha, Johnny? What the hell do you think happened?"

"I don't know. Sounds like something in the control systems. Was this your one-seventy-two?"

"No, the Piper. But then it flew fine after that."

"Any wind?"

"Nope, calm as could be."

"And you weren't doing anything unusual at the time?"

"No, I swear. Just my normal turns and stuff." Then he laughed and said, "Hell, it's a good thing Willie ain't here."

"Why's that?"

"Ah, hell, he'd say I was loaded or on drugs or something and didn't know how to fly. Some rude bullshit like that. Fucking guy." He laughed and took another pull on his beer. "Thing is. He's probably right. Hah." He laughed again and clinked his bottle against mine. "Here's to fucking Willie."

I laughed too. "Well, I don't go that way, Hondo, but I'm glad to hear you're exploring your options."

Hondo banged his beer down on the bar and gaped at me, slowly realizing what I meant. "Eat shit, asswipe," he roared with a big smile and waved at Goldie for more beers.

The door bumped open again, and Scooter walked in. Hondo greeted him.

"Hey, Scootie, man. I was just telling asshole Johnny here. I was flying along today and all of a fucking sudden, I'm fucking upside down. It was crazy as fuck." Scooter laughed. So did I. Crazy Hondo. He could drop the f-bomb into more sentences in more ways than anybody I ever heard.

I looked Scooter over for a moment. I thought I picked up an attitude from the wild eyed red headed man. Probably still pissed at me about the other night. Whatever.

Some kind of loud jumpy Cajun music started on the stereo, and people started coming into the bar. Everybody was talking louder, competing with the music. Then Mitch walked back in and joined us. He grinned at Scooter and Hondo and ordered some European import.

I leaned over to him. "I can just hear Willie bitching about the loud music. Hey, move down, will you, Hondo? Give Mitch some room here."

"Yeah, yeah." Hondo threw a peanut at me. "Hey, Scooter's telling me about his fake woman thing. Pretty cool, huh?"

Then he looked thoughtful for a moment and turned to Scooter. "How you gonna make it feel, like…real, you know?"

Scooter straightened up proudly. "I invented a natural feeling oil supply system that'll be imbedded in just the right place, so just one touch, and she'll be juiced up and ready to go."

"No shit? I knew a girl like that once." Hondo looked at Scooter with rapt interest, a lascivious memory on his face.

"Oh, yeah," Scooter went on. "It works much better than the old standards, like hollowed out bananas."

I was getting irritated. "Jesus Christ, Scooter. Who the hell are you? The Cliff Clavin of masturbation?"

Mitch jumped in. "Seriously, Johnny. You ought to give Scooter's idea some consideration. Just think how much time that would save. It's like a time management godsend."

"I don't know, Mitch. I prefer women with a pulse."

Scooter's eyes narrowed. "A pulse? Good idea. I could make that happen." He looked up at the ceiling of the bar, his mind conjuring up the required materials.

"Forget it, Scooter. Don't you think your project is kind of bizarre?"

"No way. Face the reality. There's a real shortage of women in Alaska. And guys got needs."

I rolled my eyes and shook my head. Then I noticed that Brandy was standing quietly behind me at the end corner of the bar next to the phone.

"Hey, you stalking me?" I frowned at her, pretending to be mad.

"Not even in your wet dreams," she snapped at me with a grin.

Mitch laughed, and I elbowed him. The jerk.

Trying to recover, I grinned back. "Hey, don't get the wrong idea about me. You're Willie's daughter. I don't mean nothing. I'm not interested in the slightest about what you're doing tonight or anything else besides helping Willie. I was just trying to be polite to the visiting daughter of my friend."

"Yeah, right." She winked at Mitch who was enjoying my tap dance.

"No, no, no, seriously. I'm truly not interested in what you're doing tonight."

Brandy turned back to her glass of wine with her nose slightly raised. Lifting her eyebrows just a little and cocking her head with apparent indifference, she took a sip and used both hands to straighten her napkin.

A minute went by. "So uh, what are you doing tonight?" She waited a moment, then smiled slightly and turned toward me. "You're looking at it."

"Well, okay," I said and raised my bottle. "Here's to your dad. We're all just trying to get happy."

Three stools down, Hondo was talking loud again. I looked down toward him and saw him in a heated conversation with a tourist in an L.L. Bean sweater and a baseball hat that said "Fishermen Do It Deeper."

"Oh, so you want to land on a gravel bar by the river, do ya? I know something about that." Hondo's voice rose over the sound of the music to where they could probably hear him down at DJ's. "Yeah, it might look beautiful from the air. You're flying over at a hundred feet and the trees are rushing by ya. You can go into a trance just staring at that shit. But let me tell ya, that goddamn river is deep, fast, and cold. You bust up your plane out there and you're fucked."

The tourist waved a hand at Hondo like that would never happen. His expression said "Who me? No way, I'm bullet-proof."

Hondo leaned into the guy's face. "Think you're pretty hot stuff, huh, dipshit? Let me tell ya. If you survive the crash you wait, or you walk. In the meantime you're just trying to stay alive. If you don't get hypothermia and fucking freeze to death, a goddamn bear's gonna find you. You guys all think Alaska's so wonderful, you can kiss my ass."

The tourist looked like he was about to lose bowel control, and Hondo looked like a pit bull about to have a poodle for lunch. We all knew he'd calm down in a while. Unless he was provoked. And funny thing, a lot of stuff provoked him. We knew better than to try and interrupt. The visitor started this conversation, he was going to have to get himself out of it. The guys turned to watch the show.

"That Bonanza is a nice ride, expensive too. But it's got little wheels, and a nose wheel, and a nose wheel airplane ain't got no business landing out in the backcountry. If you wreck out there, you're gonna wish you were anywhere else in the damn world. It ain't gonna seem so beautiful then."

The tourist pulled off his hat, scratched his head and wiped his brow. He looked up at us watching. His eyes flickered around the bar looking for the doors.

Hondo was just getting warmed up. "Mother Nature can be a real bitch, let me tell ya. You get in that fucking water, and the river don't care. Your measly bag of bones and pasty white ass thrashing in the current don't matter a hill of freaking beans to the river. She's seen punk ass feeble pukes like you a million times. She's dragged under moose and caribou, even grizzly bears. Beat 'em against the rocks, tangled them in tree stumps, drowned 'em and spit 'em up on some lousy mud bank to be found months later."

Hondo looked over at us watching him. Mitch and I nodded at him.

"It ain't pretty, let me tell ya, dumbass. You watch out for that fucking river. Pretty or not, she's a heartless whore."

Hondo finally stopped ranting for a minute to drain his beer and call for another. The tourist turned and practically ran toward the restroom at the far end of the bar. Hondo watched his retreat and turned back to us with a big grin.

We grinned back and raised our bottles.

"Fucking A, bubba," Hondo hollered, returning our salute. "Fucking dweeb ass idiot asked me where he could go land his Bonanza out by Resurrection River."

He looked over his shoulder but the tourist was long gone. "I guess he ain't coming back." Hondo shrugged and grinned at us again.

"Hell, I was gonna tell him some more. Educate the dumb fucker. You guys know. You wanna disappear real freaking fast? Have your engine quit over the Cook Inlet. Pilots have been disappearing in that shit for years. Ever heard of the name Merrill? As in Merrill Field? Yeah, he disappeared in nineteen twenty-nine."

Hondo launched into one of his favorite stories, just like none of us had heard it before.

"He was already a well-known Alaskan pilot, one of the originals. It was bad weather, he heads out over Cook Inlet on his way to Bethel or somewhere southwest. And disappears. Never seen again. Musta gone in the inlet."

Hondo pointed a huge finger and growled like I wasn't paying attention or something. "You better listen to this shit, Johnny. You fly over there all the time."

I was listening. I always listened to these guys who'd been up here longer than me.

"Your only chance in that water, Johnny, is to get naked."

He caught my stunned expression. "What?" I asked.

"Yeah, that's right, man. Naked. You guys have seen Cook Inlet. It ain't beautiful blue freaking water. No, sir, it's a churning horror show of brown silt. If you're in for more than a minute, the silt fills your clothes and drags you under. Just like bags of sand in your shorts. You can't swim in it. And even if you do get out of your clothes, you'll probably fucking freeze to death anyway.

"Remember last year? That Commander, you know? It was a twin-engine turbo prop flying low over the water right off Fire Island. They were training to count wildlife or some shit. A guy in a fishing boat saw them go over, thought it was odd they were so low. Radar was tracking them and then, boom, they were gone. No trace. A rescue chopper went up. Nothing.

"They searched for days with planes and boats and choppers. They even walked all over the place, screened all the nearby shorelines. Nothing. Finally had to call it off.

"The Cook Inlet, man, it's like a huge sewer system. You screw up and get in that shit, it'll flush you out to sea. Out to the Gulf of Alaska. Fish food, motherfucker. That's where they all are now. And that's what you'll be, Johnny, if you don't watch your ass. You'll be fish food too, floating around with those guys. You and old Russell Merrill. Yeah, all thanks to Mother Nature. She's a cold bitch."

He went silent and drank his beer. All of us turned to our beverages as well, thinking our own thoughts. The music was still loud, but none of us heard it.

Then I remembered Brandy sitting next to me and glanced over at her. Like the rest of us she was staring into her glass.

"Welcome to Alaska," I said. "You've just received your first safety briefing on flying the Final Frontier."

She whistled softly through her teeth and took a big swallow of wine. "Maybe I need to drink something stronger."

"Don't worry about it. Your dad always tells the pretty girls that come in here to never believe anything a pilot tells them, especially an Alaskan bush pilot."

"I know, he's told me that for years."

My cell phone rang. It was Phil in Moose Pass. "Hey, Johnny. I wanted to give you a call before it got too late. Wow, what's all that noise? You at the Yukon?"

"Uh, yeah. I'll move outside." I went out to the sidewalk and leaned against the wall, covering one ear to hear him better.

"Figures you'd be at the Yukon. Listen, our chief pilot, Dooley, was flying over the Sound today, and he saw a fire on Smith Island. You know where that is?"

"Nope, never heard of it."

"It's a flat little piece of tree-covered land about halfway between Chenega and Valdez, out in the middle of the Sound. A lot of *Exxon Valdez* oil washed up there. Anyhow, I told all the pilots what you said about looking for unusual stuff, and this qualified. He said he saw a bunch of wheel tracks in the sand out there leading up into the trees."

"What was Dooley doing out there?"

"He was taking a group down to Stump Lake on Montague, to the forest service cabin down there. We never go that direction, and usually he would be at least two thousand feet and never would have seen this."

"Why was he so low?"

"There was some weather in the area. No big deal, just a bunch of low cumulus, and he had to get low over there to get under it. No problem with the floatplane, but don't you ever do that. Anyway, that's when he saw a big fireball, like an explosion, so he swung over there for a look. But there was no forest fire or anything, just the one big poof, then a lot of smoke. He didn't see any people or any planes."

"Hmm, that's pretty weird. Okay, well, thanks, Phil. Did you call it in to the Forest Service?"

"Yup, they're going to check it out. How's Willie?"

"Not so good, I'm afraid. Still in a coma."

I went back in the bar. The guys were chatting up Brandy. She was telling them about flying the Learjet, and from the looks on their faces, I knew they were struggling between being impressed and halfway wondering if she was lying. We weren't used to a woman of such obvious aeronautical sophistication.

Scooter was trying to hide his frequent looks at her shape. She was wearing a black leather jacket that hid most of her features. But that didn't keep him from trying his best with comical glances out of the corner of his eye. His red knotted ponytail bobbed with every rapid eye blink.

She looked at me when I sat back down. "I'm on my way back to the hotel. You got a plan for tomorrow?"

I told her about the phone call. "If the weather's okay, I want to fly over to check out this Smith Island place. Let's go over and see where it is."

I walked her over to the far side of the bar, beside the tiny dance floor in front of the stage. A nautical chart of Prince William Sound was tacked onto the wall. Every piece of land or rock in the nearby waters was depicted along with water depths and other information. The heavier used areas and routes were blotched up with dirty fingerprints and smudges. I found Smith Island in the middle of open water between Green Island and Naked Island. It looked to be around five miles long and less than a mile wide.

Brandy stared at the map intently. "Where did the *Exxon Valdez* run aground?"

I pointed to the northeast and showed her where Bligh Reef was located. "Yeah, the worst oil spill area was all right in here." I swept my finger from the reef to the southwest showing her all the islands and the miles of coastline that had been heavily coated in black sludge after the wreck.

"So what time are we taking off?"

I looked at her. I wasn't thinking about both of us going out there. She caught me. "Don't even give me that look, Johnny. We're going together. Besides, I want to see first-hand how a real bush pilot handles a SuperCub out there. And I'll buy the fuel."

I cringed, knowing that if Willie overheard that, he would set her straight about what makes a real bush pilot. But I didn't bother to correct her. And I didn't argue about the fuel. I'd gladly let a high-priced jet jockey pay the way.

"Okay, okay. We can go together. You got any gear?"

"Like what?"

"Like survival stuff. We need to be prepared for anything out there."

"Yeah, okay, I've got a few things. I'll bring 'em along."

CHAPTER 13

We lifted off the next morning into a high overcast. Before we left, I checked the weather on the Internet. There was a system out in the Gulf moving to the north, so I didn't want to spend too much time out there in case it moved in faster than expected. Flight Service in Kenai didn't have much information about conditions or forecasts for the Sound, as usual. Pilots in this part of Alaska rely on each other for weather details. If you can find anyone.

Brandy noticed the lack of information. "It's been a long time since I went on a flight without a printout about the conditions," she said. "Or a copilot to keep track of it all."

I loaded our stuff behind the backseat. She climbed in with the awkward movements of a first timer, pulled on her headset and waited for me. Once preflighted and ready to go, I started the engine and flipped on the intercom. Taxiing to the south end for a takeoff into a light north wind, I moved the stick back and forth and felt it bump against something.

"Hey," she said over the intercom. "Watch out for my knees back here."

I laughed. "Welcome to the world of the SuperCub. You've got controls back there. Foot pedals for the rudders, throttle up by your left hand, and the stick, of course. But don't touch a thing."

"Thanks a lot. I can't see a damn thing from back here anyhow."

"Yup, that's right. You'll have to do all your observing out the side windows. You've got a camera, right?"

"Yeah, I bought a digital model for this trip. I'll try to get some shots of anything of interest."

I flew the most direct line I could manage, heading up the south fork of Snow River again until I gained enough altitude to get over Sargent Icefield.

I folded the sectional chart to the area I needed and stuck it under one leg. Without a VOR or GPS, I had to navigate solely by line of sight and the map. I knew that could get tricky going to an island I had never seen before. Not up close anyhow. Smith Island was just a few miles from where I had flown on my flight out to Chenega the other day, but it was almost ten miles out in open water. I never had a reason to venture that far out into the middle of the Sound before.

At least the winds aloft were calm and even though not sunshiny, it was a nice flight. High rock ridges and glaciers slid by on both sides of us until I climbed high enough to cruise over the top of everything.

"This is amazing. I've never flown this close to the terrain before anywhere." Brandy's voice gushed with static over my headset.

"Yup, you're right. People pay big bucks to see this stuff just the way you're seeing it. You can't do this around Cleveland, eh?"

She laughed. "It kind of takes my breath away."

I climbed to four thousand feet as we left the mainland and started crossing Knight Passage, a broad stretch of bluish gray water below us.

"All that water out there. Why don't you have a floatplane?"

"Yeah, right—I wish. The damn floats cost almost as much as the plane. Anyhow, saltwater tears up these planes, especially the instruments and radios. And I can do what I need to on wheels."

I think she picked up by my tone of voice that I didn't appreciate the question. Talk about your haves and have-nots. Okay, whatever. She didn't understand. I shrugged it off.

"According to the chart, Smith Island is that little green spot up ahead. Can you see it?"

She pulled herself up by the braces on the roof of the cockpit. "Barely. How are we going to do this?"

"Well, I've got to stay high until we get within gliding distance of the island, but I want to have a look before I go too low and alert anybody. Just in case they're here."

"Maybe we can swing out to the right a ways, and I'll use the telephoto function of the camera to see what I can see. And get some pictures too."

"Okay, let's try it."

I banked the airplane and made a couple of circles like we were looking at something on the surface of the water. At least that's what I hoped anyone down there would think.

"Johnny, I can see the marks in the sand he was talking about, and something blue in the trees behind it."

"Okay, take the stick and hand me the camera. Take us in another circle."

The southeast corner of the island had a flat beach and a clearing nearby where a plane could taxi. I could just make out some blue tarps in the trees and the edge of something white underneath. The wings of Willie's SuperCub were white.

"Okay, I've got the controls." I handed the camera back to Brandy. "I'm going back to the west and then check out the north side."

I repeated the routine on the other side of the long flat island and dropped altitude for a closer look. I was able to inspect the whole shoreline once we were away from the suspect beach. The dense forest only had a few wet-looking clearings. I couldn't see any likely landing spots except for the beaches.

"Brandy, you okay with landing down there? I want to check out those blue tarps. I didn't see anyone down there, did you?"

"No, I didn't see anyone. But are you really going to land down there?"

"Yeah. I think the beaches are good and solid, but I'll check 'em carefully to make sure before I set it down. I don't want to be heard if I can help it."

"How are you going to pull that off?"

"I'm going to find a good spot on the north side as far west as I can. And I'll try to keep the RPMs low so I don't make too much noise. But if anyone confronts us, we're just campers, okay? It's national forest land, so we have as much right as anyone else to be out here."

"What if there's…a problem?" she asked tentatively.

I pointed out the right window with my thumb at the shotgun case. I was glad I didn't have to look at her face as she thought that over.

I dropped the plane down to about five hundred feet and maneuvered around the west end of the island to find a place to land. A smaller island named Little Smith slid underneath us. Just a tree covered clump surrounded by water, it wasn't more than a football field long. It was low tide just like the tide tables had told me so I would have as much beach to land on as possible.

As I flew east along the north shore of Smith Island, I moved out to the left so I could examine the beach beneath us. Finally I spotted a place up ahead that looked like a good possibility. I estimated that this little beach was within a mile of the place I wanted to visit on the other side of the island. It looked to be about eight hundred feet long and smooth enough. There were a few large rocks I thought I could dodge, and my tundra tires could handle the smaller ones.

The only problem with this landing spot was it was curved. I would have to use my rudders and brakes just right to get us stopped while turning the corners. Otherwise, we would wind up in the trees and rocks.

I tried not to think too much about the consequences of cracking up out here. It could be tough to reach anyone by radio if we needed a rescue. Mitch had agreed to call Phil in Moose Pass if we didn't show up by eight o'clock. The days were getting long now, so it wouldn't get dark until after ten.

I pulled back on the throttle and lined up for a low pass on the beach. It was more like a cove, the sandy area curving like the inside of a coffee cup. High on the right side and low on the left. Over the intercom, Brandy's scratchy voice broke through the static.

"You're going to land on that?" Doubt and disbelief colored the tone of her voice.

"Not yet. Gonna roll it and make sure it's okay."

Picking my touchdown spot as close to the nearest rocks as possible, I kept my airspeed up, put in some flaps, and then let the big tires touch down and roll for just a second. Then I gave her just enough power to lift off. I banked to the left and flew out over the water again not letting her climb more than a hundred feet. Looking to my left I could see straight down into the water and saw lots of big rocks just under the surface. On this lee side of the island the water was calm, but even so, small waves lapped around the rocks leaving white ringlets in their path.

Banking left and lining up on the beach again, I sized up the wind. Coming from the south to my right, it was probably a ten knot steady flow skimming across the trees. I had the nose cocked into the wind enough to keep me headed straight toward my touchdown spot, but I knew as soon as I let the plane drop below the treeline, the wind would be blocked. Then I'd have to adjust my alignment at the same time I was getting ready to land.

It was going to be tricky, especially the stopping and turning routine that would have to be just right. But I had made landings like this before, so it felt okay.

I set the throttle and flaps and focused all my attention on the touch down point. The usual questions danced across my mind. Was I really ready for this? Did everything feel safe? Was anything talking to me, telling me to abort?

Deciding it was all good, I pulled the throttle all the way off and set her down. I hit the spot right where I wanted to, hauled the stick back into my gut and got on the brakes. The heavy duty tail wheel dug into the sand and started to wobble back and forth. I had to dance on the rudder pedals to keep from ground looping. At the same time I braked hard enough to get us stopped without flipping us ass over nose. The baggage in the back plus Brandy gave me good balance, and I was able to step down hard on the brakes. I had to manipulate them just right to keep us turning left to follow the curve of the beach. I watched out the right window to make sure the wing wasn't getting too close to any of the high rocks or trees.

 We finally stopped rolling with only about fifty feet of beach left in front of us. I turned around to see how Brandy was doing. She was grinning at me, and I could see the excitement in her eyes even behind her aviator's sunglasses. While I had the chance I taxied the SuperCub back to the highest point of the beach far from the water's edge. It was a spot well above the high tide mark. I didn't want to come back to find her floating away in Prince William Sound.

 Standing hard on the right brake pedal I gave her some gas and swung the tail left and left us facing the water. I shut her down, pulled open the right side window and latched it underneath the wing. Then I let down the door and unfastened my seatbelt. Climbing out I got a couple of rocks and shoved them under the tires to make sure she didn't roll down slope. I thought about helping Brandy get out of the backseat, but then I thought better of it. She probably didn't want to be treated like a helpless female.

 Women were funny that way. Some considered that kind of help touching and kind; others saw it as demeaning. I decided to avoid the whole thing by making myself busy securing the plane.

 She was out in a minute looking warily into the trees beside us. I reached in the back and pulled out my pack. Then I undid the bungies holding the shotgun and checked that it was loaded and on safe.

 "You ready to go?" I looked at Brandy. She had a small pack with her but only lightweight running shoes on her feet.

 She was looking all around and examining the spot we had landed in. Her movements were jerky and excited. "You know, Johnny, I've been an instructor for a lot of years, but

I've never seen anything quite like that. Makes me realize all over again how passengers have to put all their trust in the pilot. What a helpless feeling I had back there."

I wasn't sure if she had just complimented me or not. I wasn't going to worry about it. We survived the landing and the plane wasn't broken. *Let's move on.*

"So you're ready?"

"Yeah, let's do it. I think we want to head this way." She pointed in the general direction of the other corner of the island and turned to start walking.

"Wait a sec. Are those the only shoes you brought?"

"Yeah, why?"

"It's likely to be wet in there. Marshy and muddy maybe. You don't have any boots?" I was starting to regret not checking out her equipment before we left.

"I'll be fine. Let's get going."

"Okay, whatever," I shrugged.

CHAPTER 14

We climbed over moss-covered rocks and driftwood, and moved into the woods. Smith Island wasn't flat after all. We had to hike uphill for a while before the terrain leveled off. The spruce trees were thick and it got shady and much darker in a hurry. The forest floor was spongy with moss and spruce needles but dry enough in the high parts.

Without any trails our progress was slow. We had to work our way around deadfall and brush, bending under low obstacles in some places. At least the devil's club wasn't too thick. About thirty minutes went by before we said anything to each other. I was pushing the pace as best I could, and Brandy stayed right behind me.

I stopped for a rest break, sitting on an old stump. The woods were quiet. Moss and spruce make excellent sound absorbers. Only a few birds chirping nearby interrupted the silence.

"Any bears out on these islands?" Brandy asked glancing behind her.

"Yeah, could be. They can actually swim between islands, but there's not much game out here so I doubt we'll see any. But you never know. I haven't seen any scat yet."

"Any what?"

"Scat. You know—bear shit."

Dim sunlight filtered down through the trees, but there was no way to see the sky. Not being able to keep track of the weather made me nervous. I wanted to keep moving. "You okay to go on?"

"Oh, yeah, I'm doing fine. I get to the gym pretty regular and do a lot of miles on the treadmill. I'm not having any trouble staying with you."

I glanced down at her shoes again. If they got wet, it would be a whole different picture.

We pushed on. Before we'd landed, I'd seen some kind of a trench formation in the trees that seemed to lead from the SuperCub to our destination. I thought we were following it by staying on the higher ground. There was less brush and deadfall along the edge of the trough making our movements easier. I couldn't tell what had formed the trench, which was about thirty yards wide. It seemed like a water-formed drainage of some kind, but Smith Island was almost completely flat. It might even have been a manmade road at one point—unless it was left over damage from the 1964 earthquake, which made more sense. The quake, which registered somewhere around 9 on the Richter Scale was the largest to ever hit the United States and one of the largest known worldwide. A lot of the terrain in Prince William Sound had been moved around drastically. Valdez had been destroyed and relocated. The same thing happened to the little village of Chenega. Some land features had shifted over ten feet vertically within a few miles of us.

The trench let us see a little more of the sky. I didn't like the way it looked toward the south. It was a gray day anyhow, but now there was a dark area in that direction and the air felt heavy and wet.

After another hour I could see a clearing ahead. When I stopped Brandy almost bumped into me.

"Are we there?" she whispered.

"Yeah, I think so. Let's just sit here for a minute and listen."

There were more birds in this area and their whistles and calls filled the air. The wind was picking up and blowing across the clearing straight into our faces. But no human sounds. Nothing moved either. The clearing was deserted.

We moved forward, and I kept us in the treeline circling to our left. As we crept closer to our destination, I started to see water, and I could hear the faint sound of waves on the shore ahead. Then I spotted the edge of a blue tarp a hundred yards away.

I sat down again, and Brandy sat beside me. She leaned forward to peer ahead. Then she brought the camera up to her face and slowly tracked the lens around the whole area. She handed it to me. "I don't see anybody or any vehicles, but I can see what looks like trash or something up there."

I took a look through the lens. "There's also something that looks like a fire pit. Let's move up there real slow. Remember we're just campers."

We moved a few more steps when I smelled a strange odor. I stopped but still couldn't see or hear anybody. When I started moving again, my ears were straining for anything out of the ordinary. The hair on the back of my neck was tingling. Then Brandy's hand on my arm stopped me again.

"What?"

"That smell. What the hell is that? It's like cat piss but a lot stronger. You got lions out here?"

I had to chuckle at that idea. "I don't know what that is, but if we see anyone, let's melt back into the woods real fast. If we get separated, just go back to the plane as quick and quiet as you can."

"What if they see us?"

"Uh, then let's go with the camping idea. Maybe we can talk our way out of any trouble."

I shifted the shotgun strap on my shoulder making sure I could use it in a hurry. I didn't think the guys would remember me from the other night in the dark. But I wasn't going to take any chances either. Remembering the way they had kicked so viciously at Willie's head made my jaw clench. I could still feel the pain in my gut. "You ready?"

She nodded, and I started forward again. A rusted empty can of HEET, a kind of antifreeze, lay in the mossy grass at my feet. We were getting close enough to the blue tarp to see there couldn't be an airplane underneath it. It wasn't big enough for that.

We stopped and listened again. The clearing was a rough circle about five hundred feet wide with solid woods on all sides except for a wide opening pathway that led down to the water. There was no sign of anyone nearby.

"I think we're alone here. Let's look around."

I pulled the tarp back and found a white wooden frame of some kind that held a plastic tank. The smell was overwhelming, and I had to move upwind to keep from being overcome.

"Jesus, what is that?" I pulled up my shirt to cover my nose. The stench was hideous. Brandy's face contorted as she reacted to the horrendous odor. She ducked away and held her nose with one hand.

Leaving her to poke through the trash and boxes under the tarp I walked toward the other side of the path. Stopping in the middle I looked down the slope to the water and called Brandy.

"Hey, check out these tire tracks. I can see how Dooley would have spotted these from the air. Looks like someone was landing down at the beach and then taxiing up here."

"Right," she said, looking it over while she waved her hand in front of her face. "And maybe pushing some kind of a cart or something making these other smaller tracks."

Then I saw a fire ring in the trees ahead of me. An open case of HEET cans was laying beside a blackened area of dirt and there were chunks of wood laying nearby that would make good stools. Further into the trees we found dozens of empty cans of Coleman fuel like campers use. But from the looks of the area, I couldn't imagine more than three or four people had been in this group. Why would they need so much fuel?

"Hey, Johnny, check this out." Brandy waved me over to look at the paper bags she found. There must have been over fifty large bottles of Metabolife scattered around as well as assorted trash. The bottles were all empty. Cigarette butts littered the ground in all directions too.

"I know what this is," she exclaimed excitedly. "This is a meth lab."

"Meth lab? What about this Metabolife? Isn't that for body builders?"

"Weight loss too, but it's full of some chemical they use to make methamphetamine. They can buy this stuff over the counter and use it somehow in that tank over there to make the junk. Very profitable, I guess."

"Oh, brother. What's it doing out here?"

"Well, think about it. They find a deserted island, fly in here like they're camping, or come in by boat, then set up a lab, make the shit, and take it out to sell it. I remember reading about this stuff back home. They're always getting busted by people picking up on the smell. There wouldn't be any problem with that way out here."

"Yeah, no kidding." I was still holding my T-shirt over my nose. The fumes were still getting to me when the wind shifted.

"The other thing that happens is that meth labs are always blowing up. A trailer park in Cleveland went up in flames last year from a lab exploding. Look at all the gas and flammable crap they have laying around here."

"Okay," I said. "Maybe that explains the fireball Dooley saw down here. But it looks like these people cleared out. And I don't see any airplanes around, so this may not be connected to Willie's plane at all."

Her shoulders slumped. "You're right. Damn it; I was hoping we were on to something."

"Well, we're on to something all right, but I don't give a shit about meth labs. That's the cops' problem, and I ain't no narc."

"Let's walk down the beach a ways," she suggested.

"Okay, but let's not spend too much time here. Now that we know no one's around, we can fly back over here and search better from the air. Besides, check out that sky."

She looked to the south. Dark clouds were pushing their way toward us, and the wind was definitely picking up. Whitecaps were forming on the open water, and thick wet salty air was condensing on my sunglasses.

She looked at me with concern. "What are you thinking?"

"I'm thinking we better get our asses back to the plane and get back to Seward before we get caught in some nasty shit."

We made a quick trip down the beach but there were no signs of other campsites or places where an airplane could be easily hidden. Even though the beach was landable, the only tracks we found were those ruts leading up toward the fire ring.

On our way back through the clearing Brandy stopped to pick up a plastic bag filled with trash and reached inside.

"C'mon, will ya? We're about to get wet."

"Hang on. Look at this."

She handed me a credit card slip. The name jumped off the paper. Lance Holcomb's name.

I stuffed the paper in a pocket, and we started back toward the trough just as it started to rain. The wind lashed at us, and the dark forest gave us a welcome shield from the force of the sideways rain hitting us in the backs. I stopped beside a big spruce tree and pulled off my pack. Brandy did the same. I took out a rain jacket, knee-high rubber boots, and gloves. When I was finished putting on the extra gear, I looked over to see Brandy struggling her way into a cheap rain suit. The kind made out of thin transparent plastic that you can buy for about five bucks and wad up into your back pocket. They last about five minutes in the brush.

"Don't you have any boots?"

"No, I'll be okay."

"It's gonna be wet for the next hour or two. You want to wear mine?"

"No. C'mon, let's get going. I'll be fine."

Okay, I thought to myself. Whatever.

We started picking our way back along the same general route we had followed earlier. The rain increased until it was pouring down through the trees in heavy showers. The ground quickly became saturated, and every low spot was a puddle. We had to climb uphill again which surprised me. I didn't remember that much slope on our way over.

The brush got thicker. Everything was soaking wet. Pushing past ragged branches and devil's club, the sharp points snagged at my arms and legs. I knew how important it was to keep dry.

My rain jacket covered me pretty well. I had the hood up over my baseball cap, so it covered me to just above my knees. Velcro let me close it tight around my neck. The boots kept my lower legs and feet dry, and the exertion of moving through the woods was keeping me warm. The only places I was getting wet were my knees and my nose. But the moisture was fogging my glasses so bad, I took them off and stashed them inside a zippered pocket in my fleece.

The only concern I had was sweat. It was hard work slogging through wet, dense forest land, bushwhacking every step of the way. I could feel the perspiration building inside my jacket which wasn't a problem as long as I could keep moving. But if you have to stop and you become chilled, that's how you get hypothermia.

When I looked back at Brandy, I knew she was in trouble. Her rain jacket was in shreds, and she was drenched. Her running shoes were coated in thick mud, and the water oozed out of them with every step. She had on a pair of thin fuzzy gloves. Not much warmth, and they couldn't be helping with the devil's club either.

"How you doing?"

"Okay, but I'm really wet. I've got to keep moving. It's getting colder. Look, I can see my breath."

She was right, it was getting colder. Her lips were trembling, and the baseball cap wasn't keeping the rain from running down the back of her neck.

"Look, why don't you take my rain jacket? And these boots too. I should have made sure you had better stuff before we left."

"No, goddamn it. Let's just keep going. I'll be okay when we get back to the plane."

She pushed past me and plunged ahead. She was no wimp, I'd give her that. But that treadmill was nothing like the Alaskan backcountry in the rain. If we didn't get her dry and warm pretty soon, she was going to have a real problem.

I followed behind her and watched her slip and slide her way up a sloping hillside. An opening in the trees let me see part of the sky. It wasn't looking good. Dark clouds pressed all around us, and the treetops were thrashing back and forth in a strong gusting wind.

I cringed at the sight and thought about the SuperCub tied down at the beach. I hoped the ropes were holding. Suddenly our location in the middle of Prince William Sound felt like the most remote spot on the planet. We were hours from anyplace warm and dry. At least the plane had fuel we could use to get a fire going, and even though the fuselage was small, we could get inside and get out of the weather.

I plodded along behind Brandy and focused my thoughts on one step at a time. She was stumbling pretty bad and weaving. We had to get to the plane. Then we had to get Brandy dry. After that, I could try to figure out how to get us off this godforsaken island and back to civilization.

It took us twice as long to make the return trip. Finally, the edge of the forest and open sky came into view. The water was an ugly mess. Angry waves crashed onto the shore, but luckily they hadn't reached the plane. She was waiting for us right where I'd left her.

CHAPTER
15

Leaving the woods was good news and bad news. I could see the weather conditions better, and there wasn't any more brush and devil's club to deal with. But the rain hammered us unimpeded, and the wind made the conditions even more miserable. Seeing better was no blessing either. The ceiling was less than a hundred feet and a thick mist surrounded us on all sides. There was no way we could take off anytime soon.

We stumbled down a steep embankment on wet rocks and scree to reach the beach, and the shelter of the big wings was a welcome relief from the pounding rain. It echoed off the fabric with a roaring sound that I remembered from other happier times. This time wasn't happy at all.

Brandy sat on the right tire while I pulled the pack off my back and stowed the shotgun back in its scabbard. She was shivering full force now; her lips were blue and they trembled uncontrollably as she held her hands under her armpits and tried to hug some warmth back into her small frame.

"You got any dry clothes with you?"

She shook her head forlornly, her whole body rocking in agony where she sat on the tire.

"Well, you're gonna have to get out of those." I crawled into the backseat standing on the struts and started pulling gear out of the baggage compartment.

I pulled a sleeping bag out of its stuff sack. "Here, get out of those clothes and get into this. I'll get a fire going."

I headed into the woods again and crawled under the thickest spruce tree I could find. Next to the ground I started breaking small dry twigs off the trunk until I had a hand full. I stuffed them inside my jacket and started collecting small sticks as dry as I could find under the big spruce branches.

Carrying it all back to the plane I found Brandy sitting in the backseat inside the sleeping bag. Her soaked clothes were draped across the door sill. Her hair was sopping wet and matted around her face, and she was trembling hard.

"Any better?" I asked, searching her face, trying to read her condition.

She shrugged and hunched her shoulders up and down. "I'm f-f-fine."

"Yeah, sure you are."

"C-c-can we s-start the engine? G-get some heat g-g-going?" Her shaking was getting violent.

"No, it wouldn't do any good. SuperCub cabin heat ain't worth a shit. And we gotta save fuel to get home with." I climbed up on the wheel again and leaned in toward her. I put my hand on her face. Her skin was cold, clammy, and pale. With an old rag I had stuffed behind the front seat, I took hold of her head and mopped her hair. She tried to resist, pulling away in protest.

I held her tighter and kept buffing her head. She was too weak to fight and soon I felt her body relax. Instead of strawberry shampoo, now she smelled like engine oil. But at least she was getting dry.

When I had her hair as dry as possible, I pulled the sleeping bag up and around her head, pulling the drawstring tight until only her eyes and nose poked out. I held her in a tight embrace and felt her body shaking against me. I slowed my own breathing, drawing air in and letting it out in long slow repetitions. Gradually her trembling slowed. I released her and grabbed a couple old equipment packs in the back of the plane and set them on top of her. Then I climbed down to work on the fire.

Moving out toward the end of the wing I scooped a place in the gravelly sand and retrieved some bigger rocks to make a wind break. Then I arranged the twigs and sticks the best way I could and stuffed small pieces of paper underneath. With the fuel sampler in my hand I went to the wing tank and filled the cup. I didn't want to turn myself or the airplane into a barbeque, so I made sure not to spill any.

In a few minutes I had a nice blaze going. Luckily, we were in a natural wind break. The cove we'd landed in was a protected pocket. It was still raining hard but we were out of the wind. The wing blocked most of the rain from the fire. That probably saved our lives.

I looked over at Brandy, but she wasn't watching me. Her eyes were fixed straight ahead. Her body was still shaking. Probably concentrating on getting warm. I knew she was miserable. And probably embarrassed too. That kind of woman never wants to be so vulnerable and dependent. I guess no one does, but she was a particularly proud person. I hadn't known her long, but I knew her long enough to know that much. She'd had to fight her way through a lot of obstacles to get where she was, and right now she probably felt pretty worthless. I knew I would if it were me.

I went back to the woods as soon as I thought the fire could last on its own for a few minutes. When I came back I was loaded down with branches of all sizes. I piled them up where they could dry out by the fire and started feeding them in little by little.

When I had a good pile of red hot coals going, I went looking for the water bottle and coffee pot I carried in the survival gear. She peeked out of the sleeping bag when I picked up the pack I had put on her lap.

"How you doing in there, Brandy Fontaine, Learjet captain?"

She gave me a half-hearted grin. "At least I'm d-dry."

Some color was returning to her lips and they were shaking less. The rest of her was still shivering though. She turned her head to look past me while I clattered around in the baggage compartment. "That fire looks real g-good."

"Yeah, hang right here for a minute and then you can come out and get warm."

I filled the coffee pot and put it on the fire. Returning to the plane I reached under the front seat and disconnected it from its frame. I took it over to the fire and set it down in the gravel with its back to the wind.

"You ready?"

She looked at me puzzled. "How the hell we going to do this?"

"Stay in the bag, but stick your feet out toward me."

I got into the best position I could to help pull her out of the plane. "Okay, wiggle your way over here and put your feet down on the tire."

Wrapped up in the cocoon like bag it was a struggle to get her perched on the tire. I picked her up with one arm under her legs and the other under her back. With several grunts and lurches I hauled her over to the fire and plopped her down in the seat. I pulled off my rain jacket and wrapped it around her shoulders so the rain wouldn't drench her again.

"Hey, put that back on. You're going to need it."

"Just shut the hell up, will ya? I got other ways to stay dry." I tugged the rain hood over her head and grinned in at her. "How do ya like being a mummy?"

"It sucks," she grunted at me, frowning but fighting off the beginnings of a smile too.

After a few minutes, I handed her a blue tin cup of hot chocolate mixed with coffee. When she saw it, her eyes widened, and she wrestled one naked arm free on the bag. She took hold of the hot cup and sipped noisily letting the steam flow into her face.

I gave her a bite-sized Snickers bar, setting the candy on her lap. "Make that last, we don't have much else."

I climbed back in the cabin, disconnected the backseat cushion, and set it on the sand beside Brandy. I fed more wood to the fire and checked to be sure the flames weren't overheating the wing above us. I went for more firewood until we had a huge pile. Then I remembered Brandy's wet clothes and I went over to retrieve them from the plane and arranged them on sticks around the fire to dry.

Brandy watched me adjusting her bra and panties on the makeshift drying rack. "Hey, watch it, buster. I've heard about perverts like you before."

I laughed and looked at her. "Maybe you'd rather go commando for the flight back?"

"You trick all your dates into flying out to remote islands with you like this? Get 'em wet, cold, and naked, then have your way?"

"Not even in your cold wet dreams, missy."

She shook her head back and forth, rolling her eyes skyward.

I took the seat beside her, poured myself some coffee and refilled her cup. "Here's to the wilds of Alaska."

The fire crackled beside us. Ashes danced in the small breezes landing all over us both. I pulled off my soaked blue baseball cap and tried to dry my head as best I could.

"That's the first time I've seen you without your hat on," she remarked.

"Yeah, well, it keeps the rain off the thin spot in the back." I brushed my fingers over my hair rapidly while leaning over the fire.

Settling back on the seat I looked around us trying to think about what to do next. It was a strange sensation staring out at the waves and open water. Whitecaps tossed to and fro just thirty yards away. Foam and froth streaked the surface of the gray water revealing wind strength of at least twenty-five knots. Dark clouds reached down to the water. We could only see about a quarter mile. Heavy rain continued to roar down all around us, pounding out a steady percussion concert on the stretched fabric of the wing.

The coffee tasted wonderful. I tried to ignore the craving I was getting for a granola bar or a doughnut. Or a Snickers.

In my head I went through a quick inventory of our supplies. I had a package of granola bars in the survival pack as well as a few more packages of hot chocolate and coffee. A handful of bite-sized Snickers bars, and some hard candy and gum. That was it.

I looked out at the sky again. The same dark clouds were all I could see in every direction. Not a lighter spot anywhere. And I knew that weather systems like this could hang in the area for days at a time.

"Hey, Johnny, you ever see the movie *Alive?*"

"The Peruvian soccer team that crashed in the Andes and had to eat each other to survive? Yeah. But why would you want to think about something like that at a time like this?"

"Oh, no reason. I was just wondering which one of us could reach that shotgun the fastest when we run out of food."

"Very funny. Hey, don't worry. If we run out, I'll go bag us a moose."

"Oh, okay, and bring me back a Starbucks when you return, please."

Then I remembered Mitch. It was getting late, and he was going to freak that we weren't back. If he called Phil, they'd want to come out and search for us but there was no way in this shit. Or the Coast Guard might come looking with a chopper or a boat. And here we were doing just fine, camping in relative comfort on the beach. I also remembered that there was an RCO on Naked Island just about ten miles across the water right in front of us. It was just an antenna used for making position reports whenever I flew charters to Cordova or Valdez.

I went to the plane and reached in to turn on the master switch. Then I tuned the radio to the right frequency and keyed the mike. "Juneau Radio, Piper one-two-five-eight Charlie."

After just a moment's delay, Juneau Radio answered me. I told them our situation and requested they call Mitch with the information. They agreed, and I gave them his number.

"Five-eight Charlie, are you declaring an emergency?"

"Negative, Juneau. Just advise him that we're okay. We'll sit out the weather, and I'll contact him again as needed with further instructions."

"Roger, five-eight Charlie, Juneau Radio."

I snapped off the master switch to save the battery and returned to the fire. "No sense in anybody worrying about us or risking their necks to find us. We're doing just fine."

Brandy looked at me and sipped her coffee mocha. "Are we just fine?"

I glanced at her and studied my own coffee. "Yeah, we're okay for now. But we're not going anywhere for a while."

"You got that right," she muttered. It was getting dark. The wind was dying down and the rain was less intense, but a low fog was settling in around us.

"You doing okay, Miss Brandy?"

"Yeah, I'm finally getting warm. I'm just starting to feel really tired. That walk just about wore me out. Not to mention almost freezing to death."

"Yup, I'm tired too. I'd feel better if we'd found Willie's Cub or something more useful instead of a wild goose chase."

"At least we know now that these guys are setting up camps and meth labs out here somewhere."

I stared into the low flames for a while watching the coals glow and listened to the waves rushing back and forth onto the beach. It was a strange feeling to be so comfortable and so exposed at the same time.

I looked over at Brandy. She was still huddled in the dark blue sleeping bag, her legs curled underneath her. Her head was free of the bag now and her damp hair was pulled back behind her ears, but matted clumps stuck awkwardly to her forehead. I wanted to reach over and straighten them out, but I held back. Her eyes were droopy but the color was back in her face.

She looked up and saw me watching her. The firelight reflected in her eyes, and she held my gaze. For a moment I caught myself thinking I had never seen a prettier woman. I dropped my eyes back to the fire and tried to ignore the sensation stirring inside me.

"What?" Her voice was calm and husky, half-whispering.

"Nothing."

"I'll tell you what I'm thinking about. Want to hear it?"

"Okay."

"We're spending the night here, right?"

"Oh, yeah. Can't do anything about this shit." I nodded toward the water, the clouds and the fog.

"You got another sleeping bag? Or a tent?"

"Nope."

"Hmm." She leaned forward and set the blue tin cup on the sand. Reaching over with one hand she checked her clothes on the makeshift drying rack. They were still soaked. The black jeans and hooded sweatshirt were sodden and slightly steaming where they faced the flames.

I tried not to pay any attention to her underthings hanging there in front of us. A simple white bra with just a touch of lace around the edges. The tag read 34C. Her panties, bikini-cut and pink. The tag read S. I tried really hard not to think about what she looked like wearing them. I failed.

She reached for the panties and began to wave them slowly over the coals. I said nothing.

"You're enjoying this, aren't you?" She looked at me out of the corner of her eye while she waved them back and forth.

"Who, me?"

"I'm not talking to the moose standing behind you."

"Well, we could sit here all night putting it off...."

"Or?"

My mouth had gone dry. I kept staring at the fire. I couldn't look at her again.

Satisfied that the panties were dry, she pulled them inside the sleeping bag and after a series of gyrations, she resumed her former sitting position and looked over at me again. I glanced over. She was grinning at me.

"Hey, look, Brandy. I don't think you're appreciating the seriousness of this situation. We're out here in the middle of nowhere, with a couple of granola bars. The storm could sweep us out to sea, the wind could come up and destroy the airplane and us along with it, or if we're lucky we get to starve to death over the next few weeks."

"Oh, crap, get over yourself. If you were that worried about it, you wouldn't be sitting there all flustered at having a naked girl all to yourself in the Alaskan wilderness."

"I'm not fl-fl-flustered," I stammered. We both laughed, and I shook my head. "Okay, knock it off. You're teasing me, and that ain't nice."

"Who, me?" She batted her eyes playfully. "All right. We need to set up a sleeping arrangement. What's the plan?"

"Well, the Cub has a nice spot in the back for one person to sleep now that the seats are out. But only for one person, and we only have one sleeping bag. The one you're currently occupying." *Naked*, I didn't add. I was trying to ignore that important detail.

"Okay, it's getting cold. There's nowhere else to sleep but in the plane. I don't want you freezing to death in the middle of the night. Unfortunately, I need you to fly us out of here in the morning. Neither one of us is very big, so why don't we share the sleeping space in the plane."

"That could work. You sure you're okay with that?"

"Oh, please. If I can't trust you by now, do you think I'd be out here in the first place?"

"What about the…?" I was getting tongue-tied.

"The sleeping bag? We'll share that too. It'll fit us. Besides, spooning is probably the only way to fit in back there, and we'll both stay warmer that way."

"We could sleep head to foot if you'd feel more comfortable."

She laughed. "Are you kidding me? I'm not putting my head in the bottom of the bag next to your stinky feet. What are you worried about? Our naughty parts touching? Let me clue you in, bozo. They'll still be in dangerous proximity to each other no matter what strange position you dream up."

I was laughing now too. "I guess you're right about that. Besides, then my head would be downhill and it might swell up and explode like a stepped on watermelon. Don't want that."

I couldn't believe my ears listening to her. Most women I've ever known would be a wreck in this situation. Here she was totally relaxed and making jokes. My shyness evaporated.

"Okay, I'll behave if you will," I said with a straight face.

"Funny. No, it'll be okay. It's a survival situation. I can endure this. It's okay. Just don't try anything, and we'll get along fine." She glowered at me in mock seriousness.

"Oh, brother. It's time you got over yourself. I'm old enough to be your father. And you're not my type anyhow. I'm not attracted to you in the least little bit."

"Well, then. That's makes two of us. Now give me your boots and your fleece."

"What? Why?"

"Cuz I need to go take a pee in the woods. Do you mind?"

She clambered into my jacket and emerged from the sleeping bag. Slipping her bare feet into the big rubber boots, she headed clumsily into the dark. I couldn't help looking back to see her naked legs walking away under the royal blue jacket with a touch of pink panties peeking out underneath. I walked down to the water's edge and relieved myself in Prince William Sound. The rain had stopped but the fog was thicker than ever.

I started setting up the sleeping arrangement in the plane and made sure the fire wouldn't cause any problems during the night. With one of the packs for a pillow, I was stretched out in the sleeping bag when I heard her clump back to the plane.

"Okay, this looks cozy. Make room. I'm coming in."

I opened the bag and held out my arm to let her lie down in front of me.

"Oh, no, you don't. I'm spooning from behind you. I know a thing or two about you boys."

"Oh, for chrissake. You're gonna drive me to drink, woman. If we ever get out of here alive, I'm gonna become a good-for-nothing drunk, I swear."

"Well, you're making a great start."

I jabbed her with an elbow. "Take that back."

She laughed and snuggled in close behind me wrapping one arm around my waist. I was surprised at how close she pulled herself to me. Then again, what choice did she have?

As we settled in, rain started lightly peppering the fuselage above us. I could feel her breath on the back of my neck.

The goose down was doing its job trapping our body heat inside the bag. My fingers and toes were tingling and casting off the cold grip of the last several hours. I started to feel sleepy in spite of the situation.

"You comfortable back there?"

"Yeah, I am actually. I think this might work out okay. Thank you for behaving yourself. Maybe you are a gentleman after all."

I ignored her. I wanted to sleep and lose the images running through my head. Several minutes went by. I thought she might have dozed off."

"Hey, Johnny?" She whispered in a soft, little girl voice.

"Go to sleep."

"Do you really think I'm not attractive?"

"That's not what I said."

"Yes, you did."

"No, I said I didn't find you attractive. There's a big difference."

She went quiet like she was thinking that over.

"Hey, Brandy?" I know I sounded half-asleep.

"What?" There was a tinge of suspicion in her voice. Like she was trying to read my mind, anticipating my next move.

"I'm not a drunk."

"I know. Now you go to sleep."

I closed my eyes and took a deep breath, trying to get my muscles to relax. Why did I care what she thought about me? I was an idiot.

Too many pictures rushed into my head. Feeling her pressed against my back, her small breasts rubbing against my shirt and the warmth of her pelvis tucked tightly against my rear end. Those naked legs. Even through my jeans the feel of her quickly translated into pictures of the shape of her. Her forehead rested against the back of my head. Her hair still smelled of engine oil, but underneath that heavy aroma I detected another faint but familiar scent. Strawberry shampoo.

I knew sleep wasn't likely anytime soon. I pretended anyhow, squeezing my eyes tight together watching the images dance slowly by, like a peep show glimpsed through hands clasped over my face.

I think she fell asleep before I did, but I didn't really know. She might have been pretending too.

CHAPTER
16

I woke with a jolt. Where the hell was I? Slowly I became aware of my surroundings and why I was there. My neck was killing me. I raised up part way to straighten out the kinks.

"Hey, you're letting in cold air." Brandy huddled beside me, grimacing at the sudden chill.

"Sorry, I've got to sit up."

The windows inside the airplane were completely fogged over. In some places heavy moisture ran down the inside metal surfaces of the cabin and were starting to soak through the edges of the sleeping bag.

I struggled my way out of the bag and tucked it back around Brandy. I had to crawl over her to get to the front seat where I found my shoes and pulled them on. I wiped at a side window and peered outside. It wasn't good news.

It was light outside but the view was ugly. Low gray clouds still surrounded us, and patches of fog lay on the water offshore. I looked at my watch. Seven AM. At least the wind was calm. Instead of whitecaps the Sound was flat and placid ripples lapped soundlessly on the beach. I pulled open the cabin door and climbed out, grabbing my rain jacket for warmth. I thought about asking Brandy for my fleece but decided against it. The morning chill struck my bare face and hands and assaulted my lungs with every breath.

I stamped back and forth in the sand to get the blood flowing and walked away from the plane to have a better look around. Thankfully, it wasn't raining. But the sun couldn't penetrate the cloud cover. I figured we had about two hundred feet of ceiling, but it was hard to estimate without any nearby mountain sides to look at. Back in Seward I could always estimate the ceiling by how much of Mount Alice I could or couldn't see.

I could, however, see down the length of the island to the west. Walking away from the plane, I relieved myself and set about making another fire. I moved the fire pit out from under the wing, and after several minutes and a healthy dose of Boy Scout water from the wing, a good blaze was crackling in front of me. I worked on the fire, feeding it large chunks of wood when it was ready.

After a while I heard rustling noises from the plane, and Brandy emerged in the fleece jacket and rubber boots outfit from the night before with the open sleeping bag wrapped around her shoulders. Without a word she clumped off behind a nearby tree, her breath leaving vapor trails behind her. She was back in a minute and stood beside me waving her palms at the flames.

"Where's your camera? I'm sure your mom would love to see a shot of you on your Alaskan vacation."

"Up yours, jerkoff. We ever going to get out of this godforsaken place?" She glanced around at the clouds and water and visibly shivered.

"Well, good morning to you too, sunshine." I chuckled at her. There's nothing like someone else's misery to brighten your mood. I handed her a cup of coffee.

She accepted it without a word and actually moved a little closer to lean slightly against me. I don't know why, but I put my arm around her in a halfway hug and rubbed her arm through the sleeping bag.

Before she could object or pull away, I filled her in on my thoughts. "I'm thinking if the clouds lift just a bit, we can get out of here. They're pretty damn low now, and it's not a good idea to fly low over the water. What do you think? If you're not comfortable with it, we can stay put a while and wait for blue sky."

I felt her straighten up as she shifted into a more professional pilot frame of mind and evaluated the information. At the serious look on her face, I dropped my arm and busied myself stoking the fire.

"I want to get out of here, but not so bad that we do something stupid. Then again, clouds like this can hang around for days, right?"

I nodded. "We're about twenty minutes from Chenega, and we could try to make it at least that far. If it's too bad beyond that, we can stop and stay there a while. The problem is the low ceiling and fog."

"Can we fly up through this stuff? In the Lear we just burn our way up through it. There's always blue sky on top."

"I would never try that in this little beast," I said, cocking my head toward the SuperCub. "These clouds might only be a thousand feet thick, but they could be twenty thousand feet thick, and we might never find the top. Then we're stuck in the shit in a mountainous area. No thanks."

"Couldn't Flight Service tell us where the tops are?"

"We could ask, but they would only know from a pilot report. I tell you what, let's get ready to go, and if it improves at all, we can head for the edge of Eleanor Island which is just five miles west and then follow its shoreline south toward Chenega."

"All right, I'm okay with that. But you know I have to ask the flight instructor question: What if the engine quits? Where do we land?"

"Yeah, I know. Out here it's pretty iffy. There are some little beaches like this one along the way, but otherwise we put it in the trees or the water next to a shoreline and swim for it."

She gave me a dubious look. "Or we can stay put."

We worked on reinstalling the seats and packing the gear. Brandy stationed herself over the fire pit and worked on drying her jeans over the flames. I untied the wings and gave the plane a thorough preflight. When I rejoined her at the fire she was pulling on the jeans dancing on one foot at a time.

"They're not dry, but they're okay," she said shivering again and huddling over the fire.

I threw on some bigger pieces of wood and watched the steam rising from the wet fabric around her knees.

"Your body heat will help dry them too."

"I can't wait to get into a hot shower. You got anything else to eat?"

I handed her one of the granola bars and poured hot water in her cup. She dumped in a packet of instant coffee and handed it to me. Then she took my empty cup and made another cup for herself. I opened a granola bar for myself, and we chewed in silence.

After a while we walked together up and down the beach watching the clouds and talking about nothing in particular. It might have been wishful thinking, but I thought the ceiling was lifting slightly.

"I have to say, Johnny. You seem pretty calm about this whole situation."

"Maybe on the outside. This ain't my first rodeo, you know. I've been in some bad situations before."

"Well, I've never been out in conditions like this. So remote. I keep thinking back to all that stuff Hondo was saying the other night."

"I know. It's weird. You have to be aware of all the risks around here, but at the same time if you always play it safe, you're gonna spend all your time, sitting in the Yukon Bar wondering where your life went."

She looked at me thoughtfully. "You know, I think Dad feels the same way. I think that's probably why he came back up here. I probably never understood that before."

I stared to the west hoping for a glimpse of a distant shoreline. Still too much fog in the way.

"You know, I thought my flying was exciting at times, cruising the Lear at four hundred knots at thirty thousand feet at night. Living life on the edge, you know? But this—it's way different."

"Just a different kind of edge, I suppose."

"Maybe."

We picked up the pace of our walking, making big circles along the treeline down to the water's edge and back. The exercise felt good, warming our muscles. The coffee was kicking in too, making me restless and eager to go somewhere, anywhere. Sure, this was a wonderful little hunk of paradise out here in Prince William Sound, but I was ready to get back to the world.

After another couple of loops around the plane, Brandy pointed west. "Is that Eleanor Island?"

I stared hard into the distance and, sure enough, faint traces of the distant green wooded hillsides of Eleanor Island were coming into view.

"It is. You ready to do this thing? It might not be much fun up there."

She gulped and tugged her collar tightly against her throat with both hands. "Let do it."

Buckled in with our headsets on, I primed the engine and hit the starter button. I whooped out loud when the propeller turned two sluggish turns and then roared to life. The oil pressure needle jumped into the green right on cue.

"God, I love this airplane," I gushed over the intercom.

Positioning for a takeoff after a good runup, I checked the fuel levels a second time. Mentally I calculated that we would have enough to get back to Seward but not much reserve beyond that. I tried to focus on making it to Chenega first. I called Juneau Radio again and filed a quick flight plan with a description of the route I intended. Their weather briefing included the standard phrase "VFR flight not recommended." Yeah, no kidding. Visual Flight Rules meant you had to be able to see where you were going.

I shoved in the throttle but held the brakes until I was sure we had full power. Then I let her go. We hurtled toward the water at the far end of the cove, and the tail came up almost immediately. When we had flying speed I pulled back on the stick, and we lifted off with yards to spare. I banked carefully over the water as we climbed. Before I reached two hundred feet, the clouds were already starting to block my forward vision.

I backed off the throttle slightly, trimmed us out just below the clouds, and pointed her nose at Eleanor Island. "So far, so good," I said over the intercom, and Brandy reached up and patted the back of my head.

I could feel the relief in her. It matched my own. As we approached the rocky shoreline ahead, I turned left and peered out through the windshield. With the sectional chart on my lap, it was not difficult to follow the coastline, keeping the foam splashed rocks just below the right wheel. Looking that way made me nervous since the clouds and fog completely obscured the mountain sides and peaks that I knew lurked over there just out of sight. I avoided looking in that direction.

"Press on, press on," I mumbled to myself trying to calm the lump in my throat. I forced myself to take deep breaths. "How you doing back there, Brandy?"

"I'm okay, how's it look ahead?"

I strained to see into the distance but with only about a mile of visibility all I could see was a lot of water, a foggy shoreline to my right and clouds. Knight Island slid by us on the right. When we reached its southern end, open water lay ahead with no shoreline to follow. My hand tightened on the stick and my jaw clamped down hard. I could see this gap between the two islands on the map, but the sight of open water in all directions was unnerving. The visibility must have gotten worse, because I couldn't see Evans Island ahead where it was supposed to be.

"It's not much better, but Chenega should be straight ahead." What I didn't say was I could feel the edges of panic gripping me. If I didn't find that island in a minute or two, I was going to have to turn around. I shuddered at the thought of it, looking to the right and left. There were no ground reference points to guide me in a turn like that.

I forced myself to take a deep breath. *Don't make a dumb move, butthead. Press on. The chart says the next island is right there. Keep going, you'll find it. If you try to turn around, it could be all over.*

I must have looked down at the chart and back outside a hundred times in the longest minute of my life. I pushed the nose forward slightly to drop some altitude. That seemed to help the visibility, and I started to see the dark outline of another shoreline ahead. Relief washed over me as the familiar features of Evans Island and the village of Chenega Bay appeared through the mist.

"Okay, Brandy," I announced, feeling some confidence flood back into my veins. Seeing familiar territory, even just the lower two hundred feet of it, got the blood pumping again. "It's decision time. There's the airstrip at Chenega. You want to go on?"

"How we doing on fuel?"

I craned my neck to check the fuel tubes above my head. "We're good. As long we don't do too many detours."

"Well, if the conditions are going to be the same, we might as well keep going. What do you think?"

"I agree, I've flown this route in similar conditions before so I think we're okay."

"Then let's do it."

I had only fibbed slightly. Yes, I had flown this route many times when I took the marine biologist from the Alaska SeaLife Center out on harbor seal counts. What I hadn't said was we only flew in almost perfect conditions. Blue sky, unlimited visibility, and calm winds were prerequisites for those trips.

The other thing bothering me was the clouds. They were getting darker ahead and lower. But I continued anyway and flew past Chenega's wide, comfortable landing strip heading west. Seward was only thirty to forty minutes away now. We were so close I could almost feel the hot shower and warm food waiting for us.

I dropped lower to keep as much visibility as possible and worked my way around the hilltops on Evans Island. Another stretch of open water in Port Bainbridge, maybe three miles wide, sent my heart racing again, but I blocked it out. The end was within reach.

Banking left at the shoreline I flew to the corner of Cape Puget and turned while keeping white edged rocks below me on the right. What I saw ahead caused me to visibly tremble. Across Puget Bay the steep mountainside rising out of the water was almost invisible. Clouds and fog completely blocked my view of the cape that was just around the corner from Little Johnstone Bay.

I tried to shrug my shoulders and rearrange myself so Brandy wouldn't notice anything unusual, but the dark cloud ahead of me looked impenetrable. I knew it was a thick rain cloud choked with water and possibly violent turbulence. It reached all the way to the ocean and blocked any view I might have had of the mountain behind it. Turning to get around it to the left was out of the question. That path would take us way offshore into the Gulf of Alaska. No thank you.

The only possibility was to squeak between blindness and the mountain side. I knew this was potential disaster, but I hoped luck would be on our side. If it were, we'd find a way through. If not, I'd have to turn around. I shivered again at the thought of trying to turn around a hundred feet over the water in the middle of a cloud in turbulence. My jaw ached and cracked when I forced it open to yawn. My hand was cramping, and I was getting worn out trying to keep my muscles relaxed.

"Screw it. I'm going for it. It's going to get a little tight up ahead. You can help me by watching out the right side for rocks, okay?"

"What do you mean? Are you sure about this?"

"Yeah, I'm going to put the right wing tip fairly close to the mountain so I have something to look at on my way through the cloud ahead. It may get a little bumpy, so help me keep from running into anything, okay?"

Before she could answer me, wind started to batter the plane. Heavy rain hammered us, making the fabric roar. The windshield was opaque with streaming water, and I stared out the right window to find my way. All I could see was cliff.

"You got about thirty feet," Brandy called out.

I used the stick and rudder to keep the wind from slamming us into the rocks. We were flying almost sideways. A gust slapped us and tipped the wings about sixty degrees. I fought to get level.

"Less than twenty feet." Even over the headset I could hear the alarm in her voice.

I banked slightly left to get more clearance from the cliff and forced my right hand to relax its death grip on the stick.

"Thirty feet, Johnny."

I started breathing again, but I was glad I didn't have to say anything over the intercom. It was all I could do to not scream out loud like a little girl.

Then we popped through. The sky opened up in front of us and sunshine washed over brilliant blue water and green spruce forests blanketing the hillsides above Johnstone Bay. Excelsior Glacier shimmered in the distance above the iceberg filled lake, and the air grew calm as the few remaining water droplets continued to streak across the windshield.

We flew the rest of the way home mostly in silence. Breathing, counting our blessings, whatever. I tried not to worry about what she was thinking. After all, she was an experienced pilot. Maybe not in the world up here, but I was sure she'd been in tight situations before.

When we touched down back at Seward, I taxied to the parking space inwardly singing praises to five-eight Charlie. Once again she'd brought me home safe. I had asked her to perform her best tricks, in and out of the tight cove on Smith Island and the bad weather. I felt like dancing. I fell in love all over again with that airplane. Every line of her. The sound and smell and the feel of her. My euphoria was cut short when Brandy's voice came through my headset, serious and controlled.

"That was really close, Johnny. I didn't like that at all." She took off the headphones and climbed out of the plane. While I was getting out and unloading the gear, I saw her rental car heading down the airport road.

CHAPTER 17

Saturday night outside the Yukon Bar. It was raining. I pushed my way through the front door feeling an odd mixture of reluctance and glee. I was happy to be alive, happy to be home— but at the same time I dreaded seeing Brandy.

About ten people were sitting around staring at me. At least I thought they were staring at me. It took a moment to realize that there wasn't any music playing. Instead a loud, rapid-paced voice was talking about something. Some kind of accident. Everybody's eyes immediately shifted back to the TV screen above me. They'd only looked at me because I'd been in their field of vision.

Mitch was there. So was Bugeyed Larry, leaning against the wall in his usual spot next to the bucket of free peanuts. They were staring at the screen too. I took a stool between Mitch and Larry. Goldie came over and gave me a look.

"Had us a little adventure, did we?" Her expression was half-smirk, half-concern.

"Shit, there ain't no secrets around here, are there?"

"Never, Johnny. You know Seward. Like any small town. You okay?"

"Oh, yeah. Got caught in some bad shit is all."

"What kind of bad shit?"

"Clouds around the rocks, low ceiling over the water. You know." I shook off the chill running down my back.

"Sometimes you gotta do what you gotta do. What are you having?" She slid a napkin in front of me.

I loved that about Goldie. Some things she just understood. Alaska woman. She's been around. You don't have to explain this kind of stuff to someone who's lived it.

"I need a whiskey river to take my mind."

"You're shitting me, you don't drink whiskey."

"You're right. Make it beer, several beers."

She already had it in her hand behind her back. Before I could say another word, it was open and bubbling in front of me. I grinned thanks at her, but damn it, I must be too predictable. I watched her cute butt walking away, reminding me of the one that had been in my sleeping bag last night.

"Welcome back, Johnny." Mitch was turned back from the TV.

"Hey, Mitch. Sorry about the mix-up yesterday. Did Flight Service get hold of you?"

"Yeah, no problem. I hadn't even started worrying about you. They weren't too happy that you hadn't filed with them in the first place."

"Whatever. There's no requirement to file. I knew I had a much better chance telling you than them anyhow."

"Did you find anything out there?"

I told him about the Smith Island episode and the remains of a meth lab. He looked disappointed. Suddenly the cold beer bottle in my hand felt like it weighed twenty pounds.

"Damn hopeless waste of time trying to find that damned plane."

"Too bad," he said softly and turned back to the TV.

I tried to read his face but he was working hard to keep it blank. "Anything new on Willie?"

"Nope, no change."

"What's this about?" I asked pointing my bottle at the TV.

"Plane crash out in Bristol Bay. Some guy's engine blew an oil line and instead of landing it at the first beach, he tried to make it back to an airport. Landed in the drink instead."

"Kill him?"

"No, but he had his wife in the backseat and his best friend sitting beside him. The crash killed his friend, and he couldn't get his wife out of the plane. She drowned."

I looked up at the screen. A reporter was standing on a dock and behind her a tow truck crane was hauling an airplane wreck out of the water. Its prop was twisted like a pretzel, and the wings were broken but still attached. I couldn't be sure but it looked like a Cessna 172. An NTSB guy that I recognized was examining the wreckage as it slowly came into view.

"We're getting word now that he flew for about fifteen minutes after the oil line blew. Then it failed suddenly before he could get to the Naknek airport. When the rescue boat arrived at the scene, the pilot was sitting on the upside down plane still floating in the bay just twenty yards from the beach. He was screaming about his wife being caught in the backseat but by the time the diver was able to remove her, it was too late. What a tragedy to lose two people that close to you. Back to you in the studio, John."

"Jesus, I can just hear Willie if he was here. He'd be so pissed off at this guy he'd want to kill him."

Mitch gave me a curious look.

"Oh yeah, he would. Sounds like the guy was trying to keep from damaging his airplane, so instead of a forced landing on a beach, he kept going. Then the engine quit and he screwed up the landing and stalled it in, killing his best friend and losing his wife at the same time."

"How can you tell all that from what you just heard?"

"Did you look at the plane? Those wings don't bend like that unless you crash hard going straight down. Which is what happens when you try to stretch a glide and stall at about twenty or thirty feet. It just turns on its back and dives straight down." I used my hand to indicate the death spiral crash.

"That guy's going to have to live with that the rest of his life. Why would Willie be pissed at him?"

"Because it was unnecessary. He could have landed a dozen places. Instead he tried to save his plane and killed two people because of it."

"Geez, you guys aren't too compassionate about this stuff. The poor bastard was probably freaking and not thinking straight."

"Tough shit. That's the way it is up here. Some screwups are not forgiven. I didn't make this stuff up. That's what Willie taught me."

Mitch stared at his beer bottle in deep thought using a thumb to wipe moisture off the label. Goldie brought us a couple more. I got some free peanuts and went to work on them, tossing the shells to join their discarded brothers on the floor.

The bar was starting to fill up. Across the room a band with wet hair and raincoats was setting up equipment. The side door beside the stage was open and a van sat outside in the rain disgorging guitars, amplifiers and speakers onto the wet sidewalk.

I looked over the crowd. Some locals I recognized, but mostly they were visitors, tourists, bright-faced, clean-shaven twenty- and thirty-somethings. Brandy would fit in with this group, I thought to myself. Goldie was getting busy filling all the drink orders. The drummer was banging away in the background like all drummers do. Pretending to tune the drum heads, running through a few licks, but mostly just letting everybody know he was there and ready to rock the house.

"Hey, Goldie. Hobo gonna be here tomorrow?"

"Yup," she said pouring a beer from the tap, and jerking her head toward the sign above the bar.

"Hobo Jim, Every Sunday Night," it read.

I looked back at the crowd. They'd be here again for the Hobo. The tourists loved him. Good old Hobo Jim—playing guitar and singing songs about the final frontier, sloshing his glass of white wine in nonstop entertainment. He played and sang and told stories about Alaska and himself. Filled their heads with romantic images and made them laugh. The drunker they got and the drunker he got, the raunchier and funnier the songs and stories got. Stomping his foot, climbing on tables and wearing a crumpled white straw cowboy hat, yeah. The tourists all loved Hobo Jim.

One thing I'd give Hobo. The locals liked him too. Real Alaskans. If you listened to all his chatter during his shows, between the songs, he told it like it was. The cold, the ice, the hard living and tough conditions, being broke, living from one paycheck to the next. Scraping by in life. And the attitude that went along with it. Not taking crap from anybody, fighting the good fight, flipping off mainstream America. Screw the yuppies and the liberals.

That's why Alaskans loved Hobo. He filled our hearts with pride and good feelings for this big ass state. He reminded us of core Alaskan values. Hard work, hard luck, heartache, and the country, the sea, good friends, a good woman, a good laugh, go for the gusto. Locals let him sling his happy horseshit, cuz they could hear the truth between the lines. Yeah, Hobo was all right.

I was starting to feel about halfway right when Brandy came in. She walked through the door with a group of people, and I didn't see her right away. Then I became aware of her presence at the end of the bar on my right. She was wearing a white knit cap covering most of her head. The cap made her eyes seem even larger than usual.

I hopped off the stool and moved over to make room for her. She pretended she didn't notice and looked to Goldie for a drink. I was trying to think of something to say but came up empty.

Mitch rescued me. "Hey, Brandy. How's Willie?"

"I just came from seeing him. Nothing new."

"So how'd you like your Alaskan flying adventure?" he asked her.

Oh, brother. I wanted to crawl under the peanut shells gathering at my feet.

"It was quite the experience," she said carefully, glancing at me with a little smile. "I've been holed up in my hotel bathtub all day trying to recover."

"Well, I'll tell you—you're in the right hands with Johnny here. If anyone can fly you out of bad crap, he's your man."

"That's right." Goldie's voice joined Mitch's. She was back pouring more draft beer into tall glasses. "He's gotten me through some tough stuff more than once."

I didn't know who to kiss first, Mitch or Goldie. So I just took a big pull on my beer bottle and stayed quiet.

The band launched into their opening set, and the volume prevented conversation. The musicians were young and enthusiastic and after a few songs, couples were crowding the tiny dance floor, hooting and hollering.

Scooter came in and squeezed in between Mitch and me. We drank and watched the action for a while. Then Scooter started fidgeting and blinking like crazy. Every now and then he peeked around me to look at Brandy.

Uh-oh. He was working on the bottle label with one thumbnail. Something was coming. I just didn't know what yet.

"Hey, uh, Johnny?" Blink, blink.

"Yeah?" I tried to put a tone in my voice. A warning maybe. *Don't get strange on me, dude.* That kind of tone. It didn't work.

"Yeah, uh, Johnny? My thing's not working." Blink, blink, blink.

"That's too bad. You know there's pills for that now."

He didn't laugh. "No, I mean, you know, the woman thing."

"Okay," I mumbled, looking at the door.

"I need a favor." Blinkety blink blink.

I said nothing. I tried to blend into the woodwork. Wished I could be invisible. That didn't work either.

"Okay, I'm just gonna ask ya, Johnny. This is hard, but I gotta ask. A man's gotta do, what a man's gotta do. So here goes." He was blinking so fast I thought his eyeballs might hyperventilate. He leaned forward to peek at Brandy again and whispered loud in my ear to get past the music. "I need a model for the torso. Do you think Brandy would pose for it?"

I felt my face go numb. "Are you kidding me?" I stared at him hard but all he could do was blink and scratch at the bottle. I looked at Brandy but she was visiting with Goldie about something and not paying attention to us.

"No, I ain't kidding. My artist buddy told me to hire a model. I need to make a mold of her, uh, you know. And then use that to pour the compound into. Like making a statue. But there ain't no models in Seward."

"Okay, so let me get this straight. You want me to ask Brandy to let you paint her naked body with all this gooey stuff to make a mold of her snatch?"

"Well, more of her than that, but, uh, yeah. You know I'm not good with talking to girls."

"So you think I'm some kind of expert? What do you think I am, some kind of damn pimp? I gotta get women for you? Jesus Christ, you freaking moron. You're gonna have to get your own poontang, dipshit."

He looked like he was going to cry. "C'mon, Johnny. I'd ask her myself, but…I…I can't."

"Why not?"

"C-cuz I'm shy. I have been ever since Becky McDuffy in the third grade made f-fun of my b-b-blinking. You gotta help me."

"No way, loser. There's no way I'm asking her or anybody else to be a model for your perverted little phony female scheme. Jesus."

I realized then that Goldie was close enough and I was loud enough that she could hear me. Brandy turned toward us. "Hey, guys. Getting religious now, are we, Johnny? What are we talking about?"

Scooter turned bright red and looked at me in desperation. I turned away and rolled my eyes at Goldie pointing for another beer.

"Oh, boy," said Brandy. "Intrigue, mystery. Cool, just what I need to get my mind off Dad." She leaned over to look at Scooter and me, her head turning back and forth between us.

Scooter looked like he was going to explode. His eyes were bulging as bad as Bug Eyed Larry. I couldn't take it anymore.

"Brainchild here's got a project he wants your help with, but he ain't got the balls to ask you."

Goldie brought over my beer, then laid down a napkin and set Brandy's wine on it.

"Really?" Brandy said, a tone of caution in her voice. "So tell me about it, Scooter. Come on, I won't bite you."

Scooter froze. I couldn't have cared less. I refused to rescue his silly ass. If I wasn't so pissed it might have been funny. The band ended a song, and bar went almost quiet. The air was electric—just like when a guy proposes to his girlfriend in front of a football stadium audience and she doesn't answer.

Finally Goldie piped up. "Hey, Brandy. I've been listening to these boneheads. C'mere."

She leaned in and whispered in Brandy's ear. I thought Scooter was going to faint. Then Goldie straightened up and turned away with a smug grin to pour another beer from the tap.

Brandy's eyes went wide. Her eyebrows arched, and she looked at me. I leaned back on the stool so Scooter couldn't hide behind me. I tried to keep my face blank.

Brandy looked over at Scooter and took a sip from her glass of wine. "You want me to model naked for a sculpture, Scooter?"

He couldn't look at her, but he finally managed to nod nervously. His bright red face and beard bobbed up and down in time with the eye blinks. Someone walking in off the street would have thought he was having a seizure.

I was watching Brandy now, wondering if I was going to have to save Scooter from a beating. She gave me another calculating look. There was a long pause. Mitch was watching eagerly from Scooter's other side. We made eye contact and he grinned, waiting for the next move.

Then Brandy smiled and said, "That's really sweet of you, Scooter. I'd love to."

I heard an odd sound. Must have been my jaw hitting the bar. I gaped at Brandy, my mouth hanging open like a just caught salmon. Scooter's body lurched beside me. I heard him suck in a ragged breath.

"Sure, Scooter. No problem. I did some modeling for the art department when I was in college. It should be fun."

I thought Scooter was going to wet his pants. He was squirming around on his barstool until I thought he might fall on the floor. I couldn't believe any of it. Was I some kind of stranger in a strange land nightmare?

"Close your mouth, Johnny. You're going to swallow a barfly." Goldie smirked when I met her gaze. She crossed her eyes at me and shook her head.

I had to laugh. An explosive hacking cackle burst from my mouth. Holy crap. Then I had to get away. I drained my bottle with a couple of swallows and plunged into the crowd toward the john. I don't think Brandy and Scooter even noticed that I left.

When I came back they were still talking. Scooter was explaining the project, waving his hands around, describing the process. Brandy was listening intently and asking questions. Mitch motioned me over.

"The two of them talking is like watching the Beauty and the Beast. But Scooter's doing great. He's not even blinking."

I just shook my head, grabbed a handful of peanuts, and walked outside. I wanted air.

I walked down the rain washed sidewalk and leaned against the hood of the Toyota. I shelled peanuts and tossed them into my mouth. A thin mist filled the air above the wet street. The only sound was the crunch of the shells and the murmur from the bar.

I remembered the flight back from Smith Island, knowing all those islands, rocks, cliffs, and clouds were still sitting out there in the Sound. I was glad to be on the ground.

"You had dinner or you just eating peanuts tonight?" Brandy's voice jolted me out of the daydream.

"To tell the truth," I answered, "I'm getting sick of peanuts."

"Want to go get somewhere else?" She was standing under a street light with her hands in her coat pockets looking at me. There was no way I could say no to those big eyes.

I led the way to Ernie's just up the street. It was late but they were still open. We slid into a wood booth along a side wall and opened menus. I noticed that she kept her coat and hat on.

We ordered drinks and food. I waited. I knew she needed to say something to me. I was dreading this. She didn't say anything though. Once in a while we looked up and our eyes met, but she said nothing. Neither did I. Finally I couldn't stand it any longer.

What's that they say? The first one to speak loses? Hell with that. If I didn't say something soon, I might get pissed and say something stupid. I didn't like being strung along like a goddamn halibut hanging upside down on a hook, but I wasn't sure yet if she was torturing me on purpose or just not able to put what she was feeling into words.

"So are you upset with me? Did I do something wrong?"

"No, Johnny. I've been thinking about it ever since we got back. Every decision we made out there, we made together. Well, most of them anyhow. Yeah, I was upset. But I had a chance to speak up. The ceiling was low; we probably should have stayed put. We probably should have landed at Chenega. The worst part was that rain cloud against the cliff. That was Johnstone Bay, right?"

I nodded. I wanted to talk too, but something told me to stay quiet for a while.

"When you said, 'Screw it,' and dove into that rain cloud, it really scared me. How did you know that cloud wasn't miles wide instead of just a few hundred yards? How would you have gotten us out of that?"

I thought about it. "I'm not sure how to explain it. I've been thinking it over all day too. Something about the clouds and the way they were behaving. I could see similar rain clouds out in the Gulf, and they didn't look very thick. So I was guessing the one we were in wouldn't be too thick either. An educated guess, I suppose."

"Well, you were right, so I suppose I shouldn't criticize."

"Maybe I was also thinking that if we didn't come out of it pretty soon, I still had at least a hundred feet below us and without any terrain right in front of us, we could drop down and see the water pretty soon. If I had to, I could have just skimmed across the whitecaps all the way home."

She thought about that for a minute. "I decided after a while today to give you a break, because you do know the terrain here, and I don't. That's obvious, and I know that local knowledge and experience are worth a lot. Sometimes the books and all the good advice don't cover everything. Besides, I've had enough lectures from arrogant, all knowing senior pilots and instructors to know sometimes it's bullshit, and I don't want to be like that. I think mostly I just got scared. I'll own that."

I took a deep breath and sighed with relief. "Well, thanks. The last thing I need is some asshole second-guessing a tight situation and criticizing a decision when they weren't there."

"Okay, then," she laughed. "But let's make a deal. Let's not get ourselves in deep shit like that again if there's any way to avoid it."

"I agree wholeheartedly. It wasn't fun for me either." I raised my beer bottle and she clinked her wine glass against it with a smile.

She pulled off her knit cap and took off her coat. Tousling her hair with both hands to erase the helmet hair, she looked relieved. I wasn't sure if that look was a result of finally being free of the hat and coat in the warm room, or something else. Like coming in from the cold.

Our eyes locked briefly as we drank, and a sudden stir deep inside surprised me. She dropped her eyes as the food arrived.

What was that? Was I imagining things? Probably just relief. Relief and gratitude. I couldn't stand people being mad at me. When I saw her relax I turned into a puppy dog, my insides a quivering mush of happy teenage goofball.

It should have warned me. But it didn't. Something had changed for me. Did anybody know it the moment it happened? Nobody I knew. Certainly not me.

I studied Brandy's face for a minute. She was working her way through some sort of exotic looking rice and halibut dish with mango salsa. Without her sunglasses on, I could watch her eyes. Dark and round with delicate naturally long lashes, they were framed by thin graceful brows of the same dark color. No makeup. She certainly didn't need any. I was enjoying myself just watching her face while she ate.

She must have noticed that I wasn't eating. She looked up and caught me staring. Those amazing eyes lit up and she smiled. She wiped her mouth self-consciously. "Something wrong? Not hungry?"

"Huh? Oh, n-no." I shook my head and dug into the hamburger that was cooling in front of me.

"So what's next?" Now she was watching me eat.

I gulped. Hoping she couldn't read my thoughts, I swallowed and grabbed for my napkin. Making sure my beard wasn't full of ketchup or mustard, I swigged on my beer trying to avoid her eyes. I could feel her studying me. I fought the urge to get up and run. "Uh, I don't know what else we can do. We haven't come up with anything yet."

"Is there anywhere in the Sound we ought to check out?"

"How do you mean?"

"Where are these guys getting their fuel? What about Valdez and Cordova? Or even Tatitlek?"

"Yeah, we could fly over there. It's only about two hours to Valdez."

"Couldn't we drive?" She frowned at me with a worried look.

"Yes, we could drive to Valdez, but it would take all day—" I stopped mid-sentence.

She was laughing at me. "I was kidding, Johnny."

"Oh, okay. Yeah, we could fly over there. Next time the weather looks like it's going to be good for a while."

We smiled at each other and drank.

"Two days in a row of good weather could come along any month now."

She got my point. We finished up our meals and ordered another wine for her, another beer for me. I barely touched the new bottle though. I was full, but not ready to leave the cozy little restaurant just yet. Smooth jazz was playing quietly in the background, and the lights cast a soft glow through the room.

It was a very different scene from the night before. Then we had been cold and hungry, huddled on the sand beside the fire pit in the rain and wind. And now we were safe, warm, well fed, and relaxed. All within twenty-four hours. I knew that before long I would start to crave the outdoors again, but for now the comforts of civilization and the company of this young woman were suiting me just fine.

We lingered over our drinks and made plans to visit the airports on the east side of Prince William Sound. We avoided talking about Willie. The disappointments of our failed efforts in the last few days faded as we discussed what we might find on our next venture.

It was getting late and the restaurant staff was starting to clean up and shut down. Reluctantly, we pulled on our coats and went out the door. The rain had stopped.

We stood for a moment on the sidewalk. It was getting dark as the late Alaska sun had finally dropped below the mountains west of town. The peak of Mount Alice was visible again now that the clouds had moved on. Seward and Resurrection Bay plunged completely into shadow.

We walked slowly down the street. The Alaska SeaLife Center's bright glass front glistened and the wet pavement reflected the overhead lighting at the end of the dark street. There was no traffic anywhere.

Brandy started across the street to where her rental car was parked. Stepping off the high curb she stopped and looked back at me. Her white knit cap was back in place and strands of dark hair clustered above her eyes. Standing below me on the street she looked small and fragile, but I knew better.

My feet couldn't move. Neither could my mouth. I stared at her with a million thoughts choked in my throat like the Three Stooges trying to push their way through a narrow doorway.

"See you tomorrow," she said softly and turned to her car.

As she drove away, I turned too and headed for the camper. My head filled with too many questions, too much indecision, too much confusion. I drove slowly to the airport, trying to make sense of it. But it didn't make sense. There was no explanation.

I pulled up behind the office and checked on the airplane when something caught my eye. Walking out onto the tarmac, I spotted the airport beacon down at the end of the runway. A green beam flashed through the darkness under the partly cloudy sky. Then a white beam followed the green, reflecting magically off the wet pavement. A soundless light show repeating endlessly against the still water in the bay.

A dark shape was moving in the grassy area between the runways. It was a cow moose slowly making its way in the shadows past the windsock, the fluorescent cloth fluttering gently in the late night breeze. I watched until the huge ungainly beast crossed the long runway and disappeared into the trees toward the river.

CHAPTER 18

Sunday morning. I woke up early, strong sunlight streamed in the camper window and assaulted my eyes. I rolled over and lay there a while trying to get my bearings. A troublesome dream had been chewing at me throughout the night. Now I couldn't remember a minute of it. I just knew the same weird situation kept repeating, and I couldn't get it resolved.

I sat up and tried to decide whether to shower or not. I thought I could probably get away with a quick face wash and armpit wipe with a wash cloth. Then I remembered Brandy and the way she looked standing in the street the night before.

When I got out of the shower I shaved my neck and put on clean clothes. Looking in the mirror on the back of the closet door, I had to shake my head. What the hell is the matter with me? All of a sudden this woman shows up and I'm getting all twisted up inside?

Knock it off, you big dope. Come back to reality. She's only here for a few more days. If you let yourself get all shook up about her, when she's gone, you'll be a wreck. Toughen up. You're better off alone. Besides, she's not interested in you. Not in that way anyhow.

I gave myself an exasperated look in the mirror. *She's Willie's daughter, bonehead. She lives in Cleveland. She's twice the pilot you'll ever be. You're like a yappy airport dog chasing that moose like she's a midnight snack. Forget about it.*

Okay, thanks for the pep talk. I glanced at my reflection once more. *I'll keep all that good advice in mind.*

Stepping outside into the morning light, I stretched my arms over my head, working out the kinks in my neck. It was a beautiful day. I headed for the office computer to check the weather. When I unlocked the front door and entered the empty room, the chairs greeted me with blank stares. Nothing was lonelier than an empty office on a Sunday morning. Especially in the early season.

My cell phone rang. It was Brandy.

"Hey, Johnny."

"What the hell do you want?" I grumbled at her in my best imitation of a grumpy old bachelor annoyed at the disruption of my daily routine.

She laughed. "I'm at the Safeway getting coffee. What kind of donuts do you like, Mister Cranky Pants?"

Fifteen minutes later, she pulled up and I helped her carry the food and drinks as well as the Sunday Anchorage paper into the office. We spread out on the two desks and gobbled breakfast while we read news stories to each other, laughing at the silly troubles people got themselves into. The forecast looked good, and we loaded the plane together. The sugar and the caffeine had me feeling giddy. Maybe her company helped too.

After another hour of preparations, fuel, and flight planning, we were cruising up the north side of the Sound at three thousand feet. I pointed out Whittier in the distance. Smith Island was about twenty miles out to our right. A cruise ship passed below, its white wake parting the sun-sparkled blue waters.

"Sure is a different experience up here when the weather's like this." Her voice over the intercom interrupted my sightseeing.

"We're crossing Perry Island now, and the coast line ahead will take us into Valdez over that way." I pointed east and banked the plane to keep us within gliding distance of the small islands and jagged rock outcroppings ahead.

"I just can't get used to all this water around us and being this low. I hope we never have to make a forced landing around those rocks down there."

"What do you mean 'low'? We're at three thousand feet."

"You know what I mean. I fly over water like this at thirty thousand."

"You want to take her for a while?"

"Sure." I pulled my hands and feet back from the controls and watched as Brandy continued our path forward, craning her neck from the left to the right side of the narrow cabin trying to see her way ahead.

After a while she settled down and held course effortlessly. We reached the iceberg-filled waters in Columbia Bay, and she marveled at the length of glacial ice flowing down from the high mountains just west of Valdez Arm. I pointed down to the right and showed her where Bligh Reef and the *Exxon Valdez* had met company that fateful night almost twenty years before.

We held to the west and north side of the narrow entrance into Port Valdez and watched a line of tankers working their way in and out of the busy oil terminal across from the village. Valdez had been decimated in the 1964 quake and relocated to a safer location.

"Looks kind of like Seward," Brandy said from the backseat.

"We'll see what you think once we're on the ground. Why don't you set us up for the landing and then I'll take it for the touchdown?"

"Deal."

The long broad runway at Valdez lay out in front of us. My radio calls got no answers and no one else was in the pattern or on approach. At least no one was talking on the radio. I let

Brandy set up for a straight in approach and used the opportunity to look around.

The new town of Valdez was about four miles west of the airport on the end of a flat valley. The far end of the valley narrowed ahead and then took a hard left turn where it was filled with the ice of Valdez Glacier. To our right, a wide graveled stream bed ran through a low plain next to Robe Lake, which float planes used when they came to Valdez.

I could see why they'd moved the town after the quake. Aside from the fact that half of it fell in the water, the old site was definitely in a flood plain. Probably got washed out every spring. Seward had a similar problem. Building towns on alluvial plains comes with its share of risks. Maybe Mother Nature was trying to tell us something. The old broad certainly had power on her side.

The airport itself was huge. Thanks to its use by regular commercial carriers from Anchorage, a large terminal building sat off to the right side. But it was not busy enough for a control tower. I counted the hangar buildings below us, wondering if Willie's Cub was inside one of them. It seemed doubtful.

The Valdez airport was a little larger than Seward's and somewhat busier because of the airlines that came here. They wouldn't come to Seward anymore. Not enough business. Other than that, the small airplane scene was similar to Seward's. Only one company on the field offered scenic flights or air taxi services.

In Seward the local pilots kept a close eye on anything going on around the airport. Anyone acting secretively would attract lots of attention. I figured Valdez would be similar, but I wanted to check it out anyhow.

Brandy had us lined up expertly and when we were drifting down to short final, I took over.

"Thank you, captain. I've got the controls."

"You've got the controls, sir. That was fun. Would you believe that was my first stick time ever?"

"You should do some landings next."

"Okay, great. How about if I fly from the front seat next time?"

"No way. I ain't gonna fly this crate from back there, blind as a bat. Whaddaya think I am, crazy?"

She laughed. "You don't want me to answer that."

I bumped down way long of the numbers to minimize the taxi time and turned right for the small hangars. On pavement the big tires rolled along like riding on pillowy doughnuts. There was still no one in sight even at the terminal building at the far end.

"So where do we start?"

"Well, it's a Sunday morning. Maybe some local guys will be hanging around that we can talk to. I'll let them know we're from Seward, so they won't treat us like Outsiders quite as much."

I parked in front of a row of hangars. We walked around the entire complex, but all the doors were closed. No cars came up while we were poking around.

"I don't see anything unusual, do you?"

"Nope. Is this how it always is? Where is everybody?" Brandy asked.

"I've been over here a few times now, bringing passengers, and it always seems kind of empty. Unless, there's a plane from Anchorage, and even those guys seem to bug out as soon as they can."

"Why don't we head down to the terminal?"

"Yup, that's the plan. We might as well taxi down there and fuel up."

"Are we low already?"

"No, but it's a good idea to keep the tanks full around here. In case something comes up, we might need it."

On our way to the fuel pumps, I noticed the security fence in place all around the field. Another difference between Seward and Valdez. Homeland Security and 9/11 had brought a lot of those kinds of changes to airplane operations all over the country. Even small airports like Valdez were getting locked up. Somehow, Seward still managed to avoid the chain link fences and security code gates. None of us wanted the changes that would mean.

I was still thinking that Valdez was a dead-end for us. When we pulled up to the fuel station there was another plane there. The first person we'd seen was standing on a ladder pumping fuel into the wing tanks of a Cessna 185. I walked over to say hello. I didn't think I was going to need a cover story this time.

"Hey, there," I called up to the guy on the wing. "You a local pilot?"

He looked down at me. "Yeah, who's asking?"

"We're from Seward, just looking around. Have you—?"

"Goddamn it. Look what you made me do." He jerked the pump handle out of the wing, and tried to jump out of the way of the overflow. He danced an awkward little dance on the ladder, holding the wing with one hand and wrestling with the hose with the other. I watched as fuel rushed down the wing and ran onto his pants. I moved toward him thinking he might fall.

"Hey, sorry. I—"

"That was a goddamned lousy time to ask a guy a question, dontcha think?"

I was about to say that actually it was a lousy time for him to answer a question, but I thought better of it.

"Can I help you with something? I can take that hose for you." I kept my tone civil. So much for getting some friendly pilot-to-pilot information.

"No, I'm fine by myself," he snapped.

I watched again as he struggled his way down the ladder. When he got back down to the pavement he swiped at his pants with a red rag. On his way to the other wing, he stopped to deal with me. I could tell by his impatient look, he wasn't going to be much help. "I'll be out of your way here in a minute if you're getting fuel."

"Yeah, thanks. I just wanted to ask a local guy a question or two. Like I said we're from Seward."

He looked me over, then shifted his eyes to Brandy. He was probably in his sixties, tall and lean. His neat appearance and clean clothes told me he probably worked with tourists and might be getting ready for a scenic flight. He had a look about him like he had been flying for years and years. Maybe too many years.

"What do you want to know?"

I gave him a little background on the airplane theft. "So you seen anything unusual around here? Something that might fit in with my friend's plane?"

He picked up the ladder and turned to refuel the next wing. "Nope, can't help you with that one," he said, shaking his head. "That's a law enforcement problem, anyhow. You a cop?"

"No, we're just trying to find the plane if we can before it's destroyed. The cops aren't moving too fast for some reason."

He climbed the ladder, but before he started pumping fuel he looked down at us again. "I'm in a hurry here, but I haven't seen or heard anything about any of that stuff." He squeezed the pump handle and turned his head away from us to watch the pump counting out the gallons.

"How about a black SuperCub? Anybody like that come by for fuel?"

He shook his head without looking at me.

"Well, thanks anyhow." I turned and walked back to the plane rolling my eyes at Brandy.

"I don't think that guy wanted anything to do with us or our problem. Is everybody over here like that?" she asked.

"No, not at all. Usually pilots are really friendly. I don't know what his problem is, but I believed him about not knowing anything. Let's go inside while we're waiting."

We walked across the tarmac toward the terminal building. On the way we passed the airport fire station and crossed a wide red line painted on the pavement. A glass double door opened in the middle of the terminal and a young woman emerged holding the door and motioning at us.

"Excuse me, sir. You need to stay off the loading ramp. I've got a flight on the way in."

I headed for her feeling like I was treading on wet paint.

"No, sir. You can't come in this door. This is reserved for our passengers."

I stopped twenty feet from the door, staring at her.

"You need to use the gate at the end of the building." She pointed down the tarmac another two hundred feet in front of us.

I continued to walk across the sacred loading ramp ignoring her annoyed frown. I noticed there were no airplanes anywhere nearby and no sounds of one on the way in either. The gate held a sign with instructions about what code to use when we wanted to come back out.

"Sheesh," Brandy said. "How far did you say it was over to Cordova?"

"Shouldn't take us more than an hour. What? You're not getting a warm and fuzzy feeling for Valdez?"

"I guess I'm not used to being one of the little guys on an airport anymore."

"Jet jockeys," I shook my head.

We used the restrooms and walked around the inside of the modern terminal, looking at the historical pictures and plaques on the walls. It was like a lot of small terminals except it was almost completely deserted like the rest of the airport. Only two people were around: a cleaning lady and one counter agent. Even the small gift shop was closed.

"I've spent a lot of time in small airports. Mostly in my training days, before the Lear job came along. You know, those long cross-country trips building time either on my own or with students. Usually everybody's really friendly, like you said. What's going on here?"

"Ah, it's not the locals' fault, I guess. I've noticed the same thing you have. It's always made the little places my favorites. It's when there's an airline on the field that changes everything. They got all their rules and the airline people have this attitude. Like they know the airport depends on them for its survival so they can act all high and mighty and push the little guys around. It's probably what's making the guy at the fuel pump so grumpy."

"It's too bad. I guess I've forgotten what it's like outside the corporate flying biz."

"Yeah, that's why I like Seward. We got airport dogs walking around, no fences, no painted lines that anybody pays any attention to. People drive their cars and motorcycles across the tarmac whenever they feel like it. Although there's some folks that think we ought to be more professional, we locals like it just the way it is. We don't have any problems there.

Hell, it's been over a week since a dog got sucked up into a jet engine."

Brandy laughed. "So when can we get out of here?"

We took another way back to the fuel pumps, out the front door of the terminal, across an open field, and through the back gate of the empty fire station. At least it looked empty. A couple of fire trucks sat inside, their shiny paint jobs reflecting through the small windows in the roll up doors.

"You'll like Cordova better. It's a small village. Smaller than Seward. They've got two airports over there. A big one like this way out of town and then a little municipal field I use on the edge of town. It's a short little gravel strip right next to a lake with water on both ends."

"Sounds good," she said. "You know anybody there?"

"Yes, I do as a matter of fact. Friendly people over there. The folks I know fly all over the Sound and the Copper River Delta. They'll know if anything weird is going on nearby."

When we reached the plane, Brandy reached in back and pulled out a paper sack. "Want a sandwich? I picked some stuff up at the Safeway."

I helped myself to a big bite of an overstuffed sourdough bun and wiped my mouth on my sleeve. Then we pushed the Cub closer to the pumps in the vacant space left by the 185.

Still chewing a mouthful of turkey and cheese, I retrieved the hose and the ladder. While I was waiting for the tanks to fill, I let myself think for the first time about what might be waiting for us in Cordova. If we didn't find out something about Willie's SuperCub there, I wasn't sure what to do next.

More of my thoughts revolved around Brandy. We had planned an overnight stay in Cordova, but I hadn't let myself think about it much. At least not until now.

The pump produced a forceful stream filling the tanks in a matter of minutes. I was careful not to make the same mistake the other guy did. Lapses of concentration could be deadly. Distractions and Alaskan flying didn't mix.

It wasn't cold out and the weather was still spectacular. But I noticed that my hand holding the pump handle was shaking. I forced myself to quit thinking about Brandy and watched the fuel streaming into the tank.

CHAPTER
19

It was early afternoon when we lifted off the runway in Valdez. I banked over town giving the pipeline terminal a wide berth. One tanker was at the pier taking on a massive load of the black gold. Another waited its turn anchored offshore a mile away.

I pointed out the oil tanks against the south hillside for Brandy. "There used to be a flight restriction over the area right after nine-eleven, but they've relaxed it now. I keep my distance anyhow. Can you feel the eyes watching us?"

She sounded surprised. "You think so? Yeah, I suppose you're right. It would be a simple thing to load a plane full of explosives and fly right into those tanks. That's creepy to think about. We could get there from here in about three minutes."

I could feel her shudder even though she was sitting behind me. Or maybe it was me who was shuddering.

"That's why I think someone's watching us. Anyhow, I hope someone is. Someone with a missile or something that would knock us out of the sky if we looked like we were up to no good. Creepy is right."

It wasn't easy to imagine death and destruction, fireballs and suicidal insanity on a beautiful day like this one. The snow-rimmed mountaintops around us split the blue of the sky from the azure water below in a dazzling panorama as I banked left and crossed Port Valdez for a gap in the high country called Jack's Notch.

The snow line still reached from the peaks almost down to the water's edge on the forested hills and valleys that passed below us. Only the lowest points of riverbeds and low-lying meadows were snow free, and they glistened up at us green and inviting in the afternoon sun.

I flew over Tatitlek at five hundred feet, but not a single airplane was parked anywhere around the long wide gravel runway. Without any hangars or other structures capable of hiding an airplane, I decided not to land. I climbed back up to three thousand feet, and we flew over Port Hidalgo, Port Gravina, and then the east edge of Orca Bay. The marina at Cordova came into view, and the closer we got the more boats we could see in the waters all around. Fishing boats mostly, working their nets.

"There's an airport here?" Brandy's voice came over the intercom.

"Yep, it's around the corner just past town to the left up there. You'll see it when I turn into that valley."

I throttled back, pushed forward on the stick and let the Cub descend over the water outside the marina. I turned into the opening and followed the south wall of the canyon that held Eyak Lake. I pointed down to the left.

"There she is." Cordova Municipal Airport was a narrow strip of gravel just eighteen hundred feet long with the waters of Lake Eyak on both ends. A steep mountain shoulder bordered it on the north.

"Cordova traffic, SuperCub one-two-five-eight Charlie's on a left downwind for two four." I grabbed one notch of flaps and studied the airstrip as we flew by.

"SuperCub traffic, eight-eight Victor's on short final for the lake. Where are you?"

I jerked my eyes back to the front and spotted a floatplane descending in front of us. If I hadn't seen her and continued with my base turn in the normal spot, we would have collided in about thirty seconds.

"Roger, eight-eight Victor, no problem, I'll extend."

"Roger that, hey, Johnny. That you?"

"Hey, Junior. What's happening?" The radio went quiet again as we both concentrated on our landings.

As I added power to stop my descent, I watched out the left window until Junior flew his big yellow Beaver past us and settled onto the glassy surface of the lake. Banking left onto base and then again to final, I flew straight ahead until I intercepted a good glide path again, then chopped the power, added the rest of the flaps and dropped us in at the end of the strip.

"Nice landing, Johnny," said Brandy. "This doesn't look like an airstrip; it looks more like a road headed out of town."

"That's exactly what it is. The taxiway doubles as a local road. Around these parts they squeeze in an airport wherever one might fit. Let's go meet Junior."

I pulled the SuperCub across the road to park in an open area against the hillside. A local guy in a pickup truck was coming down the road at the same time, but he stopped for us as we taxied across. As I was turning around, he drove on by, waving to us as he left.

"This place feels better already." Brandy climbed out and stretched. She was busy tying down the wings while I put things away in the cabin and secured the stick with its locking handle.

We walked into the sunshine toward the dock on the west end of the strip. A pilot in a red plaid shirt, blue jeans, and rubber hip boots was helping an older couple climb down the Beaver's little ladder to stand on the float before stepping across to the dock. The tourists were grinning from ear to ear gushing about their flight and snapping pictures of each other in front of the plane. We waited and watched while they pulled Junior over to stand between them. Brandy jumped forward and took their camera to capture the images I imagined would soon be framed on their mantle at home in southern Illinois or wherever they were from.

They pumped Junior's hand vigorously and thanked him for showing them the most beautiful scenery they had ever seen in their lives. Junior smiled humbly. A big stocky man with a lumberjack's full beard and a smile that made him friends everywhere, Junior said goodbye and turned toward us.

"Hey, Johnny. Thanks for not ruining my landing." He swallowed my hand in his huge mitt and looked from me to Brandy. "Who do we have here?"

"Watch it, buddy. She's a Learjet jockey."

After introductions and catching up on small-town gossip as he unloaded gear from the Beaver, I told him what had happened to Willie.

"Whoa, no bull? We got an email the other day about a stolen plane from Seward with the N-number but I didn't know that was Willie's. Holy shit."

"Yeah, that's why we came over here. Brandy is Willie's daughter. We were hoping you or someone around here might have seen something unusual out in the Sound or in the delta? Or a black SuperCub?"

"Gosh, I don't know about that. Black SuperCub, eh? Let me think about it for a minute. You think these guys came this way?"

"We really don't have a clue yet, but we wanted to look around anyhow, just in case."

"Yeah, I don't blame you. Cops helping any?"

When I shook my head, he nodded. "Figures. I think they take a dim view of the way you operate."

I looked at him. "What do you mean, the way I operate?"

"Don't worry about me. Hell, I think it's funny. If they can't take a joke, ..."

I had to chuckle. "Yeah, that's kind of the way I look at it, too, but those guys…no sense of humor. I'm just trying to create a little justice here and there."

Junior lifted his cap and scratched his head. "Maybe you heard, I'm the only act in town now. Jake and his wife packed it in at the end of last season." He nodded down the runway toward a hangar that used to hold an air service that had been in Cordova for years. The sign was missing from the building and the planes I had seen there on previous visits were nowhere to be seen.

"That's too bad. I always liked them. What happened?"

"I don't know. I think they finally just got tired of fighting the fight, you know?"

"Well, more business for you, right?"

He shook his head and groaned. "Yeah, too much, I'm going to be swamped this summer. Too much of a good thing. You know? It's gonna wear my ass ragged. Hey, why don't you come over and fly with me?"

"Oh, nah, thanks, but I've got enough where I am. Besides, I couldn't walk out on Phil, you know."

Junior laughed. "That old bastard's still kicking? The son of a bitch has a good deal with you flying for him."

I had to laugh. "Yeah, I'm always reminding him of that, but he fails to be impressed."

"Well, make sure to tell Phil hello for me when you get back. I go way back with that miserable so and so." His big grin made me laugh.

"Let's go up to the office. I got more flights coming up, but let's see what anyone else might know. The other guys have been flying to Montague and Hinchinbrook lately. Maybe somebody's seen something."

As we walked across the road, Brandy went ahead and entered the log building. Junior pulled me to the side and wrapped a massive arm around my neck and bent me over in front of him in friendly hug. "Damn, it's good to see you, little buddy."

Then he whispered to me. "So you hooked up with the little filly yet?"

I pulled away in mock horror. "No, no way, man. Get your mind out of the gutter. She's Willie's daughter; this is strictly professional. I'm just helping out a visiting pilot, that's it."

"Yeah, right, you dog. What's the harm in tasting a little forbidden flesh?" He dug his fingers into my side, getting off on tormenting me. I must have turned red, because he threw back his head and roared.

"Why don't you guys hang out for a while and then have dinner with Deb and me?" he suggested. "Heather will be back by then, and you can ask her what she's seen lately." Junior had another pilot flying for him. Besides the Beaver on floats, he also had a 206 on floats. Heather flew the 206 but she was out on a flight and wouldn't be back for a couple of hours.

I picked up the gear and climbed the stairs to his office. I envied his setup. The comfortable open room had a long counter across the middle of it, and a neat office space on the other side with telephones, computers, and a couple of desks. Pictures and animal heads covered the blond wood walls beside wide picture windows. Rugged but cozy couches and easy chairs sat in the customer waiting area where we were standing.

"God, that's awful news about Willie. He gonna be okay?" Junior asked.

Brandy and I looked at each other uncomfortably. "Hard to say," she said, looking down at her shoes.

"Hey, don't worry. Willie's a tough old bird. I flew with him out west for a few years a long time ago. He'll get over this, you'll see."

"Say, Junior," I jumped in. "Is it okay if we walk around a bit and look the place over? I thought I'd ask some other people if they might have seen anything too."

"Yeah, good idea. Like I said, I'm gonna be busy a while. Make yourselves at home. We'll strap on the feed bag about six. Do whatever you like. Okay?"

With the last remark, he gave me a big wink. I quickly turned away and headed for the door desperate to hide a nervous grin.

"Seems like a great friend you've got there." Brandy caught up and walked beside me. I was headed for the empty building down the line.

"Oh, yeah. Junior and I used to work for Phil up in Moose Pass a while back. Got to be great friends. That guy can put away some beer, let me tell you. A hell of a pilot too. And the Beaver. What a great plane for the bush."

Cordova Municipal is more like a wide place in the road than an airport. Built on a shelf of land on the lake there are only two hangars. One was Junior's and the other one was in front of us. Junior said it was abandoned, but I wanted to see for myself.

The large bifold door that enclosed the front end of the hangar was about sixty feet wide. It had a smaller, normal-sized door cut into it, and it was locked. On the far end from us another small windowed door indicated a small office. It was locked too, but looking inside, I could see the remains of a business operation's paperwork scattered across an old wooden desk spilling onto a chair and the floor. Another doorway at the back of the office probably led into the main hangar space, but it was closed.

"Doesn't look like anyone's been in here for a while," Brandy said, cupping her hands around her eyes and peering through the dirty glass.

"I know; let's look around back. There's usually a back door in these places." I knew I could break the glass to let us in, but that didn't seem like a good idea.

A beat up and weathered work shed sat next to the hangar. Its door hung open, revealing old tires and gas cans and trash. A pile of brush partly filled the small alley between the shed and the tall aluminum siding wall of the hangar. Before we went around back, I wanted to be sure we had a good cover story. I knew that having Junior as a local contact would help, but I also wanted to be able to explain ourselves to any locals who thought we looked suspicious.

"Hey, if anyone asks us what we're doing," I said to Brandy, "we're here to see about renting out the hangar, okay?"

"You got it, Ace." She was smirking at me.

"Ace?"

"Ace Ventura, pet detective?"

I rolled my eyes at her and took a look back at the airstrip and the road. We were alone. I headed to the back of the hangar. Once back there, the mountain side climbed almost straight up leaving little room to maneuver. And there was trash back there as well, blown in during a windstorm and then buried under heavy snow.

As expected, we found an old, beat-up door with a deadbolt lock above the handle. I leaned against the door jam and removed the tool kit from my jacket. Selecting my favorite wrench and pick, I winked at Brandy, who was watching me intently.

I slid the wrench into the opening of the key slot and put slight clockwise tension on it with the fingers of my left hand. Then I inserted a pick feeling the tiny pins inside the lock. They all moved easily up and down in their cylinders except for one. I relaxed the wrench tension just a bit and the pin popped loose. I felt the familiar slight jerk as it lined up with the edge of the lock tube. Then the other pins moved one at a time and also clicked into place with the corresponding tiny movements.

Except for one. One of the pins wouldn't set. I started over. Relaxing tension on the wrench, I heard the pins click back to their original seats. This time I was more careful with the key pin. It clicked easily like the first time, and then all the other pins moved into their proper places with ease. The tube turned slightly and the lock was sprung. But the deadbolt was stuck. I wasn't surprised with the door being so exposed to the weather. It had probably never been lubricated.

I took a medium flat-tipped screwdriver from another pocket, inserted it in the lock and carefully twisted it until the deadbolt screeched in its housing and pulled back into the door. I turned the handle and the door swung open. We were in. I looked at Brandy who had been standing right next to me the whole time watching every move. She looked up at me in amazement, her mouth hanging slightly open.

"I didn't know you could do that." Her eyes held a fascinated twinkle. She squeezed my arm with one hand and kept looking back and forth from the door to my face to the tools I was putting away.

The cavernous interior of the hangar yawned before us. It was completely dark inside and I moved in carefully until enough outside light spilled into the room to reveal some details. The strong musty smell of mildew and dead air filled my nostrils.

There was an airplane inside. It was positioned closer to the front door on the other side of the hangar floor from us. Brandy followed me into the darkness. As our eyes adjusted, I could see more sunlight filtering in through cracks in the front door and sidewalls.

As I moved forward I ran into a metal bucket on the floor. It clattered loudly as it fell over. Some kind of liquid spilled onto the floor. Brandy and I both jumped. She reached out and grasped my coat with both hands. I turned and grinned at her.

"Leaky roof. The bucket was there to collect the drips."

"Scared the crap out of me," she whispered, giggling.

As we moved forward it was clear that there was only the one plane in the big room. And it was just a fuselage sitting on saw horses. No engine, no skin, and parts of all kinds were strewn on the floor. A pair of stripped wings were leaning against the wall to our left.

"Damn. This ain't it."

"How do you know?"

"Cuz this is somebody's project plane. It's not a SuperCub. Looks more like an old Taylorcraft or something, with side-by-side seating in front and real doors. Besides it looks like it's been here a long time."

"Yup, I think you're right. This place hasn't been disturbed in a long time. Look at the dust bunnies all over the place."

After a quick look around, we left. Another dead-end. Out back again I pulled the door closed, inserted the screwdriver, and relocked the door. Brandy was leaning against me as I put the screwdriver back in my pocket. I could feel the warmth of her, close and soft. It reminded me of the night in the plane.

"Uh, excuse me, miss. I'm not used to such close supervision when I'm breaking the law."

She giggled and put an arm around me. "I just can't believe how easily you did that. That was so James Bond."

Her eyes were twinkling at me again. I thought about kissing her. I really did. She looked ready for it. But then I thought it would be better to get the hell out from behind the hangar before someone spotted us.

I pulled away from her, tested the door to be sure it was secure and looked over the area around us. Everything was back in place. Only a few footprints left any trace of our visit, and they would disappear after a couple days of rain. I led the way back through the alley and out to the road. There was still no one around.

We walked to the end of the runway and looked out over the lake. Canadian geese were flying overhead, headed north. Their honking filled the air. We turned our heads toward a familiar rumble behind us. We watched Junior taxi the Beaver away from the shoreline, the big radial engine coughed white smoke and chugged with a distinctive low guttural rumble.

"Johnny, this place is just so amazing."

"Yeah, this is Eyak Lake. Ain't it great?"

"No, I mean the whole thing. Alaska. Everything I've seen, everything you've shown me."

I said nothing. We walked down the road beside the lake and watched a group of bald eagles swirling in the air currents high above us.

"Johnny, I need to apologize."

"What for? You do something bad?"

"No, well, yes." She took hold of my arm and pulled me slightly toward her. "I'm serious now.

"I've been behaving like a real bitch to you, and I don't need to be that way. I was feeling like I was stuck with you, because you're the only one around with a plane that could help out. I put a lot of pressure on you and even got nasty, calling you a drunk and stuff like that. And you've been nothing but terrific. I just want you to know how much I appreciate it."

"Aw shucks, it's nothing." I was embarrassed. Didn't know what to say. I glanced at her quickly, and she was looking directly at me with those big soft eyes and a little smile. I looked away as quickly as I could. It was hard to tear myself away from whatever it was I was reading in her face.

"Well, tell you what, you can buy this old drunk a beer. How about that?"

"Always with the jokes, huh?" She put her arm around me again as we walked and pulled me in tight. "You're not old and you're not a drunk."

I was going to say, "I'll drink to that," but that would have been another joke. I let her hold me. Are you kidding? I put my arm around her shoulders and we turned back toward the airstrip enjoying the easy way our bodies fit and moved together as we walked.

To hell with a bunch of eagles and geese; I was flying higher than any of those dirty birds. We walked and talked about Alaska and places she hadn't seen yet. She talked about her life in Cleveland and the weight of responsibility she felt about her mother. I listened and offered a thought here and there but mostly just listened. Her voice was hypnotic, and my mind traveled far and wide just drifting on the spell of her.

I don't know how much time went by. I didn't care. But the sound of a 206 increasing power for a landing on the lake interrupted my reverie, and we watched as a yellow floatplane banked across the lake toward us and flew onto the water headed toward Junior's dock.

"I'll bet that's Heather," I said, picking up the pace toward her.

The rest of the afternoon and evening swirled by in a blur. We met Heather, and I could see Brandy was impressed with the short, stocky powerhouse in hip boots. Heather moved around her plane like a spider, climbing up to check the wing tanks and clean the windshield. She dove in and out of the cargo space through the double doors of the 206 offloading gear and cardboard boxes. We chipped in to help her carry the load as we visited, but at first she didn't have any good information to add to the mix. Most of her recent trips had been out to Montague Island.

"You know, come to think of it. I saw a SuperCub north of us yesterday. Not sure if it was black but it was pretty dark.

So it could have been black. I remember cuz it was low over the trees near that old lumber site north of Patton Bay. I figured it was hunters looking for bears or something."

Dinner with Junior and Debbie came and went in their cozy cabin down by the marina. They took Brandy in like an old friend. We drank and ate lasagna, sharing stories and laughs with their two young kids around a big wooden table in the kitchen.

A shaggy dog named Clem lay at our feet offering her belly to anyone with a spare hand that wasn't otherwise occupied. *Hey, you. You ain't busy. How about a scratch?* I had a thing for dogs of almost any kind but especially big hairy calm and friendly creatures like Clem. Brandy apparently did too, and Clem had us figured out in a flash. She squeezed herself right between us. We found ourselves taking turns patting, scratching, and cuddling her the whole evening.

When it got late, Junior helped us collect our packs from the plane and dropped us downtown with a couple of suggestions for places to stay. We said our goodbyes and then found ourselves on an empty street in front of a bar. It was just a hole in the wall next door to an old hotel that looked like something out of a western movie.

"Let's get a nightcap," I suggested, and Brandy took my arm as we headed into the bar.

I'd been there before, as I remembered. It had been a while but once in the front door the place was familiar again. I led the way to a booth against the wall. Brandy surprised me by scooting into the same side as me and we ordered drinks.

"Want anything to eat?" The waitress looked young enough to worry the ID police, but we waved her off pleading full stomachs from Debbie's excellent lasagna.

A slow rhythmic blues ballad was playing on the sound system. I could feel Brandy's body moving gently against me in time with the music. The next time I set my beer bottle down her hand was there, and I rested mine on top of it. It was warm. I looked down at her and she turned into me so naturally that our lips met before I even had time to think about "Should I, or shouldn't I?"

CHAPTER 20

Her lips were warm and alive, quivering against mine. Her touch was electric. The effects of a long day of flying, eating, and drinking swirled in my head. The feel of her next to me was overpowering. I had to admit it to myself, the tide had been tugging me this way for a long time. I just wanted to let myself go and surrender to the pull.

I let my lips mingle with hers, lightly at first, then with energy. I reached up and stroked the side of her face with my hand. Ran my fingertips into her hair and tucked it behind her ear, saving her the trouble. Her eyes closed, her warm breath smelled of wine. She leaned into me, and I could feel her whole body relaxing into the kiss.

Emboldened, I flicked my tongue between her lips. Only a gentle probe. Testing. Her jaw relaxed and I felt a movement within. Lightly returning my exploration. Tongue tips dancing, tripping the lights fantastic. I think I could have stayed in that booth making out like teenagers for hours. Like kids again, we were fogging up the windows of a fifty-seven Chevy. Or a SuperCub in the rain for that matter. Sprinkles drumming on the wings and fabric, softly serenading young lovers in the night. Caressing us with a warm breeze that flowed through our hair, tantalizing the millions of nerve endings from our heads through our souls.

I released my mind and forgot about everything else that could have possibly mattered in that moment. To hell with missing SuperCubs, to hell with thieves and police, to hell with the rain and the fog, cliffs, and rocks of Prince William Sound. All that mattered in the world at that moment in time were those lips tangled with mine.

But all good moments must end. And yet, this one held promise. The promise of more to come. I sat back and took a deep breath. Her eyes opened slowly, taking me in. I was lost in the smoky green look of her eyes, lost in her gaze. I kissed her eyebrow beside one of those emerald pools of bottomless immersion and whispered, "Don't you dare go anywhere. I'll be right back."

She smiled and made room for me to leave the booth. I headed for the men's room. I hated myself for breaking the spell. I prayed I would get it back. Like one of those dreams where you wake up and try desperately to sleep again. Perhaps to dream. Begging for another chance. Another dream, the same dream.

My bladder had intervened. Some realities don't care about lust. I took care of business and washed my hands. I ignored the mirror, avoiding the reflection. *You stay out of this. Let a guy live, will ya? When am I ever going to get a chance like this again?*

When I returned to the table, she was gone. I tried not to panic. Surely she had gone to relieve the same need. Of course, that's all it could be. I couldn't have misread a kiss like that. Could I?

The next few minutes were some of the longest of my life. When she finally returned, grinning at me with a twinkle in those lovely green spheres I thought I might never catch my breath again. Then I realized that she had come from the wrong direction to be returning from the ladies' room.

She sat down beside me, kissed me quickly on the mouth, and said, "Let's go."

I've been known to be slow in some situations. Reluctant to follow direct orders out of sheer stubbornness or independence. But not then. I was out of that booth in record time, leaving money on the table without a care for calculating appropriate percentages. To hell with that; I would follow this woman off this edge of the earth.

She had my hand and pulled me behind her out the door and down the sidewalk. I stumbled behind her as best I could carrying both of our packs in my other hand. She giggled every time I tripped over my feet glancing back and winking at me. I was laughing too, completely giving in to her insistent towing without taking the time to question our direction.

I became vaguely aware that she was pulling me up the stairs of the hotel next door and pushing open the old and weathered wooden door with creaking hinges. Cut crystal glass window panes reflected sparkles of dim chandelier light through the ancient wood floored lobby. Not a soul in sight to witness the fevered pace, we climbed the interior stairs. The old wood squeaked under our weight as it had for countless souls before us. Many of them as heated as we were, I'm sure. It wasn't until we reached the first landing and turned down a gray-tinged worn carpet that I managed to say anything.

"Hey, where we going?"

She continued hauling me down the hall but turned and without a word waggled a clattering plastic room key at me with a wide eyed, smiling mouth. Room 209. The door appeared behind her and after a brief struggle filled with giggling and fumbling, the door opened and we tumbled inside. I dropped the packs and slammed the door behind us.

A dim street sign outside the dusty window cast lazy beams of light into the room. But otherwise, darkness was our only witness. She turned toward me, pulled off my hat, and took my face in both her hands. A tinny wind chime made from dinner utensils hung above the window. The breeze created by the closing door tickled it into an enchanting tune.

I heard a little voice from somewhere calling a warning. I pulled back and looked at her dreamy eyes swimming in sensation.

"Are you sure…?"

She pulled me back. "Shut the fuck up and kiss me," she whispered huskily.

I obeyed and pressed my lips deeply into hers. With both hands I went to work on her jacket stripping it off her shoulders. Multitasking with the fervor of a child on Christmas morning, I kicked off my shoes and pulled at the rest of her clothes with reckless abandon.

Our tongues dove at each other in a fever. No more careful testing and gentling probing. The pre-test was over; midterms and finals were here. Her hands dropped from my face to my waist, and I soon felt the cool air of the empty room flowing around my bare knees.

Her sweatshirt flowed up and over the head and flew across the room. When her head reappeared, her hair was scattered in all directions. She looked up at me through the bangs hanging in her eyes and tossed her head with another lusty giggle. She watched me as I reached behind her and unfastened her bra with both hands, using the closeness of the embrace to lock my lips with hers again. She pulled back and with a shimmy tossed the bra straps off her shoulders into my waiting hands. A dramatic toss sent the lacey garment sailing in the opposite direction from her sweatshirt.

While I gazed down at her breasts in the shadowy light, she pulled my sweatshirt and t-shirt off as one and pressed her naked chest to mine pulling me in tight. Her hands slid down to grasp my buttocks and pulled me in even tighter. Perky pink nipples stabbed into my chest.

I stabbed my tongue deep into her mouth and slid both hands inside her jeans and down her hips. Her pants melted to the floor, and she fell giggling backwards onto the bed, pulling me along for the ride.

Here I go, off the edge of the world. I didn't care. Nothing mattered now. The point of no return couldn't have been more clear if it had been a flashing neon sign emblazoned on the ceiling.

But I wanted to slow the pace, let the party prolong the pleasure, make it last. Squirming our feet and legs to remove our socks, I buried my lips deep in her neck. She wriggled and crawled backward, giggling in a vain effort to escape the tickling contact of my beard and mustache against her pale smooth skin. I leaned against my left elbow and slowly slid my right hand up the side of her leg, cruising gently up and over her hip bone, dancing lightly across the silky smoothness of her belly to cup one breast.

Her back arched and she let out a small moan as I slid my mouth from her neck and across her chest to take a nipple between my lips. Flicking and sucking in turns, I felt her legs beginning to thrash, her heels digging into the bed.

I pulled away and gazed down at her lying in my arms. Her hand reached up behind my head and pulled me down kissing me again and again.

I pulled back once more and walked two fingers into her navel loving the sight of her. "Oh, my, you are still so completely overdressed," I murmured, running one finger under the silky pink line of her panties waistband low on her abdomen.

"That's your fault."

"True. Allow me to redeem myself."

She arched her back and raised her hips while I removed the last remaining obstacle between us. I knew it was going to tickle her, but I didn't care. I leaned in and kissed a spot on her inner thigh just above her knee, and felt her cringe and then give in. Kissing my way slowly up her thigh her back arched again, and when I ran out of thigh, I could tell she didn't care either. She took the back of my head with both hands and held me as I moved.

Her moans grew louder, and her legs seemed to lose control. Cradling her with both arms to keep my place, I felt her heels pounding my back and digging into my flesh.

When her struggles slowed, I kissed my way to her navel again greeting it like an old friend. Suddenly she levered me over with one leg and crawled on top forcing her mouth over mine.

I let her have her way with me and watched through the slits of half open eyes as she slid her body over mine, raising up and then lowering herself slowly, deliciously. Her head pulled back and turned to one side as she bit her lip at the electric sensations racing under her skin. My head started to thrash from side to side, and I arched up to meet her. Her eyes squeezed shut. Then they opened, but her gaze was unfocused. In a dream state. If she was seeing anything it was far, far away.

She rocked back and forth letting the feelings take over until her eyes squeezed together tightly again and a high-pitched groan escaped her lips. Her whole face contorted in a pained grimace that I knew wasn't pain at all. I held her hips in place against me and met her thrusts with thrusts of my own.

Her breathing finally slowed. She relaxed above me, gradually melting, and then she slid down beside me gasping in the shadows. I laid my hand between her breasts, felt her heart thumping wildly inside her ribcage, and watched her belly rising and falling slower and slower. I wiped wet hair back from her forehead and lightly kissed her shoulder.

Finally, smiling up at me, she breathed a deep sigh. She reached up and placed her hand along my face, running her fingers through my beard. Above us, the little wind chime jingled a sweet melody of random pings and tings dancing in a tiny breeze that sneaked through the cracks in the window frame.

"You can do anything you want to me now," she murmured with her eyes closed, a happy half-smile curling her lips.

So I did.

CHAPTER
21

Outside the hotel, nighttime marched toward the dawn. A billion stars and planets sparkled in the northern sky. An almost full moon crept gradually to the west. Like celestial twins peeking in at us, the street light and the moon filled the window together for a time bathing us in shadows and glow.

The lonely darkness of another northern night vanished under the double beamed illumination. Then the moon moved on, fate and physics pulling her away to resume the journey alone. Brandy slept beside me curled in my arms. I nuzzled my nose deep in her hair and listened to her slow breathing. Strawberry shampoo and sweet perspiration filled my nostrils through the damp strands of her soft hair. The smell of her was the last thing I remembered as I drifted off into space. Foolishly I tried to memorize the sensation of her closeness so I would never lose the feeling again.

When I woke up I was still in full glow. So was the whole room. Bright sunlight flooded through the window. Almost immediately I felt the distance. I was always like that on a trip. I never really relaxed until my plane was tied down back in its own spot, safe and secure. The distance from home always lay in my mind like a wide puddle I needed to leap before I could be completely comfortable again.

I heard the shower and soon Brandy came out of the bathroom with a white towel around her torso and using another to dry her hair. I gawked at her still in awe, taken with how she looked so much smaller and girlish without clothes on. But I didn't mind. I really didn't.

Noticing I was awake, she grinned and spun for me in a playful pirouette. "Hey there, tiger. Like my outfit? You better get your ass in the shower."

She pulled me to my feet, kissed me, and danced away when I tried to grab her towel. "Oh, no you don't. What's a girl going to do with a brute like you?"

"As I recall, I think you know exactly what to do."

"Oh, thank you, sir. C'mon now. We need to hit the friendly skies."

The tub was an ancient masterpiece of early nineteenth-century bathing décor. Clawed feet below a huge yellowed porcelain base made my mind wander to the possibilities. Candles, bubble bath, back rubs...I had to force myself to focus on my task.

I let the hot water flow over my head and took my time. A full-force shower was a real luxury when I was used to the alternating cold or scalding hot dribble in the camper's shower. It was either that or a two-dollar shower at the Harbormaster where, ready or not, the water cut off after six minutes. I used to kid Willie that I would tell the guys he had suggested a way that we could each save a dollar by sharing the shower. The look of horror on his face at the threat helped relieve the pain of the punch to my shoulder that quickly followed.

My mind reviewed with wonder the events of last night. Brandy had been so...fun. It was the best description I could come up with. She had taken charge, and I had let her. I shook my head in amazement at the memory of it all. She knew what she wanted and without pretense or games of any kind, she made it happen. We seemed to click. The two of us had simply merged. I said something funny, she laughed. I said something stupid, she came right back with a quick reply that set us both roaring. I chuckled at the way she giggled; she laughed at the sight and sound of my laughter.

And it wasn't just alcohol. Sure, that had helped, loosened us up a little. But we didn't drink that much. We were a couple of lightweights. And then when we weren't talking anymore, the physical give and take was simply a dance of ecstasy. Every way I touched her, she answered with a move or a murmur, guiding me, informing me, encouraging me. Thinking back, I realized that she had made sure to get what she wanted and needed, and then she did the same for me. Unselfishly and honestly, a partnership of passion had formed between us, an understanding of mutual need and desire. We had found relief for a time, a respite from the hidden ache of loneliness carried deep inside.

I was already starting to miss her when I finally shut off the water and grabbed a towel. I glanced in the mirror. That was a mistake. Stupid, I thought to myself. What would Willie say? Letting myself fall so hard for a pretty woman. Willie? Oh, crap. Willie and Brandy? *Jesus Christ, what have I done?* I looked in the mirror again, but images in the shadows from the night before fogged my view. I shook my head violently to clear the cobwebs.

Turning my thoughts to the flight home, I remembered the sunlight through the window. A good sign for flying weather.

"Hey, Brandy," I called from the sink as I combed my hair. "Maybe we can check out Montague Island on our way back. If there're no clouds, we might spot something interesting."

When I didn't get an answer, I finished up at the sink and went to pack my stuff. The bedroom was as empty as a broken promise. She was gone.

I looked around for a moment and noticed her pack was still next to the bed. The towels were on the floor and her clothes were nowhere in sight. I opened the door and looked down the hall, but it was deserted and quiet. No one walking, no one on the stairs at the end of the hall. Had she just gone for coffee?

Back in the room I spotted her purse on the floor and her sunglasses. No self-respecting pilot would go outside on a sunny day without sunglasses. And I'd never seen Brandy outside without them. Maybe the lobby had a coffee pot. Then I saw the note.

Scribbled on the back of a hotel brochure, a large sloppy scrawl read, "Stop looking for us or she's dead." I stood staring at it, frozen in disbelief. I ran to the window and wrestled it open, cursing the old paint and blistered wood frame. Leaning out and craning my neck left and right I saw no one but an old guy walking his dog.

Shit! I fought to stave off the panic building in my chest, but I could hardly breathe. I paced back and forth through the room pulling on my clothes trying to stop my hands from shaking. How did they know where to find us? How did they even know we were looking for them? What the hell was going on? *Anthony.*

This couldn't be happening.

Yes, it was, idiot, pull yourself together. The note was left on the chair by the bed in plain sight. We must have been followed. Or somebody made a call. Whatever. She was gone. Taken against her will.

I grabbed up everything that was ours and ran from the room carrying both packs. There was no one at the front desk. I rang the bell repeatedly, and a teenage girl finally came out of a back office. When I asked if she had seen Brandy leaving with anybody, she just shrugged her shoulders at me and looked confused. I dashed outside and scurried up and down the street, but it was deserted.

I half-ran, half-walked the two miles as fast as I could to Junior's office at the airstrip. I paid no attention to the quaint weather beaten white frame houses that passed on both sides of the streets. Summer flowers were starting to appear in boxes under the windows, but I ignored them. My breath was ragged and my throat was burning when I burst in the office's front door.

Debbie was behind the counter. She looked at me with alarm and listened as I croaked out what had happened.

"I'll call Tom Doogan," she offered. "He's the only cop we got."

"No, Debbie. Don't do that. These guys are dangerous. They might…" I couldn't finish the thought.

I showed her the note. Her eyes grew wide and she sat down in disbelief. "What are you going to do? Nothing?"

"Where's Junior?"

"He just left on a flight to Kayak Island. Heather's out too; she's up near McCarthy."

"Damn it." I stared out the window trying to think. It would be hours before either of them returned.

"Any other airplanes take off out of here this morning?"

"I heard one earlier. More than a half-hour ago. It flew over the house before we came out here, but I never saw it."

That would have been about the right time. "Can I get fuel here, Deb?"

"Sorry, Johnny. We just used our last drop, and the fuel barge doesn't get in until tonight."

I turned back to her. "Okay, look, I'm going to go look for her. You can tell Junior what happened but that's it. Nobody else, and Junior has to keep it to himself too. We can't take any chances. It's Brandy's life we're talking about here."

Debbie looked uncertain but she nodded and watched me nervously as I left and headed for my Cub. Before I put Brandy's pack in the back, I opened it and dug out her camera. The pack smelled of her, and I closed the flap as quickly as I could. Her scent grabbed my gut and twisted it. I hurriedly went about a preflight, reminding myself that it was distractions that killed more pilots in this country than any other hazard. I couldn't let myself get careless.

Hanging the camera around my neck, I started the engine and taxied to the end of the strip. In a few minutes I was airborne climbing over town and Orca Inlet. Hinchinbrook Island lay in front of me and beyond that the high peaks on Montague Island waited in the distance.

Forcing myself to be calm was almost impossible. My thoughts were racing. But the SuperCub trundled along just like always, making about eighty-five knots when my mind wanted to go the speed of sound. The emptiness of the backseat yawned behind me. The weight of Brandy's camera around my neck was the only connection I had left with her. It pulled uncomfortably at me and got in my way when I pulled back on the stick, but I just shifted it to one side and flew on. I reminded myself to pay attention to the instruments, oil pressure, oil temp, fuel, airspeed, altitude. All the stuff that would keep me in the air.

I had to get her back. Damn it. Of all the goddamn worthless bad luck. Why had I agreed to take her along? Why wouldn't she listen? Shit. Not only had I lost Willie's plane, now I'd lost his daughter too.

I climbed to five thousand feet. That slowed the Cub even more, the tedious pace ground at me. *Take it easy, don't push the river, it flows by itself.* I remembered the old saying from somewhere.

I wasn't going to take any chances. If I stumbled on their camp flying low, they would recognize my tail number and take it out on Brandy. I settled for the only thing I could do.

The long skinny island lay across the water in front of me in a line running north to south. Flying down the east shoreline I waited until I was over the area Heather had told me about the night before. Setting the camera on full zoom, I leaned out the open side window and took several shots as the terrain passed below. I tried to hold the camera steady but the buffeting wind made it difficult. Doubtful that I got anything that would be useful, I pulled the window closed and glanced up at the fuel vials. They were getting low. Gritting my teeth, I stared down at the hillsides and meadows below one last time and then turned reluctantly for Seward. I needed fuel and I needed help.

Flying along I reviewed the shots on the back of the camera and pulled in on them as close as possible with the zoom. The vibration in the plane and the bright sunlight made it hard to see. I wasn't sure if I was seeing anything or not in the photos, but there plainly was an old airstrip along a rough road next to Bench River. Commercial logging had stopped there a long time ago, but some run down cabins and sheds had been left behind. No one flew in there anymore that I knew about. The only decent cabins for tourist drop-offs were along the beaches miles away, and they had their own landing areas available at low tide.

The rest of the way back I worried about Brandy. I didn't know if she was okay or not. I hadn't heard any struggle when they took her, so they must have used a weapon or something to scare her into shutting up. How long had I been in the shower? Six or seven minutes? Certainly long enough for them to get in, stick a gun in her face, and pull her out the door. Down the stairs and out the door into a vehicle before I even got the soap out of my eyes.

Who the hell were these people? It had to be Anthony and the other guy I had barely seen. *Why didn't they jump me in the shower when they had a perfect chance? What are they doing to her now?* I felt sick.

CHAPTER 22

"Willie, we gotta talk." I sat beside his bed and watched the sheet rise and fall slowly with his breathing. The strong smell of disinfectant filled my nostrils.

I gathered my thoughts and leaned forward. It felt strange talking to a silent shape but I had to get this out. I reached out with one hand to play with the sheet while I spoke. My other hand stroked my beard nervously.

"Willie, listen, man. We're in some trouble here, you know? I don't know how to tell you this, but Brandy's been, uh, taken. We were over in Cordova trying to find your plane, and I think the same people that jumped us kidnapped her to make us stop searching. Now I don't know what the hell to do."

I sat quietly for a minute and stared out the door of his room. The woman at the nurses' station was writing in charts and putting them in slots on the wall behind her.

This would be the tough part. I started to talk again and felt my tongue getting thick.

"And, uh, Willie? There's something else too. I didn't mean to sleep with her, man. I really didn't. It just happened. She's very, uh, she's just very friendly. No, I don't mean like friendly with everyone. She's not like that. Not at all. In fact we didn't even like each other at first, but we're over in Cordova and we had dinner with Junior and Debbie. Remember them? Yeah, they're doing fine and all, but…. Anyhow, I, uh, one thing led to another, and we were getting close. And then it was probably too many beers. You know how that is, you know?"

I looked at him, but only saw the breathing.

"I just thought you should know."

I stood up and turned to go, but then staring at my shoes, I thought of something else. I didn't want to say it, and my throat tried to seize up. I pressed on anyhow. "And, uh, one more thing, Willie. We need you back here. I mean I need you. I'm drowning here, man. I don't know what to do by myself with all this."

I walked to the door.

"J-Johnny?"

I whipped around in surprise.

"Willie?" I leaned over his bed and looked down at him. His eyes were fluttering and his head was rolling back and forth. He struggled to open his eyes and squinted, trying to bring me into view.

"Have I been strange lately, Johnny?"

I couldn't believe he was awake.

"Well, you've been much more horizontal than usual lately. But otherwise, I dunno. How are you doing, man?"

I took hold of his arm and smiled at him. Then I felt the smile drain from my face. "How long you been awake, Willie?"

"What? What do you mean?" He looked around, a bewildered expression in his eyes. He tried to sit up and then he saw the cast on his foot.

"Holy crap, what happened to me?" He looked at me blinking his eyes and I watched the confusion twist his features into a startled gaze. He reached up, felt the bandage on his head and collapsed back on the pillow.

"Holy crap, did they get away?" He reached over and grabbed my arm. "The Cub, did they get the SuperCub?" He was remembering as if it had happened hours ago instead of a week.

I nodded my head with a grim look and sat down beside him again. He rolled his eyes back and brought both hands up to cover his face, groaning in misery.

"Yeah, Willie. We're working on it, but there's a lot of stuff you need to hear about. Are you ready?"

He just stared at me in shock. His blank expression had me worried. The nurse came in then.

"Well, well, Mister Maxwell. Welcome back to the world. How are we feeling?"

Willie continued his fixed stare, but then he looked at her, still too dazed to answer. He worked his mouth and coughed, but no words would come.

"You'll have to leave, I'm afraid," she said looking at me as she took Willie's pulse. "I need to call the doctor."

"Has he been awake before now?" I asked her.

She shook her head paying attention to the pulse. She reached for a blood pressure cuff and started fastening it around Willie's arm.

"Willie, I'll be back as soon as they let me." As I left the room I motioned with my finger at the nurse and waited outside the door. When she finished the blood pressure and came out of the room, I whispered to her as quietly as I could.

"Can people in comas hear stuff?"

She gave me a look. "Oh, yes. Or so I've been told, anyhow. I think it's time you left now."

I gave a guilty glance in Willie's direction. "When can I visit again?"

"Now that he's awake we have a lot of procedures to do. It'll be several hours. Now if you don't mind…."

I got the message. I turned and left. On my way to the airport, I called Mitch and told him what had happened.

"Can you get into Montague with your boat?"

"Damn, Johnny. I've been over there with a boat and there's beaches I can land on easy enough on the south end. But it takes a while to get there."

"How long?"

"At least three hours depending on winds and currents. What are you planning to do?"

"I don't know. I don't know if I can do anything. These guys might be capable of anything. To come in a hotel room like that and kidnap somebody in broad daylight. Jesus. It's scared the crap out of me, Mitch."

"Yeah, no kidding. Don't you think the cops need to take over now?"

"No, goddamn it. Everybody wants the cops to do this, but it's not going to work that way. And I can't sit around waiting while they take their time getting organized."

"Well, let me know what I can do, Johnny. I've got charter work going on, but let me know, okay?"

"Thanks, Mitch. I'll call you."

I spent the day studying maps of Montague Island and reviewing everything I knew about the place. I almost forgot the pictures I had taken. I moved them from the camera to my laptop and studied what I had. The larger screen and steady platform made it a lot easier to analyze. I had taken twelve shots from the airplane that morning but half were just fuzzy blurs.

The others were workable and showed various angles of the old loggers' airstrip. A small valley widened in the middle of the island in a small bowl formed by high mountains on three sides. An old dirt road and wide flat area that looked like a gravel bed looked like a possible landing place. But only for a SuperCub. Any larger plane wouldn't have enough distance to get stopped. Not before hitting big rocks and trees.

I searched the treelines in all the pictures at maximum zoom until my eyes burned. There was one spot that looked like a possibility. I thought I could see a tarp-covered structure of some kind in the trees. It wasn't a blue tarp though; it was brownish green, almost the same color as the trees around it. And it looked big enough to hide an airplane.

If that was their camp they had picked a good spot. It was in an area no one visited anymore. Not since the logging operation quit.

I called Mitch again. "Hey, man, tell me what you know about Montague. These assholes might be hiding out there somewhere."

"Well, the attraction of Montague Island is the beaches. Especially on the east side. It's over sixty miles long and totally exposed to the Gulf of Alaska. That beach catches all the wind and currents for thousands of miles across the Pacific. Dumps all kind of stuff on the beach. Every new storm sends more. Driftwood of all kinds and sizes, huge logs, trash, and all kinds of things dropped overboard from boats. Not to mention shipwrecks. Stuff collects there from all over."

"So beachcombers hang out there? What's the big deal?"

"Japanese glass floats. Out of fishing nets. That's one of the big prizes. They're made out of glass. Dark green, blue and red anywhere from handheld to basketball size. You've seen them. They've got some on the wall at the Yukon."

"Yeah, I've been there once or twice."

"Right, smartass. But Montague has another reputation too. It's cursed."

"Cursed? What do you mean?"

"Well, bad weather for one. It's the only high ground across a thousand miles of ocean. All that moist air lifts on Montague's mountains and forms thick clouds whenever the conditions are right. And the conditions are right most of the time."

I knew that from experience. Almost every time I flew within view of the big island, the mountaintops were obscured by clouds. Fog was another frequent visitor. Just like it had trapped us the other night on Smith Island, it crept over Montague Island in frequent swift assaults.

"Another thing, Johnny. The island has a reputation for ill-tempered animals, namely grizzly bears. And not from a natural habitat either. No, Montague Island was used for years as a penal colony for misbehaving bears that had been relocated from Anchorage and other communities. After a second offense of raiding dumpsters and trash cans, they were tranquilized and taken by helicopter out there. Some of the bears escaped by swimming for miles. But plenty remained."

"Doesn't sound like a good place to go camping." But it would make a good hiding place for bad guys, I thought. "What about airplanes out there?"

"That's where the curse comes in. You've heard of Harvey Nelson. His outfit operated out of Seward for years taking hunters to Montague. He used the airstrips along the beach and took folks to the Forest Service rental cabins. Harvey always said, 'Watch out for Montague, I've had six wrecks out there. That island eats airplanes.'"

"Yeah, I've heard that one. Lots of fog out there. Two of his planes took off in fog one time, almost zero visibility. Before they could get enough altitude to break through, one of them turned the wrong direction and hit a mountain. Killed himself and two passengers. Idiots. Phil won't take people out there anymore. Says it's not worth the risk."

"Yup, I heard that too. So you think these guys are out there? You think they have Brandy out there?"

"I don't know. Did you hear Willie woke up? Want to meet me there when the docs are finished?"

"No, I can't. I've got a sightseeing charter."

"Okay, I'll catch up with you tonight."

Back at the hospital Willie was looking much better. At least he was sitting up. Now that he could talk, the doctor decided he didn't need the collar anymore and his head bandage was smaller too. The guy almost looked normal.

"Dude, what's happening?"

He gave me a crooked smile and tossed his hands with a helpless gesture.

"A week? I've been here a goddamned week? Laying here like a motherfucking gutted halibut. Shit." He wasn't smiling anymore, but he sure sounded normal.

"It's great to have you back, man, but I've got bad news."

"Did you say something about Brandy this morning?"

"Yeah, she's missing. The same people that grabbed your Cub, I think."

"Holy crap. I haven't talked to her in years. Then she gives me a couple days notice that she's coming up."

He stared at me waiting for me to say more. I didn't want to overload him, but I told him the whole story. Well, not the whole story. I decided to leave out some of the details. With him staring at me like that, I just couldn't bring myself to confess any intimacies again.

"So you think the plane's on Montague? And Brandy is too?"

"It's the only lead I've got. I called around this morning and no one knew of any operation using that old logger's strip by Beach River."

"I went in there once years ago, and it's short. Almost cracked up." He was giving me that look. The hard look, the warning look. The look that would help me if I was smart enough to listen. "Look, Johnny, we've got to find Brandy, but I really need to get the plane back too."

Something in his tone made me study his face closely.

"Yeah?"

"Yeah, listen." He looked out in the hallway and motioned me closer. "There was a duffel bag of mine in the back of the plane. You've probably seen it around. I've had it for years."

"That old Army one? Yeah. What about it?"

He looked uncomfortable. "There's important stuff in there. I got to get it back."

I frowned at him. "I have been trying to find the plane, but look where it got me. Maybe we should just turn the whole damn thing over to the cops."

"No." His eyes went wide. He grabbed my arm and squeezed hard. "You don't understand. We gotta get it back fast. My whole life's in there."

I was puzzled. But I didn't have a chance to ask any more about it. The doctor walked in with the nurse and a cart of equipment. They looked at me expectantly as the nurse pulled the privacy curtain between Willie and me. I left, wondering what the hell Willie was trying to say.

Driving back to the airport, I thought about what he'd told me. I knew he had some collections of stuff. Coins, books, even some old walrus ivory he had been hoarding for years. He always talked about how valuable it all was. I didn't know he had them stashed in the plane or if that was even what he was talking about.

As eccentric as he was, I didn't put it past him to get paranoid and hide his collections in the plane. Now he was obsessing about it. And not thinking straight yet. After the head injury and all.

Still, I was relieved to see Willie doing better. All of a sudden I didn't feel so lonely. Even if he was in a hospital bed, at least I had my partner back.

But hell, now I had another problem. Goddamn Willie and his stupid duffel bag. We lost his airplane and we lost his daughter. Now I gotta worry about a stupid coin collection? Shit. No wonder Brandy was estranged from the guy. He had a weird sense of priorities.

Thinking about Brandy twisted my gut again. I didn't want to think about her. What was I going to do? Willie would be in the hospital a while longer, I guessed. I needed help. I was way out of my league., but there was no way I was going to grovel in front of the damn cops and submit to their arrogance. I couldn't stand the thought of them pushing me out of the way and taking over the case. But the idea of taking these guys on by myself made my gut flutter.

I checked the sun and my watch. Late afternoon but still lots of daylight left. And getting more everyday. It would build like this until summer solstice when there would only be an hour or so of darkness. Then slowly the days would start to shorten again. I felt the need to do something. It was eating at me. Montague Island was calling me. A low whisper from the back of my skull, it wouldn't leave me alone.

I thought about driving to the Yukon. Drown the voice with beer. Right. That impulse lasted about half a millisecond. I couldn't even imagine sitting in the bar while Brandy was tied up somewhere wondering if she would live to see another day. A twist in my gut hit me again. I couldn't even think about drinking a beer. Just the idea of it brought me to edge of puking.

Passing the Safeway reminded me that I hadn't eaten all day. I pulled in and bought a sandwich and a cup of coffee. I moved fast hoping to avoid anyone I knew. I didn't need anything slowing me down. I was starting to get an idea. The food helped. Especially the caffeine.

If I could get somebody to go with me, I wanted to fly out to Montague while there was still some light. I drove down the highway juggling the coffee and the sandwich and pulled out my cell phone to call Hondo. It was times like these when I dreamed of an automatic transmission. A huge RV whizzed past spraying my windshield with tiny pieces of gravel. I almost dropped the coffee in my lap while I listened to Hondo's phone ring and ring with no answer.

When I got to the airport I fired up the laptop again and reviewed the pictures I'd taken of the island. I scoured my sectional chart, the Alaska atlas I had, and I even brought up Google Earth to eyeball the area with the logger's airstrip.

I wished I had a picture of that asshole, Anthony Baxter. The sonofabitch was due for some payback. Sure he had me intimidated, but he couldn't be that smart. Stupid jerk. Coming up here and ripping off fellow pilots. Stab-in-the-back bastard. So maybe I couldn't beat him down like Mike Hammer or Dirk Pitt, but I'll bet I could out maneuver him. Either that or die trying. It was coming down to that. I needed to make something happen even if it cost me some pain. I'd outsmarted plenty of these dipshits before. Why not now?

Then I remembered the pictures Brandy and I had lifted in Soldotna. Where were they? I last remembered them being in her rental car. Standing up and looking out the office window, her car was still parked where she left it before the Cordova trip. I reached in a desk drawer and took out the handy slim jim I kept there. The car door was locked but it didn't matter. In two minutes I had the pictures and was back in the office spreading them out over my desk.

Baxter's familiar face looked up at me in several of the shots. I studied the backgrounds for any clues. One caught my attention. He was standing at the tail of an airplane with trees and a ridgeline behind him. Something about that hillside looked familiar.

Jumping back and forth between that shot and the ones I had on the laptop, I finally found it. In that picture of Anthony the ridgeline west of the airstrip on Montague had an odd rock formation that formed a shape like a capital L. The rocks were whitish colored, probably from lichens and moss dried in the sunlight. One of the images on my laptop had the identical rocks on a hillside. They had to be the same ones.

I sat back and stared at the opposite wall of the office. My mind was spinning. This was it. This was the proof I needed. Anthony Baxter standing by an airplane on the airstrip on Montague Island. Slap me stupid if that wasn't the hideout we'd been looking for.

I left the office and ran to the hangar. The entry door did its usual sticking routine, and I had to wrestle with it for a second before it jerked open with a loud screech. Raw metal scraping concrete was an ugly combination. Rock music blared from the speaker system set up in the office. I spotted Scooter on his back underneath an airplane. Nuts and bolts and pieces of muffler lay all around him on the floor next to an oily drip pan.

"Scooter, what are you doing?"

He rolled out from under the plane, metal wheels squeaking. His stocky body filled the protesting dolly underneath him. His red ponytail dragged on the floor and trailed through a puddle of oil leaving a snail like slime behind him. While he was rolling, he turned his head to locate me and the corner wheel of the dolly rolled over the ponytail.

"Aw, shit." He grappled with his hair and the dolly for a minute trying to free himself, eyes blinking frantically. Rolling to his hands and knees, he couldn't get the hair loose. Finally he picked up the dolly in his arms and stood up. He turned toward me, holding his head at an odd angle with the dolly still tangled in his hair, the ponytail dripping oil on the front of his shirt.

"Hey, Johnny. What can I do for ya?" Blink, blink, grimace.

"Here, I can help you with that, Scootie." I grabbed a pair of scissors from a red rolling tool box and reached for the ponytail.

He backed away in a horrified rush clutching the dolly tighter to his chest. The tighter his grip, the more he pulled his head sideways until he had to turn ninety degrees to the left to keep me in view.

"Relax, Scoot. Look, I'm in a hurry here. You seen Hondo?"

"No, man. I ain't seen him. This is his plane here. I'm doing an annual on it, but he ain't been around lately."

I watched him tugging on the dolly while he was talking. The wheel finally came loose taking a sizeable clump of red kinky hair with it.

"Scooter, you got a gun?"

"Uh, yeah, got a forty-four under the seat in my pickup. You need it?"

"You up for an airplane ride?"

"Sure, always, Johnny. Where we going?" He wiped his hands on the rag hanging from his back pocket and stared at me like an Irish setter that was just promised a ride in the country. His tattered coveralls and an oil smear under his right eye made him look like a battered fullback lining up for a third and long.

"How many hours you got now?" I motioned for him to follow me.

"Just the fourteen I done with you."

I'd been teaching Scooter to fly over the past year when he could scrape together money for fuel. I knew I was going to miss Brandy's flying skill in the backseat, but what the hell. We were going to have to make do.

"Okay, grab your gun and some survival stuff and meet me at the fuel pumps. I gotta make some calls and get my gear. We're going to Montague."

"No shit? Cool." He started toward his truck. "Hey, Johnny, why do we need a gun?"

"Bears, Scooter. They got bears out there. Just in case, you know."

I jogged to the office and started getting the plane ready. The sun was still plenty high, but I knew I was pushing it. I put in a call to Mitch's number, but all I got was voicemail. Damn it. I left a message with a quick rundown of my plan and told him I'd be back by dark. As an afterthought I told him I'd have the marine radio with me. I checked the survival bag in the plane to be sure the batteries were good.

With Scooter in the back and full fuel tanks, the Cub felt heavy, but we lifted off without hesitation. I pointed her nose to the east and before I turned through the notch, I took a backward glance at Seward. Evening shadows were starting to creep across town. The sun was partly blocked by Mount Marathon, and the hospital and the Yukon were already in the shade.

CHAPTER 23

I followed my usual route over Day Harbor and the bays along the south shoreline until I crossed Port Bainbridge. Chenega village came into view and I used the hatchery below to make my turn to the right. The map told me that would line us up with Beach River on Montague Island.

Looking out the right side window, I double checked that the twelve gauge was still strapped into its scabbard. At the same time I noticed that way out on the gulf, a low layer of fog lay right on top of the water. Probably moving slowly our way. I hoped it wasn't going to cause us a problem.

Heading due east with the sun behind me, I climbed to five thousand feet to cross the wide expanse of water between Latouche Island passing beneath us and Montague straight ahead. The strong side lighting from the sun outlined the ridgeline that I knew led down to the airstrip, our destination. When we were within safe gliding distance of the shoreline I chopped the throttle and let her descend steeply for the ridge.

Thick cumulus clouds were bunching up along the mountains just to the north, but the way ahead was clear. If I hadn't been so focused on the task ahead, I would admired their beauty for a minute. Puffy cotton clumps sat on the high mountain peaks like Cool Whip on a dangerous sundae.

"Hey, Johnny. It's getting late, ain't it?" Scooter's voice sounded a little concerned in my headphones.

"No sweat, Scooter. I figure we just cruise around over here for a while. See if we can spot Willie's airplane, and then head for home. No big deal." I tried to sound calm and light. I didn't need Scooter getting freaky on me.

"Okay, Johnny. It's not a problem anyhow. I brought food and some extra clothes just in case."

"You're a good man, Charley Brown."

"Survival gear. Just like you taught me, Mister Flight Instructor."

So Scooter wasn't the sharpest spike in my bed of nails, but he was doing alright. It was good to be reminded that somebody looked up to me. I wished I felt more deserving. If people really knew what a wuss I was sometimes.

I wished I had Hondo and his powerhouse of muscle and aggression with me, but I was starting to feel better about Scooter. I thought about my own survival stuff and mentally reviewed its contents. Rain gear, food, signal mirror, hatchet, matches, bug juice, fishing stuff, et cetera, et cetera. Wished I had a satellite phone but couldn't afford that luxury. Besides, the pack was straining at its seams already. Without any room in it for the marine radio I'd stuffed it in my coat pocket. I could feel its bulk pressing into my hip where it was jammed against the cabin door.

I let the plane slide over the top of the ridge noticing how smooth the hillsides were below us. Almost immediately we were over thick trees. The high timber was out of reach of the hungry chainsaws that had ravaged all the lower slopes nearby. The open valley along Beach River lay in front of us and I spotted the airstrip down to our left. Moving out to the right slightly I set up a turn just above the treetops and flew along the valley walls until we crossed the beach and were back over the ocean. Then I banked and headed back toward the strip. I hadn't seen anything suspicious yet, but I was in the wrong place to look for that dark green tarp.

That's when the first bullet struck. Like driving over an unseen speed bump or hitting a bird in flight, the whole plane jolted. The bullet must have hit the carburetor. I immediately smelled gasoline, and the engine stopped.

"Oh, shit." I wished I hadn't said that out loud, but Scooter knew there was a problem.

"What happened?" His voice pitched up and I could feel him pull against the back of my seat as he tried to see ahead.

"We're going down, Scooter. Get ready."

"What? No. Not out here. Holy Christ."

I had to ignore him. Tundra tires make for drag. Tons of drag. We were only a couple hundred feet high and dropping fast. I racked the throttle back and forth. Nothing. I switched fuel tanks and slammed the mixture all the way in just out of habit. Still nothing.

Peering ahead I could see the rough logger's road right in front of us and just beyond, the airstrip. Could I reach it?

I set up to land straight ahead. There wasn't anything to the left or right within range. Tall trees and big rocks were everywhere. My only option was forward. I glanced at the airspeed indicator. My eyes bugged when I saw how slow we were getting.

Don't stall, don't freaking stall. The ground was rushing up at us now, and we sank below the tops of the trees. All the horror stories flooded my head. The ones about SuperCubs stalling and turning on their backs and crashing nose first. I pushed the stick forward and tried to keep the wings level. The prop kept turning but there was no power to save my ass whatsoever. The engine was just a big dead weight now, and if I didn't get us landed and stopped it was going to be sitting in my lap in about thirty seconds.

The river was right beside us. Side channels and dry ditches filled with big rocks crossed in front, one after another. I fixed my eyes on a place in the shadows ahead just past an ugly trench. *Damn, we were moving fast.* That's a good way to avoid the stall but a really bad way to meet rough ground.

North To Disaster

I took a deep breath and reached down for the flap handle. Pull it too soon and we were dead. Wait too long and we'd never slow down enough to stop before we hit the trees looming above us. We were headed for the final ditch just short of the strip. I tried not to picture the Cub crushed nose first against its wall.

Forcing myself to keep a light hold on the stick I milked it for every last inch of terrain I could cross. Tweaking it to pitch up slightly and keep some altitude. Then relaxing it forward to keep from stalling. They tell you in training, Don't try to stretch the glide. Yeah, well, screw that. If there was ever an exception, this was it. If we went into that ditch, we were dead. It would be just like a head on collision. Our only prayer was to stretch just beyond the edge of the ditch, so the big tires could flop down on flat land.

With less than twenty feet to go, I yelled over the intercom. *"Hold on."* Scooter didn't answer. I tried not to picture his bright red hairy face straining behind me, eyes bulging with panic.

At the last second, I pulled up hard on the Johnson bar to get the flaps down. We slowed and lifted, and I thought we just might clear the ditch. I had to push forward on the stick again to keep from pitching up too much. The ground was right there.

You know that moment everybody talks about? The one right before you think you're gonna die? Where they say your life passes before you? Like a wild instant replay at super warp speed. You supposed to see all the important events and all the important people from your whole life.

What a bunch of shit. All that was going through my mind was one thought.

"Get this motherfucker on the ground."

All I could see were big rocks and the edge of the deep trench right where we were going to hit. I hauled back on the stick for all I was worth.

Momentarily, for just a flash, I remember thinking, this is it. The end of everything. I wondered how long I would feel the painful impact of the jagged rock headed for my face. Then my mind went blank. I forgot about everything else.

Forgot that my beautiful airplane, my magic flying carpet, my livelihood, my ticket to blue skies over wilderness paradise was about to become a wretched pile of twisted metal and torn cloth.

That last pull on the stick grabbed us a little altitude. Very little. The jagged rock passed just below the cowling. For a fraction of a nanosecond I thought we were going to make it. I thought we might clear the ditch and land normally on the flat graveled surface in front of us. Just like so many other landings over so many years. Not all of them had been pretty. Some had banged down a little too hard. But mostly I made nice landings. For that split second I fantasized a beautiful, smooth end to the terror.

I was wrong.

The tires hit the edge of the ditch. The landing gear crumpled with a sickening crunch and the nose slammed onto the airstrip like slapping a counter top with a flat hand. The cabin of the plane rose into the air like the small kid on a teeter totter with an evil bully on the other end. We were stopped cold, hanging in mid-air pinned by the propeller whose turning blades crumpled and pretzeled against the ground. But the tail hadn't run out of energy yet. She wanted to keep flying. Or at least keep moving. So she did, spinning us in a half circle while the momentum slid us forward ten or twenty yards on the gravel. The grinding, screeching metal and fabric tearing underneath the fuselage assaulted my ears.

Then all sound stopped. I wondered if I was dead.

"Damn, man." Scooter's voice sounded strange until I realized my headphones had been thrown off my head. The impact had blasted open the side door and I could see the river rushing past just past the wingtip that was resting on the ground. The fiberglass wingtips were in shreds.

The river was close enough I could hear the soft rushing roar of the water bubbling along its rocky path to the sea. My hands hurt. So did my shins. I looked down and saw blood seeping through the front of my jeans. I moved my legs and feet carefully. They weren't broken, but my left hand hurt like a bitch. I clenched my fist repeatedly thinking I must have been holding the flap handle in a death grip when we hit.

I twisted around to look at Scooter. His eyes were bulging and blinking, but he looked alright.

"You okay, Scooter?"

"Yeah, I think so."

I smelled fuel. It must have been seeping from the damaged engine underneath us. The *hot* damaged engine. I thought about the scraping metal on rock and the potential for sparks.

"We got to get out of here." I kicked the battered door open and unfastened my seat belt. The right tundra tire was pushed up beside the cabin almost blocking the door, but I was able to crawl out through the space between the tire and the wing. Looking in at Scooter I wondered if the big man was going to be able to get through the small opening.

While he worked at getting loose from his seatbelt I walked around and looked at the plane. The propeller was completely twisted and one side was curled under the plane. The tubing of the landing gear was bent double, but the tires looked amazingly fit. Still inflated and round, their fat doughnut shapes were only scuffed with dirt on their sides. An idle thought passed through my head to write a thank you note to the manufacturer. The cushion-like tires had acted like air bags, saving our lives.

The fuel leak wasn't serious, and I was surprised to see that the wings looked alright and so did most of the tail section. When I got back around to Scooter he was trying to come out of the cabin head first.

"Don't worry," I said to him. "I don't think we're going to catch on fire. Hey, hand me my pack, will ya?"

"How's the plane look, Johnny?"

"Well, I don't think we're gonna fly it out of here."

"No shit?"

"Yeah, but I don't even think it'll cost that much to repair." Hell, I was feeling happy that we'd survived the crash.

I bent over to look under the cowling where the fuel was dribbling out of the engine. That's when the second bullet hit us.

The terror of the landing had completely wiped my brain clean of why we were here in the first place. I must have been in some kind of shock. I ducked and tried to look down the valley, struggling to remember. Something automatic took over and I dropped flat and spread out on the gravel.

"*Get out of there, Scooter. We got trouble.*"

When I didn't hear any response, I looked up. Scooter's dead face stared back at me. He wasn't blinking anymore. A huge hole in the middle of his forehead pumped blood down his face. His body hung in the opening with one arm dangling limp beside him.

My legs turned to stone. My hands fluttered to my mouth. I felt an uncontrollable urge to scream. I wanted to run but my legs wouldn't move.

My eyes went frantic. Everywhere I looked my vision was jerking around like a bad movie projector. I looked back down the valley. Still nothing. Rising up just slightly I looked down the airstrip to the spruce trees on the far end. They stood five hundred feet away, a dark hillside behind them climbed to higher ground where clouds were beginning to creep down the mountain side.

I scurried on my belly to the back of the plane scraping my palms on the rocky ground. When I had the body of the plane between me and where I guessed the shots were coming from, I ran.

Fixing my eyes on those trees I gritted my teeth against the pain in my legs. I pushed myself forward, gasping for air and fighting past the ache in my neck and hands. Every second I could feel a bullet in flight chasing me, flying down the runway behind me. Targeted at the back of my skull, I could see it screaming in, tracking me like a smart bomb on short final. I wondered if I would feel the impact or if the end would just happen, followed by the big empty.

If it was going to happen I wanted the head shot. In the back would just wound me. Probably fatally, but not before a long cold, agonizing ordeal of slow death in an Alaskan rain shower, flat on my back and helpless to stop the insidious creep of death's steely grip choking off my life in its final whimper.

Automatic movements took over again. I found myself zig-zagging and ducking randomly right and left as I stumbled over the uneven field. Clumps of grass and stumps reached up to grab at me in a cruel effort to give my invisible attacker a clean shot. But no shots came. Five hundred feet felt like five hundred miles, and when I reached the trees, I collapsed on the ground and spat dead leaves out of my mouth, gasping for breath.

I crawled then, deeper into the trees and brush. Instead of blocking my way and sticking my fingers with their spines, the devil's club had become my friend. The further I crawled the safer I felt. That's if sheer panic and terror can possibly feel safer than something else.

I didn't stop until I was invisible. So buried under leaves and deadfall my attacker would have to step on me to get another shot. I concentrated on slowing my breath. Tried to get my wits together. How was I going to get myself out of this shit?

I surveyed my location. I was about thirty yards into the treeline from the airstrip in thick brush. The mountain side rose above me and the first wall of its lowest ridge started only ten yards away. To the left the ridge flattened in the direction of the river. I remembered seeing from the air how the water curled against the side of the steep embankment next to the clump of forest where I was huddled.

There was no escape to the right. The walls of the canyon blocked me in that direction unless I made an almost vertical climb. The thought of that made me shudder. Even if I could climb like a gecko and avoid breaking my neck in a fall, the shooter would have me exposed.

What the hell was I doing here? What had I stumbled into? Here I was in the middle of Prince William Sound on freaking Montague Island. Night was coming on. Clouds were building above me. It felt like rain would start any minute. And somebody was trying to kill me?

My thoughts jumped back to Scooter. Why was he killed? He didn't have anything to do with any of this. Unlucky bastard. Goddamn it, that was my fault. Bringing him all the way out here. And why?

My stomach turned sick again. My Cub. The last sight I had of her crumpled in the dirt came back in stark detail. I had no money for repairs that bad. No airplane, no income. And no way to get off this island.

Stupid, so stupid. Damn it. I balled my fist and started to bang my forehead, but the pain from just clenching it cancelled that idea.

I looked down and rubbed the sore places on my shins. I pulled up my pants legs one at a time where the blood was seeping through. I had identical bloody dents on the fronts of both shins. The impact had thrown my legs up under the instrument panel. The dents were perfect impressions of the metal edge. If our speed had been any faster I'm sure both legs would have broken.

The other pains were in my hands. The left one was the worst. The momentum at impact must have slammed it straight down from where I was holding the flap handle. My right hand had been holding the stick and it probably gave some when we hit, so it wasn't as bad. At least I could make a fist with it.

Then I heard a metallic sound. Someone was at the plane. I couldn't see in that direction, and I wasn't about to stand up and take a look. Someone was kicking at the plane. I knew it wasn't Scooter.

"*Hey, Wainwright.*"

I froze.

"Wainwright, Jonathan? P.O. Box 4993, Seward, Alaska." The voice calling me out sounded familiar, but nobody called me Jonathan. The sonofabitch was reading the SuperCub's registration. I kept it in the pouch on the back of my seat.

"Nice SuperCub you used to have here, asshole."

Used to have?

"You need to come out now, man. If you ever want to see her fly again, that is."

There was no way I was answering. Huddled under all that brush, I could feel him listening. Trying to pick up any sound that would give him a clue. Bits of leaves chafed inside the neck of my shirt, and my legs ached. The musty smell of soggy moss and decay drifted up my nose.

"Nice shotgun you got here. The dead guy's got a nice gun too. Too bad he ain't gonna need it no more."

I thought about my survival gear. Everything was in the plane. When I ran I left it all behind. Rain jacket, food, water, guns, everything.

The voice was Anthony's. I was certain of it. He could tell I didn't have the stuff I needed. But he probably wasn't sure that I didn't have a hand gun with me. He was a good shot with the rifle he'd used on Scooter. No question about that, but he wasn't about to let me take a shot at him. He was out in the open by the plane, but there was no way I could get to him across the flat expanse of the airstrip without giving him a clear shot.

"*You need to come out of there now, asshole.*" His voice pitched up and I remembered that's exactly how he sounded the night he stole Willie's airplane. Pissed off to the max. Enraged that someone would screw with him.

What was it he had screamed over and over that night?

"*You couldn't leave me alone, could you? You goddamn idiot. I just want to be left alone out here. Give me a fucking break. But no. Not you. You gotta play Mister Hero. Who the hell do you think you are?*" His voice was getting closer. He was working his way toward my hiding place.

"*Well, you can kiss your airplane goodbye, unless you come out right fucking now.*"

More silence, more listening from closer now. I tried not to breathe. There was no way he was going to come into the dark part of these woods and start kicking every clump of leaves. If I could wait him out, maybe he'd leave and give me the chance I needed.

"*What are you worried about? I ain't gonna do nothing to you.*" He laughed. A high pitched bitter cackle. The kind you hear at the bar around closing time. Just before a fight breaks out.

He was walking the edge of the wood line. I could feel him peering into the gloomy thicket stepping carefully and listening. He didn't need to shout anymore. He was close enough to hear the smallest sound. He shouted anyhow.

"*Okay, Jonathan Wainwright. Maybe you don't care about your airplane, but we got your lady too.*"

He let that sink in for a minute. It occurred to me that Brandy must be nearby, but not that close nearby. Or he'd be dragging her along, making her scream. Then I'd have no choice.

"*Yeah, she's real pretty too ... and soft.*" He sneered those last words letting them sink in for full effect.

I closed my eyes and tried to squeeze out the images flashing through my mind. Make it stop, make this madness stop.

"*Now we got us a situation here, don't we? What are we going to about this little mess you created, asshole? Huh? What are we going to do about this?*"

I created? I wanted to shout back. No, you're the asshole.

His voice was moving away now. He was walking the edge of the airstrip, moving toward the river. He might have been thinking I wasn't in the woods after all. Maybe I had managed to slip over that direction somehow. I wish. The river was my only way out of here.

I heard the crackle of a hand held radio and muffled words.

"*Yeah, Lance. Get up here and bring the bitch with you. He's hiding somewhere around here. I'm at the far end of the airstrip. Hurry up.*"

There was a static filled answer, but I couldn't make it out.

"*I know it's a long way. Do it anyhow.*" Anthony spat the words into the radio. His voice was getting louder again. He must have made it to the river and seeing no sign of me was started back.

I tried desperately to think of something I could do, anything. If he brought Brandy up here, there was no way I could stay hidden. My only chance, our only chance was to get away. If I surrendered, I knew he'd kill us both. He'd already murdered Scooter in cold blood. If I gave up, pretty soon all three of us would be hidden under the dirt. It wouldn't take them long to dispose of and hide the pieces of the airplane either. We might not ever be found.

No, I had to get away. And I had to do it before he got Brandy up here. I was guessing she was down near the beach where I had seen that green tarp. It would take a while to get here, but not that long.

I strained my ears to pick up any sound of Anthony. I thought I heard his foot steps moving slowly and carefully the other way. Along the tree line but toward the hillside the opposite way from the river. I started to crawl.

If I could get on the river bank and its gravel bar, maybe I could work my way upstream and put distance between us. Low crawling careful and slow I stopped every minute to listen.

Then I heard his voice again. Angry. *"Where the hell are you?"*

It didn't seem like he was talking to me. Something about his tone was different. Sure enough, I heard the static from his radio again. The answer must have thrown him into a rage.

"I don't care if it's gonna rain. Get your stupid ass up here now. You think you're gonna melt?"

He was far enough away that I thought I could stand up. Moving in a half crouch I worked my way closer and closer to the edge of the woods where it met the river. Making sure to step over every single stick and branch was slow hard work, but finally I could see a brighter background where the trees ended.

I peered out and stared down at the river where it moved toward the airstrip. There was no one in sight as far as I could see. I dreaded seeing Brandy in the hands of some guy with a gun. Then I'd be finished.

I studied my position. I was standing on a river bank about three feet high. A six foot bed of gravel separated me from the river. The water ran by in a rush, cutting a path twenty or thirty yards wide. There was no way to wade across it. It looked to be at least four or five feet deep and fast. If I tried to walk into it from where I was, the current would take me downstream and right out in the open. No cover.

Across from me, the other side of the river was almost identical to my side but the woods didn't start for almost a hundred yards. Again, way too much open ground to get across. Anthony would have my ass for sure if I tried to go that way.

My only chance was upstream. Looking over my shoulder in Anthony's direction, I heard nothing. The sound of the water masked any chance I had of hearing anything anyhow. It was decision time. Goddamn it.

Hide or run? I knew I could hide again, and they never would be able to locate me. But that would mean lying up in the woods and listening while they tortured Brandy in front of me. Or I could get the hell out and try to give us the only chance we had.

Sorry, Brandy. I eased out of the wood line and let myself down onto the gravel bed. I looked down stream again for any sign of the other guy. Somebody down there would have a clear look at me if he came along now. Walking as carefully as I could I started moving up the river. The water curved around the ridgeline and disappeared around a corner to my right. If I could get around the bend out of sight, I could move faster.

Hiking up the gravel was easy. Beach River was one of those streams out of the high country that run hard and fast in the spring and then reduce to a trickle when the snow cap was gone. By late November or December it freezes solid and waits for spring.

This was late May. Spring runoff was still in progress with another month left. The water in front of me ran strong and cold. But the gravel bed I walked on was almost clear of debris, flushed clean by frequent rain storms. There were no logs and stumps like those found in so many flat Alaskan river beds.

It was around the corner when I spotted the problem. The river turned to the right around the sharp ridge I had been hiding below, but the bank and the gravel bar dwindled to nothing on my side of the water. I was going to have to cross the river. If I didn't and Anthony came around the corner behind me, I'd be stuck in a dead end.

I walked as far as I could. The gravel bar was getting steep, and the bank became a cliff. Looking it over, I decided I needed to climb along the water line as far as possible, because when I went in the water it was going to carry me downstream toward Anthony and his partner. If I could get across the river to the other side I had a chance to get into the woods there, climb the ridge and get away. But first I needed to cross the damn water without getting carried back down under the muzzle of Anthony's rifle.

When I couldn't move any further upstream I leaned against the wall of the river bank and looked at the water. I couldn't tell how deep it was. It was murky and filled with silt, and it was fast. Rumbling against the rocky floor it moved with relentless force. As it came down from the mountain into a steep ravine, it picked up tremendous speed before turning the corner and reaching the flatter part of the valley floor. I looked across the twenty feet or so of rushing turbulent water and tried to calculate a path across, including a likely point I could reach on the opposite bank if I had to swim.

I thought about drowning, and I thought about getting shot. Not much of a choice. I moved into the stream. The cold bit into my ankles and shins as soon as the water penetrated my shoes and socks. I took a deep breath and kept moving. The pull against my legs was impossibly strong. I held my arms out for balance and turned to face upstream. The water got deep in a hurry and by the time it was over my knee, there was no way to stay upright.

I tried to shuffle my feet sideways against the rocks on the bottom of the river, but almost immediately the water took me. I fought to stay in a crouch, and my knees and hands banged on the rocks as I went face first into the flow. Scrambling sideways like a crab on a hot plate I was doing okay for a couple of seconds. Then the force was much too strong. It turned me around and threw me into the middle of the torrent. My hands and feet could no longer reach bottom, and it was all I could do to keep my face from going under. The water was brown and thick with spring runoff. It splashed into my mouth and grated between my teeth like a mouthful of sand.

I knew I only had a second or two to get through it. If I couldn't reach the other side right away, one of two things would happen. Either the river would take me under or a bullet would end the struggle once and for all. In the water the cold would paralyze my chest and all my muscles. I would drown in seconds. All I could do was try to battle the water long enough to reach the opposite bank.

    I don't know what kind of swimming stroke I was using. Some kind of panicked dog paddle. I had to keep my head above water. The cold hit me, and I felt the shock grip my chest. It was bad. The cold crushed the breath out of me. If I couldn't grab the other shoreline, I was through.

CHAPTER 24

The river had me. I only had one chance left. Clamping my lips tight, I pounded at the water and kicked for all I was worth. My eyes bored ahead and spotted a rock stuck in the mud just ten feet away. I focused all my strength, all the energy I had left, on reaching it.

With a final lunge I got one hand out of the stream and grabbed the rock. But the water wasn't ready to quit fighting. Beach River was determined to kill me, or deliver me downstream where Anthony could do it. The raging torrent ripped at my legs. I felt the strength draining out of me as I clung to that rock. The river swept my legs downstream, and I had to fight like hell to get my other arm out of the water.

My hand slipped. I thrashed in vain to reach the rock again, but there was no way. I thought I was finished. But just as quickly as the river had taken me, it spit me out again. The momentum of the water swept me off that rock, but after dropping me into a trough it turned me toward the far bank.

The current did the rest. My body ground to a halt on the gravel, half in and half out of the water.

I blinked my eyes desperately trying to clear the blur. Amazingly, my sunglasses were still on. I couldn't see shit, and I realized the lenses were coated with muddy water and silt. I pulled them off and did what I could to clean them.

I rolled onto my back and stared up at the sky. Heavy gray clouds looked back at me with indifference. My legs didn't want to move, but something drove me to sit up and look around. I was a still a long way from safe.

My clothes were drenched. I was wet from the top of my head down. I couldn't believe it, but my hat was still on.

I was having trouble breathing. I may have even been hyperventilating. I didn't know. The cold water had paralyzed my chest. The muscles I needed for breathing didn't want to work anymore, but I knew I had to move. I crawled to my knees and looked downriver. I was still alone. The roar of the water masked all other sound.

Then I saw them. A hundred yards away Anthony was running up the opposite bank, stumbling in my direction. Further down, I could just make out the blurry shape of two figures in the distance. One smaller than the other.

The river had carried me down almost back to the treeline where I'd hidden from Anthony. Somehow I found the strength to get to my feet, and I ran. More like a shuffle, but fast enough to get away. I had to get around the corner of the ridge again. On this side of the river, there were trees and brush nearby if I could just get to them before Anthony got to me.

I caught a glimpse of him with his mouth open and shouting at me, but I heard nothing. And I wasn't going to hang around to listen either. In a low scramble, I made my way up the gravel slope, willing my leaden legs forward, ignoring the wet chafing drag of soggy jeans tugging at my knees. My jacket felt like it weighed five hundred pounds. Goddamned fleece. The stuff was like a sponge.

Just before I reached the trees, I heard the crack of a bullet sail over my head. Looking up I saw wood splinters fly from the trunk of a huge spruce only a foot higher than my head. The adrenaline hurtled me forward. There was no way I was going to survive a plane crash and a frigid near drowning only to get shot in the back. I launched myself up and over the low bank and threw myself into the woods.

After a twenty yard mad dash with branches striking me in the face, I collapsed behind a dead tree trunk lying on the ground and tried to catch my breath. My lungs burned. My throat ached from the exertion. I cursed every cigarette I had ever smoked in my entire life. Even though I quit years ago, I knew the damage was still with me.

Another shot rang out. I could hear it rip through the leaves and branches well above me, but I wasn't taking any chances trying to get a look at Anthony again. From where he was on the opposite side of the river, he had no direct line of fire at me. There was no way he could see me. I took a minute to regroup. It would take him a lot of time to get across the river and reach me. If he even wanted to risk the water. Damn, that shit was cold.

I waited for a few minutes, just breathing and trying to let my body heat build and spread through me again. Then I crawled carefully back toward the treeline to see what he was doing. That last shot made me think he was losing hope of catching up to me. Why else would he take a blind shot?

I kept a screen of bushes in front of me and scanned the river banks below. I finally spotted him and didn't think he could see me through the leaves, but I wasn't feeling that sure about it. If I saw him raise the rifle, I could duck before he got off a shot.

He was pacing near the spot I went in the river. He studied the dirt at the edge of the water, then looked in my direction. I tried to read his thoughts as he weighed the situation. Wondering what would happen if he tried to cross. Carrying the rifle, he was going to have a hard time of it. I started hoping he'd go for it. Then I might have a chance to smash his goddamn head with a rock while he tried not to drown.

Forget that nonsense, idiot. As much as I wanted to attack him, I didn't like the prospects.

Anthony looked things over for a few minutes. Then with a disgusted kick at the gravel, he turned and walked fast toward the others. Probably to get Brandy up there where he could force me to come out.

I watched him until I felt reasonably sure there wouldn't be another rifle shot. Then I turned and headed further into the woods. I didn't know what was ahead, but I knew it was better than the disaster downstream.

The terrain got steep in a hurry. But at least now I could breathe and take my time. I stopped and leaned against a tree feeling the temptation to just drop and sleep. My knees cried out for rest, but I knew better. I couldn't give in to it. Not if I wanted to live through this.

It was still light but barely. The clouds were growing darker and sunset wasn't far off. In the thicker parts of the woods, I strained to see the branches that kept trying to knock off my hat or poke out an eye.

I was warmer, but I knew it was only because of all the exertion. If I stopped and cooled off, hypothermia would have me in a matter of minutes. Without any sunshine ahead of me for hours or even days, getting dry any time soon was impossible. I had a battle to wage and couldn't afford to rest.

I sat down on a stump and pulled off my fleece. Twisting it with my hands, my knuckles and fingers ached. I squeezed as much water out as I could and did the same thing with the sweatshirt, grimacing through the pain. Then as miserably wet as they still were, I pulled them back on and tried not to shiver.

Standing there in the woods on the side of a steep hill on Montague Island, I felt completely lost. In every direction wide open nothingness stretched for miles. I zipped up the jacket and clenched my jaw. How the hell was I going to get out of this mess?

I sat down and pulled off my shoes and socks. My feet looked like starved and abused refugees from a foreign war. I wrung out the socks and pulled them back on over the battered, callused creatures and tied up my soggy black shoes. Finally dressed again but still damp, I looked around and tried to remember the hills and valleys from the air. My memory of the flight was hazy, but as I thought about it, images of the sectional chart, Google Earth, and the flight with Scooter started to seep back into memory.

Montague Island was a long and narrow rectangle with a spine of high mountains running down its middle. The north end of the island featured towering peaks almost three thousand feet high with permanent snowfields and icecaps. I had only seen them a few times before because the island was usually covered with thick clouds.

There was no way I was going to try to sneak back down toward the airstrip. They had all the advantage down there.

I wracked my brain to remember. The long valley I was in curled up into the mountains, and if I recalled accurately, the valley below me connected to another, forming a passage through the mountains from east to west. I had been so focused on the airstrip while I was flying that I hadn't looked down that much. But the photographs I'd taken had shown it too.

I stood up and tried to see my way to the west, but from that spot I couldn't see anything. The only way to get a real clue of a route was to climb higher. I was exhausted, but climbing was the only option. It would get me further away from Anthony and his rifle, and I might be able to spot a way out of the maze.

Before I started to walk, I pulled up on my jeans and tightened the leather belt by one notch. They were dragging heavily and must have made me look like a teenaged gangsta wannabe. I felt a heavy bump on my lower back. The marine radio had slipped into the middle of my back, and I had forgotten all about it. I slipped it off my belt and turned it on. The LED panel lit up and looked normal.

Suddenly the possibilities lit up too. If I could get higher on the mountain I might be able to reach somebody. My heart started pounding. I switched off the radio to save the battery and began to climb. I had a plan. Get to the west side of Montague. To the opposite side from Anthony. Put the whole mountain range between us, and I might have a chance.

The higher country would be less clogged with brush and vegetation too, making it easier to move. The only thing it wouldn't have was cover. I looked at the skies and wondered if Anthony might come looking for me in an airplane. The low clouds moving in and the approaching darkness made that seem unlikely.

I climbed slowly but steadily, stopping every few minutes to catch my breath. I had to stop more than I wanted to, but my legs demanded it. There was no trail to guide me so it was slow going. Pushing my way through clumps of devil's club and alders and climbing over and under deadfall was exhausting. I kept thinking that any minute around the next bend or over the next lip I'd reach timberline and break out into easier climbing, but it wouldn't arrive. It grew darker, until without looking at my watch, I knew it had to be almost midnight.

A vague trail formed in front of me. I hadn't given bears a thought until then. But now the signs were unmistakable. I was on a game trail. It was just light enough for me to make out a few tracks in a soft muddy patch. One distinctive human foot like shape with long claw marks stood out in fresh detail.

Great, just what I needed. Why can't I just be alone up here and not have to worry about being eaten alive? Was I ever going to catch a break? What was that Anthony had shouted? *Why can't you just leave me alone?*

"Hey, bear. Hey, bear," I called out as I walked. "Don't want no trouble with you. Believe me, Mister Bear."

Finally reaching the treeline, I moved up and beyond the high brush and scrub alders onto a rocky slope. From a position on the ridge I could see down toward the river. Enough dim light gave me a view almost to the ocean on the east side. The layer of cloud was only a hundred feet above me, and without trees to block it, the wind pushed at me from the south swirling over the peaks and valleys.

I took a break and pulled my collar tighter around my neck. The wind tried to take my cap when I looked south, so I tugged it down snugly too. I strained my eyes, trying to catch a glimpse of my SuperCub back at the airstrip. The crumpled memory of it was seared into my brain, but I couldn't help looking for it and wondering what would happen next.

I didn't have to wait long for an answer. I'm not sure if I heard a whooshing sound, but something echoed up the canyon toward me. Then a fireball appeared, rolling into the air above the airstrip. Just for a moment it burned bright red, then there was only smoke. I couldn't see the source of the flames, but with overwhelming dread I watched a coil of dark smoke rise above the treeline far below. The wind caught and scattered it into the gloom.

I felt sick. I didn't want to admit to myself what that had to be. I turned and started to climb again.

I didn't know what else to do. I had to keep moving. My feet and legs weighed a thousand pounds each. Every step became an ordeal. The wind whipped at my soggy jacket trying to suck away precious body heat. I thought about the matches and granola bars in the survival gear. I craved a cigarette just for the heat. I wasn't really hungry, but I could feel my energy level sinking like a fuel tank dangerously close to empty. Somehow I kept going.

After an eternity the slope finally topped out. I reached a saddle formation where a ridge rose to the right and the left and past a flattened out bowl area a valley headed down. I guessed I was about dead center on the island. At the highest point I would need to climb, I hoped.

I figured that I'd traveled less than two miles, but it had been a steeply cruel climb. I wasn't sure I could do anymore. The only thought that sustained me was believing I had reached the crest.

I clung to the hope that if I could connect the valleys in front of me, I might be able to work my way down to the ocean on the west side of Montague. Walking flat and then downhill would go faster. The shoreline was at least another three miles away. Hopefully more straight line. In the bowl the wind dropped off for a while.

But the last of the climbing wasn't over. I plodded ahead into the night, my mind wandering. Sometimes my route took me down a slope, then other times I had to climb again. I stumbled a lot. A few times I even fell, landing on my hands and knees on the rocky scree. One time I tripped and my glasses flew off. That gave me a scare, but they didn't break. I put them back on carefully and stood still for a minute to calm myself. *Take it easy, you nearsighted old bastard.*

What was I doing here? What did I do to deserve this agony? Images of Willie's bandaged head and Brandy's smoky green eyes haunted me. I tried to banish them by focusing on each step, planting my feet carefully. Taking my time dodging boulders. And worrying about my route. Was I headed into a blind canyon with cliff walls I couldn't get over? I racked my brain to remember from the flight over if there were any deadends in front of me, but I had no way of knowing. All I could do was push ahead and see where I came out.

It started to rain. Lightly at first, just a sprinkling mist. The clouds reached down from the sky and the wind gusted in my face. Patches of fog spread across the ground in front of me, and freezing droplets slid down the back of my neck. It quit after a while but not before the clothes that were almost dry were completely soaked again.

I was moving down across the upper edge of a wide valley in loose gravel when I fell. Hard. I slid on my face for several feet before finally grinding to a halt against a big rock. I was so tired I just laid there trying to catch my breath. Just a little rest. I didn't know how much longer I could do this.

Couldn't I just stop and wait to be rescued? Wouldn't somebody come along and take care of me? Please?

My mind drifted helplessly back in time. Back to other times where I'd had no control. Or when I'd done things I'd regretted. I couldn't shake the memory of Scooter's dead face staring at nothing. He'd caught a bullet that was meant for me. *Scooter, I'm so sorry, man. Here I am blabbering on and feeling sorry for myself, but look at what I did to you. I never should have asked you to come along. I hate myself for getting you involved. I work alone. I always have. And this is why. No one deserves what happened to you. I had no right to bring you out here. I got you killed. How am I ever going to live with that?*

My thoughts wandered and lost their grip on reality. *Off in the distance, I saw a white rowboat on a dazzling azure lake. It was floating beside a blue-white iceberg on a clear summer day. The air was still. The only sounds were birds in the distance and water lightly lapping at the side of the boat. Slowly I realized it was me in that boat, lying in the bottom* and staring at the ice looming above me. I couldn't make sense of it. Didn't know why I was there. I was curled in a fetal position with one ear pressed against the hard floor of the boat. Sounds from the deep filtered up through the wood. Like I was listening to an ancient recording, every sound made in the lake since the beginning of its life. From before the time the glacier formed, the rains, the snow, whipped by ancient winds and storms, the freezing and then the slow melting. Dripping, dribbling, running downhill, water collected in pools and grew. Crackling and rumbling, the sounds of tectonic plates moving across the horizon through the millennia. Eerie sounds of wind and rain and silence. Finally a whisper. Soft at first, then louder. I couldn't make out the words. A voice was trying to tell me something, but all I could hear was a soft whistling whisper. A raven flapped in noisily and landed on the iceberg. Sitting on the pinnacle it stared off in the distance like ravens do, but kept an eye on me at the same time. He was a raggedy beast with rumpled black feathers and a crusty, dirty beak. Well past his prime. I sat up slowly and peered over the side of the rowboat at the iceberg that floated just a few feet away. I reached out with one hand but couldn't touch it.

Looking down into the milky blue water I thought I saw something. I leaned closer straining to see down into the silty murk. A face rushed up at me so quickly I jerked backwards in a panic. The boat rocked violently and threatened to turn over. It was a young face, a sad face, the loneliest face I had ever seen.

My eyes snapped open, and a fierce shiver shook me awake. I don't know how much time had gone by. It was raining again. My right ear was numb. I reached up and realized it had filled with rain. I shook my head to get the water out and jammed in a little finger to clear my ear canal.

I groaned at the cramps in my legs and struggled to stand up against the rock I had been laying beside. Every muscle in my body felt tight and spent at the same time. Wrapping my arms as tight as I could around myself, I stamped my feet and paced in small circles trying to get warm. My feet felt like blocks of concrete. I was surprised looking down at them that they weren't huge. I dreaded to think what they looked like inside the muddy, scuffed, and torn black shoes. I could feel blisters that had formed and split.

The rain. The goddamned rain. I wiped my wet face as I paced. Had it saved me? Or doomed me? To more of this. Was I fated to wander the planet alone for eternity? Wet and painfully cold?

It was getting lighter. Early morning twilight. Everywhere I looked rain clouds filled the sky, a ceiling of gray as far as I could see. I was still shivering. Clamping my eyes shut for a moment, I did the only thing I could think of to stay alive. I put one foot in front of the other and started walking again.

I wasn't giving up. No way. I thought about the face in the lake and shook my head violently to dispel the image. I was not going to join the kid under the water. The bastards were not going to beat me, they were not going to win. I was going to get them even if it killed me.

I came around the corner of a ridgeline on a clear slope just above treeline. Stretched out in front of me was water. A huge expanse of glorious open water. Montague Strait. It had to be. As exhausted as I was, I felt my face break into a huge grin. I'd made it. My chest ballooned with a deep breath, and I raised my tired arms to the horizon as if embracing a new life. At least I was still alive and on the opposite side of the island from Anthony.

The rain had let up. Low fog hung in the trees below me. True to Montague Island's reputation, the airstrips along the beaches had to be socked in. The air was dead still, which wouldn't help move the fog along. I was a little warmer after walking for a while. The shivering was less, and the cold cramping pains all over my body had let up. Or maybe I'd just gone numb.

I worried for a second, thinking that maybe I'd dropped the radio somewhere up above. There was no way I could reverse course and climb back up to look for it. I let out a deep sigh when I found it on the back of my belt again. I'd grown so accustomed to its weight back there, I didn't feel it anymore. I slid it out of its case and turned on the switch.

Nothing. *What? Nothing? Wait a minute. That's impossible.* I'd just checked it a while back. I banged the radio with my hand and shook it like a baby's rattle. The monitor window on the front stared back at me, empty of any response. I turned it off again and waited.

This couldn't be happening. I looked out and saw a boat in the distance. Easy enough to see as dim light spread across the islands and water in all directions. But there was no way to get them to see me. My signal mirror was back in the airplane. I winced at the memory. My bent SuperCub, Scooter's dead face, the river.

The river. The goddamned river. Was that the problem? Was the supposedly waterproof radio wet inside?

I fumbled through my pockets and found my cell phone. I knew there wasn't any signal out here, but I checked it anyhow. The panel's cover was filled with moisture, and no information was visible. I turned it off with the power switch and then turned it back on, but it was still dead.

With a dime from the front pocket of my jeans, I unscrewed the battery compartment on the bottom of the marine radio and pulled it open. There was moisture all around the electrical contacts. I spread the different pieces on flat rocks in front of me and went to work. I bent over the parts, trying to will life back into the device that could save my ass. Without it I could only imagine wandering through the brush and rocks for days trying to find help.

My hands worked feverishly as I examined every surface and part looking for any secrets to its revival. With the driest spot of my T-shirt, I wiped and rubbed and massaged every nook and cranny. Hunched over it to keep out any stray raindrops, I reassembled the parts and pieces, taking all the care possible. When I had it done, I held it in my hands and stared at it for a moment.

What if it didn't work? No, scratch that—it *had* to work. I put all the hope and positive energy I could conjure into this device succeeding. For Brandy. For Willie.

I turned the switch again. A little light flickered inside the panel and a channel number appeared. A faint sound of static came over the speaker. I pressed the channel button and the numbers changed. I pushed the button until channel nine was displayed.

"Any station, any station, this is aircraft five eight Charlie, over."

I waited. Nobody answered me. Just a static buzz. I figured out how to adjust the squelch and the static stopped.

"Any station, any station, this is aircraft five eight Charlie, radio check, over."

I waited a couple more minutes. I decided that the quiet was too unnerving and readjusted the squelch so that I could hear something even if it was just the noisy rush of static. Anything was better than dead quiet.

Still nothing. I switched to channel sixteen, the emergency channel, but I didn't push the transmit button yet. I had to think this over.

The Coast Guard monitored channel sixteen. So did the commercial boats. I had no idea what kind of range my handheld model could broadcast or receive. What would I tell the Coast Guard? Help, I've fallen, and I can't get up? I hated the idea of contacting the authorities. I never wanted them in my business. I thought through all the possibilities.

I was okay for the moment. Scooter was dead, they couldn't do anything about that. My airplane was wrecked and maybe worse. They wouldn't do anything about that either. I could try to get them to go after Brandy, but would they believe my story? Or would they think I had lost my mind with an unbelievable fairy tale? No, the Coast Guard would only come and get me. With a boat or a chopper, they'd find me and take me back to Seward. Is that what I wanted? To call for help and give up any chance I had of personally solving the problem. That felt like quitting. I knew I could never forgive myself if something happened to Brandy because I quit.

I didn't have time to think about it for long. I heard an airplane. It was coming from the valley behind me. Anthony.

CHAPTER 25

I ran for the trees and dove behind the first cover I could find just as a black SuperCub crossed the ridgeline above me. I watched it from underneath a pile of dead branches. It was flying slow and close to the hillsides like hunters searching for game. I thought about the radio again, but there was a good chance Anthony had a marine radio too and might be listening. I stayed quiet and watched.

The plane made a few passes up and around the valley behind me. I didn't think they were any tracks they could spot, but some of the places I fell might have left signs. Then the SuperCub turned to the south and disappeared. The sound of the engine grew more and more quiet until it was gone.

Cautiously, I crawled out from under the branches and brushed myself off. Staying close to good hiding places, I worked my way south. From the top of a rock I could see almost to the end of the island, and I could just barely make out a silent shape flying low back and forth along the shore. Then it flew out of sight to the east. If that was Anthony, I hoped he was headed back to his base.

Marine radios are like airplane radios. They need line of sight between the stations to connect. I took a chance that if Anthony was monitoring, the mountains between us would block him from hearing me.

On channel nine again, I keyed the mike.

"Any station, any station, this is aircraft five eight Charlie, over."

The immediate answer surprised me. "Aircraft calling on channel nine, this is the Jolly Roger, over."

I looked around nervously. I didn't want to get jumped by the black SuperCub again while I was yakking on the radio. The answer was so loud, I thought the boat was right in front of me. The *Jolly Roger* wasn't familiar to me, but that didn't mean much. Seward and the whole area was home for hundreds of boats. I didn't know very many of them.

"*Jolly Roger,* uh, I'm having a situation here. I need to contact a party in Seward. Uh, what's your location? Over."

"We're south of Day Harbor, off Cape Resurrection. Who's your party? I can relay a message."

Oh, man. I was making progress. The guy sounded helpful and wasn't asking too many questions. That was good. I gave him Mitch's phone number and his boat's name.

"Roger, five eight Charlie. Stand by."

I listened as he made his call, but I couldn't hear whatever answers he was getting, if any. I waited, afraid to get my hopes up. Time went by.

It felt good to sit and let my legs rest, but the exhaustion was pulling me down. I was feeling my age. Hiking all night on blistered feet in the rain had worn me down. Not to mention the strain on my nerves.

I was hungry too and thirsty. Looking around I found a pool of rain water. Stretched out on my belly I drank my fill. The cold liquid hurt my teeth as I sucked it down, but I didn't care. I needed water more than I needed food. Lying there next to the puddle, I started to close my eyes, but feeling sleep about to overtake me, I jerked up and got to my feet. If I let myself go, I might never wake up.

"Aircraft five eight Charlie, Jolly Roger, over."

I grabbed up the radio. "Five eight Charlie."

"Roger, your party's on the water near Johnstone Bay. Contact him on channel seventy-four. *Jolly Roger,* out."

I couldn't believe my ears. Mitch? At Johnstone Bay? That was only thirty miles away. I switched over to channel seventy-four.

"Lonesome Sailor, this is aircraft five eight Charlie, over."

"Johnny? That you? What the hell's going on, man?"

So much for radio protocol. Mitch's voice was the sweetest music I'd heard in years.

"Hey, Mitch. Thank God, it's you. I've, uh, had a little problem out here. I'm on Montague."

"Are you okay? When we didn't hear from you last night, we weren't sure what to do. We called the FAA, but they had no flight plan from you."

"Well, I'm okay, but the, uh, the airplane's wrecked, Mitch. Can you come get me?"

There was a long pause. I could picture Mitch's face looking puzzled and serious. "Johnny, I've got Hondo out here with me. We were out delivering supplies near Little Johnstone, and I brought him with me in case we heard from you."

I thought that one over. I had a ton of questions, but my mind was starting to shut down. I knew I had to get rest and food before my brain quit altogether. I gave Mitch directions so he could find me and begged off answering any more of his questions until I was aboard.

It had started to rain again. The wind picked up too. I stood up, switched off the radio to save the battery and started downhill through the trees. My nose was running bad. I tried to wipe it on the sleeve of my jacket, but that just wet my whole face. I headed for the rocky shore down the hill and straight across from Latouche Island which I could just barely see as the rain, mist, and fog rolled in.

You'd think walking downhill would be a lot easier than climbing. It takes less lung power and less exertion at first, but after a while it kills the feet, legs, and knees. My blisters were raw and screamed out at me every time I stepped on them wrong. It felt like walking with razor blades in your shoes.

The worst part of dropping below treeline was the brush. Down in the thickets again forward progress was a bitch. I had no strength to push through heavy alders or to climb over deadfall.

I started to worry that Mitch wouldn't find me. Especially if I couldn't move fast enough to make it to the shore by the time he got there. We had estimated three to four hours to meet up, but I wasn't traveling fast at all. I began to pray for a game trail. Anything to get me through this stuff.

Just eat me, Mister Bear. I don't give a damn anymore. If life has to be this painful I don't want to live. It ain't what I signed on for. Just do it quick, okay? Have a heart, you big hairy sonofabitch. Finish me fast. Take my skull in your jaws and give it a crunch.

I was getting delirious. I tried to talk to the bears, tried to let them know I was just passing through their neighborhood. My words came out in a mumble, so I rattled branches as I pushed my way through, hoping I was making enough noise to be heard. My delirious mind might have welcomed death, but the rest of me wasn't interested. At my core, a kernel of desperation burned to live on.

Back off, Mister Bear, you self-centered sonofabitch. Get your lunch somewhere else.

I walked and I staggered. Brush whipped my face and I didn't care. I fell several times. More than once twisting a knee or an ankle, but it didn't matter. I knew I had to pull myself back up and keep moving. So I did. Like a prize-fighter hammered to the canvas. Relentlessly hauling himself up on a rope before the count expires. Then turning to face the enemy one more time. Propelled by pride and sustained by survival instinct when just laying still and surrendering would be so much easier.

Then I began to hear waves. An ocean breeze swept across my face, chilling the sweat. The trees thinned out and a low grassy meadow lay in front of me. Blue lupine blooms stood silently and swayed in the wind watching me trudge by. When

I reached the waterline, I stood still, unable to think. I knew I should be celebrating or dancing or something, but I was incapable of anything but standing there like a tattered zombie from *The Night of the Living Dead* staring across the water.

Time went by. A lot of time. I lost track. I leaned against a driftwood stump where Mitch could see me and tried to remain conscious. I wasn't sure I saw the boat slowly working its way across the strait toward me. But I must have realized my journey was over. My eyes closed, and swaying like a lupine, I didn't hear the crunch of gravel and I didn't feel the impact when the back of my head met the west shore of Montague Island.

* * * * *

I came to coughing and sputtering. Hondo was leaning over me trying to pour water down my throat.

I fought him off and knocked the plastic water bottle to the floor. "Hey, what the hell—?"

"Easy, man. Easy. Just trying to get you rehydrated. You okay now?"

I looked around bewildered. We were in a small weird-shaped room, closed in on all sides. I was lying on some kind of cushioned seats that made me think I was in a camper. But the floor was moving weirdly, up and down. There was a blanket on me, and my wet clothes were gone. I gave Hondo a hostile look and drew my knees up protectively. Then I noticed my feet. My shoes were gone. Band-Aids and gauze covered my feet in several places.

"Relax, Johnny. You're okay now. We had to get you warm and dry. You've been out for almost four hours."

I looked at my watch. No shit. I took a deep breath, but the air in the tiny room was hot, thick and heavy. It smelled like wet dog and dead fish. No, I guess that was me. The floor moving was about to make me sick.

I was on Mitch's boat. In the cabin below deck. Hondo's bulk filled most of the space. His sweaty face was staring at me with concern, but he had a crooked grin too. I knew I had to get out of there.

I moved to stand up, but I was so unsteady I had to put my hands out for balance and sat back down.

"Here, dude. Put these on." He handed me some dry clothes. "What the hell happened to you? And where's Scooter? Didn't he come out here with you?"

The memories rushed back as I pulled on the clothes.

"Oh, Jesus. What a freakin' disaster. Scooter's dead. He's been shot."

Hondo dropped onto the seat across from me. His mouth fell open. "You're kidding me."

The hatch above us opened then, and Mitch stuck his face down the ladder. "Hey, you're awake."

The floor moving and images of Scooter's face made me bolt for the opening. I pushed past Mitch and leaned over the railing but all I could do was dry heave.

I heard Hondo telling Mitch about Scooter and when I'd recovered enough to turn around they were both standing in the back of the boat looking at me. Waiting for me to talk.

I took deep breaths of ocean air and drank the water Mitch handed me. Gradually my head started to clear and my stomach quit trying to escape my body. Seeing the horizon helped. So did the air.

I took another deep breath and felt the pain around my bruised ribcage. I twisted my neck in all directions hearing it crackle in protest. Then I told them the story.

They listened to the details of my flight over, the low pass over Beach River valley, the gunfire, and my forced landing. I told them about Scooter getting shot and Anthony hunting me, and my swim across the river and hiking all night to get away. Then I remembered the fire and told them about that too.

"They torched your airplane, dude. God, that sucks. But the guy shot Scooter?" Hondo's face was scrunched tight, his eyebrows screwed together and his eyes burned into me with a fire I'd never seen in him. Hondo was a drinking buddy and a guy who helped me with stuff in his workshop. I'd never seen him like this. He turned to stare at the island speechless. We were still sitting next to Montague.

Mitch handed me a sandwich. I waved it away.

"Eat something, Johnny. I thought you were dead when we saw you collapse on the beach. You looked like hell. Actually you still do."

The smell of ham and cheese came to me then, and I realized how hungry I was. I reached for the sandwich and started eating like a man shark.

Mitch talked to me quietly while I ate. Catching me up. "We've just been sitting here fishing, waiting for you to wake up. We didn't want to leave until we knew what was going on. Or if we needed to wait for Scooter. We didn't know you'd been through a goddamned war."

He handed me hot coffee and watched me chew. Whenever I swallowed, he pushed more stuff toward me.

I slowed down and slurped the coffee greedily. The hot liquid burned its way down my throat. I took my time, savoring the sensations, appreciating nourishment more than I had in a long time.

"And what about Brandy? What are we going to do?"

Hondo came over and joined us. "Yeah, Johnny, what now?"

I stared at them and took another sip of coffee. I looked up at the mountain peaks and thought back over the past twenty-four hours. The high valleys and ridges I had traversed in the dark hovered above us just a couple miles away. Images and memories rushed back at me like hail stones in a gale.

The food and caffeine were hitting my bloodstream, filling my gut and pouring adrenaline into my brain and energy into my hands and feet. My mind was spinning. I remembered that meadow and the trench in front of the Cub on our way down. I tasted the bile in the back of my throat again as I shouted at Scooter to get ready. I heard the crunch and felt the sickening impact down to my core. I could even smell the acrid stench of hot metal, fear and sweat from the crash.

I'd left blood on that island. I'd left my airplane on that island. They'd killed our friend, and they still had Brandy. They still had Willie's airplane too. But for how long?

"I'll tell ya what we're going to do. We're going after those sonsabitches. That's what."

They stared at me. Mitch had a look on his face wondering if I'd lost my mind.

But Hondo was a different story. His face lifted. His eyes widened, then narrowed again. He grinned widely, and I could see the juices starting to flow. He pulled open his jacket to show me a huge handgun in a shoulder holster. Then he stood back with his legs spread wide and his hands on his hips. "Fuckin' A, bubba. Let's get it on."

Mitch looked back and forth at us. "Are you guys serious? What about calling the Coast Guard or something?"

"We don't have time for that. These assholes don't know where I am, or even if I'm still alive. We have to do something before they split. Grab those charts, Mitch. I've got an idea."

I sat down at the small table in the center of the wheelhouse, took a pencil and started drawing a diagram. Trying to recall as many details as I could, I traced out the east shoreline, Beach River, and the place where I guessed Anthony had his camp. Mitch got the boat ready to move. He tapped me on the arm at one point and pointed to one of the walls. Strapped into a rack was a Winchester Forty-Four Magnum hunting rifle with a high-power scope mounted and ready to go.

Hondo and I went over the options. We studied the map and made notes and arrows on the drawing. Mitch drove the boat north. We had a few hours to travel and equipment to get ready.

It was a gray day, and it rained on and off as we moved deeper into Prince William Sound. The low lush expanse of Green Island passed us on the left and we entered a channel that would take us to the north end of Montague.

When the plan seemed ready to go, Hondo and I went over it several more times. We filled in Mitch who nodded nervously in agreement. I knew he was reluctant but he could see the fire in Hondo's eyes. When he looked at me I stared him straight in the eye. "We gotta do it, Mitch. It may be Brandy's only chance." He nodded and turned to navigate us through the rocks and jagged hazards, guiding us with a sonar unit next to the wheel.

Hondo went in search of gas cans, and I went below to find the head. In the tiny compartment, a small mirror on the wall gave me a start. A scratched and tired face stared back at me. I wiped sand out of the corner of one eye. My hand was trembling. I clenched my fist several times and looked deep into the eyes in the mirror watching myself wince at the pain.

"Just hold on, Brandy," I whispered to the tired face. "We're coming. Just hold on."

I looked down at my hands and continued to flex and clench. The pain subsided somewhat as I pictured those hands wrapped tight around Anthony's neck. I was squeezing and squeezing, finding strength from somewhere deep inside. The harder I squeezed the more his eyes bulged, panic building as he ran out of air. I was surprised by the power I felt and let my hands relax. With a final wink in the mirror, I gave myself a tight grin and left to get ready.

CHAPTER 26

Twilight, gray skies and rain surrounded us as Mitch's boat crept quietly down the east shore of Montague Island. Ice capped peaks blocked out the sky high on the starboard side. Mitch kept us just off shore, out of reach of the foam splashes that danced off rocky outcroppings moving beside us in the gloom.

I positioned myself carefully at the bow and got ready as we moved past high ground called the Purple Bluffs. Mitch idled the boat expertly and brought us to the shoreline where I hopped off onto a large flat rock. A steep hillside climbed straight up from the water and left me only a narrow slice of graveled beach to make my approach. After pushing the boat back into deeper water, I crouched next to the rock and studied the area in front of me. Calm seas and low tide swirled in the gravel under my boots and low fog rolled in offshore.

I watched the boat back out into the surf and turn back to the north. Mitch was going to swing out into the Gulf and move south pretending to be a fisherman. With less than a mile of visibility he wouldn't be far away. I could see Hondo checking the gas cans stationed at the stern where he had checked them at least a dozen times already.

The guy was a professional. I could see it in the way he prepared, mentally calculating every possibility and planning every move. He had prepared me too, reviewing the plan and checking my gear. Made sure I had the radio and the handgun and my Leatherman, checking that they were secure. We went over the plan again and again until we were all clear on each step. It seemed simple enough. Hondo would sneak onshore with the gas cans and set them up as diversions to draw Anthony and the other guy away from their camp. That would give me the opportunity to move in undetected. Every possibility had a response. We even agreed where to meet if everything went to shit.

It was easy walking for the first quarter-mile or so. Driftwood logs were strewn along the way draped with seaweed. A five-foot skeleton lay exposed to the weather, the remains of a seal. Its skull grinned up at me from some private hell. I wondered what evil the poor critter had committed to deserve eternal captivity thrashing back and forth on the gravel, a victim of every passing wave and gust of wind.

A stream flowed down from a break in the bluffs, but I was able to work my way uphill to a place where I could easily jump across. The only noise was the sound of small waves running up on the beach. I couldn't see a soul, but a light breeze in my face smelled of wood smoke. I couldn't tell where it came from, but my heart started racing. Someone was nearby. That was no forest fire.

Then I heard voices. I hunkered down in the brush to listen and watch. The calm, dead air amplified every sound nearby like we were inside a drum. Metallic sounds repeated in a strange but familiar pattern. In a crouch, I crept forward tracking the sound. Someone was playing with a Zippo lighter, snapping it open, then snapping it shut.

"Knock it off, Lance. You're making me crazy with that shit." It was Anthony's voice. The metal noises stopped.

My mouth went dry. I melted back into the low bushes against the hillside and laid down on my belly. I checked my watch, then reached inside my jacket and carefully pulled Hondo's revolver out of its holster. Another hour to wait while Hondo got things set up. I maneuvered where I could see down the beach, but there was no sight of Hondo or the boat. The fog kept me from seeing past the spot where Beach River sliced through the gravel bar and spilled into the Gulf. But I could see some large rocks and a raised area where Hondo was probably going to place one of his loud surprises. I was hoping to figure out if Willie's airplane was nearby.

The voices seemed to be coming from a small clearing behind a row of brush and alder bushes. I moved closer, keeping vegetation between me and them. I recognized the area from the flight the day before, but seeing it from ground level was so different I got disoriented. I needed to get uphill. I glanced at my watch again, wondering how Hondo was doing.

Deciding there was enough time, I turned around and headed back to an area I had already passed, which sloped up to the bluffs. Before long I had a view looking down into the meadow. The layout became much clearer. The water line was fairly straight and the beach was wide enough at low tide to make a nice landing strip. Then there was a line of alder growth about thirty or forty yards wide that ran parallel to the beach. Behind that was a clear corridor also parallel to the beach followed by more alder thicket.

A couple of tents were set up behind the first patch of brush on the edge of the meadow, which hid them from the water. One was brown and the other was dark green, making them tough to spot from the air. Next to the tents was a camouflage-patterned tarp stretched over the top of what had to be an airplane. That meant there had to be a passage out to the beach. The clearing didn't look long enough to handle takeoffs and landings—even with a SuperCub.

I licked my lips. My mouth was getting dry again. I checked the revolver for the hundredth time. I made sure it was secure in the holster and started back down the hill. The sky was growing dimmer, but the fog seemed to be thinning out. Now and then gaps of blue sky appeared above me. It was growing darker. I estimated the fog to be only a hundred or two hundred feet thick above the water.

I found a position in the alders where I could watch the tents and not be seen. I heard a zipper being opened and watched as a tall man crawled out of the green tent. It wasn't Anthony. Had to be his sidekick. The guy named Lance on the credit card slip.

There must have been a small campfire on the other side of his tent. Lance walked in that direction and soon after I saw smoke kicking up above the tents like he was working on the fire. Then he came back around and started taking down the camouflage tarp.

My heart moved into my throat as I watched the white wings and red markings of Willie's plane appear. When the tail number was clearly visible, I reached for the marine radio and turned it on. I kept the volume setting at its lowest mark and pressed the transmit button twice, paused and then once more.

Anthony emerged from the same tent and tossed sleeping bags and a pack out the door.

Shit, they were leaving. Where was Hondo?

I moved backwards to get some distance and keyed the transmitter again. This time I turned it up just slightly and huddled over the speaker cupping it against my ear.

The static I could hear suddenly broke. Once, twice, and after a pause, a third time. Hondo was ready.

When I could see both men, I keyed the switch again. I pressed my lips against the mike and whispered, "Go."

The sound of a boat engine roared just offshore. Anthony and Lance looked at each other and dropped the things in their hands. Then they dove for the tent and pulled out rifles. Moving cautiously they headed toward the sound of the boat. I waited until they were in the brush and almost out of sight before I keyed the mike again. "They're on the move."

A shot rang out. I could hear the bullet whip through the air well above me, but it had the desired effect. Anthony and Lance dropped to the ground. I watched as Anthony motioned for Lance to head inland. He curved his hand pointing out for

Lance how to proceed. He waited a moment for Lance to disappear and then he began to creep toward the beach.
When they were both out of sight, I called Hondo again.
"Fireworks," I whispered into the radio.
Another shot rang out and an explosion lit up the fog bank over the beach. Gas can number one.
I heard a shot closer to me. Anthony was yelling at Lance.
"You see him?" he screamed.
"No!" Lance's voice answered from a distance.
I keyed the mike twice and made my move. Standing up but staying bent over low, I ran toward the tents with the pistol drawn and ready. The green tent's door hung open, but it was empty. The brown tent's fabric split open easily with a quick slice from my Leatherman. A shape wrapped in a sleeping bag was thrashing around on the floor of the tent. Someone was trying to sit up.
I grabbed at the bag and wrestled it open. Pulling at the hood I finally got it over the head of dark hair inside. It was Brandy. She blinked hard and stared up at me. Her face was flushed and lined with creases from the sleeping bag. There was a welt on one cheekbone and she had a black eye. She looked dazed, but I was in a hurry.
"Brandy, you okay? We gotta move."
I tore at the zipper on the sleeping bag. She groaned as her muscles started to move again. "C'mon, c'mon. I don't know how much time we have," I whispered furiously."
She began to fumble for her shoes but they were nowhere in sight. I grabbed her arm and hauled her toward the opening. Outside the tent she stumbled along in stocking feet as I half-dragged her toward Willie's plane. More shots rang out down at the beach and another explosion lit off. *Gas can number two,* I whispered to myself. I forced myself to take a deep breath and felt my heart hammering in my throat.
"You okay? We gotta get in the plane, Brandy."
She nodded and started moving. "Yeah, I'm okay, I'm okay."
I let her walk on her own and reached the SuperCub's door before she did. It was latched. Running around to the

other side I slid back the left window and leaned in to open the door.

"Get in the back," I whispered as loud as I dared and motioned to her through the glass. She started to climb in. Her socks and feet were covered with dead grass as she pulled herself inside. I ran in the direction where I'd last seen Anthony.

Sure enough there was a small corridor in the stand of brush just wide enough to fit the plane's wings through. The gap was stuffed with brush, maybe six to eight feet high, and I could see the evidence of freshly cut alders where they had hacked a path into the hiding place. I scurried back and forth tossing branches in every direction, clearing the way.

"One's coming back your way," Hondo hissed over the radio.

"Need more time," I whispered back, dropping the branches and turning toward the plane. My knees were starting to shake violently, and I took a deep breath to focus. I reached for the revolver, but the holster was empty.

Shit. I looked around frantically but there was no sign of it.

More shots rang out down the beach. I heard leaves rip nearby as bullets shredded their way through the thicket.

When I got back to the plane, Brandy was settled in the backseat with her headset on. I climbed in and quickly checked the fuel tanks out of habit. There was fuel but not much. There was no time to calculate anything. I pulled on the headset and flicked on the master switch.

"Brandy, see if there's anything in back we can use for protection. These maniacs are going to try and kill us."

I felt her lurching around in the seat to search the back of the plane. I shoved the primer back and forth as fast as I could. The back pressure against the tiny plunger made it move with maddening slowness. I held my breath, hit the master switch, and jammed my thumb against the starter button.

The engine turned over briefly, then died. I froze, staring straight ahead. *What now?* I racked the throttle back and forth once and looked over the instrument panel.

Mixture, you stupid asshole. Jesus Christ, why had I been born with shit for brains? I slammed in the mixture knob and hit the button again.

The starter groaned, and the prop began to slowly rotate. Then it caught, and the engine chugged to life. I didn't have the luxury of a run up. Breaking every rule in the engine management book, I poured the coals to her and listened as the pistons slammed back and forth in their cold cylinders. We started to roll, and with a hard shove on a rudder pedal, I swung a violent turn to the right out into the meadow. By the end of the turn we were lined up on the gap in the brush.

I prayed Hondo had heard the engine roar and was in position to keep Anthony and Lance occupied. I knew they'd heard the engine start too, and one or both of them had to be running this way.

In front of us, the gap was still half clogged with brush, but I didn't care.

"Hang on!" I shouted to Brandy.

Plunging into the thicket, the propeller hit branches like a weed whacker on steroids. The noise was deafening. The engine was howling and brush flew around us in a tornado of wood chips and leaves. Then we burst through the final barrier and exploded like a bouncing green bomb onto the beach. The gravel sloped ahead of us down to the water. There was open beach to our right, a natural airstrip, but I could see Anthony running toward us with a rifle in his hands like an assault trooper in full charge.

In a snap decision, I aimed the nose for the water and shoved as hard as I could on the throttle even though it was already full against its stop. We seemed to roll forever. The big tundra tires bounced and tumbled slow motion as we picked up steam. I was focused straight ahead willing the plane into the air, but the speed wasn't there.

Out of the corner of my eye I saw a huge flash and a motion that must have been Anthony diving to the ground. Gas can number three. That was it. Either I got the damn plane in the air, or they were going to be fishing us out of the surf. Probably just pieces of us, tangled in driftwood and wrapped in the flotsam and jetsam from thousands of years across thousands of miles of open ocean.

The incline of the beach to the water steepened slightly. Gravity began to help. I felt the tail come up. Fighting the urge to haul back on the stick, I kept the elevator as flat as possible, doing everything I could to reduce our drag to the minimum.

The water line was approaching fast. The ground below us was already wet. At a higher tide we would already be swimming. Just as the big tires were about to smash into the first small wave, I pulled up on the Johnson bar as hard as I could. We leapt into the air.

On the ragged edge of a stall I pushed the nose down and aimed at the water. Glancing quickly at the airspeed indicator I could see the needle dropping fast. It was all I could do to keep the nose down until we were really flying.

Wind. Where the hell was the wind? If there was ever a time I wanted wind, it was now. I remembered the slight breeze coming from the south blowing that wood smoke toward me. As gently as I could with a tense fist on the stick, I banked us slightly to the right.

I was sure the right tire or the wingtip was going to kiss the water. We were so close to the surface I could see details of foam and tiny ripples right beside the plane. Then little by little the wings caught some of the breeze and the power of lift pulled us up and out of danger. I whispered a prayer of thanks to the aviation gods, the genius of Daniel Bernoulli, and the dogged persistence and guts of Wilbur and Orville Wright. If I could have, I would have kissed their hairy faces right on the lips.

But our troubles weren't over. In fact, they were just beginning. Low fog in every direction forced me to stay close to the ground. The clouds to the south looked especially thick and foreboding. I turned back toward land and watched Mitch's boat pass by underneath us. A heavy wake behind them told me they were getting the hell out of Dodge too. He was headed for a thick fog bank just in front of them.

The oily gas can fires that Hondo had set off with his rifle were still burning down below. A heavy smokescreen floated across the beach just like we had planned giving Mitch's boat some cover. But in an opening next to the alder thicket I spotted Anthony aiming his rifle at us. In a split second decision I pointed the nose right at him and shoved the flap handle back to the floor.

We were hauling ass now, and Anthony knew it. I saw his eyes bugging out as he threw himself to the ground to avoid the Cuisinart on the front of our plane. Again, I had to haul back on the stick to avoid the alder thicket, but with plenty of flying speed, she soared skyward.

That's when the bullets hit us. I didn't know if it was Anthony or Lance who got off the shots as we roared overhead. In a sickening repeat of a recent nightmare, I felt at least two impacts rock the airplane. Then everything went straight to hell.

CHAPTER 27

"Brandy, you okay?" I tried to keep the panic out of my voice, but we were headed for the trees.

"I…I'm h…here." She sounded weak and small, her voice barely audible over the intercom.

"Take the stick. Now. I got nothing up here."

I was serious. I had no control. The airplane tilted hard right and nosed up. I grabbed for the trim handle, but the nose kept rising. It was all I could do to keep the ball in the center, shoving the rudder pedals right and left. The window filled with trees and the mountain side was coming at us fast.

I twisted around in my seat as far as I could. Surprised at how easily I turned, I realized I'd never put my seatbelt on. Brandy was holding the stick, but she looked woozy. She was staring down at her hands, not looking outside.

"Brandy, you gotta fly. I got no stick."

She looked up at me puzzled. I held up the severed control stick with one hand and waggled it at her. One of the bullets had ripped through the lower end of the shaft leaving me with nothing but a worthless hunk of metal, not connected to anything but my sweaty palm.

Her eyes went wide. In that split second I saw it register. The cobwebs cleared, and she shook her head like she'd been given an electric shock. Her instinctual reflexes developed over years of flying took over. She pushed forward on her stick and leveled the wings.

My relief that we weren't going to stall quickly disappeared. We were still headed straight for a steep rocky wall just below a thick bank of fog.

"Left. Turn hard left."

"Hang on a sec; this bag's in the way."

"We ain't got a sec. Left now!"

I heard her grunt and the plane lurched down and left. The cliff swept by on the right only a few feet off the wingtip. We were deep into Beach River valley now with fog above us, trees and river below and canyon walls on all sides. Except back toward the beach where Anthony and Lance and gunfire waited.

High country lurked behind the fog ahead. That was the valley I'd hiked into the night before. Flying up there in the clouds would be suicide.

"Head back for the beach, Brandy."

"I can't see shit back here, Johnny. You're going to have to guide me."

"Okay, turn left. I can do the rudder but you got the only stick."

"Yeah, I'm aware of that."

I looked down and searched frantically inside the cabin for some way to reconnect the control stick. But there was no way. I had to let Brandy do the flying. All I could do was sit and watch. We weren't about to crash anymore, but there was no way I could relax. We were stuck under a fog bank in mountains with only one way out. And that's where the killers were.

I stared at the ground ahead as far as I could, searching for Anthony and Lance. We were flying down the edge of the valley far enough from their camp that I hoped we were out of range, but there was no way to be sure.

"Okay, Brandy, we got to go up through this crap. Take us up. Put all that instrument time to some use, will ya?"

"Sure, no problem, that's just great. Except I don't have any instruments back here."

"I know. Welcome to the backseat of a SuperCub. It shouldn't take us too long. I saw gaps in the clouds a little while ago. It should only be a couple hundred feet thick. Lean over so you can see these instruments." I tapped on the turn coordinator and the altimeter until she had them spotted.

"Okay. Where's the attitude indicator? And the directional gyro?"

"Uh, they haven't been installed just yet."

"Are you shitting me?"

"I shit you not."

"Well, Jesus Christ. This isn't instrument certified! What the hell are we doing?"

"Oh, you wanna file a complaint with the FAA? Or do you want to crawl into the baggage compartment and let me take over back there?"

"Screw you, I can do this," she muttered into the mike. "I got the rudder and the throttle too. Just keep giving me feedback, directions, altitude, that kind of stuff."

"Yeah, yeah, we'll tag-team this baby."

She pushed the throttle all the way in and we started to climb. Just before we were engulfed in cloud I looked down toward the campsite again. Movement caught my eye and I peered down in disbelief. A dark shape was rushing down the beach straight toward us. Just as we disappeared in the clouds I saw it lift off.

"Holy shit. They had the other plane down there too?"

"Yeah, the black SuperCub. Belongs to Anthony. They had it hidden on the other side of that meadow."

"Damn it. I looked all over down there and never saw it. It just took off behind us."

"Never mind that now; you got to help me get through these clouds."

"Right, okay. Looks good. Climb at seventy. Altimeter's moving. We're at three hundred feet."

Thick cloud surged past us on both sides. I looked over the side of the cabin but only saw more cloud below us. Leaning my head back, I looked up through the skylight. Solid gray up there too. We were totally surrounded by soggy dense fog. Beside the skylight, the fuel gauges reminded me it was going to be close getting back to Seward.

The gray started to lighten ahead. I thought we were about to pop out of the clouds when it went dark again. The engine sounded strong. Everything felt fine, but something nagged at me.

"Brandy, how's it feel back there?" She was still leaned forward and resting her left shoulder against the side window craning her neck to see the instruments.

"Well, this position's awkward as hell, and I got all this crap all over me, but otherwise okay. Seems like we should have broken out by now."

"That's what I was thinking too." I looked out both sides and above us again. Still nothing. I studied the instruments. Something was different. The ball was in the middle of the turn coordinator but the compass was slowly turning and the altimeter was dropping instead of climbing like before. The airspeed was over ninety.

"Shit, we're turning and diving."

She made a small movement with the stick and the compass turned faster.

"Other way, other way!"

I felt the plane respond as she made a gentle correction to the left. The compass slowed and held but the altimeter was still dropping. We were still only at four hundred feet. "Okay, we're straight again but still diving."

My gut settled toward my knees as she pulled back on the stick. We started to climb again.

I watched for a couple of minutes. Brandy kept the compass steady on one eight zero, the airspeed on seventy and the ball centered. When the altimeter reached six hundred feet, the clouds lightened again, and in another minute we broke through.

"Man," I crowed in relief. "Nice job."

Brandy sighed into her mike. I felt her sit back in the seat. "Whoo, finally. My neck's killing me. Which way?"

"Turn right and head for those mountains."

Snowcapped peaks on the Sargent Icefield loomed in the distance poking up through a thick cloud layer as far as we could see.

"What is all this shit?"

As I turned to see what she was talking about, she dropped a heavy plastic package over the seat and into my lap. It was about the size of a half a bag of flour. Felt like it too. A white powder leaked out of a hole in the duct tape that was wrapped around it.

"Where the hell you'd get this?" I turned around again to see her brushing white powder off her jeans and jacket. A rumpled old canvas bag was stuffed between her and the cabin wall.

"I pulled this out of the back when you said get something for protection. It fell on the floor and I think a bullet hit it."

I touched a taste of the white stuff to my tongue with one finger. It left a tingly sensation and then the spot went numb. "I'll bet this is cocaine."

"You've got to be kidding me."

"I kid you not. They say anything about it?"

"No."

"Is that what these guys are doing? Running coke?"

I kept looking behind me watching Brandy fly the plane. She stared at me, thinking back. The airplane rumbled around us and the clouds passed below us like an enormous container of cool whip.

"They kept me inside that sleeping bag in a separate tent. Couldn't hear much."

"Well, there's over ten pounds of it in there. Gotta be worth—"

"Wait. They were laughing about something one time I remember. Said something about '...just dropped in our laps.' Something like that."

"Damn it! They're not gonna let this get away if they can help it."

"To hell with that. I'm getting the shit out of here. That's the last thing we need."

She reached for the side window and slid it open. Something made me stop her. "No. Wait."

I grabbed for the bag and stuffed the package she had given me back inside.

"Let's keep it for now. We got bigger problems."

As I was sliding the window closed again, I had a perfect view of the black SuperCub popping out of the clouds behind us and turning in our direction.

"They're following us. What the hell?"

Brandy tried to look behind us.

"You just fly, okay. I'll keep my eye on them." I turned backwards on my seat and sat up on my knees, grimacing at the sore places on my shins. I couldn't remember ever feeling more helpless, sitting backwards like that in Willie's plane, like a little kid, watching Brandy handle the controls.

The black Cub was gaining on us, but not very fast. I turned back around and reached for the mixture.

"Brandy, don't freak out. I'm gonna lean it out some for max performance."

I pulled out on the mixture knob slowly and watched the RPMs. As soon as they started to drop, I added some back. I checked the fuel tanks. The left tank was barely registering, but the right tank had about an inch showing. I leaned down and switched the fuel selector to the right. The instruments all looked okay, so I turned in the seat again to look for the other SuperCub.

It was directly behind us and closer. I wondered if they were going to try to shoot at us from back there. They couldn't shoot straight ahead because their prop was in the way. I thought ahead to what might happen at the airport. How the hell were we going to avoid that rifle when we had to land?

Just then I saw them turn right to take a thirty-degree angle away from us.

"They're leaving. We might be in the clear."

But it wasn't going to work out that easily. I kept my eyes trained on them out the right side of the plane. They were about a quarter mile away, still moving out to the right. I got a creepy feeling and noticed myself crouching down in the seat trying to get more of the cabin wall between me and them. Looking down I saw a ragged hole in the side wall where a bullet had passed through. The severed control stick lay on the floor where I'd dropped it. Its jagged edges sent a frigid chill down my spine. How that bullet missed hitting me, I'd never know. I squeezed my eyes shut for a moment, trying to block out the memory of Scooter's lifeless body.

The thin aluminum was no protection. I forced myself to sit up straight again and looked out for the black SuperCub. I felt like one of those metal ducks at an arcade shooting gallery. We were marching along in plain view while they lined us up.

Then I saw a muzzle flash. I ducked.

"Dive, Brandy."

Without hesitation she shoved forward on the stick and we dove for the clouds. She leveled us off where we could cut through the tops but still see where we were going.

"Where are they?" I was amazed at the calm in her voice. No panic, no hysteria, no screaming. Just business.

"Straight behind us again. He can't turn out to the side like that and stay with us. Go that way." I pointed the direction for her as we skipped through the top of the cloud bank. From the high peaks off to the right, I figured we were passing Johnstone Bay.

"If you spot any holes in the clouds we need to get down through 'em," I said. "Just don't make any turns."

I wracked my brain trying to figure out how to get out of this. If only I had the controls, I knew I could dive and turn and weave in and out of the rocks and canyons that were my familiar playground. I was guessing Anthony didn't know the country as well as I did.

But I didn't have the controls. Brandy did. While she was doing great, she knew less about the terrain here than he did. I turned backwards again and shifted from side to side in the seat trying to keep them in sight. They were closer.

"Fuel status?" Brandy's captain voice commanded my attention.

I looked up and tried to calculate.

"Fuel status?" she repeated.
"About twenty minutes remaining on the right tank."
"And the left tank?"
"Zip."
"And our ETA?"
"Maybe fifteen minutes."
"Lean out the fuel mixture some more. Maybe we can squeeze out a few more minutes. Or will that overheat us?"
"Good idea. I'll tweak it a little. Running too hot is the least of our problems."
"No shit," she grumbled.
I turned around to adjust the mixture. When I turned back around Anthony was sliding out to the right again.
"He's lining us up for another shot. Can you dive?"
"There's some gaps up ahead. I can see the water."
I turned around and stared down. The white edge of the shoreline flashed up at us through small holes in the clouds.
"Go for it. Then turn left."
We left blue sky and sunshine behind and dropped into the fog. Almost instantly we were through the murk and under a heavy dark gray blanket about three hundred feet over the water. The steep walls of Cape Fairfield loomed off the right wing.
"Hug that wall." I twisted around and caught a glimpse of Anthony descending out of the clouds behind us. The dive gave him some speed. They were gaining on us.
"C'mon, baby. C'mon!" I urged Willie's SuperCub forward. "Day Harbor's coming up."
The sky in front of us was not encouraging. The cloud layer obscured the ridgeline between us and Seward. The only clear way around was out to our left at the far end of Resurrection Peninsula. We didn't have enough fuel to fly all the way out there.
As we started across Day Harbor, I strained to see up the valley to the right. The ice of Ellsworth Glacier in the distance lay cold and sullen with a layer of thick cloud masking its upper reaches. We didn't have enough fuel to go that way either. We'd have to make the looping circuit up to Lake Nellie Juan, connect over to the south fork of the Snow River,

and then bend around by Bear Lake north of Seward. That was way too far. Plus, that path depended on clear sailing through the passes. Not likely. Our only choice was straight ahead.

I clicked on the radio and tuned to the Seward airport weather recording. I didn't expect to pick it up yet since we were low and blocked by mountains. Sure enough, the channel was silent. I switched it to the Unicom frequency to see if I could hear any other traffic. As we reached the halfway point over the harbor, a voice came on.

"Wainwright, you listening?" It was Anthony. His voice was so loud and clear it made me jump. No way was I going to answer. I didn't even want to listen. "Why couldn't you leave it alone, jerkoff? All you had to do was walk away. What are you, some kind of hero or something?"

Shit, don't ask me questions. You wanna kill me? So kill me. Don't screw with my head.

That's what I wanted to say. But I knew better. *Don't let 'em get inside your head. Don't let 'em see you sweat.*

"Listen to me, Wainwright. It doesn't have to go down like this. We already trashed your plane. You want to die now? Just land at Seward and drop the dope out the window. We'll pick it up and fly away. You'll never have to deal with us again."

I still wasn't going to answer.

"Drop the dope and walk away. All the dope. No free samples. Otherwise we'll have you before you can even get your plane stopped."

I reached up and snapped off the radio. I wasn't listening to that lying bastard another second. Brandy said nothing. We flew across the water in silence.

"What are we doing, Johnny?" I could hear tension in her voice. No surprise. The west side of Day Harbor was a solid wall. We were headed straight for it. Trees filled the hillside all the way up to the snow line. There it met the clouds.

"Remember the notch?"

"Yeah, sort of. Not really."

"Aim that way." I pointed out the ridgeline that lead up to the only gap in the rocks that might let us through.

"Up there?" She craned her neck to see around me.
"There's nothing but cloud up there. And mountain."
"Yeah, well, that's where the Notch is. Follow the ridge up. Get real close to it."
I looked behind us. Damn, Anthony was getting close. Would he follow us up there? If I could get him to chase us into the clouds behind the ridgeline, there was a good chance he'd either lose his nerve or run into a rock. He was probably figuring he could stay with us if he got real close. It was either that or he'd have to make another turn to try another shot. But we were getting really close to the notch. He was going to have to make a decision quick.
"See the saddle there? That's the bottom of the notch. Aim for that."
"I can't see shit back here."
"Okay, okay. Just do what I tell ya. We'll get through this." I hoped I sounded sure of myself. I'd flown this patch of rocks and cliffs plenty of times. So many times I used to kid my passengers that I could do it with my eyes closed.
But when I'd hold my hands over my face they'd all scream bloody murder and beat me until I quit. It was always good for a laugh on a scenic flight.
The cloud bank was hanging thick above us. Its wispy base filled the floor of the notch, leaving less than twenty feet of space between cloud and rock. That's not what had me worried. My throat went dry looking into the gap.
We were headed into solid cloud behind the notch. Even if we made it through the tiny space, we might get swallowed in the gray and lose sight of the ground. Then we'd be surrounded by rock with no way out. That's how so many people died flying in Alaska—trying to squeak through a pass in bad weather. I shuddered, remembering pictures of broken airplane bodies strewn all over Merrill and Lake Clark Pass.
"Okay, Brandy. Here's what we're gonna do. When we get through the notch here, we're gonna drop down a little and when I tell you, you need to turn us right. Then we should be able to drop into the gorge that leads down to the prison. Okay?"

"Okay." She sounded tentative, but I ignored the uncertainty in her voice.

All my concentration was on the clouds and rocks in front of us. I glanced behind me. Brandy was straining to see her way ahead, leaning hard to the left side of the plane. Anthony was right on our ass. He had no room to turn out and take a shot. That was the good news.

The bad news was if we couldn't shake him here, the showdown would come in about ten minutes at the airport. They had high-powered rifles, and I had a Leatherman. Brandy didn't even have that. She didn't even have shoes on. In other words, at the airport we had no chance.

We were almost in the notch. "Drop us down just over the surface. Ten feet or less if you can do it."

Brandy aimed for the saddle. I could feel her fighting the urge to abort and turn out before we got there. If she did, we were finished. I had a couple of other ideas, but neither one gave us a good chance of shaking Anthony.

I wanted that stick in my hands so bad I could feel it in my grip. To steady my hands I clutched the top of the instrument panel and hunched forward as if being a foot closer to the clouds would help me see a way through.

Then we were in it. I saw the rocks slide by just below us. The clouds were so thick, I couldn't even see the rising slopes of the notch on either side. A steep valley dropped off to the left in a long slide down into Thumb Cove. I could have gone that way, but Anthony would have followed us easily.

"Okay, cut back to fifteen hundred RPMs. Our right turn's coming up."

Brandy throttled back and we slowed and dropped toward a snowfield.

"See that waterfall there to the right. Turn over there and follow it."

We were still dropping. Clouds swirled around us. The only way I could see was straight down. Everywhere else was fog, mist, and gray death. I wanted to turn and look for Anthony, but I didn't dare take my focus off the rocks.

"Johnny, that's a shear cliff in front of us. I won't be able to turn around in here." It was true. The walls of the gorge we had entered were so close to both wingtips, there was no way to turn.

We were getting closer and closer to the waterfall. Directly in front of us, I could see globs of water vaulting into space and falling hundreds feet below. A cloud of mist and fine spray formed down below.

"Now! Full power." I shoved in on the throttle just in case Brandy hesitated. "Pull up! Full flaps coming on."

Brandy hauled back on the stick and we pitched up. I yanked the Johnson bar all the way up.

"More!"

I felt the elevator straining against the stops as she pulled. My eyes must have been huge as I watched out the side window. The tire just barely passed above a slice of ice covering a small pool at the top of the waterfall. The stream poured out and launched into space. We were climbing almost straight up. The cloud swallowed us.

My jaw clamped down until my teeth ached. I wasn't breathing. The ice disappeared. Dark gray murk surrounded us. We might have been upside-down for all I knew. I waited, knowing that if we dropped altitude a second too soon, we'd hit the ice.

Then I couldn't bear it any longer.

"Okay," I croaked, gasping for air. "Drop us straight down." I pushed in the detent button and slowly brought up the flaps.

Mentally, I prepared myself for the impact. It was all guesswork. One second of miscalculation and we were dead. I felt Brandy working the stick to bring the nose down while she cut the throttle.

I couldn't help pressing slightly on the right rudder pedal. There was a rock wall to our left just off the wingtip. I couldn't see it, but I knew it was there. I could feel it. Then again, moving to the right too much was a bad idea too. This was a narrow gorge I was trying to guess our way through. Another cliff wall just like the one on our left was hiding inside the clouds not far to our right.

I've had nightmares like this. More than once. They all end the same way—with me jerking awake in a cold sweat, staring into the night for a long time before sleep comes again. I loved these mountains and these rocks. I just didn't want them to be my final resting place. Not yet anyhow.

I clenched my teeth and tried to keep air flowing into my lungs. I could picture what would happen if we drifted left another few feet. The left wingtip would hit first. Its outer edge would scrape along the flat rock wall for a moment. The plastic shield over the navigation light would burst. Tiny flecks of red plastic and clear glass from the light bulb would sprinkle like parade day confetti. Then the friction and drag would slow the left wing enough that the whole plane would pivot in that direction. Not long after that the whirling propeller would hit rock as the front of the plane slammed into the cliff.

Spinning momentum would carry the right wing into the wall next, smashing it backwards and rupturing the fuel tank inside. The red hot pipes of the exhaust system would meet the cloud of vaporized gasoline and erupt in a fiery ball of flame about the same time the tail section joined the pieces of disintegrating wings and propeller.

The whole package would then begin a flaming tumble down the cliff wall. The sounds of the explosion and cracking aluminum ribs and tubes, shattering glass and shredding fabric would drown out even our loudest screams. And that was only if we hadn't already been bashed unconscious by the initial impact.

By the time the thousands of pieces of wreckage hit the ice, nothing resembling an airplane would remain. No one would witness its thousand foot slide down the frozen rock-bound chute.

Many long moments would go by before it all stopped moving. Even the burning pieces would soon extinguish, and the high rocks would again be alone to stand sentry over the icefields and canyons with blank uncaring stares.

I didn't want to die, and I didn't want Brandy to die either. And I didn't want Willie's SuperCub to join the countless others crumpled in a remote pass somewhere in Alaska's vast emptiness. The victim of human weakness and corruption. Most of all, I didn't want it to be my fault.

But, of course, it would be my fault. I had gotten us all into this mess. I had made every decision, taken every step, committed every act that placed us all in this exact predicament. And I was the only one who could get us out.

Or was that just ego speaking? I felt out of control, but at least I had a guess about where we were. Brandy might have had the flight controls, but all she could do was follow my directions and hope that I knew what the hell I was doing. I hoped she was right.

Where was the goddamn "do over" switch? Every decent video game gives a player unlimited retries. Where was my second chance? Where was my "pause" button? Why couldn't I fast forward through the hard parts? Reality was such a bitch.

Why was all this crap running through my mind while we hung in the clouds surrounded by rocks and instant disaster? I was a man without a clue. I just hoped we were in the right canyon.

The bottom of the ice chute below started to appear as we sank out of the cloud, but there was always the chance I'd dropped us into a dead-end gulch with no way to turn around and no way to out climb the walls all around us. There were plenty of wrong choices in this area. I'd seen every one of them during earlier flights.

All I could do was sit and wait while Brandy flew the plane.

CHAPTER 28

At first all I could see was cloud and cliff. We continued to drop out of the sky. Then gradually, the ice chute below us appeared. It was split by a turbulent stream of water tumbling away from us and down the steep ravine. Silently I begged for the view we needed to survive.

"Yes!" I cried out. "Start turning left."

There it was. Green color came into view as we sank out of the cloud. Way below and ahead I could see Fourth of July Creek and the alder thickets that grew along her banks. I had picked the right canyon to plunge into. Godwin Glacier filled another valley to the east. All we had to do now was head left and follow the creek into Resurrection Bay. Seward's airport was less than five miles away.

"Full power, Brandy. Take us home." I reached for the throttle but she was already on it.

"Jesus Christ, Johnny. I can't believe what just happened."

I turned around to look for Anthony, but we were alone. I didn't know if he had turned away or if he'd hit a mountain. Either way, we had breathing room to make our escape.

Brandy's face was flushed and her mouth hung open in stunned silence. When she saw me looking at her, she broke into a nervous smile.

"Unbelievable. Un-fucking-believable," she murmured, pulling her gaze away from mine to look for the airport.

"I love it when you talk dirty to me." I grinned at her.

"Zip it, buttface. We could have been killed fourteen different ways in the last hour. We have any fuel left?"

I glanced up at the fuel vials. I couldn't see fluid in either one.

"Not much," I admitted. "Stay as high as you can until we get there."

"Good idea." She backed off the throttle slightly. "Can you lean it anymore?"

I backed off the mixture just slightly until the engine felt rough. Screw it. The engine was just going to have to run rough until we were back over land. The SuperCub sailed over the prison below us and headed out over the bay.

I thought through what might happen once we landed. If Anthony was out there somewhere, we only had a ten-minute lead. We could land and get away in a vehicle, but how were we going to protect Willie's airplane? After all that had happened, I couldn't let them destroy it while we ran. Then again, screw the airplane. We had to survive first.

I switched on the radio and called for any traffic. Just in case someone at the airport was listening in. No one answered. A knot gripped my stomach when I remembered that Scooter was usually the one to answer the radio in the hangar. Scooter wouldn't be answering this call.

I reached for my cell phone and saw that its front panel was still waterlogged. I pressed the power switch. Nothing happened. I thought of my office. We had to land and get to the phone there. I could call 911 and get the cops rolling.

Brandy interrupted my thoughts. "How far will this thing glide?"

Her voice was calm and her question a good one. The answer wasn't easy. I looked ahead to the alluvial plain abutting the airport. Red buoys in a circle held herring nets just offshore. If we ran out of gas where we were at five hundred feet in the air over the water, we would probably splash down a hundred yards from shore. Right next to those buoys. The big tundra tires made for lots of drag.

I was trying to decide how to answer when the engine began to sputter. I stared in horror as the RPMs started to drop. The steady roar of the engine went silent, and the airplane headed for the water. We were still more than a mile from shore.

I jerked my head from side to side looking for a boat. If someone could reach us in the water, we might have a chance. Otherwise, the frigid liquid would paralyze us in a matter of minutes. But there were no boats. It was a cold rainy day in Seward. Even the fishermen weren't interested.

"Best glide, seventy-five." I snapped at Brandy rapping one finger on the airspeed indicator. We were dropping fast. There was no way we were going to make it to the shoreline. The fuel could not have run out in a worse location.

North country pilots fear water landings more than any other emergency. You can do everything right and still freeze to death or drown.

Then an old mantra from long ago flashed through my head: "Fuel, mixture, mags, and switches," said a voice from somewhere.

My shaking hand flew to the fuel tank selector switch. I turned it to the left tank. Immediately the engine roared back to life. I almost fainted with relief. Even though the fuel indicator read empty, there must have been a few drops left in there somewhere.

"Go, Brandy, go." I jabbed my hand frantically at the runway out ahead of us. I didn't dare look back at her. I'm sure I had panic written all over me.

"Good idea, Johnny." There was a terse efficiency in her tone. Not like resignation. More like acceptance of the absurd. We were in a living nightmare. There was no point in protesting or complaining. All we could do was react and wait for the next fiasco. Watching the prop turn, I felt the plane flying with power again, and I made a mental note to thank Phil for teaching me that emergency mantra so long ago.

"Now, Johnny. How do I land this thing?"

I'd completely forgotten that she had never landed a SuperCub. I wanted to curse. I wanted to scream. I wanted to shake my fist at the sky. But instead I just shook my head to myself. What else could possibly be more screwed up than this? I wanted to pound myself on the side of my head. What else could possibly go wrong?

"Uh, heck. Nothing to it," I said. Nothing like a little false bravado to disguise the panic. "I'll talk you through."

She aimed us right at a good place where we could turn to land. The wind sock was easily visible in the middle of the airport up ahead. Its orange fabric fluttered in a ten-knot direct crosswind.

"Line up a final to land in the parking area beside my office. We can't mess around up here anymore."

Brandy pulled back on the throttle and slowed us down. Traffic on the highway below flowed by in its normal routine. Drivers dodged potholes and impatiently followed too close behind plodding RVs and slow tour buses. Just another normal afternoon in Seward, "The Fun Capital of Alaska." So said the welcome sign they were driving past just below.

"Yeah, turn base now. I'm gonna put in some flaps. Hold about sixty until we turn final. Then slow to forty-seven and I'll put in full flaps."

She followed my directions without comment.

"Okay, turn final and aim for my office. Your touchdown point is the pavement just past the grass. Can you see it?"

"Got it."

"Can you see your airspeed?"

"Yeah, got that too," came the reply.

"I'll help you with the throttle and the rudder when we set down so we don't ground loop in this crosswind. When we touch just keep the stick all the way back."

"Okay."

"And don't fight me when you feel me on the controls."

"Good idea," she said calmly.

She banked right, and the SuperCub angled into the wind setting up a cockeyed lean. I pressed on the left rudder pedal to straighten us out. The landing picture in front looked good so far. I pulled up on the Johnson bar. The plane slowed noticeably and as we dropped down past the telephone wires strung along the highway, I could feel the familiar floating sensation of short final.

"Okay, you're doing great, Brandy. Bring the nose up a little. Hold this and just ride it down."

I glanced at the airspeed indicator. It was steady at forty-seven. "Hold it, hold it. This looks good. Here we go."

I gave it just a touch of power. The grass slid by, and we sailed over the asphalt. The right tire touched first as we leaned into the wind and landed on the wet pavement. A wind gust pushed at us, and grabbed the tail as we slowed. The nose started to wobble to the right but I caught it with opposite rudder. I danced my feet on the pedals and kept us straight while we rolled toward the office. The neon window sign on the front porch gleamed out of the gloom.

We were still thirty yards away when the engine went quiet. The propeller stopped turning as we rolled to a stop. The last fuel tank had finally gone bone dry. I dropped open the lower door with a crash and fumbled to latch the upper section to the wing. Hauling myself up by the crossbars on the roof of the cabin, I threw my legs out and tumbled down to the pavement.

"Get that duffel bag," I shouted at Brandy as I ran for the office.

I fumbled for my keys but then I remembered changing clothes on the boat. I'd never switched over my wallet or my keys. Brandy came limping toward me in her stocking feet across the wet pavement lugging the old canvas bag in both arms.

I thought about breaking a window into my office, but the hangar was only fifty yards away. An outside light was already on, glowing in the mist. There was a phone in Hubert the mechanic's office and the back door was always unlocked.

Then I heard the sound of an airplane approaching over the bay. Brandy's face went white. She stood shivering in the mist, staring at me and waiting for me to do something.

"They're coming." Her calmness in the plane was gone, her eyes quivered and her chin trembled.

"C'mon." I pulled her by the arm and ran to my camper. It wasn't locked. I jumped inside and grabbed a pair of old rubber boots.

"Put these on. Quick."

As she stumbled into the boots, I looked across the field. The black SuperCub was following the same approach we had used. The field was deserted. We had less than five minutes. There was a grassy meadow at the west end right beside the airport road. If we tried to drive out now, they could easily spot us and cut us off. We were going to have to make a stand right here somewhere.

I looked around the airport for anyone who could help but didn't see a soul. The woods on the other side of the airport road stood dark and silent. I took Brandy by both shoulders and peered into her eyes.

"Okay. Here's what I need you to do. See the woods over there. Run in there as far as you can and hide. Don't come out until I call for you. Okay?"

She nodded her head rapidly and turned to go.

"Wait. Let me take that." I reached out and took the duffel bag from her. "This is what they're after."

She ran for the woods, and I ran for the hangar. The back door's lock was still broken and hanging loose. It opened easily and I let myself in. The hangar space was dark as hell inside, but I knew my way around. I took it slow letting my eyes adjust to the darkness as I moved. I headed for the office on the far side, ducking under an airplane wing and stepping over a pile of parts on the concrete floor.

The office had been built into the southeast corner of the hangar out of drywall and two by fours. It was a simple arrangement with an eight foot ceiling, sitting like a shoebox jammed into the corner of the open hangar space. Storage space on top of the office was reached by a simple wooden ladder nailed against the wall.

North To Disaster

The office door was locked, but my foot pushed it open without much effort. Hubert frequently forgot his keys and had pushed through the door with one shoulder many times. I reached for the light switch out of habit, but then stopped myself. No lights. Use the darkness. The phone was usually buried under a pile of old paperwork or parts. Hubert always had to search for it along with everything else he ever needed. I knew thrashing around in the dark for it was futile.

I waited another minute to let my eyes adjust some more. Standing there quietly in the dark, I heard the chirp of Anthony's tires landing on runway one-five. I couldn't see the phone anywhere. Running my hands all over the two desks, I located a phone console and put the receiver to my ear. Nothing. It was dead quiet. There weren't any lights on the console either. And an old cord connected to nothing was wrapped around the base. It wasn't hooked up.

Damn it. *Hubert, if I live through this, I'm gonna kick your goddamned disorganized ass.*

I kept searching. I knew he had a working phone somewhere. I finally started opening desk drawers with shaking hands. In the back of my mind, I tried to picture Brandy stumbling through the dark alders and devil's club thicket where I'd sent her in those ridiculous oversized boots. But at least she'd be safe.

In the last drawer in the second desk, I finally located the phone console underneath two phone books. The tiny lights twinkled at me in the dark. I put the receiver to my ear and dialed 911. I realized I was holding the phone with a death grip and while I listened to every electronic click and distant phone circuit switching unit buzz and connect, I forced myself to relax.

"Nine-one-one, what's your emergency?" The bored voice of the operator was businesslike and professional.

Just then I heard the SuperCub pull up to the front of the hangar and stop its engine. Looking down I realized the duffel bag was laying right by my feet.

"Hang on," I hissed into the phone. Grabbing the bag I stepped back out the door and heaved it up the wall onto the office roof. I winced at the hollow thump it made landing on the plywood flooring just a few feet above my head. Then I jumped back to the phone.

"I need cops at the airport. The main hangar. Hurry." I spoke as slowly as I could, making sure their tape would get every word. No response. My eyes went wide.

"Hello, hello." The line was dead.

My teeth clenched together so tight, I thought my jaw would break. I could hardly dial again my hands were shaking so hard. I didn't have a dial tone and had to hammer the button repeatedly until finally the receiver hummed its ready signal again.

"Nine-one-one, what's your emergency?" Same voice, same bored tone, but I never got to answer.

CHAPTER
29

Out of the corner of my eye, I saw Lance enter the office and lunge toward me. With one hand he grabbed my head. The gun he held in his other hand smashed into my face. Holding me by the back of the head, he forced the barrel into my mouth and levered me to my feet.

"Hang it up, asshole," he hissed, pressing his face in my ear. When I dropped the phone he reached down, grabbed the phone wire and yanked it out of the wall. Then he dragged me out into the hangar.

"Where's the coke?"

When I didn't answer right away he shook my head between his hands rattling the huge forty-five back and forth and chipping several teeth.

My arms dangled uselessly at my sides. I gestured with one of them, and he relaxed his grip enough to pull the pistol out of my mouth. He jammed it against the side of my face instead.

"Talk. Where is it?"

I stalled trying to think of something. I pretended that I couldn't speak, cringing and twisting my neck and jaw like I was hurt. He wasn't buying it.

"You think you're hurting now? Keep fucking around and you'll wish you were dead, motherfucker. Where is it?"

"I don't know," I grunted.

He laughed with a bitter rasp. "Yeah, right. What's this on your shirt, idiot? Powdered sugar? You stop off at the bakery on the way over here?"

I looked down. White powder was splashed across my chest. He gripped me tighter and pressed the pistol in harder. I felt the skin give way and blood began to flow.

"Okay, okay," I said. "Up there." I pointed with one hand.

He was over six feet tall and probably weighed well over two hundred pounds. I was no match for his physical size. We both knew it, and like most big guys he used his bulk to maximum advantage. Jerking me around like a bag of laundry he spun and stared up at the storage space above the office. I could see the gears turning as he tried to figure out his next move. He looked across the hangar, probably wondering where Anthony was. I was wondering the same thing.

He knew he couldn't climb that ladder and leave me behind. And he couldn't let me go up there by myself.

"Okay, you first." He shoved me to the ladder and motioned with the forty-five for me to start climbing.

I stepped up on the first rung and he shoved the pistol against my rectum. "No funny stuff. You better pray I don't slip."

He had my total attention. As I climbed I prayed all right. I didn't even know where the bag had landed. As my head reached the storage flooring I spotted it half concealed by a wooden box to my right about ten feet away. But I pretended not to notice. The flimsy plywood creaked under my weight.

"This floor ain't gonna hold both of us," I said.

When he was up the ladder and standing beside me, he bounced his weight on the plywood and the whole surface flexed like a trampoline.

"Where is it?"

I pointed.

"Go get it. Real slow."

He put the gun to the back of my head and shoved me forward. When I reached the duffel bag I bent over and tussled with it on the floor. I kept my back to Lance and repositioned my feet.

"It's caught on a nail here. Hang on."

"C'mon, motherfucker. Bring it—"

I flung the bag at his face and rushed him. His hands flew up to protect himself. I braced my spine into my best imitation of a battering ram and launched. My head connected with his crotch, and I felt him lose balance. His arms flailed as he fell backwards. I don't know how, but I managed to grab the edge of the ladder and watched as he hit the concrete floor flat on his back. The Smith & Wesson skidded across the floor and disappeared under a nearby tool chest.

But he wasn't out. He stared up at me, his face contorted and his teeth bared like a wild animal. He struggled to get up. I dove off the top of the ladder before he could get his arms or legs up and landed on my hands and knees directly in his soft middle.

I heard the air leave him in a rush, and he laid still.

"How'd you like that, dumbass? The bigger they are, the harder they fall." My voice rasped and wheezed in my chest.

I rolled off him and fought to catch my breath. I wiped at the blood dripping down the side of my face with my sleeve. Looking around, I spotted some of the black plastic tie wraps that mechanics use on airplane engines. I used two for his wrists and two for his ankles. The big sonofabitch weighed a ton. It was all I could do to roll him over, but by the time I was done he wasn't going anywhere.

One down, one to go. Where the hell was Anthony? I still didn't have a weapon and with the phone out of commission, my only choices were to run like hell or break into my office. I considered finding a box inside the hangar to crawl into and hide, but then he might find Brandy before he found me. And he might just take the opportunity to torch Willie's plane.

I picked up the duffel bag and worked my way over to the back door again. It was quiet and dim outside. The gray foggy overcast covered the area with a thick soundproofing blanket. Even highway noises a mile away were muffled.

I peeked out the door carefully but there was no one in sight. A small building next door blocked the view toward my office. I had to expose myself to look around the corner of the hangar toward the runways. As I crept toward the corner straining to hear any sounds of Anthony, Brandy's voice rang out.

"Don't move, Johnny."

I looked up and froze. She had just stepped out from behind a telephone pole twenty feet away and was pointing a shotgun right at my face.

Instinct took over. I flung the bag in her direction and threw myself back into the dark interior of the hangar. A huge blast went off and smacked into the metal wall of the hangar where I had been standing. I heard pieces of the building flying past my head.

What the hell?

I scrambled on all fours into the darkness. Knocking over a table loaded with parts started a cascading crescendo of falling metal and fiberglass. I kicked at another stack of boxes nearby causing more debris to fall between me and the half open door. I thought I heard a scream outside, but in all the noise around me I couldn't be sure.

Remembering Lance's forty-five, I scurried across the floor in a crouch. I couldn't believe what had just happened. I expected more shots and went into automatic reaction mode. I had to get that weapon. It was my only chance. Once again there were two people trying to kill me.

Wait a minute. Was that really Brandy shooting at me? What the hell is going on?

I didn't have time to think about it. I had to defend myself. All I knew was that enemies pointed guns. I was really tired of bullets and guns pointed at me. Especially in my face.

Back over by Lance's still form, I looked around trying to locate the Smith & Wesson. I laid down flat on the concrete floor. Its cool surface smelled of wet dirt, dust, oil, and avgas.

I found the tool chest near Lance. It was one of those tall red cabinets on wheels with drawers. Like everything else in

Hubert's hangar it was stacked high with old coffee cups. Some of them half full of old coffee and the others filled with nuts, bolts, and sheet metal screws. I crawled toward it sweeping my hand across the floor in the dark. Under the cabinet jammed against one of the wheels in back, my hand found the cold steel of Lance's forty-five.

The thing was a goddamn cannon. I pulled it out from under the cabinet and crawled backwards under a table beside a stack of smelly old tires. I grabbed some nearby cardboard boxes and an empty plastic trash can and arranged them around myself until I was completely out of sight with a view into the open area of the hangar.

This is where I'll make my stand, I thought. I pulled back carefully on the gun's slide and felt inside to make sure there was a cartridge loaded in the chamber. Feeling for the safety I pushed it back and forth wondering which position it was in. It was too dark to see, and I couldn't remember if pushing it up with my thumb would make it ready to fire, or if that was the safe position.

The hell with it. I'd leave it the way it was and if it didn't go off on the first pull, I'd push it the other way.

I sat then and listened. Several minutes went by. I strained to hear but only picked up a few muffled bumps and thuds in the distance. My thoughts were whirling, trying to make sense of the situation. Had I completely misunderstood what was going on? Whose side was Brandy on? Was she not who I thought she was?

Frantically I went back over every interaction I'd had with her. Hadn't Willie said his daughter was coming to visit? Yes. But I realized I had never seen the two of them together. Willie had been in a coma when we were in his room at the hospital together. Holy shit.

But what about her being kidnapped?

I didn't see it happen, so who knows? Come to think of it, she looked awfully surprised to see me when I found her out at Montague.

Wasn't she tied up? No, she actually wasn't tied up. She was inside that sleeping bag looking like she was tied up, but in my hurry I didn't look her over that carefully.

What about the black eye? Yeah, but that didn't have to mean she was a prisoner.

My mind was racing. Could I have been so wrong about her all this time? What about Cordova? Was that all an act? I thought about the coke. Is that what she was after all this time? Was she an impostor? I felt my face reddening. *Idiot. You stupid idiot. Goddamn fool. Stupid sonofabitch. Jesus, how damn dumb can one guy be?*

Wait a minute. I couldn't be that wrong about her. If she was acting she had to be the best con artist of all time. I thought I was good at that shit. Had I just been taken in by the all time champion? *I'm such a moron.*

The silence inside and outside the hangar was broken by the sound of an airplane engine starting outside. The sound moved toward me. *They've got the coke; they're leaving.*

I crawled out of my hiding place and moved cautiously toward the front door of the hangar. Pressing my ear against the door, I could tell the plane was right outside the building. But I had a weapon now. Now I could do something about it.

The door was locked. But it was one of those deadbolt jobs that I could open from the inside. I shifted the forty-five to my left hand. My swollen fingers ached at the effort to hold the heavy weapon, but I ignored it and twisted the handle. Like always, the damn metal door stuck in its frame and the metal scraped against the concrete door jam as I pushed on it. Finally, another shove with my shoulder flung it open.

Anthony's black SuperCub was starting to roll. I could see him sitting in the front. The back seat was empty but another shape loomed behind that. It had to be Brandy. He had her stuffed in the baggage compartment. The door and side window were still hanging open.

Okay, this is it. Take the shot now or watch them fly away. I braced myself in my best shooter's position. Half-crouch, weapon in my right hand, left hand wrapped around my right.

The SuperCub's engine accelerated and the plane started to roll faster. The blast from the prop blew dirt in my face, and I had to raise my arm to block its flow. Squinting against the dirt I aimed again, but they were moving away. Then the engine cut back to idle. I heard yelling from the plane. I pointed the gun at the right wing and pulled the trigger. Nothing happened.

Shit. The safety was on. I found a button on the handle and pushed it. The magazine slipped loose and almost fell completely out of the pistol. I shoved it back in, and pushed the button again. The magazine slipped again. Shit. It wasn't a safety; it was the goddamn magazine release. I stared down at the weapon trying to figure it out, but the plane was too far away anyhow. I ran after it. The engine was making strange sounds, revving and faltering. The Cub was still rolling but slower now, moving away but barely. This was my last chance. I finally located the safety as I ran. Coming to a stop, I lined up to take a shot.

Suddenly a lurching shape bolted out from behind a shed. Somebody was blocking my line of fire, limping and running toward the plane carrying some kind of stick. Whoever it was wore a familiar dark blue jacket.

Shit. It was Willie. I stared in disbelief. With a big cast on his left ankle he was hobbling as fast as he could toward the open door of the plane. He had a crutch in his hand, and he was charging with it in front of him like some kind of a crazed knight on horseback.

The SuperCub's engine continued to cough and sputter. The crutch disappeared through the door into the plane. I started to run again in their direction and watched as Willie pulled the crutch back out and slammed it in again and again. He fought like a demented plumber with a plunger from hell until he lost his balance and fell to his knees. The still moving plane knocked him over with the tail section and kept rolling forward.

I reached Willie first. He was struggling to get up.

"Willie, you okay?"

He gaped up at me standing over him with the forty-five in my hand. His mouth twisted in a teeth baring snarl. His left eye was blackened and an ugly purple bruise covered most of the left side of his face. A white patch above his ear had replaced the massive bandage I'd last seen him wearing.

"Get him! Shoot the motherfucker!"

"What about Brandy? She just tried to kill me."

"Shut up, dork. She was aiming at him. Then he jumped her. Now get him."

I looked up and saw the plane roll to a stop. I was there in two seconds and with the gun ready I jumped into the doorway and aimed into the front seat.

"Freeze, mother—" I didn't need to finish. I stood there pointing the weapon and stared. Red lights flashing from Airport Road reflected off the glass windows of the Super-Cub's cabin. Willie hobbled over to me, grimacing at the awkward painful gait he had to use to maneuver. His eyes flashed with venom. His fists were clenched and he was visibly shaking. Adrenaline was coursing through his veins so fast and furiously I thought he might rip the airplane open with his bare hands.

"Shoot him, goddamnit!"

"No need, man. It's over."

Willie looked in at the battered body. Anthony's face was a bloody mess. The left side window was cracked where Willie had slammed the poor bastard's head against it with the crutch. I thought he was dead, but then I spotted a bubble of blood form on his lips as he exhaled, sucked in a ragged breath, and groaned.

"Gimme that." Willie grabbed the forty-five. I let him take it.

"Okay, but don't shoot him. The cops are almost here. They'll take care of this."

I moved to look in the back of the plane. Brandy was lying twisted and contorted, slumping over the back seat. A rope was tied through her mouth and her hands were knotted behind her. It looked like Anthony had tried to tie her into the baggage compartment, but she'd gotten loose and somehow had managed to squirm her legs up and over the seat back. Then she'd jammed one of her bare feet against the back seat throttle knob and blocked it from moving forward.

Evidence of the struggle was obvious. Her foot was bruised and bleeding, and blood seeped from the left side of her head where Anthony must have knocked her out before he tied her up. She was out cold, but I could feel a pulse in her neck.

I untangled her foot from the throttle and straightened her leg out the best I could. I reached for my Leatherman to cut the rope tying her, but the pouch on my belt was empty.

"Hey, Willie. You got your Leatherman?"

I looked over at him but he was busy trying to wrestle the duffel bag out of the baggage compartment. His eyes were even wilder than before. He tugged on the bag in frantic desperation. The police lights were rounding the corner of my office only two hundred yards away.

"No, man. No!" I jumped on him and wrapped both arms around his chest pinning his arms.

"Let me go, goddamnit! That's my shit."

"No, Willie. No." We stumbled backwards and I tripped over his cast. He screamed as we fell to the pavement. He kept struggling but I held on with all my strength.

The first cop car skidded to a stop on the other side of the plane and the second one slid to a stop right behind him. I could see even more red lights pouring off the highway. Their frantic glow crossed the tracks and headed our way.

"Freeze, you two. Oh, shit. Johnny?" It was Betty. She lowered her weapon and signaled her partner to check the plane.

"Hey, Betty. Boy, it's sure good to see you." I know I sounded like an idiot. Somehow it didn't seem to matter anymore.

"The one you want to arrest is in there." I pointed to the plane. "And there's another one in the hangar."

One of the other officers moved toward the open hangar door with his gun drawn.

"He's tied up on the floor. Or at least he was the last time I saw him," I added for good measure. I figured it was a good time to be a responsible citizen assisting local law enforcement in any way I could.

The officer at the plane was busy putting cuffs on Anthony, who was conscious now and cursing at the pain. White powder had spilled in his lap.

"Whoa, what's this all over you, mister?"

Betty was staring down at Willie and me, but the question got her attention.

"What is it, Paul?"

The guy holding Anthony held up the top of the duffel bag. White powder had spilled out. He reached in and removed one of the duct-tape-wrapped bricks.

"Looks like we hit the jackpot here, ladies and gentlemen," he crowed with a big grin.

Anthony began to protest. "That's not my stuff, man. That belongs to them." He jerked his jaw in our direction.

The cops looked at each other. There were five of them now standing around us. They all looked at the coke, and they looked at Anthony. Then they looked at Willie and me. We were still standing up and brushing off our clothes. I held on to Willie, holding him steady. He was looking a little calmer. At least he was breathing regular, but his eyes were still wild.

I nudged him in the side and he looked at me. Made eye contact just for a second. I shook my head just barely and dropped my eyes. So did he. I felt him relax and little by little I let my grip loosen so it looked like I was helping him stand up. Not holding him prisoner anymore.

The cops looked back at Anthony. Then they started laughing.

"Yeah, right, dude," one of them said to Anthony. "Do you know how often we hear that line?"

The cops all roared. Willie and I glanced at each other. Then we started laughing too. Just chuckling at first, but as the cops got into it, pretty soon we were bellowing along with them.

Betty walked over to Anthony.

"Yeah, that's a good one. 'It ain't my stuff, officer. Honest. I was just holding it for somebody.' How about this line? *You have the right to remain silent.*"

CHAPTER 30

It was the next night. I pushed open the heavy door and felt a wave of warm air and blues rush into my face. The Yukon Bar smelled of beer and cigarette smoke. I couldn't remember a friendlier fragrance in my life. The crack of pool balls broke my concentration. I looked down and watched as a white cue ball bounced off the hardwood floor and rattled toward me. I stopped it with one foot.

"That'll be a dollar, mister. Put your cash in the oh-so convenient fishbowl right here." Goldie's voice rang out over the bedlam of music, television noise, and loud voices.

"What? That's bullshit. It wasn't my fault," protested the pool table offender. I handed him the ball and headed for the bar.

Goldie smiled at me and flopped down a napkin as I took a stool in the Revenue Corner.

"Yeah, get Johnny whatever beer he wants," Willie piped up, pushing dollar bills at Goldie. "Domestic, that is."

I grunted. "Thanks, butthole. Just when I was getting used to drinking without your interference around here."

Willie's head jerked back with a silent grin. Then he poured beer down his throat and wiped his moustache with the back of a hand. When Goldiè brought me a cold bottle and popped off the cap, I leaned over and clinked it against Willie's. Mitch and Hondo were pulling up stools on his other side.

"Goldie, my dear. Please bring these gentlemen whatever they want. And Hondo too. I can't tell you guys how much I appreciate what you did for me out there."

Hondo laughed. "Hell, that was the most fun I've had in years, but Mitch here is a little pissed off about the bullet hole he got in the boat."

I looked at Mitch, but he waved away my concern with a smile. "Think nothing of it, Johnny. That guy was a better shot than I gave him credit for. We were just into that fog bank when one round hit the windshield. I can show it off to my passengers all summer."

I shook my head. "How about that Hondo commando?"

Hondo grinned and blushed like a little kid trapped in a three-hundred-pound fortress of muscle and lard. He used his napkin to wipe his shiny head.

Mitch laughed watching the big man's embarrassed expression. "He was a sight, wasn't he? Running up and down that beach with the gas cans. Used every shell he had pinning those guys down for you, too. He looked like Mister T out there. Very impressive."

I raised my bottle and the four of us banged them together again and drank. Then we fell quiet and turned back toward the bar, all avoiding the same thoughts.

The front door was standing open behind us to reveal evening sun lighting up Mount Alice with a golden glow across the bay. Sailboats on the water danced on the evening breeze a mile distant.

"Sorry you lost your airplane, Johnny," Mitch murmured low.

I nodded and looked away. Took another swallow of beer.

Willie glanced at me and said to Mitch, "He probably can't talk about that just yet."

Everyone went silent again until I couldn't stand it anymore.

"Aw, shucks, Mitch. Willie's going to fly me out there with a few wrenches and some duct tape. We'll have it back in the air in no time."

It was a feeble attempt at levity, but the guys chuckled anyhow. They knew.

When the music got loud, Mitch and Hondo started jawing about some damn thing I couldn't make out. I leaned in toward Willie and spoke quietly into his ear. "Cocaine? What the hell was up with that?"

He let out a big sigh. "That was my retirement plan."

"Retirement plan?"

"Yeah, that's why I went out to Bristol Bay."

I just looked at him and waited. I was used to this with Willie. He drank more beer and glared at the speakers that were pumping out a raucous Caribbean tune.

"Goddamn shit's too damn loud. Stupid pothead music anyway."

"Yeah, no good if you're into coke." I gave him my best "What the hell were you thinking?" look.

"It wasn't for me."

I waited.

"I never told you this story. Hell, I never told anyone. Years ago when I was flying out there, a guy I knew was flying up to Nome. He disappeared in a snowstorm and was never found. But I found him. That next spring I found the wrecked plane with his dead body in it and a shitload of coke. I hid it away and kept my mouth shut."

"You were gonna sell it?" I gave him a confused stare.

"Yeah, I know, I know. But a guy's gotta do what a guy's gotta do." His shoulders slumped and he studied the label on his bottle of beer.

I nodded. "Yeah, I hear that."

"I know a guy in Anchorage that was going to move it for me."

"Sure you do."

"I'd have been set."

"You sure would have."

We drank without talking for a while. The music changed to southern rock and roll. A mournful guitar solo and snare drum back beat echoed through the bar. Glasses clinked together and laughter erupted from time to time. A loud argument about football four stools away was interrupted by the loud crashes of glass bottles being slammed into the plastic garbage can under the bar.

"Coulda made a million bucks," I said, just guessing.

"Not that much."

"How much?"

"Maybe a half-mill."

"You know, Willie, I been thinking."

"Don't think. Drink beer."

"Is that your bumper sticker?"

"Yup."

"I been thinking your Cub's worth about sixty grand, and my normal fee's half of what it would cost you to replace it. So I figure you owe me thirty grand."

He sniffed and sat back folding his arms across his chest. "Goldie, bring this man another beer on me."

"Okay," I said. "Thirty grand minus two beers."

"Since you just gave away my half-mill, let's call it even."

"You know, you might have told us about it. Brandy almost threw it out the window."

He thought about that for a minute. "Yeah, maybe. But it was a secret."

"You got any other secrets?"

"Who, me?" He winked at me and clicked his bottle against mine.

Goldie brought beers over. She leaned over the bar toward me and laid one hand on mine. Her skin was cool from the frosty bottles. She gave me a soft look.

"Betty stopped in earlier. Said the Coast Guard sent a chopper out to recover Scooter's body. There's a service tomorrow."

I hung my head. Goldie squeezed my hand and hung on for a minute without speaking. Some guy at the other end of the bar called for a refill.

"Keep yer pants on," she yelled down at him. She turned back to me.

"I'm off early tonight if you want to talk." She gave my hand another pat and moved down the bar.

Mitch came over, dragging a big laundry bag behind him. He put his arm across my shoulders. "Don't worry about Scooter, Johnny. It wasn't your fault. He was a good kid, and he died doing what he loved."

Willie elbowed my arm too. "That's right, man, and they're gonna fry that bastard, Anthony, for it too."

Someone tapped me on the shoulder then and when I turned I saw it was Rainey. She gave me a quick hug. "Hey, Johnny. Glad to see you're still kicking."

"Rainey. What the hell you doing here? Came down to slum with the working people?" I smiled at her, enjoying how her blond splash of sunshine could light up a dark bar.

"Oh, yeah. Well, I couldn't miss celebrating with the 'gang that couldn't think straight.'"

Where had I heard that expression? I reached for my beer and was about to tilt back a cold rush of mood medicine when Willie raised his bottle high and his voice higher.

"Hey, everybody, here's to Scooter. He was a good man and a good pilot. He lived for the sky and he died helping a friend. May he rest in peace."

The twenty people crowded around the Revenue Corner raised their glasses and bottles. Even Bugeyed Larry looked up from rolling a fat lumpy cigarette of dubious ingredients.

"To Scooter," twenty voices roared in unison.

Mitch reached down and placed the laundry bag on the bar.

"I went over to Scooter's place this morning," he said. "To call his family and make arrangements, and I found this on a pedestal in the kitchen. I think he would have wanted us to see it."

He untied the top of the bag and pulled it partially open. A flesh-colored shape came into view, but Mitch left it mostly covered by the bag. He arranged the shape so that it sat by itself on the edge of the bar. He reached inside and removed an extension cord that he plugged in to a nearby outlet.

"You all may remember that our friend, Scooter, was a creative individual. What you probably didn't know—hell, I didn't know either—was that he was also a skilled sculptor and inventor. Ladies and gentlemen, for the sake of modesty, I will leave his final work of art draped, but I invite you to reach in the bag here and discover for yourself the genius of lifelike sensation that Scooter created."

He stepped back and the group went quiet, staring at the shape on the bar. No one moved. I noticed Hondo leaning on the bar, gaping with his mouth open. Larry's disjointed eyeballs ran over the shapely curves under the cloth. Even covered by the bag there was no mistaking the swell of obvious hips and waistline and more.

Still no one moved or said a word. Goldie came over and looked at us all standing there speechless.

"You boners just gonna stand there with yer hands in your pants all night?"

"All right, all right." Hondo laughed and stepped over to the shape on the bar. His face went bright red but with furtive glances at all of us watching him, he slowly reached inside the bag and let his hand move over the contents. Then his eyes went wide and glazed over. His mouth dropped open again.

"Holy shit," he whispered in a kind of rapture. Then, as if remembering we were all staring at him, he jerked his hand out and hurried back to his stool.

Okay, enough of this baloney, I had to check it out for myself. I approached the bag cautiously and reached in. Goldie was watching me. She shook her head, rolled her eyes, and frowned at me. Then she turned away.

The shape was warm and felt amazingly like real flesh. I cupped the place that felt exactly like a woman's waist with a lifelike hip bone underneath. I was captivated. I took hold of the other hip and jostled the form slightly. It even moved naturally. My hand wouldn't stop exploring. I moved lower and stroked the top of the buttocks with the back of my hand. My knuckles brushed against inviting cleavage. It felt familiar somehow. A chill started in my low back, then ran up my spine with a rush.

I must have visibly shivered. I looked over at Hondo who was watching my every move as he sipped his drink. He slowly shook his head back and forth, still in awe.

Gradually, I let my hand slide forward and move around the hip bone. My thumb passed along the top of the thigh and my fingers brushed past the smooth skin of the hip. Suddenly my thumb felt a lot warmer. I followed the warmth.

Then I became aware of the people around me again. I realized that I was feeling up a piece of rubber with a crowd watching me. I must have turned a hundred shades of red and purple.

The door swung open and a woman walked in. I jerked my hand out of the bag and moved away like I'd been bitten by a snake. Everybody laughed. Brandy smiled and walked toward us.

"Hey, there, cute shoes. How you doing?" She reached for me with one arm, settled her purse on the bar and crawled onto my bar stool next to Willie. Then she noticed my bright red face.

"What's wrong?"

Speechless, I sputtered and reached for my beer. She noticed the group of people staring at the half covered torso. Reaching for the bag, she pulled it open and looked inside. After a couple of moments, she looked at me. Then she looked at all the people standing around us. She pulled the bag free and exposed the torso perfectly balanced where it sat on the edge of the bar naked to the world. It was an exact nude replica of beautiful feminine form. Except for missing a head, chest, and lower legs,

Brandy turned around, stepped back and held both hands toward the fleshy creation like Vanna White demonstrating a new car.

"Voila." She grinned at the crowd and a cheer broke out with laughter and applause. Goldie handed her a glass of wine and she clinked it against our bottles.

"Came out real nice, didn't it?"

I tried not to look, but I couldn't help myself. The form was damn near perfect. Even down to the little dimples in its cheeks. I couldn't speak. I just shook my head in wonder.

A burly man with a cigar clamped in his teeth pushed his way through the group for a closer look. After a quick inspection, he pulled out a checkbook and turned to Mitch.

"How much?" he asked as he clicked a pen and got ready to write.

Mitch didn't skip a beat. "For the night, for the weekend, or forever?"

Before I could hear anymore, Brandy picked up her purse and pulled me by the arm to join her outside. As I followed, Rainey caught my eye. She cocked her head at me without a word and raised an eyebrow. She pointed two fingers at her eyes, then one back at me and looked away with a half-smile.

The big door slammed behind us and then we were alone on the sidewalk. Music and laughter in the bar were instantly muffled.

Brandy turned toward me and looked in my face. "I wanted to let you know I'm taking off. I've got an early flight out of Anchorage tomorrow, so I'm turning in early."

My disappointment must have shown. *Damn it. I hate when I do that.* "Oh, I thought we might—"

"No, I don't think so. Probably not a good idea. I've got to get back to my mom and the job. Long distance things and all that...."

So many things I wanted to say stuck in my throat. I fought the urge to cut and run with a quick "See ya" and dive back into the bar. I could feel my tongue growing thick and useless, but I couldn't bail that quick.

"Did you and your dad talk at least?" I was curious but stalling for time too. Maybe stalling for courage more than time.

"Oh, yeah. We had a great talk earlier today. He feels bad about leaving us, but this is his home up here. I understand that now." She turned and sat against the hood of a car parked at the curb. "I know he loved us. He still loves us even though Mom's really gone now. He doesn't express himself that much. Well, you know him."

"What about you?"

"What about me?"

"I dunno. You okay with everything…I mean, all the stuff that happened here?"

"Am I okay? Oh yeah. What about you? You're the one that lost a plane and had to climb a mountain to keep from being shot. You're my hero, Johnny. You took a big risk to save my bacon. I'll always love you for that."

I blushed and looked away. "Aw, shucks," I mumbled and watched my toe pushing at the sidewalk. "I'm going to miss you…."

She reached up and pressed a finger to my lips, stopping me. In a reflex I pulled her in and kissed her. She pressed herself against me and held me tight. When our lips finally parted, I kept holding her close with my mouth against her ear. My eyes closed at the scent of strawberry shampoo.

"Look, Brandy," I whispered in her ear. "I can do alone. Been doing it a long time. But your being here, flying with me and everything…I-I liked it. I liked it a lot. I can't quit thinking that maybe…."

She pulled away and looked me straight in the face. Her smoky green eyes filled with mist. She pulled her hair back behind her ears with shaking hands. "I can't."

Her words hung between us only for a second. Then she pulled me in for a last hard kiss, her body trembling against mine. Her cheek was wet against my beard. Then she turned and ran, disappearing around the corner.

I leaned back on the hood of the car staring at the empty sidewalk. I thought about running after her. But I didn't. In a moment I heard her rental car starting and pulling away. It didn't take long for the sound to fade, until it was replaced by the cries of seagulls and a dog barking in the distance.

I sat there for a while not trusting my legs to carry me just yet. Then I walked north. Stayed in the alley as long as there was one. It was five miles, a couple of hours, to the airport. I needed it.

The air was salty and thick walking through town. A steady breeze was bringing weather. I could see rain clouds on the edge of the blue evening sky moving toward me.

Everything was back to normal in Seward, the Fun Capital of Alaska. Small seaside town in the final frontier. Three thousand people or so—more in the summer, less in the winter.

When I got to the airport, I kept walking along the runway, headed toward the bay. I was tired but not ready to lie down yet. Not sure where I was going or why. Just seemed like the thing to do. The place was deserted. As usual. A northern wind pushed at my back.

Low soggy clouds flooded down the hills behind me. Gloomy patches of mud coated the pavement in places. Left there by last night's heavy rain. I glanced behind me to see the muddy footprints my shoes were making. Off in the distance cars and pickups continued their relentless pursuit of whatever they were always pursuing along the highway. I told myself I didn't care.

Walking straight ahead with my head down, I watched the grass next to the runway rippling in the breeze. I listened to my shoes slapping quietly one after the other on the asphalt. Up ahead there was clear blue sky over the south end of the bay. The moon was sinking, red and full, into the ocean. Her reflection in the water was pointing straight at me, a pathway of endless possibilities. Just to the right the twinkling lights of town glistened in the darkening sky sharing the calm water's surface for a late night samba.

I could feel the slipping. The adrenaline rush of the past few days fading. Sliding quietly back into the simple existence of boring days and repeating routines we all did just because. It was too soon to start dreading the cold winter days ahead, but that was in there too. Was this my day of glory? Like Travis Bickle in *Taxi Driver* said, "I want to do something big." Just before he fought the bad guys and saved the girl. Is that what just happened with me? If that was the glory, it sure was slipping away fast. At least Brandy said she appreciated what I'd done. Right before she walked away. It started to rain. I walked on.

The rain picked up force, showering me with a drizzling flow. I looked back over my shoulder again, toward the highway. I don't know why, nothing to look at anyway. The muddy footprints behind me were fading in the rain. In another hour there would be no trace.

Mount Alice would still stand tall to the north, maybe hidden behind wet clouds, but for sure it would wait there patiently. Waiting for the return of autumn showers to leave fresh snow creeping further and further down her craggy sides like they had every fall for twenty thousand years.

I thought about the burned skeleton of my SuperCub lying by itself in the weeds out on Montague Island. I knew that image was going to hurt for a long time. I shut my eyes and hunched the collar of the fleece tighter around my neck. I turned around to look at the moon again and forced the bad pictures out of my mind.

In front of me, the pavement was coming to an end. Not a plane in the sky, not a soul anywhere around. Thousands of feet of paved runways and tarmac all around me in the middle of one of the most beautiful places on the planet. I stood there alone, wondering about that. The dozen or so small planes parked nearby sat silently on the tarmac, tied down and dripping, the rain drumming on their wings.

I stepped off the pavement, still not sure where I was going. I took one last glance behind me. Nothing there, even the muddy footprints were gone.

Then my cell phone rang. I wrestled with the zipper on the front pocket of my fleece and finally got the damn thing out. I was amazed to hear it working. The moisture inside the panel was almost gone.

"Seward Air," I said, trying to keep the mood out of my voice.

"Hey, there, Johnny. I'm back at the Yukon. Wanna buy a lonely girl a beer?"

After a few more words I stuffed the phone back in my pocket. Then I turned and started to jog back up the runway.

ACKNOWLEDGEMENTS

In memory of Donny Hauenstein, Alaskan pilot and skilled aircraft mechanic who had innumerable friends, countless airplanes and the messiest hangar on the planet. Rest in peace.

A lot people helped me get this work ready. I'll be forever grateful. Sue Nolan, Duane Hallman, Vern and Lura Kingsford, Jack Hart, Denny Hamilton, Jim Barkley, the Windings Readers Book Club in Westminster, Colorado, you're all the best. And, Genean, love of my life, the best cheerleader ever and my best friend.

Thank you, Sue Collier, LeadDog Communications, for a masterful job of editing and Dennis Treadwell, Starbird Studios, graphics artist extraordinaire, for the cover.

A special thanks to Sue Cummings, owner of the Yukon Bar, for that true gift of Alaskan atmosphere and, of course, the beverages and free peanuts.

For information on air taxi and scenic flights in Alaska, go to www.sewardair.com